MW00627704

RECLAIMED LOVE

ALINA LANE

XOXO,
Alina Lane

VON RIPS PUBLISHING

Copyright © 2021 by Alina Lane

All rights reserved.

No part of this book may be reproduced in any form or by any electronic or mechanical means, including information storage and retrieval systems, without written permission from the author, except for the use of brief quotations in a book review.

Names, characters, businesses, places, events, locales, and incidents are either the products of the author's imagination or used in a fictitious manner. And any resemblance to actual persons, living or dead, businesses, companies, locales, or actual events is purely coincidental.

Designations used by companies to distinguish their products are often claimed as trademarks. All brand names and product names used in this book and on its cover are trade names, service marks, trademarks and registered trademarks of their respective owners. The publishers and the book are not associated with any product or vendor mentioned in this book. None of the companies referenced within the book have endorsed the book.

ISBN: 978-1-7368977-0-6 (ebook)

ISBN: 978-1-7368977-1-3 (paperback)

Cover Design by: Y'All That Graphic

Edited by: Jessica Snyder Edits, Happily Editing Anns and Editing by Gray

Printed in United States of America

https://alinalane.com

❀ Created with Vellum

JOIN ALINA LANE'S NEWSLETTER

Want to receive exclusive news, content, specials and giveaways!

Subscribers are always the first to hear about Alina's new books and projects.

See the back of the book for details on how to sign up.

For Nickolas.
You found me in the dark and taught me to embrace the light. I love you endlessly.

KATE

RUSHING THROUGH THE HOSPITAL DOORS, I'M HIT BY THE STALE smells of disinfectant and lingering anxiety. I have general directions, so I bypass the reception desk and aim for the elevators. My hands shake and nerves swirl around the pit of my stomach as I take five quiet seconds in the elevator car to steel myself against being in the same room as Arik for the first time in twelve years.

He's always made himself scarce during my sporadic visits back home to Idaho—to benefit himself or me, I don't know. I've always appreciated that I don't bump into him when I'm in town. It's been years, but every time I remember what he said to his friends, it leaves behind the hollow ache of the young brokenhearted girl I was. Those feelings are something that time and distance haven't erased.

The elevator doors don't fully open before I'm out and headed to the nurses' station. Speaking to the first nurse I reach, I introduce myself and ask if Gram is out of surgery. My voice wobbles on the word *surgery,* so I clench my back molars to hold it together.

With a compassionate smile in place, the nurse taps away

on the keyboard. After glancing at the monitor and checking my ID, she informs me, "Mrs. Palicki is finished, and she's about to move to recovery. The waiting room is down the hall and to the right. A doctor will be out to speak to you soon."

Turning from the desk, I head toward the waiting room, the multitude of questions I have bouncing around like chipmunks on crack in my mind. How bad is the break? What's the recovery time? How much help will she need? Is she going to need a nurse? How do we get her home? The gray walls give way, and I'm at the waiting room entrance before I'm ready. Stepping inside the room, I expect to find Arik, but he's not the first person I see. It's the elderly gentleman sitting next to my once best friend. Mr. Dawson, my history teacher from tenth grade, has his head in his hands and is slumped forward in the chair, worry and concern radiating from him.

What the hell is he doing here? My brain blips and stutters trying to put the puzzle pieces together. *Error: does not compute.*

Arik waves me over. "Kate, come on in and sit down. Are you okay?"

A shiver works its way down my spine from the rough and gritty grumble that is Arik's voice now, and the thought that adulthood has been gracious to him arcs across my mind like a shining beacon of—*nope, not going there.*

I drag my eyes away from Mr. Dawson to find Arik, the giant Viking look-alike with door-wrecking shoulders, walking toward me. Eighteen-year-old Arik was tall but nothing like the size of an adult Arik.

Involuntarily, I shy away from his outstretched hands in a flinch that's irritating. Besides a flex of his jaw, he shows no sign that my aversion to his touch affects him at all. Why would it? I'm nothing to him, never have been.

He drops his arms, hands closing into fists as he stands there staring at me. Breaking the awkward eye contact, I look at my feet as I skirt past him to sit down in the chair next to Mr. Dawson, keeping him between Arik and me.

I'm setting my bag on the empty chair next to me when Mr. Dawson reaches for my hand, his features worried. His palm is hot and sweaty, but I don't pull my hand back. I'm still confused as to why he's here, so I wait for some sort of explanation.

"I'm so sorry, Kate. The edge of the bed was just there, and the next thing I knew, Hedy was rolling off, and she hit the ground so hard…" he trails off, and my jaw falls open as I gape at him.

Errrr, what?

Snapping my mouth shut, I need something, anything to get me out of the landmine I stepped in. Yes, landmine, because apparently Mr. Dawson and Gram were rolling around *in bed* when she…*fell.* My stunned stupid expression must be comical, because I catch Arik's smirk out of the corner of my eye.

"Um…I'm sorry, what did you say?"

Mr. Dawson looks me over and frowns, taking in my confused expression before realization settles on his face.

"She didn't tell you about us, did she?"

"Tell me about what? What was there to tell?" Honestly, I don't know if I want this information or how much more I can take before my head simply explodes.

Gram and I have a standing phone date on Sunday nights. I call, or video chat her if I'm available, and we catch up routinely.

There was never any mention of her dating anyone, let alone my favorite teacher from the horrible high school experience. When did this start? How did it happen? *No, brain, I don't need the visuals, thank you very much. Abstract thought is sufficient for now.* Taking a deep breath, I try in vain to halt the blush that curses all redheads.

"Why don't you start at the beginning?"

Mr. Dawson clears this throat like he's starting storytime. *Thanks so much for this, Gram. My revenge will be sweet.*

"Okay, well, um...Hedy and I started spending more time with each other about two years ago. At first, it uh, it started as friends at book club before it, uh, progressed to more. I guess you could say we both fell in love. I finally worked up the courage to ask her to marry me last night and"—his eyes find his shoes on the linoleum before he continues—"she was a little more...*ahem*...spirited this morning. Before I knew it, we were rolling off the bed, and I couldn't catch her. I thought she told you about us."

Holy mother of God, what did I step into? Shutting my eyes tight, I try to stop the image-producing side of my brain, the one currently locked on the fact that *my grandmother has sex.* I give up trying to rein in the blush staining my cheeks, the heat of it scorching as it climbs. Let's not forget that she has *spirited* sex that can lead to a broken hip. Lucky fucking Gram, pun intended.

Awkwardly patting the hand still clasped tightly in mine, I offer a smile.

"It's okay, Mr. Dawson, it was an accident. Not your fault at all. I'm gonna go find the vending machines for a soda." I need caffeine if I'm going to sit in a room with an elephant that size.

Standing, Arik offers, "I'll show you where it is."

Sheer willpower keeps my groan from being unleashed. Could this day get any worse?

"No, that's okay. I'll find it on my own."

"I want something too." Dismissing me, he turns to Mr. Dawson, asking if he wants anything. When he gets a negative in reply, I resign myself to more time in Arik's presence.

Charging out of the waiting room and taking a left, I get about six whopping feet before his voice stops me.

"Uh, Kate, the vending machines are this way."

The slight tilt of his lips tells me he's amused at my escape attempt, but I don't find the situation funny at all. Now that we're past the weird explanations of how my Gram got broken—which I'm still not thinking about—the worry rushes back in, and stress pings between my already tight shoulders.

Keeping my eyes on the floor, I follow Arik's lead but maintain a substantial distance between us. He doesn't try to make small talk or comment on my giant personal bubble, and I thank every deity there is when the alcove of vending machines comes into sight. A dollar lighter and a frosty Coke in my hand, we're headed back to the waiting room before he speaks again.

"It's been a long time. You look good."

I'm curious if what he means is since I dropped almost sixty pounds, I look different than the chubby girl who used to follow him around with the misguided assumption he was my best friend. Hating the needy self-conscious girl I used to be, I remind myself I have a backbone now, and his attention is unwelcome, his observations unwanted.

Has Gram kept him in the loop about me? Or is he astonished? Regardless, I have to pick my battles. I'm in no mood to continue this line of conversation when I'm already dealing with a grandparent sex-induced broken hip and rearranging my life to make an emergency trip to Idaho, a state I don't want to be in. Keeping my face as expressionless as possible, I only offer a nod in reply, then quicken my steps to pass him in the hallway.

I'm almost to the waiting room when I feel a hand firmly grip my wrist, accompanied by Arik saying, "Kate, wait a second."

Mindless muscle memory kicking in, I twist my wrist and reverse the hold, stepping around him while giving a firm jerk. I pin Arik's forearm to his lower back. My cheeks heat again, the connection from touching him still electric, but I force myself to speak through gritted teeth.

"You no longer have touching rights. Keep your hands to yourself." I release his arm, and he whips around to face me.

Challenge flares in his eyes, and there's that tic in his jaw flashing and gone in a second. A stiff nod is all the reply I wait for before turning back to the waiting room, once again settling into the uncomfortably hard chair while I wait for the damn doctor to come in and tell me what the hell is going on with Gram.

KATE

TOTAL HIP REPLACEMENT. MINIMALLY INVASIVE PROCEDURE. Six to twelve weeks of recovery for mobility. In-home nurses, not to be left alone, optimistic release tomorrow, picture of health, came through surgery with flying colors.

The doctor's words float around in snippets, my brain trying to piece them together as I sit beside Gram's bed in recovery. Arik's gone to check into a hotel, and the relief that comes from his absence is welcome. Ben—"don't call me Mr. Dawson, you're not one of my students anymore"—is quietly reading a paperback novel in a chair across the room.

Looking at my grandmother lying in a hospital bed is a sobering moment for me. While we talk with regularity, I live almost a thousand miles away. I was able to fly directly into Idaho Falls and grab an Uber to the hospital, but my concern-addled brain is screaming that the distance between Arizona and Idaho is too far.

Wine-red curls streaked with silver, the color passed down to me, lay limply across her pillow. Laugh lines and creases around her eyes betray her age but also her ability to laugh through the most trying times. Like being saddled with a two-year-old granddaughter when her teenage mother skips town. Gram is the only parent I've ever had. Sure, there was Grandpa, but he passed away when I was six, so I don't remember him much.

A lot of her traits and characteristics passed to me as well. A love for books, our voluptuous figures, the typical redhead temper that takes a lot of effort to tame when we get mad. Traits of hers I don't possess are the ability to forgive quickly and to let go of old hurts and move on.

Sunspots sprinkle the back of her hand, which is cool and dry in my palm. Instead of allowing my broken heart to rule and fleeing after prom, I should have been here for her.

Glancing up, Mr. Daw...I mean, Ben is looking at me, watching while I stare at Gram's prone form, and he takes pity on me, answering some of my unspoken thoughts.

"She's always so proud of you. Hell, I'm proud of you, and you aren't even my granddaughter yet. Neither of you has had an easy life, but she's never regretted a minute of it. She talks fondly of you, and your Sunday night calls are a high-light of her week. The distance is hard for her, but she understands you needed to make your own choices, and she's never begrudged you leaving Felt."

He's holding his place in his book with an index finger, looking at me, assessing me, probably reading the guilt that's all but yelling into the room. Since the doctor came out to talk to us, his concern and worry have calmed, and he's almost smiling as he reassures me that I'm not a horrible granddaughter.

"Thanks, but I should have been here for her."

"That's understandable to think given what's going on, but you need to remember you're entitled to make your own life and follow your dreams, dear. Your grandmother would be the first person to tell you that."

The room lapses back into silence, and we both sit, the steady hum of machines providing a backdrop of noise.

"Do you mind if I step out to make a call? I need to touch base with my boss about work arrangements."

"Not at all, dear. I'll come to get you if Hedy wakes up before you get back."

Grabbing my phone from my bag and quickly slipping through the door, I call Olivia. It's been almost seven hours since I left Arizona, so she should have wrapped up her workday by now, and the phone doesn't even ring a full time before she's picking up and talking.

"Kate, how are you? Is Gram okay? What's going on? Do you need me to come out? Because I can be there in a couple of hours."

Her concern for Gram is one of the reasons I love her, never mind that we've been inseparable since my freshman year in college.

"Hey, Liv, she's out of surgery. They had to do a whole hip replacement. We're waiting for her to wake up, and they're talking about releasing her tomorrow. You don't need to fly out. We're good here for now, but if that changes, I'll call you."

"Wow, they're already letting her go home tomorrow? How can I help? I went to your apartment and packed a bag for you. I just need to know where to send it."

When I got the call from Arik that Gram was hurt, I grabbed the first flight I could find, meaning I have my purse, the laptop and charger I hastily shoved in it, and the clothes on my back. I can pick up the essentials from somewhere until we get back to Gram's house.

"Yeah, they did the procedure a different way, so she's allowed to go home tomorrow pending any complications, but she'll be in a wheelchair for about a week. Thank you for the bag. Send it to Gram's house in Felt, and I need to ask a huge favor."

"Of course, doll, anything you need. What's up?"

When the doctor was detailing the treatment and recovery plan, I realized that Gram would need a lot of help, including me staying in Felt until she's on her feet again. None of this comes as a surprise to Olivia since she's the next thing to family to us.

"Whew, what a Tuesday for you."

And I haven't even told her about pinning Arik's arm when he touched me.

We plan for me to work remotely before going over what projects we have running between now and the end of July. June and July are always pretty sparse on her calendar, something I am thankful for now. With only a few things in August, it shouldn't be hard for us to manage the distance over the next six to eight weeks.

"Are you going to stay the night in the hospital with Gram, and if you are, do you need me to cancel the hotel room I booked?"

"Yeah, if you could, I'd appreciate it. I can't leave yet."

"You're leaving?" The harsh grate of Arik's voice interrupts my call with Liv.

Whipping around, I find him standing in the doorway to the waiting room.

Speaking to Liv, I wrap up the call.

"I've got to go. I'll catch you up soon. Love you." Disconnecting the call, I let the disappointment and anger coming from him fuel my own. How dare he be upset with me? He's the reason I've felt unwelcome in my hometown for years and part of the reason I was so far away from Gram when she was hurt.

"Excuse me?" I narrow my eyes at him, hackles raised. A

surprising amount of resentment rises, and for once, I don't bother trying to choke it back.

"You just fucking got here, Gram is *still* in the hospital, and you're *already* making plans to leave?"

"Not that it's any of your business, Arik, but I was making plans to work remotely. I'm not going anywhere."

His eyes flash hot azure fire at me.

"Bullshit, Kate. You said you *can't leave yet,* which implies you're leaving. I guess I should have expected this from you, especially with the vapor trail you left when you bolted after prom. But this is low, even for you."

The venom in his words fire angry daggers at me, hitting the bullseye of guilt harbored over not being here. Old feelings of inferiority well up, and I fight them back, holding on to the confidence I've built over the years by the skin of my teeth.

Clenching my jaw, I rein in the temper that wants to ignite. "Once again, not that it's any of your business or that I owe you any explanations whatsoever, but my boss was offering to cancel my hotel room. So, I'm able to *stay here* with Gram. Which is why I was telling her I'm unable to leave *the hospital* yet. If you had heard the whole conversation, you wouldn't be jumping to conclusions, so butt out."

Fuck him. Fuck Arik and his shortsighted assumptions about my life, a life he knows nothing about.

He says nothing, his expression locked down. I match him, choosing instead to stare at him in stony silence. Full minutes pass as neither of us gives ground, and it isn't until Ben pokes his head around the corner that either of us looks away.

"Uh, hey, you two. Hedy woke up." The tension between us is evident, making Ben's words cautious, like he's trying not to step in between years of festering resentment and distrust. I don't blame him. I've spent years avoiding Arik and everything that comes along with thoughts of him.

Following Ben back into the hospital room, I dismiss all thoughts of Arik.

Gram's bed is in a slightly elevated position, and she's propped up with pillows. Her eyes are half-mast, heavy from what I assume is a side effect of the pain medication she's on. Moving back to my seat by the bed, I reach for her hand.

"Gram, how're you feeling? Are you in any pain?" Ignoring the audience at my back, I take in her coloring, looking for any indication she's hurting.

Glazed green eyes look me over before she responds. "I feel like if they replaced a hip, couldn't they make them a little narrower?"

A choking laugh escapes me and then tears are spilling down my face. Her form blurs on the bed, and I valiantly try to stem the waterfall running down my chin, sniffling back the snot that always shows up when I cry.

"Gram, don't you know…our hips don't lie." The words fall flat; my voice is shaky and sad.

"Oh, come on now, Kate. Other than a missed orgasm, I'm okay. No crying now."

I am not going there. Reaching for a box of tissues, I mop at my face and tell Gram, "Ben's been worried about you. You shouldn't give an old man like him a scare like that. It's not good for his heart."

"Hey now, I'm not so old." Ben takes his seat on the other side of the bed while stroking the back of Gram's hand.

That's when Gram finally realizes her beau is sitting next to us. Her expression turns to apprehension and guilt.

"I'm sorry I didn't tell you, Kate. I didn't know how to bring it up."

"It's okay. Ben caught me all up. I do, however, want details from *you*."

My sixty-six-year-old grandma has the grace to blush, face turning red, and she's quiet for a minute.

"I'll tell you. But first, before I fall back asleep, I want to know what's going on."

"Of course, I can page the doctor." When she waves that away, I give her the rundown. "Pretty much, they're hoping you'll be released to go home tomorrow and then we'll start physical therapy next week. You should be up and participating in acrobatic sex acts in about six to twelve weeks."

"*Kate*." The blush beats hard against her face, making her skin almost match her hair, and I laugh at her embarrassment, having experienced the same at her hand growing up.

"I'm teasin' you. I'll be here for a while helping out with the bookstore and around the house. We'll get you back on your feet in no time."

"What about your work? I love Olivia, but I know she'd be lost without you."

I wave away her concern. "It's already taken care of. I'll work remotely in the morning and evening, on-call as needed. My days will mostly be free to work at the bookstore."

"I'll be helping too. With school out for the summer, I'll step in at the bookstore as needed," Arik says from behind me.

There's a flash of worry across Gram's face, gone before I pinpoint it.

"What's going on? What is it?"

"I'll let Arik fill you in. He knows what's going on. I won't lie to you, Kate. It's not good, but I'm so exhausted I could sleep for a week."

My smile turns strained, but her eyes are already starting to droop. Instead of arguing with her, insisting I don't need Arik's help, I hug her closely and kiss the top of her head.

"We'll figure it all out. You rest."

"Gonna close my eyes for a bit. You get some food and rest. You're looking too skinny and pale."

My eyes roll at the familiar comment because I'm neither tired nor hungry. I brush her hair back from her forehead. Once I'm sure she's asleep, I scoot back from the bed. Grabbing the bottled water from my bag, I drink deeply to wash away the leftover tears and tightness in my throat.

"She's right. You're gonna need help at the bookstore. I'll be there to give her a hand at home when she needs it. I'll also help get her to and from physical therapy. We might be able to arrange it at the house, but I couldn't tell you the first thing about running the bookstore."

"Thanks, Ben, it's okay. I'll figure it out."

"Kate, a minute, please?" Arik motions to the door behind him as if I'll jump up and follow. Little does he know, I don't hero-worship him anymore, and I have no intention of following him anywhere.

"No need, I'll figure the bookstore out on my own. Thanks for the offer of help though."

Pulling my laptop out, I open it, intending to get some work done while I wait, only to have it shut gently on my fingers.

"Can I please talk to you outside for a minute? It's important and about the bookstore." His jaw keeps ticking away like he has a million things to say to me and bites back each one.

Glaring at Arik, I set aside my laptop and follow him out of the room. Saying nothing, I lean a shoulder against the wall and wait, letting him fire the first shot.

"The bookstore isn't in the best shape."

"What do you mean it's not in the best shape? Physically or financially?"

"Either really, but financially the most. With a lot of book sales going digital, there hasn't been a high demand for print books, and even less so in our small town. We're pretty much in the middle of nowhere. Physically, a water pipe burst after the last blizzard and went unnoticed until it started to warm up. The store flooded, causing mold. The removal process was lengthy and expensive, so much so that Gram didn't have enough money to repair the actual water damage to the shop. Readers' Haven has been closed for two months."

Shock steals my breath. Ignoring the fact that I didn't know Arik did anything for the store in the first place, I try to stay calm to get details.

"This is news to me. Gram always told me the bookstore was doing well, keeping her busy, that sort of thing. Why wouldn't she tell me if it was hurting or something like this happened?"

"I can't speak to her reasons. My guess is she didn't want you to worry about it with you being so far away. Not much you could do to help."

I don't bother correcting him because he's wrong. I could do a lot to help. I have connections to authors and people in the publishing industry that would make a difference. That's not even considering the degree I hold with a minor in marketing. Hurt flashes through me—hurt Gram wouldn't ask for help, hurt she felt like she had to hide the business troubles from me, hurt that she would think I'm incapable.

The thought that she didn't reach out because she doesn't believe I have what it takes to help her circles like a vulture.

I hate that she felt she had to deal with this all on her own, that I'd been so out of the loop in her life. Not only does she have a new fiancé, but her business is struggling and in jeopardy.

"How bad is it?" I ask quietly.

"It's bad, Katie. Unless we get it fixed up and start generating profits, she'll likely have to close for good."

She must have been pouring her own money into the

store to keep it alive, making things worse. My heart gives a sorrow-filled pang at the thought of closing the store.

My grandparents opened Readers' Haven in their twenties. Gram was in charge of everything relating to the book world and community—signings, poetry readings, book clubs, children's storytime, and community outreach. My grandfather ran the store's business side, which ultimately fell to Gram when he passed away. Readers' Haven is an institute in Felt.

I grew up amongst the cedar-lined bookshelves, the smell of new and old books giving a bookworm the best kind of high. Big comfy couches and chairs were my home away from home after school as I disappeared into children's books, or as I grew older, the newest releases from all of the big-name authors. It was one of the few places in Felt not tainted in my memories. The thought of it closing, no longer existing, causes panic and heartbreak to tear through my chest.

He sighs and continues, "I don't know how to fix it. Gram only lets me handle some of the numbers, but I do know something needs to change."

Embracing change could have been the motto for my whole life. No more Mommy? The little two-year-old me blossomed when I had steady, loving Gram picking me up from preschool, reading to me each night.

Chubby and bullied through school? I used that motivation to get healthy and lose weight, falling in love with my body and everything it could do along the way.

My childhood best friend kissing the biggest of those bullies at the prom he asked me to, and then the humiliating words he said around his *real* friends? That heartbreak got me through twenty-one credit semesters over and over again until I graduated summa cum laude.

Change took me from a master's in business administration to being the best personal assistant and agent to Olivia Carter, an international best-selling author. Change allowed me to push back that voice in my head telling me that I'd never be good enough, that I'd never have any worth, and diminish it until it disappeared almost entirely.

Change doesn't scare me.

Plans forming, I mentally make a list of things that would bring Readers' Haven into the digital age while setting it apart as a top independent bookstore. I know I'll have my work cut out for me, but I can do it and do it well.

Firming my jaw, I lift my eyes to meet Arik's, his shrewd gaze taking in my determination.

"Once Gram is settled, I'll be shaking things up at Readers' Haven."

The fact I'll have to set aside my distaste for working with someone who had ripped my heart out leaves a bitter taste in my mouth, but I can't do this without him. Master of business degree or not, he's been on the ground with the bookstore longer and that gives him a familiarity I lack. I need Arik, though it galls me to admit it.

I only tell him to be prepared before heading back to the hospital room. I'll get what information I need from him and then avoid him as much as possible for the rest of my time in Felt.

Reopening my laptop, I start putting the connections cultivated through my years in the publishing industry into place.

ARIK

THE TETON MOUNTAINS CREST MAJESTICALLY OUTSIDE THE window over my kitchen sink, snowcapped peaks in a constant state of change depending on the season. Standing there, staring into the view, the feeling in the pit of my stomach is unnamable.

There's a slight ache in the ball of my shoulder when I move my arm, and it makes me grin every damn time, as sadistic as that is. The last thing I would have expected when I reached for Kate was her jacking my shoulder to shit and back. She didn't learn that from me, which just showcases the differences in her.

As much as I resent her for taking off years ago, the oddest surge of pride fills me, knowing she can defend herself if she needs to.

Her personality is leagues away from the girl I grew up alongside. The Kate that strode into the hospital waiting room was confident and outspoken, traits she'd only shared with me before. She knew what she was doing, and God save you if you got in her way. It's a damn sexy look on her.

Her only stumble was coming across Ben. The memory of

the look on her face when he explained how Hedy broke her hip makes me chuckle, and if I weren't trying to actively *not* think about that, I would give Ben and Hedy some credit for being as enthusiastic as they are at their ages.

Trying to push away thoughts of Kate and her return to Felt, I glance at my phone, hoping for a distraction, but I only have a missed call from Ma.

With a fortifying inhale, I click on her name and wait for the onslaught.

"Hi, honey. How's Hedy doing? I heard Kate is back. Have you seen her yet? Do you want to talk about it? Do you want to come over for dinner? You could bring Kate. It would be like old times, and I haven't seen her in years."

When she pauses to take a breath, I jump in.

"Hi, Ma. Hedy's fine. Ben said she got settled alright, and they'll start therapy to rehab her hip soon. Yes, Kate is back in town. Yes, I saw her. No, I don't want to talk about it, and no, I'm not inviting her over for dinner."

The motherly huff that comes through the phone makes me smile. While my mother has a backbone of steel, I won't budge.

She takes the gentle approach and wheedles, "Well, that poor woman, all cooped up in her house with so little company. You think she'd like a casserole and some chatting company? I could bring the makings for some hard lemonade if she's allowed to have it."

"Ma, come on. She just got home, and she doesn't need the likes of your nosiness in her house. Let her rest."

"Arik Aramis Beaumont, I would never." My balls draw up at that because nothing good ever comes from the full name.

"Ma, I'm only sayin'..."

Mom-guilt is a real thing, and Meg Beaumont wields it with the precision of a brain surgeon's scalpel. "If I want to take one of my oldest friends a casserole and some company, then I'll do just that, and that's the last on it I'll hear from you. What kind of friend would I be if I didn't go visit anyway?"

Resigned, I try to mitigate some potential damage preemptively.

"Okay, and you remember while you're interrogating Gram, that Kate flew out here a week ago. She's still working full time while trying to figure out how to take care of her grandmother. That's all on top of the heap of problems she's gonna have once I get the financials for the shop over to her."

"I'm not gonna call for pitchforks or waterboarding. It would just be nice to lay eyes on Kate. I haven't seen her in over a decade. I went from you two rambling about town daily to never hearing from her again. I never did get the details of what happened out of Hedy, *or you for that matter*, but I miss that girl. I thought…" she trails off, and I know what she thought. Hell, I thought it too. The velvet box buried at the top of my closet is proof of how much *I thought*. There's a saying about best-laid plans, and in my case, it couldn't be more accurate.

"I gotta get these documents over to Readers' Haven. I'll catch up with you later, Ma. Love you.

I grab the file folder off the desk and do my best to quell the nerves that threaten to take over. As I'm heading out and climbing into my Jeep, my phone rings, and I snatch it up, eager for the distraction. I'm dropping off the files, not lingering, no matter how much I want to. Nope, not learning about this new, still fascinating Kate. Not learning about how much of her is different than the girl I knew.

How much of her is the same? Does she still nibble on her lower lip when she's reading a book? Is she still as clumsy as always?

Irritated with myself, I swipe my screen to answer my boss's call, one I've been waiting on for weeks.

"Hey, John, how's it going?"

"Hey, Arik, no complaints. You enjoying your summer?"

I hear the answer before he says it, and abandoning pleasantries, I ask, "They shot down the proposal again?"

A weary sigh is all I hear on the line before John replies, "They did. Unless we can come up with the funds for the tablets through fundraising, the best they'll do is table it until we get some room in the budget."

The fucking budget. I hate that word. Teaching history and math to students is hard enough, but doing it with severely outdated materials is worse.

It's already June, and they want us to fundraise the money needed for three hundred tablets by the start of the new year.

"I got with the PTA, and they think that we can put together some events for the rest of the summer to raise a portion of the funds, but it's going to be a tight timeline."

Textbooks used when I was a student are now falling apart and have little relevance in education these days. That's what the bureaucratic asshats expect us to use to teach these kids and then question us when they continually score lower than their peers in annual state testing.

Frustration at the brokenness of the education system firms my resolve. I'm getting those damn tablets if it's the last thing I do this summer.

"Have the PTA call me so we can get started."

"Will do, Arik. Let me know what we can do to help."

"I will."

Disconnecting the call, I pull into an empty parking spot for Readers' Haven, noting the lack of cars in the surrounding lots. This is part of the problem that Gram and other business owners are facing. There isn't enough traffic for the store to stay viable in a small town without events to

ALINA LANE

draw in people. Tourism is our primary source of income, Felt being only a short drive from the ski resort up the mountain. People find themselves staying in town when they don't want to pay the inflated resort prices during the winter.

Summer months are a little slower around here but popular with campers and people who enjoy hiking and rock climbing. Gram should be looking toward retirement. But instead, she's spent the last five years fighting tooth and nail to keep the shop open, and I commend her for it, even if it is to her detriment.

I don't blame her for keeping the shop's state a secret from Kate. There wasn't much she could do from Phoenix. There was no sense in stressing her out or hurting her if Hedy didn't need to.

If I'm being honest, I don't have a lot of faith in Kate's ability to bring the shop back to life. But I won't say that to her—I value my life after all. I am curious about what she has planned for the store though.

Pushing the worn oak door open, I step into chaos as the tinkling bell rings. There are boxes of books everywhere. Both hardbacks and paperbacks blanket the floor. The checkout area is a mess of wires and covered in papers, and the furniture is shoved around and used as tables for everything else. The back wall has been ripped down to studs.

When did that happen?

I stare, dumbfounded at the amount of work going on. If this is her plan to get the bookstore back in shape, my lack of faith is justified.

Inching my way past the stacks, careful of where I'm stepping, I head for the back of the store, where the storage room and an office of sorts are, calling out as I go.

"Uh…Kate? You back there?" I hear a muffled curse and some shuffling around before the door opens.

Holy fuckfire.

My first look at Kate stepping around the corner of the doorway has my breath stuttering and my mouth going bone dry.

Dressed in those yoga pants that women practically live in now, not one inch of her is hidden in the form-fitting clothes. A tank top shows defined biceps and flows out over hips that would fit my hands nicely. Her collar bones peek above the neckline of the tank and were made for teasing bites and nips. Her red curls are bundled at the top of her head, tied in an artful knot that defines female trickery.

Face devoid of makeup, there's a small smudge of dirt next to the mole that hugs her slender nose. My attention drifts down, and I notice she's barefoot, a shimmering toe ring matching the bright gold polish she's wearing. She looks like a mythical goddess rising from an ocean of books.

Blood pools in my groin, and I've never been happier to be holding a file folder to hide behind. I'm so engrossed in cataloging each inch of her that it takes me a minute to catch she's talking to me.

"Arik…you okay?"

Forcing my eyes back up to look into her emerald gaze, I shove down the less than gentlemanly thoughts begging to be unleashed on a physique that lush.

Clearing my throat, I croak out a response. "Yeah, uh, hey, Kate. I'm good."

Eyebrow cocking in question, she waits me out. "I uh, brought those financials for the store." I start to wave the file but stop, thinking better of it since this file and my Wranglers are the only things between her eyes and my erection.

"Oh, that's great. Thanks for getting those put together for me." She's walking toward me with a hip-swinging gait that does nothing for my efforts to think with the brain north of my shoulders. After I hand over the folder, I shove my fists down my jeans' front pockets, hoping for a little more cover.

She misses it all, flipping the front page open to glance at the documents inside.

"So, how's Gram doing?"

Her attention is pulled from the contents of the folder, looking at me like she wasn't expecting me to make small talk, and the look of dismissal she's shooting my way gets my dander up.

"Gram is good. She's adjusting, and they already have her in a walker and out of that damned chair. Having Ben around has been a huge help." Straight and to the point, not any better, but at least she's talking to me.

"Yeah, Ben's a good guy. I'm glad he's there for y'all, but I'm here if you need me." Rambling, the words escape before I stop them. Wishing I could snatch them back out of the air, I stay silent in hopes she'll ignore them.

That's not the case as her jaw clenches, eyes going flat. Confirming my thoughts, her voice is monotone. "While I appreciate the offer, I think we'll be good. If I need anything from you about the store, I'll call."

About the store. I don't miss the qualifier, and my irritation spikes. I reach over and quickly snatch the file folder back out of her hands, an idea forming before I think better of it.

Kate's arms chase after the papers, but I hold it up out of her reach.

"What are you...give those back, Arik."

"Nope." I end the word with a pop. She wants to play? That's fine with me. I'll keep upping the stakes until she folds. I'm done with her avoidance and done with this stalemate.

"This is what we're doing? You're acting childish."

"Well, darlin', so are you and I reckon it's about time we cleared the air between us. You want these files, you come up

24

to my house tomorrow. We'll eat dinner and talk. You hear me out, you get the file. Otherwise…" I let the words trail off as I look around the wreck of the shop.

"You manipulative son of a bi—"

Cocking my head, I cut her off. "Sure you wanna finish that sentence, honey?"

"Arik, I have Colby coming by today, and I need those documents to get started here. I'll come to dinner, but I need that file."

"I was born at night, Kate, but it wasn't last night. You'd bail quicker than a novice cowboy in the chute if I hand these over. Dinner first or no documents."

Her shoulders are practically touching her ears at this point, and based on the emerald fire sparking out of her eyes I'm two seconds away from getting roasted. Walking backward, I hightail it back through the store as she furiously stomps after me.

"Get my address from Gram. See you at six."

I don't stop my quickstep till I'm in my car. Aware of how Kate can be, I head toward Gram's house to prime the pump.

Winding my way through the other side of town, I pull up to the sprawling ranch house that's been in Gram's family for years. The white shutters and wraparound deck paint the prettiest picture against the backdrop of rolling fields and towering mountains. Gram's gardens are a thing of beauty, not just the flowers and foliage, but the vegetable garden as well. The grounds are landscaped both for efficiency and aesthetics.

Many summer nights I've sat on the back porch in a rocking chair visiting with Hedy. There were summers spent hauling mulch, soil, and fresh flowers, pulling weeds, watering, and providing a strong back for the heftier projects. All of this in between running wild with Kate. The Palicki house holds an abundance of happy childhood memories for me.

The blue Honda sedan parked in the driveway is familiar, and I'm surprised it still runs as Ben has had it for decades. The white Ford Escape is also typical, but newer as I went with Hedy when she purchased it last year in Idaho Falls. Pulling alongside both cars, I exit and make my way up the porch, its pretty carnations in planters popping against the slate blue of the door.

I haven't knocked on this door in years, so the subtle urge to grab the brass knocker has me shaking my head. Ignoring my idiocy, I push the door open, stepping into the great room. Not much ever changes in here. No TV, because Gram believes *the family room is for conversation and friends, not television.* Paintings obtained from the local gift store showcase the creative talent we have here in the valley. It's a room that makes the house warm and welcoming, and I've always felt at home here.

"Hey there, Arik. How're you doing?" Ben's greeting comes from the kitchen entryway, where he's wiping his hands on a dish towel. His voice is slightly hushed, and when I look over, Gram is snoozing in her reading chair with an open book next to her.

"Hey there, Ben. I'm good, how're you and Gram doing?" Ma's stern voice rings through my head, reminding me that no matter my urgency for answers, it doesn't negate the need for manners, so I slow my roll.

"We're doing fine, getting into a routine around here. You want some tea? I made a pitcher yesterday."

"You know what? That sounds good right about now."

He waves me back into the kitchen. "I've just gotta wake Hedy and then I'll help her in here, and we'll have some tea and cookies while we catch up."

The kitchen is more updated than the rest of the house, with stainless steel appliances, granite countertops, and white cabinetry that shows off the sage-green stoneware through glass fronts. The old-school farmhouse table has enough seating for eight. I pass it up in favor of grabbing glasses for us and pulling the tea out of the fridge.

The shuffle step that comes behind me reminds me Hedy moves a bit slower since the accident, all too different from the confident stride I'm used to her having. Looking over my shoulder, I greet her with, "Hey there, gorgeous, sleep well?"

Gram grumbles at me as she gingerly sinks into the end chair at the table, shoving her walker to the side. "I hate napping—feel like I'm wasting my day away—but those dang pain pills make me so sleepy. What brings you over today?"

"Well, I wanted to check on you for one. Let me get this tea poured and we'll chat."

Gram gestures for me to grab some cookies from the jar that looks like a laughing cow. Armed with drinks and snacks, I carry everything over to the table before handing it all out. I'm not sure where to start the conversation, so I begin with the store.

"I stopped in at Readers' Haven to drop off the financial reports for Kate this morning. She's got the store in a right mess."

Embarrassment covers her face, and while I don't blame her, there's a sting that comes along with knowing that one of the women I admire most is hurting.

"We haven't talked about it much yet. How was she this morning?"

"Kate's about as fussy as you would guess with her feelings toward me. Which is one of the reasons I'm over here."

Her lips purse at first and then she opens her mouth, but I cut her off and continue.

"Gram, level with me here. What happened after our prom? What chased Kate hundreds of miles away? What put that betrayed look in her eye every time I'm within spitting distance?"

Silence reigns around the table. Ben, who's aware of our past, sits quietly, sipping his tea and nibbling on a cookie. Gram shakes her head slightly, lips turned down in a frown.

"Arik, as much as I want to give you the details, I can't. It's not my story to tell. The only thing I'll say is she was hurt and brokenhearted like only a teenage girl can be. If you want to know, you should ask her."

Irritation surges, and I scrub a hand along my beard to stop from yelling. I get the same answer every time I've tried to pry the details out of her, and then out of Ben when they took up together. Ben knows my side of things, since he's been a large part of my life since college. But neither of them ever offer up details, so I'm left stumbling in the dark. Now I have a new weapon in the form of financial paperwork Kate needs to move forward with her plans.

"Honey, I know you're frustrated, and I know you care for Kate. You were two peas in a pod growing up. I'm sorry, but the only thing I can tell you is this is a conversation you need to have with Kate."

Hedy's explanation means it's time to pull out my trump card.

"Well, that's the thing, Hedy. How am I supposed to get answers from someone who continues to shut me out? How do you propose I break down that barrier? I refuse to bloody my knuckles knocking at the door over something that happened when we were teenagers. I get so twisted up around her that I'm holding the damn financial papers hostage until she talks to me. She drives me that insane."

"You're holding the reports for the store hostage? What do you mean?"

"Kate got snippy with me—pissed me right off—so I took the file back. I told her that it was past time we clear the air, and she has to come to dinner tomorrow if she wants the papers."

Sly appreciation covers her face. "Do you think she's going to go?"

My reply is deadpan. "Yeah, I'm sure she'll show up. She's practically the picture of cooperation and all."

The sinister twinkle I get in return has my shoulders hunching. I know what the twinkle means, and it's not good news for the person it's targeting. "I'll get her to dinner. Just you wait."

I don't know whether I should be thankful or hesitant at Gram's promise, but at this point I'll take what I can get.

KATE

A SINGLE WEEK. I'VE ONLY BEEN BACK HOME A WEEK, AND Arik's pushy ass is playing games. I spent most of my morning buried in plans to rearrange the store, set it up in a less ramshackle way, and bring a sense of order to the shelves. Books litter the floor that I have a precise layout plan for. I had expected to pore over the store's records in the later part of the afternoon, but Arik had to shove his nose where it doesn't belong.

My face is still hot with the angry flush I've been sporting for hours. I gather my things while preparing to close the store. If I'm unable to get information from the paperwork— which I fully intend to get eventually *without* having to submit to dinner—I'll get information from Gram instead.

We haven't had a real conversation about the store yet, partly because she's exhausted and the pain pills are keeping her tired. I'm also not ready for the argument that is sure to come when two fiery redheads go to battle. It's easier for me to ask her forgiveness after making the necessary plans and adjustments than asking for permission and giving myself a concussion by beating my head against her sense of independence.

Stepping out of the store, I pull the door shut, locking it behind me. A cool breeze drifts over me, and the fields are blooming with wildflowers popping against the grass in a sea of color. I would be roasting in Arizona's arid desert, and the cool summer evening is a welcome change. Painted shades of pink, indigo, purple, and red, the sky darkens as the sun sets a blazing path past the horizon. Sure, we get some pretty sunsets in Arizona, but they don't have anything on the ones right here in Felt.

Main Street showcases our local businesses in the almost two-mile stretch that runs through town. There's the post office, Corner Drug, Buffalo Diner, Mountaineering Outfitters, Louis' Pizza Pizzaz, and a few other stores that keep this place on the map.

Unlocking my bike from the lamppost, I prepare for the ride home. Biking three miles to and from the store will help keep the country cooking off my hips and my expenses lower by not having to shell out money for a rental car. I refuse to borrow the bigger vehicle that's easier for Gram to get in and out of. I'm about to turn down the road that leads to Gram's house when there's a *beep-beep* of a car horn behind me. Slowing to a stop, I turn around and gape at the vaguely familiar blonde poking her head out of the SUV window while she pulls off to the side of the road.

"Ally Sawyer. Holy shit, is that you?" I abandon my bike before rushing over to the now open car door. She barely clears it before I'm wrapping my arms around her and we're both jumping around and squealing like crazy teenagers.

"Kate freaking Palicki. Look at you. You look so good! How are you? How have you been? Tell me everything."

She smells like sugar and vanilla. I'm so unprepared for

the familiar face of an old acquaintance that tears sting my eyes. I didn't realize I needed the hug and happy welcome until now. That's when I start crying in earnest.

"Oh, oh no. What's wrong? What did I say? I'm so sorry. Please stop crying. I didn't mean to upset you."

Her panic makes me chuckle through the tears.

"No, not at all. I'm sorry I'm such a mess. You didn't do anything. Here, let me look at you. Gosh, it's been so long." I hold her at arm's length. The leggy cheerleader from my memory is now a stylishly put-together woman, and I am so happy I ran into her.

"You look amazing. What's new with you?"

The Ally I knew in high school defied the stereotype. Two years behind me, her brother Jackson was in my grade. We didn't exactly run in the same circles—she was younger, outgoing, and popular—but she and her brother were never mean to me and always called Christina on her shit. We lost what little touch we had when I left for college, and a little guilt for that surfaces.

She must recognize the expression on my face because she says, "Don't even worry about it, Kate. You had to do what was best for you, and if leaving Felt in your rearview is what did it, that's okay with me. Now, that doesn't mean I'm gonna let you out of catching up."

Grateful, I give her a small smile while offering, "How about a drink at O'Malley's? Do you have time?"

"That sounds great. Let me clear it with Mama. She's watching my twins, Elle and Emma, but she should be good with it." Pulling her phone out, she shoots off a text, and almost immediately her phone chimes.

Still looking down at her phone, she says, "Yep, she's good with it. You wanna load your bike in the back here and I'll give you a ride?"

It takes some maneuvering, putting the seats down and shifting stuff around, but we both get the bike in the back. As I climb into her passenger seat and buckle in, Ally hands me some napkins from her glove compartment to clean up the mess on my face.

"So, twins, huh? How old are they? What are they like? How's your Mama and brother? Are you married now?" I have so many questions they just ramble out.

Clearing her throat, she takes a second to reply. "Yeah, uh, not married. I'm divorced. The girls are six and pretty much exactly like us at that age. They're crazy, and I'm ready for them to head back to school even though they just got out. I own The Sweet Tooth bakery here in town. Mama and Jackson are doing great. Jackson's a park ranger now, no surprise there. Mama's fully retired, and she watches the girls during the summer for me, and before and after school too. As she puts it, she left her day job for her career in being a grandma. The girls love her to pieces, and it's a mutual love affair. You should swing by sometime and meet them."

"I'd love that, thank you."

"Me too." She shoots me a sunny smile.

Pulling into the parking lot of O'Malley's, I note the wooden porch and the saloon-style doors pinned back to frame the entry. It's how a modern-day western bar should look. The interior is unchanged from the faint memories of eating here occasionally with Gram and then later with Arik. The walls still sport the mounted animal heads and framed sports memorabilia from my youth.

There's a big-ass bar situated under the second floor that houses more seating, a dancing area, and a couple of lounging chairs and couches. The lighting is dim, but it looks like they have a setup for an actual band, though there's no music playing.

The hostess seats us in a booth near the back, which I appreciate as Ally and I won't have to shout over the noise from the televisions that play by the bar. As we get situated, I watch a gut-curdling blast from the past walk to our table.

"Well, look who we have here. Kate Palicki." She says my name like she's tasted something nasty, and she hasn't changed a bit. Her trademark sneer firmly in place, memories flash. The cruel taunts about my weight, the horrible pranks—like taking all of my clothes and throwing them out of the locker room while I showered after PE class, then telling the football team the shared locker room was empty.

I look up at the bleached-blonde hair and overly caked makeup of the girl who was the center of my high school misery—Christina Hathaway, meaner than a rattlesnake and bully extraordinaire. I physically restrain myself from launching my fist into her cheap nose job and instead level her with a polite smile. Gram raised me with better manners.

"Hey there, Christina, how have you been?"

"I'm great, so sorry to hear about Hedy. It's such a pity with her being laid up and the bookstore closed and all." Offhandedly she adds, "Hey, Ally."

Old insecurities are everywhere in this town. Those feelings of being ugly, of being overweight, of not fitting in have constantly tried to bring me down since being back, but I've fought them back every time and I'll continue to do so, Christina be damned.

Fixing her with my best bless-your-heart smile, I say, "I'm actually running the bookstore now, and we'll be reopening soon. But thank you so much for your concern." Uninterested in her fake bullshit, I open my menu, dismissing her.

Steam might as well come out of Christina's ears when Ally jumps in. "I think I'm ready to order. How about you, Kate?"

"Yeah, I'm ready. I'll have a margarita on the rocks with a glass of water, and a plate of the loaded nachos, thanks." As I pass her the menu, my stomach chooses that moment to unknot and loudly growl. I'm officially starving again.

Venom I lost patience with a long time ago comes out sugary sweet in backhanded concern. "Oh wow, that sure is a lot of calories. Looks like your eating habits haven't changed much, but I understand the need for comfort food. I bet you've just been so stressed out."

Ally's jaw pops open. Maybe Christina's rude side is reserved for only me these days? I'm not a pushover anymore, though. If she wants to get into a battle of wits and insults, she's gonna lose.

"Christina, I bench press weights higher than your IQ. I'm not overly concerned with a few extra calories, comfort food or no. As I'm sure you're aware, I'm doing fine regarding my caloric intake." I'm damn proud of my body. I compete in obstacle course races, triathlons, and hike routinely. Christina probably has trouble lifting the trays that serve as her paycheck.

Eyebrows shooting up before her gaze narrows, she obviously didn't expect me to be more than the meek, quiet patsy she used to love tormenting. The triumph that spreads through me is vindication at its finest.

She opens her mouth, no doubt to deliver a scathing retort, but Ally speaks up first. "I'll have the same. Thanks, Christina. That'll be all for now."

There's no reply as she leaves our table to go put in our food order. I don't care if it's petty or beneath me. I'm proud of myself. There's a part of me that was afraid that coming back to Felt would mean losing all the confidence and backbone I grew during my time in Arizona, and I'm pleased as punch that's not the case for the most part.

"She's as delightful as ever," I comment while spreading out the napkin on my lap. Looking up, I see Ally is staring at me all wonky. "What?"

"Holy shit, Kate, that was *awesome*."

"Eh, it's been twelve years. I don't take shit like that anymore."

"I'll say, but yeah, she's about as pleasant as a pissed-off hornets' nest being poked on a hot summer morning. I don't think I've ever heard you talk to someone like that though."

I laugh, because she isn't wrong. "What can I say? I grew pretty outspoken while I was gone."

Head cocked, she says, "Tell me all about that."

So, I do. As we eat I tell Ally all about being away for college and how meeting Olivia was the best thing for me. I tell her about how I dropped the weight and how I learned to love myself. How I used lifting weights, self-defense classes, and hiking to challenge myself and combat the insecurity that was a second skin for so long. I'm out of breath and my eyes sting when I finish. Ally has been mostly silent and listening to me or tossing in questions here and there between bites of food.

"That's about it for me. Tell me about your life since high school."

Ally jumps in, talking animatedly about her girls and about working at the big resort. How she thought she was in love with the owner's son, Daniel, after dating a short time. How she married him when she found out she was pregnant with the twins and then divorced him within a year of them being born.

"Now I run Sweet Tooth. You know the old bakery the Sheltons owned for years? They were ready to retire and none of their family wanted it, so I bought them out, and it's been about four years now. You should come in and grab a coffee. I make the best lattes in town."

"It's a date."

We pay our bill and make our way out of O'Malley's. Just as I'm pushing through the door, Ally offers, "Let me know if you need any help with the bookstore, assuming you don't mind the girls tagging along when Mama can't watch them. I'd love to get my hands in there."

I shove the door open while talking to Ally, so I'm not paying attention and I ram straight into a man-sized brick wall.

When I stumble back, hands grab at my wrists, wrapping around my forearms to prevent my fall. My neck prickles, and the zing that climbs up my arms gives me an inkling of who collided with me. Looking up into lake-blue eyes, I start to stammer my way through an apology before I remember that I'm still pissed at Arik and let the apology die in my throat.

I try to step away, tugging ineffectually at my trapped arms, but his hands are warm and strong as his thumbs draw small circles on the inside of my forearms. I hate how good his fingers feel skating across my skin. With a shiver, I glance up to find his eyes warm, lips quirked in a slight smile as he asks, "You okay, Katie?"

His nickname for me has me yanking hard, and he finally gets the hint to let go, showing no outward signs of emotion other than that fucking smile.

"I'm fine, thanks." I turn to Ally. "You ready to go?"

There's a curious gleam in her eye, a glimmer that makes me suspicious, and she addresses Arik. "Hey there, Arik, how's it going? Grabbing some dinner?"

"Nah, I already ate. I wanted a drink and the game high-lights, so I decided to get out of the house."

His glacial gaze bounces back and forth between Ally and me as they chat. Fiddling with my bag's strap, I try to ignore his looks, the argument from earlier still fresh in my mind. I don't want to jump in and interrupt Ally, but I also don't want to stand here and be under his scrutiny longer than necessary.

"Oh, well, Kate and I should get going. I'll catch up with you soon." Ally's farewell is part tease and part threat.

Clueless male that he is, he just says, "You betcha." With the proverbial hat tip to Ally and a rumbled "Kate," Arik disappears through the door.

"Sorry for making you wait. Let's get out of here—you look cold."

I don't even realize I have curled up on myself until she points it out, but yep—my arms are wrapped tight around my middle, shoulders rounded and hunched in. I shake off the tension.

"Nope. Not at all. If you wanted to pop the back, I'll grab my bike and then head on home."

"Kate. I'm not letting you ride your bike home at eight thirty at night. I'll drop you off at Hedy's. Come on, let's go. You may not be cold, but it is chilly out here." She's right, with the sun almost completely gone and the breeze cooling off the heat of the day, there's a chill in the air.

The car ride home is quiet. I ruminate on the argument Arik and I had this morning. I need those records from him, because while I trust Gram to lay out the whole story of how bad a shape the shop is in financially, I still need the hard figures before I can make any definite plans.

Once I have those papers, I'll prioritize building revenue for the store. But that doesn't mean I couldn't use some input from another business owner, and she did technically offer to help.

"Did you want to come to the shop sometime this week and help me with the layout plan? It's a lot of moving stuff around right now, but I wouldn't mind the company, and you're welcome to bring the girls."

"Wow. Yes, I would love to. I know you said you're changing stuff up, but with it being closed for so long, a lot of people were unsure it was going to reopen. We all thought that Readers' Haven was done for."

"No, not at all. If I can fix it, I'm going to."

"If?"

"Yeah, I'm having some problems getting the financial reports for the store."

"Arik does all the…oooh."

"Precisely. Arik won't give me financials until we hash out the past. I think he wants to sing 'Kumbaya' or some such nonsense."

"I never did find out what happened that night. I remember you hauling ass out of the gym crying, but you lit out of there while I was getting you tissues, so I never got the full story. If you don't mind me asking, what did happen between you two? Maybe I can help."

"I don't think so, but pretty much I got my hopes up and he dashed them. I was young, naive, and too trusting, and it came back to bite me in the ass."

"Hmmm."

The noncommittal response has my brain whirling. Is she involved with Arik? Their conversation outside of the restaurant didn't give the impression they're involved. I hate myself for it, but I ask anyway.

"You and Arik…y'all friends or is there something more there?"

A coughing snort pushes its way out of one of her orifices before Ally dissolves into giggles. Once she has herself mostly under control, she says, "No, *God, no*. Arik and I are just friends. He and Jackson are super tight, and they fish together all the time. That would be so awkward."

I shouldn't be relieved. For all I know he's with someone else, but considering how beautiful Ally is—that bright sunny hair, hazel eyes, and petite frame—I can't help it. *Something is wrong with me. I shouldn't care if Arik is involved with someone else.*

But the sinking feeling threatening to consume me proves that I do care. And that's a problem.

KATE

WEDNESDAY MORNING, I'M STANDING AT THE STOVE WHEN Ben comes in from the backyard. After slapping his gloves on his thigh, he pockets them in jeans that look older than I am. He's been out working in the gardens so Gram doesn't have to get up and down to weed. I fell a little in love with him when he suggested she sit on the patio to enjoy the fresh air.

Seeing them together is still surprising, even after a week. Since I can remember, it's always been Gram and me, ready to take on the world together. We've always had each other's backs. Now Ben's belongings are scattered around the house, little pieces of their lives merging evident in my childhood home. I never expected her to find love again since she never went looking for it when I was younger, but I'm glad she has it now.

My mother got pregnant with me at sixteen. I'm not even sure she knew who my father was, other than a bull rider on the rodeo circuit. Two years of being a mother convinced her parenthood wasn't really for her anymore, and after dropping me off with Gram, she lit out of town and we haven't heard from her since.

Over the years, idle curiosity had me googling her name for what I could find. Besides a couple of arrest records and a three-year prison stint, there isn't much information on Stephanie. But I don't have the same wonderings I did before. She did me a favor by giving me to Gram, and I got over that childhood hurt a long time ago.

Looking over at Ben, who's grabbing a couple of mugs from the cabinet, I ask, "You and Gram ready for some breakfast? I thought that we could eat on the patio and enjoy the morning."

"Sure thing. Let me take this coffee to Hedy, and I'll come in and help you cart it all out there."

While he gets coffee together, I decide to plate everything for us. A country breakfast is on the menu—eggs, hash browns, bacon, sausage, and biscuits with some of Gram's jelly from the cellar. I have everything ready to go when the front door opens and closes. Wondering if Gram was planning to have friends over, I tuck my hair behind my ear and stick my head around the partition wall that separates the living room from the kitchen.

Meg Beaumont is hanging her purse at the coat rack with one hand while an enormous casserole dish balances in the other. I'm stunned stupid at the sudden appearance of Arik's mom standing in Gram's living room. She turns to me, and the same platinum-blonde hair she passed to her son swings from a chic bob around her pixie-like features.

Stephanie opted out of raising me in favor of living a life free of responsibility, and I've always respected that Meg is the polar opposite. Pregnant at seventeen, she dropped out of school. Between working at the fancy resort in housekeeping, night classes for her GED, and raising Arik singlehandedly, she's always been someone I admire.

"Katie Bug. Oh, it is so good to see you. I've missed you

something fierce. How are you? Getting used to the pace of Felt again?"

The shotgun blast of her foghorn voice makes me smile. For a small woman she has the most resonant voice, almost as if she's smoked for years, when in fact she never has. Huge grin stretching my cheeks, I rush over to her, wrapping her in a hug. She barely has enough time to set the casserole on the entry table before I envelop her.

The scent of cinnamon and *Mom* surrounds me. Her dainty arms squeeze me tight, and she's surprisingly strong for a woman who resembles a pixie. How she created a giant like Arik I'll never understand. Unexpectedly, my eyes sting, the hot prickle of tears trapped while I enjoy the embrace. Her hand pets at my hair while she sways side to side, and I bask in the motherly comfort.

After a few seconds, I pull back while clearing the tightness from my throat.

"Holy cow. I'm good. How have you been?"

Laughing lightly, she brings her hands up to cradle my face, the gesture so familiar, I ache. She touches her forehead to mine, and her voice is a little watery when she replies. "I've been right as rain, pumpkin. Come on, let me put this casserole in your freezer and we can catch up."

Remembering the forgotten plates of breakfast, I ask, "Have you eaten yet? Gram, Ben, and I were about to sit down to breakfast. We have plenty if you want to join us."

"That sounds delightful. I think I'll do that." We walk side by side through the house, our arms linked, pausing only to grab plates and flatware before heading out to the patio.

The sun's painting a pretty picture across the Idaho sky, and the temperature is still mild enough that we won't swelter while we eat. Meg drops a kiss on Gram's cheek, hugs Ben, and pleasantries are exchanged before we're all sitting around the table digging into our food.

"Hedy, I stuck a tater-tot casserole in your freezer. Figured I'd save someone from having to cook dinner tonight."

"Meg, you didn't have to do that, but thank you. We appreciate it."

Meg waves off Gram's thanks, and I watch two of my most influential female figures chat about who's who and what's what in Felt. I miss this kind of thing living in Phoenix—the small talk, the history, and the unwavering sense of community. After running into Ally last night and then Meg this morning, I realize that I lost a lot of the good memories when I worked to shut out all the bad ones.

I catch Ben's gaze as he's putting his coffee mug down, and there's a teasing glint in his eyes, an understanding of how much I'm enjoying this. Smiling at him, I settle in, letting conversation and good company surround me.

As we're wrapping up the meal, the conversation moves to the bookstore. Keeping my plans vague as Gram and I haven't discussed everything yet, I walk them through what I've got going for the day.

"On the topic of the store, though, did you ever have a website set up?" I ask.

Orange juice snorts out of Gram's nose and she chokes on the liquid. We all grab napkins and thrust them at her.

"Are you okay?"

Waving us off, she wipes her face and clears her throat.

"I'm fine, I'm fine. It just went down the wrong pipe. I don't think we've ever had a website for the store. Why do you ask?"

"Just something that's been bothering me. I was trying to secure a domain name for the store to build a website, but the one I want isn't available. The site that has it is down for maintenance. I don't know of any other bookstores with the name Readers' Haven, and a google search didn't pull anything up so it's just confusing. I do have a couple of alternatives though, so I'll just go with one of them."

Ben's face is bright red as if he is the one that choked, Gram's eyes stay on her plate, and Meg stares off in the distance. They're all acting weird, and as much as I want to ask what's going on, I have to get some work done for Olivia before I head into the shop.

Turning to Meg, I ask, "Is Arik busy today? I could use some help moving book boxes and some of the bookcases. He offered to help, but I don't have his phone number." After he called and informed me of Gram's accident, I tried to call the number back, but it belonged to the local hospital instead of his cell like I had originally thought. If I'm going to trick him into giving me those reports without the humiliation that comes with dinner, I need to get him alone.

A delighted grin covers Meg's face as she pulls her phone out. "Let me get that number for you."

Unlocking the door to the shop, I flip on the lights and navigate my way around the mess of boxes that are full of books, all labeled neatly and noted with their new home. I'll be moving them today so Colby can come in and measure everything before drawing up specific plans. His walk-through of the store yesterday was thorough enough that I asked him to fit in the repairs as soon as possible. Every day that we're closed is a loss for the store, and missing the Independence Day tourists is hard enough to reconcile.

Pulling my phone out of my pocket, I fire off a text.

Me: Hi Arik, this is Kate. Is your offer of help still open?

Not even thirty seconds pass before my phone buzzes in my hand.

Arik: Sure thing, what'd you need?

Me: I was hoping to move some of the bookcases around the store, but they're too heavy for me.

Arik: Yeah, when did you need me?

Me: Whenever you have time today is okay. No rush.

Arik: Give me an hour.

Staring down at my phone, I'm glad that wasn't as unpleasant as I thought it would be, especially when his demands are still fresh in my mind. I tuck my phone away and head back to the storage room, hoping to clear some space.

Noting the small area that I'm working with and how it limits the amount of stock we can carry, I resolve to clear out the second floor of the shop to turn it into a more formal storage area.

The stairs to access the area are blocked off to avoid creating a liability, making the studio with its full bathroom and loft the perfect place to renovate, giving us the ability to carry a larger reserve of books. I jot down the changes on the plan to talk about it with Colby.

I'm shoving the last of the papers into a decrepit filing cabinet when I hear the bell chime at the top of the front door. I poke my head around the corner of the storage area. Instead of the towering Viking I'm expecting, Jackson Sawyer, Ally's older brother and high school quarterback turned park ranger, is pushing into the bookstore. His bright green eyes dance over me, a smile tugging at his lips.

"Hey there, Kate. It's been a while. Arik said you needed some muscle to move the shop around."

Warm pleasure shoves aside my irritation at Arik passing off the work, as Jackson sweeps me up in a bruising hug. He's a foot taller than I am, and my feet leave the ground as he spins me around.

"Jackson Sawyer as I live and breathe! It's so good to see you."

"Katie Belle Palicki in the flesh. How are you?"

"I'm great. Certainly not expecting to see you, that's for sure."

Some of my irritation leaks away because Jackson clarifies, "Arik's on his way, but he asked if I would come give him a hand with the heavy lifting."

I'm happy to see Jackson, but Arik didn't even bother to ask me if I wanted anyone else's help before just making the decision himself, and that's aggravating. It's not Jackson's fault his friend is a bonehead, so I let it go. The extra hands should make everything go quicker. Then I'll weasel the papers out of Arik and after that, we can ignore each other.

"Thank you, I do appreciate the help." Settling onto a couple of stools, we go through the general pleasantries, the how-are-yous and the what's-new-with-you spiel I'm doomed to repeat until the town settles in with the fact I'm back home.

Jackson is finishing a story about the recent increase in raccoon wildlife when the door opens to let Arik in. The pleasant feelings of catching up with an old friend die as I watch the bearded blond behemoth clear the threshold. I'm still pissed at his antics yesterday, but I plan to use honey rather than vinegar to catch this fly.

Giving a smile to the guys, we get down to work. It's quick work, so less than an hour later the guys are carting the last of the boxes of books back to storage.

As the last box gets tucked into place, a chime sounds from Jackson's pocket. Pulling his phone out, he fires off a quick message and says, "Hey Kate, we all good here? That was my partner, Connor, and they have a situation they need me for up at the station."

"Yeah, that was all I needed today. Thank you so much for coming and lending a hand. I appreciate it. Next time we catch up I'll have to buy you a drink."

"Sounds like a plan."

Lingering near the reception desk, Arik's engrossed in its overflowing contents. The papers, printouts, and schematics I have spread across it hold his attention.

Mentally girding my loins, I approach the counter.

"Hey, can we talk?"

His gaze meets mine, and I can't tell what he's thinking. It's so much harder to read him now. I get the impression he's reserving the right to rip my head off while I work on charming him to my side.

"So, I'm going to be in town for a couple of months, and I know you're close to Gram. I don't want us to have to walk on eggshells around each other." Sticking my hand out to him, I offer, "Friends?"

The flash of disappointment that flickers in his gaze is gone before I'm sure I saw it, but the stone-cold façade is firmly in place as he takes my hand but doesn't shake it. Tingles spread up my arm with my palm enclosed in his, and I hate that even after everything between us, he still affects me this way. I'm willing to set aside our differences and be friendly, but no, my traitorous body still reacts to him like I'm seventeen.

We were teenagers, sitting by the lake, as I confided my hesitation about prom. Those blue eyes, a perfect match to the lake water, looked at me like I was something to cherish before his lips dropped to mine. The lightest of brushes, it was the sweetest first kiss. I remember him carving the memory of the day into the bark of a tree after I agreed to be his date to prom the next night.

Now, his slow nod has me settling into complacency when he opens his mouth and says, "You want to be friends? Then I'm looking forward to us talking tonight. It'll be nice and *friendly* to get everything out in the open."

Relief gone, I yank my hand out of his grasp, giving up the charade.

"Goddamnit, Arik, I don't want to have dinner with you. I don't want to rehash the past. Why can't you understand that?"

"I understand it's in the past, but you left for twelve fucking years, Kate. I deserve to know why."

While I disagree that I owe him an explanation at all, I need those reports. If he's going to dig his feet in, then I might as well get this over with, but I make demands of my own.

"Fine, you want to talk it out, we'll talk it out. After that, I want that file, and I don't want you around unless it's necessary while I'm here."

ARIK

KATE'S WORDS PLAY IN MY HEAD ALL AFTERNOON. I TOSSED out the ultimatum about dinner to get all the shit from the past out into the open. I never expected her to kick back with one of her own, but I should have. While everyone else looked past her or only noticed her perceived flaws, she's always been outspoken and fiery with me.

I don't want you around unless it's necessary while I'm here. Those words are a fist to my gut because I'll lose the chance to get my best friend back unless I work this right.

Leaving the shop was the only option left to me after nodding dumbly at her demand. The shock that she'd demanded me not come around—it fucking hurt. I cleared one hurdle with her agreement, but keeping her at dinner is gonna be trickier.

I need a lot of help. Fast.

Being a creature of habit, I have a few different outlets when I'm feeling frustrated or need a break from life. Driving the back roads in my old beat-up Jeep, I head out of town and up the dirt roads that lead me to Packsaddle Lake. It's about a twenty-five-minute drive requiring a four-wheel-drive vehicle, but it's still early enough that there isn't anyone on the back roads while I let the breeze blow through the open windows.

I pause near the shoreline where the forest goes right up to the water, some of the trees sprouting from the lake's shallow shores. There's an old makeshift diving board someone way before my time fashioned out of a cut-down tree. A few of the trees have ropes tied around the branches creating rudimentary swings. Coming up here as a kid was always fun. We used to walk out on that board as far as we could before jumping—or falling—into the lake. The tree serves as the backwoods version of a dare and is a son of a bitch that shakes and wobbles, taking a nimble grace to make it more than halfway down the thirty-foot length. There are steep inclines to clamber up only to run down and swing from ropes into the waiting water below.

Not interested in taking a dip today, I pull the Jeep off to the side of the firepits along the shoreline. I haul my gear over to a sandy bank, spreading out my pole, tackle box, and a camp chair—essentials for any last-minute fishing trip.

The hunter-green Jeep that pulls up beside mine sports a state park decal on the side, and I watch as Jackson and Connor climb out of the SUV.

"Hey, guys, how's it going?"

I wasn't particularly close with Jackson other than a greeting here and there in school. It wasn't until after we both came back from college and he talked to my students about forest fires that he invited me to go fishing. It's tradition now—usually if one of us ends up out here, the others follow. The simple text I sent while leaving the shop ensured that.

"Did you coerce Kate into dinner by keeping vital paperwork about the bookstore from her?"

The question takes me by surprise, but then realization

hits. Ally and Kate were at dinner last night. If Kate said something to Ally, then Ally most likely said something to Jackson. For siblings those two are pretty close.

"Yeah, I did. Well, kinda."

"I thought Ally was bullshitting me when she called me at the station earlier. And what do you mean 'kinda'?"

"I am keeping the papers from her, but only so she'll be reasonable and tell me why the hell she lit out of town. I have a general idea, but we still need to talk about it."

"First off, when has a woman ever been logical when it doesn't suit her? Secondly, you still don't know why she took off? I figured as close as you are to Hedy, she'd have told you by now. That was, what, twelve years ago?"

"Yeah, it's been about that long," and *God,* thinking about it burns. "But Hedy's never said anything to me about what went down. I don't blame her—it's her granddaughter *and* something that Kate and I should work out ourselves."

Connor is tying off a knot on a hook attached to a bobber as he speaks up for the first time. "What's the endgame here?"

"What do you mean?"

"I mean, what's your plan? Say it all goes perfectly and you get her alone. Y'all talk it out. What then? You aiming to be just friends with her? You want more? What's the goal here? Why rip out the past to examine it if you don't need to?"

I want my best friend back. The thought comes to me before Connor finishes speaking, and it's true. I don't want to have to stay away when Kate is visiting, sporadic as those times have been over the years. I want her to feel comfortable coming to see Gram. I want to clear the air between us and bury the hatchet.

I want to know what she thinks happened that night. I always assumed she saw Christina kiss me while we were dancing, but that wouldn't explain the devastation on her face every time I try to bring up the past. I'm also pissed off she ran instead of coming to me. The more I think about it, the angrier I get that she would run instead of confronting me, that she would assume the worst about me.

Maybe trying to persuade her to talk it out in a more private setting wasn't the way to go. As soon as I have the thought, I dismiss it. If I left the ball in her court it would stay there until we were dead. The woman avoids conflict more than any other person I've met in my life, so I used the only leverage I have to get her to talk to me.

"I want my friend back. I'm not afraid to admit that her leaving left a hole in me. It did. It hurt." *It still fucking hurts.* "But if everything works out perfectly, I'll get my friend back."

Connor doesn't let me off the hook just yet. "And what about what she wants? Based on what you've said and what we've heard from Ally, she hasn't been interested in a stroll down memory lane."

There's always this heartbroken and betrayed look in Kate's eyes when I'm around her. I want to erase it, and maybe that's the reason I'm pushing so hard for this talk. I want to understand. I want her to understand that I would never intentionally hurt her. I can't tell that to Connor though. It isn't his business, so I leave it at, "I have my reasons."

"Then what's the strategy here? How are you planning to pull this off?"

"I'm not trying to *pull* anything off." That makes it sound like I'm nefariously plotting against Kate. "I want to talk to her, to clear the air, and maybe make it easier for her to be home helping Gram out. I have no illusions she's planning on staying."

"And you think talking out what happened all those years

ago will make it easier on her? Or easier on you, considering your connection to the shop?"

A few years back I found Hedy crying on the back steps of the shop. After considerable effort on my part, it came out she didn't have the capital to go on with the store. There was a mistake made by the accounting firm in Boise who did the taxes for the store, and she was going to have to close. She was so close to calling Kate, who was in her master's program at NAU, and asking her, begging her to come home and help clean up the mess.

There was so much grief in Hedy, and I understood that grief. She and Greg had built the store from the ground up. They were a fantastic team—working together and doing so smartly.

The combination of Greg passing away and corporate bookstores appearing made the business harder to run, but Hedy had made it work for many years. Then there was the evolution of bookstores turning to primarily digital sales and the emergence of e-readers taking business from independent bookstores.

Throw in Hedy hiring a sketchy firm for the accounting after the last accountant retired instead of taking the time to learn how to run the store's business side, and it all combined to create a recipe for disaster. Time and market trends were about to force one of the women I'd admired my whole life to close down the last physical reminder of her husband. I couldn't stand for that, not when I had the means to help.

As much as I wanted Kate home, I didn't want to put her in the position of having to save the day, the same place she was in now. So I'd offered to help to give Hedy some breathing room, and I started handling the books. She began to turn a corner and get some profit back into the store when that damn pipe burst and destroyed her chances.

I don't regret it though. I grew up in Readers' Haven alongside Kate. We did our homework together while I waited for my ma to get off work and come pick me up. Afternoons and weekends were spent browsing the stacks. I shelved books for extra cash when I needed to save up for the newest graphic novel or Stephen King horror. Readers' Haven was a second home to me.

"My question is, are you doing this to make it easier on her or yourself? That's what you need to decide."

Connor's question gets my mind working, but I don't have an answer for him.

"Honestly? I don't know. I'm just hoping she'll listen, and we can put this behind us."

A snort rips out of Jackson and he's shaking his head. "Like reason, I've never known a woman to listen when she doesn't want to. I'll wish you luck, Arik, because you're gonna fucking need it. This is gonna take some serious finesse. What do you have planned for dinner?"

I hadn't thought that far ahead yet. The goal was to get Kate to agree to come to my house, where we'll have privacy. Where we wouldn't have to worry about Gram and Ben overhearing our conversation—or anyone else for that matter.

I don't want you around unless it's necessary while I'm here. Not only do I have to bare my soul about what happened on prom night so long ago—something I'm not proud of—but I also have to explain the part I play in her inheritance.

I'm hopeful for friendship, but if I'm really honest with myself, I'd like to touch her again. I want to taste her, feel her. I want to bury my hand in all that red hair and tug at the silky length to put her right where I want her.

There isn't a way for me to go back in time and change what happened that night, no matter how much I want to rewrite our history. The only option open to us is to find our way through and move forward. To hopefully remove that crestfallen look in her eyes when I'm around. While it's been twelve years, I know her wounds are still raw, and I'm about to add to them.

Changing the subject, Jackson asks, "How is your mission with the tablets coming along?"

"We're hosting a car wash at the school Monday and then every weekend through the summer. It's going out in the paper tomorrow, and we're hoping for a good turnout. After that, we have other plans in place. It's a tight timeline but I feel like we'll meet our goal, especially if I can convince people of the merits of replacing those books at the town council meeting Thursday night."

John's call this morning about the parents pushing back against getting the tablets has my blood boiling. Parents around the valley would rather use the funds the PTA raises for new athletic uniforms rather than the tools needed to educate their children. The blatant lack of support is just one more thing to handle. I have the school faculty's help, and they'll show up in force at the council meeting, but that may not be enough to convince parents that the school funds need to be used for more academic reasons.

Jackson, Connor, and I hang out at the lake for the rest of the afternoon, planning and working out the details on what I should do to help win parent support, and I'm grateful to them. For two guys uninvolved with the school, they have pretty good advice. The drive back to town is peaceful, and I remind myself I have to keep it simple and not let my own emotions cloud the situation, no matter how much they riot the closer I get to dinner tonight.

KATE

THERE ARE PAPERS ALL OVER THE KITCHEN TABLE. PRINTOUT after printout of the repairs that need to be done to the bookstore. Cost projections, material lists, and a breakdown on the rough schedule and labor calculations are spread across the gleaming wood surface.

Hours. I've been staring at these printouts for hours, and the numbers are starting to bleed together. Getting up, I grab another cup of coffee and take a short break to rest my eyes.

I don't have any idea of the capital available in the store, but if the bleak look in Arik's eyes when he talked about it at the hospital is any indication, I have to assume I'm working on a thin financial margin. That's okay, though, because the buy-in agreement I had drawn up allows me to make a large enough investment to cover the repairs and renovations to the store—assuming I get Gram to agree with it.

As if on cue, the front door opens and closes. Gram and Ben are back from physical therapy. I stand to put the kettle on for tea but stop when Gram's voice cuts through the house.

"Of course it'll work. We have everything in line."

"I'm just saying we need to have a backup plan if they catch on."

"Oh pssh. They're both so wrapped up in figuring each other out right now, they have no idea what's about to hit them."

No idea what they're talking about, I ask loudly, "Who has no idea?"

A short yelp is my answer before Gram enters the kitchen.

"Oh goodness, Bug, I thought you were still at the store. I didn't see your bike out front." The critical eye that circles the printouts littering the table isn't overly tired today, and that's an improvement. Gram is still moving slowly, but she's getting around with more mobility this week largely due to the walker she'll be using for some time. Physical therapy should help with her halting gait in the coming weeks.

Scooping up the papers and shoving them into a file folder, I arrange some cookies on a plate for us to nibble on.

"Don't deflect. What was that about?"

"Uh, what was what about?" Gram's eyes shift between Ben and me.

"Who isn't going to know what hit them? Who is so wrapped up?"

"I'm sorry, Kate, we can't tell you. That's official Cowboy Course information," Ben tells me, a light pink blush crawling across his cheeks. They're both acting cagey lately, but I have bigger things I need to cover today, so I let the subject drop.

"Come sit down. There are some things I want to go over with you."

Ben helps her over to the table, and he fusses with her until she's comfortable, making my heart sigh. Sitting down, I get right into the information I want to cover.

"Okay, so first order of business, the finances. I don't have the reports yet, and you've said you're not a hundred percent sure of what's going on there, so I drew up a couple of different business plans to account for the different possibilities."

I detail the individual setups, how we'll attract more readers to the shop both in person and digitally, melding the two worlds. Then I outline the changes that have occurred in the bookselling industry since the start of digital reading.

"High time here in Felt is the tourist seasons. You have people who vacation here during the summer, and then the skiing booms every winter with the resort's guests. While Felt isn't the closest town to the resort or even the largest, we are the closest with a non-chain bookstore. We're going to capitalize on that by hosting events during the summer that bring more people into the shop. I also reached out to Dolly over at the inn and came to an informal agreement to get a coupon in their room folders for a book purchase, so if any vacationers stop in, it'll increase the chances they buy from us. In return, we'll refer authors to the inn, so there's something for both sides there. Still with me?"

Gram looks over the papers, and after a couple of moments, she nods in understanding.

"Okay, next, as part of my job, I have connections in the book industry and put out some feelers. This year's tours are tight, but a couple of the agents and authors I've worked with before agreed to have an impromptu signing here the first weekend of August. The count as of now is sitting at ten authors, not including Olivia, who will be participating,"—I hand over a printout of the authors who've confirmed and continue—"and they'll be promoting the signing on their social media pages. I have a promotion schedule here as well for the social media pages I'm creating. The signing will, of course, bring more readers into town. While our goal is to get them in the store for the signing, the readers bring additional business to the town overall and boost our business through the digital storefront I'm designing."

"My word, Kate, you've been busy." There's a measure of awe in her voice as she looks at the pages. "All these authors confirmed to attend a signing here? Stella Nova, Norma Marie, Fancy Roberts, Tara Carr, Iannah Roberts…" she trails off. I mentally finish the list, *Hattie Harte, Robyn Elyse, Tamara Karr, Breanna Lynn, and Claire Hastings.*

"This is what I do, Gram, so it hasn't been much work. We're calling it Romance at Readers' Haven since that's the primary genre of the authors." I work to keep my reply light. The reality is the store is in some serious trouble, and unless we start increasing the income, then Arik's prediction will be right, and the store will fail—and that's not something I'll allow.

"What did Colby say it was going to cost to fix the damage?"

The numbers won't decrease her stress, which hardens my resolve to fix this for her.

"Don't worry about the cost of repairs right now; we'll figure it out. I have plans to update the store as well, and I'll cover that once I get all the details hammered out."

The tiny sigh that slips past her defenses has Ben running his hand down her back in comfort.

"It'll all work out, Hedy. Let's listen to what Kate proposes and then we'll think about it. I may not be knowledgeable about running a bookstore, but so far, her plans are smart and business savvy. Let's trust her to know what she's talking about and hear her out."

"Okay." Gram's hesitant agreement coupled with her determined nod is the okay I need to continue outlining what I've come up with so far.

"Next, along the same lines as the digital storefront, I've taken liberties to create a more comprehensive website with affiliate links to the digital bookstores. I couldn't find contact information for the owner of the domain that I wanted, so we went with an alternate. The more people we get here in Readers' Haven, the better, but for instance, if we don't have a book they're looking for and they use our website to order it from an online retailer, we get a slice of the sale."

These business practices should have been done years ago. The store should have been updated and grown with the times. Gram has always done her best, but her avoidance of this exacerbated the problem. She could have told me she needed help sooner. Instead, her stubborn insistence to handle everything herself has created a mess I'm scrambling to clean up.

While I brush off the work I've put in, I can't help a tiny bit of resentment at the late nights and early mornings plus the extra hours put in on the planning outside of the time I'm at Readers' Haven, while I try to keep up with Olivia's schedule. Cutting my sleep down to less than four hours a night, I'm starting to get ragged. This week alone, I missed two critical documents that if Liv hadn't caught, we would have been in a world of trouble with the IRS for the third quarter tax filings. Double dipping on work is taking a lot out of me. I'm always running, and I need a break soon, or I'm going to crash.

I get that I'm young and new to the book industry, but my work over the years should have meant that she felt comfortable telling me about the store's problems, which would have ensured that she never got to this point. Shoving the useless thoughts away, I plow ahead.

"Any questions so far?" The next subject is going to be touchy, but I promised myself I wouldn't keep information from Gram no matter how badly I want to shield her from it.

"None so far. These plans are smart business, Bug. Thank you for doing all this."

Waving away her thanks, I pull the next stack of papers from another folder, saying, "I asked Rob to draw up partnership papers that detail me buying into the store, bringing in an influx of cash that'll help with the necessary repairs and upgrades needed."

Gram's face goes stony before she says, "No, absolutely not. I'm not taking your money. No." Closing the folder, she gives it a little shove across the coffee table, dismissing it and my efforts and offer to help.

I knew when I had the papers drawn up that she would balk, that this would be a point of contention between us, but I'm not budging.

Cocking a brow, I pull out every bit of attitude I have.

"No, you won't take my money, but you'll pull funds from your retirement accounts to keep the store open when you're barely earning enough to pay the taxes on the building? There's that business acumen our family is known for."

My assumption she's been pulling from her investments is a shot in the dark. I can't imagine where else she's been getting the money to run the store, though, because Arik won't give me the financials, but it's a logical assumption.

I don't mince words because, as frail as she is at the moment, I know she'll walk all over me if I handle her with kid gloves. Silence sits heavily between us. I get comfortable there until Gram squirms in her seat, her gaze flickering back to the folder. Seizing the moment, I go in for the kill.

"The documents in that folder protect my investment— the money I've already put into the store and the money I've used to create the digital storefront. I don't have to go into a partnership with you. I'd give you the money either way, but this way protects us both."

Sliding open the folder, I pull out the expense report I've been keeping in my proverbial back pocket. Handing it over, I watch her eyes bug out. There's a measure of satisfaction that comes with her shock. The total of what I've paid out so far isn't staggering, but it's not insignificant either.

"I've noted the costs associated with the signing and the percentage of income we'll make in profit—the profit that'll cover a new website's cost and the various changes I've made to our ordering process, equipment, and technology. Gram," —my voice is as exhausted as I am—"the register behind the desk is older than I am. You don't even have a setup to accept debit and credit cards, which is essential."

Taking a sip of coffee, I catch my breath before continuing. "Letting me buy into the store means you don't have to eat these costs and allows me to make a pretty smart investment since I have experience in this world that you lack. It gives us enough capital to keep going until there is a profit margin for operating again. You don't have a choice. Not if Readers' Haven is going to stay open. I have to go to the bathroom. I'll give you a few minutes to think about this."

It's a big decision, and while her motivation is to stand on her own feet, this is the only way. I don't have to use the bathroom. Instead, I head down the hallway before slumping against the wall to rest just a moment. The dark circles under my eyes were hard-earned this week. I made more progress in the store in a week than anyone else had in almost two decades.

"What do I do, Ben?" she asks in the kitchen. Sadness saturates her tone and makes my own eyes tingle as tears gather. I never want to upset Gram, and yes, my words were harsh, but this is her business. A business I'm trying to put back together.

Peeking around the corner, I watch as Ben wraps his arm around her shoulder and pulls her in, letting her lean on him. *Come on, Ben, don't let me down now.*

"I hate that she feels like she needs to come in and take care of me. Her leaving was hard on me, but she needed to spread her wings. I'm glad she's home, but I hate she has to deal with this burden."

My heart clutches at those words, but Ben's steady cadence catches my attention.

"What's the harm in letting her buy into the store, Hedy? In my opinion, it's a win-win situation. She buys in as a partner, which according to any standard partnership agreement does protect you both, and you work together to bring the store back, and…" Ben's volume dips and I can't make out what he's saying. Still, it must be persuasive since Gram is nodding along with him. Taking that as my cue, I head back in, purposefully making noise so they know I'm coming. Luckily Gram doesn't leave me hanging long before speaking.

"Okay, Katie, I'll let you buy into the store. But you'll need to edit that agreement and get someone else's approval."

"Who." It's not even a question. The sinking sensation in the pit of my stomach has pieces of the puzzle clicking together before she confirms my thoughts.

"Arik. Arik bought into the store years ago. He needs to be included in those documents as well."

KATE

THE SUN IS STILL SHINING BRIGHTLY AS I MAKE MY WAY DOWN the dirt path leading to Arik's house. After Gram dropped her little bombshell about Arik owning part of the store, rage so acute I've never felt anything like it took over. It took the combined efforts of Gram and Ben to calm me down. I have my temper locked up tight right now, and that's the only reason I'm comfortable having this conversation with him. Otherwise, I would have bailed on dinner, with or without the documents. Gram's words of wisdom urging me to go to dinner ring through my mind on a continuous loop.

"It's better if you both get everything out in the open. There are things you don't know, things that happened after prom, and I feel like they could shed some light on the past and the store."

"What do you mean things happened after prom? What happened?"

"That's not my story to tell, Bug, but I think you deserve those answers, so go get them."

Fed up with everyone keeping secrets from me, I work hard to rein in my reigniting temper. The carefully crafted outfit I was planning to wear tonight for the supposed air-clearing dinner went out the window. I'm still wearing the ratty yoga pants I decided to lounge around in while working at the store and home today.

Not my best look for confronting him.

Hawks Road is one I'm familiar with. It winds its way up one of the steeper inclines on the outskirts of Felt. Arik and I used to come up here during our summer adventures around town when the only thing to do was entertain ourselves and make sure we were home before dark. The road backs the Hawkinses' land, and I don't recall any houses up this way, but it's been a long time, and maybe that's changed.

I breathe deep to maintain my tenuous calm while navigating around the last turn. Arik owning part of the store is just another problem to handle. I refuse to go in there guns blazing, no matter how much I want to rip his ass for keeping his involvement with Readers' Haven from me.

I crest the top of a rise and sure enough sitting pretty as a picture, painted by the sunset, is a sprawling ranch style home with a wraparound porch.

At least he has good taste in home design.

I take in the intricate river rock masonry that brackets the lower half of the house rising into a deep blue color.

Of course, he would have a beautiful home.

Blindingly white shutters frame expansive windows with a rustic-looking garage door. Not one, but two chimneys jut from opposite ends of the house.

Phoenix homes don't boast this kind of design; stucco is everywhere with tiled roofs. The differences in houses is not something I'm used to anymore.

While shopping for my condo in Arizona, I never thought much about the interior or exterior of a place. Not like when I was growing up in Felt, because there are some beautiful houses here.

My main concern in buying my place was functionality.

I'll admit there's an undeniable pull to the picturesque house with the evening light playing across it. The house has to be over three thousand square feet. Why does he need all this space?

I let gravity pull me down the hill and give my legs a much-deserved break from biking across town. The grounds of the house are stunning. Aside from the concrete driveway, there's a landscaped mulch bed surrounding the porch saturated in English lavender and wildflowers to break up the sea of purple. The grass is so green it stands out against the surrounding fields' rustic browns. The house itself looks new, probably not older than five years, and it sits right at the beginning of the Hawkinses' land.

I drop the kickstand after pulling the bike up to the porch and climb the steps.

Each step is harder than the last.

The door opens before I have a chance to knock, and there's Arik in a dark red Henley, his blond hair damp as if he's fresh from the shower.

"Hey, Kate, come on in." His easy welcome makes me think Gram called ahead to warn him. His bare feet pad backward after he pulls the door wider, allowing me to enter.

My curiosity gets the better of me as I step into an honest-to-God foyer. Built-in cabinets line the entryway with hooks and benches for shoes and coats. The dark mahogany floors gleam, and soft overhead lighting illuminates the space. Taking off my lightweight cardigan, I hang it up before turning to Arik as he speaks.

"Did you ride a bike here?" The irritation in his tone takes me aback, but his gaze isn't on me, but on the bike on his porch.

I counter with a question of my own.

"Why didn't you tell me you bought into Readers' Haven?"

His eyes bore into me, all icy intensity. The colors often change depending on the mood he's in, going from ice blue to warm cobalt. I've heard them described as frigid, though I've never agreed with those opinions. Then again, I also know how they warm up in affection and amusement.

Finding my voice, I can only assume he has a problem with the bike, so I answer his question first. "Yeah, I've been using Gram's old bike to get around. I don't feel comfortable leaving her without a car, especially if Ben isn't going to be around during the day."

"Kate, it's eight fucking miles from Gram's to here, most of it uphill."

"And?"

"And you're a damned idiot for riding that far when it'll be dark soon. Why didn't you use Gram's car?"

Pulling out the voice reserved solely for whiny editors and nagging agents, I crisply inform him, "It wasn't necessary. Since I'm standing here, I made the trek in one piece."

If it's possible, his expression turns even grimmer before he bites out a reply. "I'm driving you home tonight. You don't need to be riding a bike that far in the goddamned dark."

"We'll see." I don't bother to keep the sass out of my reply, and it doesn't go unnoticed that he hasn't answered my question.

Scrubbing a hand through damp locks of platinum, he growls—actually growls—in response. "Still like Gram."

I smirk at the intended insult before parrying, "Always will be."

Helpless not to grin at the chuckle he lets out, the tension dissipates as we stand in the open doorway looking at each other. It feels like old times, the less complicated times when we would argue over stupid, pointless stuff.

Breaking the stare, Arik swings the door shut and says, "Come on, we need to talk." I follow him through a tastefully decorated living room with a TV the size of a barn wall mounted high above a massive fireplace. Dark leather couches and chairs sit on an immense rug. The tables match, and the lamps' soft light give the room polish, leading me to believe he had help with the house's interior. With the bare walls and lack of window curtains, it's as if someone purchased furniture for the house but no one actually lives here.

Wordlessly, we head down a hallway, and as we step through the wide opening, the floor shifts from hardwood to a light tile.

I have officially entered heaven on earth.

Boasting a shining stainless steel six-burner range with a smoke hood, double ovens, and a deep farmhouse sink, his kitchen is magnificent. A composite resin table with a slab of a tree running through the middle of it eats up the far side of the room, and if I counted the chairs right, there are eight place settings. Spacious is the only way to describe the house, and I have so many questions. Reaching under the counter—where I see a wine fridge built into the island—Arik pulls out a bottle of cabernet.

"When did you move in here?"

Turning from the bottle of wine he's opening, he says, "I talked Mark Hawkins into selling me a piece of his land he wasn't using about three years ago. Got with a contractor friend, and we put the plans together for the house. Took about a year to build it the way I wanted it, but I've been here for about a year and a half now."

"Where were you before?"

"I had an old fifth-wheel trailer parked on the lot. It was cramped while we were building, but I made do. Before that, I lived in the apartment above the bakery."

"This place is nice. What is it you do again?"

"I teach here in Felt, at the high school."

"I didn't know that. What do you teach?"

"Algebra and History."

"Like Ben did?"

Arik struggled in school. It wasn't a secret, but also not something he broadcasted. The fact that he's a teacher for one of the subjects that used to give him trouble fills me with pride. Pride that he pushed himself outside of his comfort zone to overcome those obstacles and pride that he pursued something most people would have given up on considering his past.

He nods. Being nosy, I decide to push in hopes of receiving a less succinct answer.

"How does a high school teacher afford a house this nice?"

As if he was expecting the question, he has his reply ready. "I dabble in trading stocks and investments. I've done pretty well for myself. I also invest in small businesses here in town as needed, which you're aware of."

That brings us full circle to the reason I'm here.

"You never answered my question. Why'd you buy into the store, and why didn't anyone tell me?"

My abrupt change in the topic doesn't bother him as he fills two wine tumblers, handing one to me.

"Gram was in trouble and needed help. I offered her the money, but she demanded I buy into the store before she would take it."

"Yeah, I got that part, but that doesn't answer why no one told me about it."

Throwing up his hands in exasperation, he says, "Kate, what were we supposed to do? It was around the time you were finishing up your master's degree, and you had your hands full with that. Gram also asked me to keep it between us. Not that I could get in contact with you even if I wanted to, which I didn't since it wasn't my place and would only hurt you."

"That still doesn't excuse you for not telling me since I've been back. You've had plenty of opportunities to bring it up. Also, I'm a grown woman. I don't need you or Gram protecting me from something that might hurt me."

"When was I supposed to bring it up? Every time we are in the same room, you spit fire if I so much as look at you for too long."

The irritation in his tone ignites the smoldering embers of my temper. Biting back the sarcastic retort on the tip of my tongue, I try to speak as calmly as possible. "I appreciate you helping Gram. That's not why I'm upset. You should have found a way to tell me."

"I was planning on telling you tonight over dinner."

That takes me by surprise. "You were?"

"No, I was going to keep it a secret and hope and pray you didn't find out."

I let the sarcasm go, the last of my energy to maintain the fight gone.

Changing the subject again, I ask, "What's for dinner?"

"I have Gram's pot roast in the oven. We have about thirty minutes until it's done."

"Gram's recipe, huh? Not that confident in your cooking abilities?"

Chuckling at the slight rosy hue that colors his face, I have managed to catch him off guard.

"I cook just fine. I guess since you're here, I might as well give you the tour. Follow me." He points to a door I assumed was a pantry. He disappears through it, leaving me to trail after him down to what I believe is a basement. Flipping on the lights, I can't help but whimper at the sight before me.

A fully padded and insulated floor holds a home gym so wide-ranging I wouldn't be surprised if it spans the house's length. Centered in the room there is a squat rack with the accompanying attachments, weights, and add-ons. Cardio equipment, medicine balls, balance balls, and dumbbells line one side of the room. The entire back wall hosts floor-to-ceiling mirrors with a barre mounted in place. Another giant TV on the rear wall is currently off.

"This was one of the first things I put in. After the community center couldn't secure the funds needed to keep their fitness center going, I invested in having a home gym. It's not as extensive as a traditional gym, but I usually spend several hours a week down here, so I expect it to get the job done."

"I'll say. Holy cow. You have a Rogue Rack set up in the bottom of your house. I might be friends with you so I can use it." As soon as I say it, I wish I hadn't, but Arik steps right through the door I opened.

"You're welcome to anytime. There's a whirlpool here in the back for soaking." He points off to a tucked-in small room separated from the gym area.

Curiosity has me by the teeth so I can't stop my next question before it jumps out, filter completely gone in amazement of the weightlifter's dream in front of me. "What do you bench?"

"Uh, about two twenty or two thirty on a good day. You?"

"I can handle a buck forty when I have the right motivation."

"The right motivation? What would that entail exactly?"

"Honestly, usually margaritas. The only things I love more than lifting heavy weights are tacos and margaritas."

"I'll have to grab some tequila and find out what you're made of then. When did you start weightlifting?"

"My freshman year in college. I signed up for a gym membership but didn't know what I was doing. My friend Rob saw that I was overwhelmed, so he stepped in and taught me."

The comfortable back and forth between us edges with flirty, but it's mostly friendly and cautious. I'm dead set on keeping my distance, but I can't help but admire the way his jeans hug the solid muscles of his ass as we head out of the gym.

Someone doesn't skip his squats.

Praying I don't blush for once in my life, I keep my eyes trained on my feet as we walk back through the kitchen.

Leading me down the first hallway off the living room, he points out guest rooms. Some are empty, but there are a total of six bedrooms in this house, not counting the den he uses as a home office.

His laundry room alone would make any organization nerd weep with the efficient use of the space, with shelving for baskets and a mounted ironing board. I want to find out who his contractor is if I ever build my own house.

At the end of the hall, he points to the closed door with a mumbled, "That's the master bedroom." His explanation is lacking in comparison to how detailed he was when showing me the various other rooms.

"Well, let's see what your closet space is like." Reaching past him, I turn the knob and push the door open.

"Uh…Kate, wait a minute." Arik tries to stop me, but I'm already stepping into the room. A huge four-poster bed looks small in the massive space. Like his living room, the bedroom furniture is obviously from a matching set. There are two side tables, a long dresser, and its matching tall bureau cornered in the room. Huge windows let in the breeze while a sliding door opens out to the back deck. Turning to check out what I assume will be a large walk-in closet, a picture over the dresser stops me in my tracks.

Red hair in pigtails, purple huckleberry juice spread out across my lips, I'm about eight in the picture. Arik's arm is slung over my shoulders, the mess around his mouth matching mine as we both smile widely into the camera.

I remember when Gram took the picture. We had been picking berries all morning, soaking in the sunshine. We ate more than we put in our buckets, the sweet but tart juice getting everywhere and turning our fingers a dark blueish purple. I even chased Arik down and rubbed some of the liquid in his light hair, giving it an indigo tint. He responded by smearing it across my whole face. Shrieking in the fun that only best friends can find together, we ran wild that day, the sound of Gram's hooted laughter a backdrop as she watched us roughhouse.

My voice is tinny in my own ears, and I try to ignore the lump in my throat. "Where'd you get this?"

"Gram gave it to me right after you left. I had it made into a canvas." His voice is deadpan like he's trying *not* to feel when that's all I do, the messy memories of happier times sitting like lead in my chest.

Its placement on the wall isn't insignificant. It's hung to catch the early morning light, directly across from his massive bed. Arik wakes up to a canvas of *us* every morning.

Suddenly uninterested in what his bathroom and closet might contain, my snooping no longer holds the appeal it did five minutes ago. I'm afraid of what else I might find hidden in the depths of this man I don't *understand* anymore. My eyes find my shoes again.

Unsure of what to say, I clear my throat, hoping my voice doesn't come out watery. "So, uh, how about a refill on this wine."

I turn to exit the room but don't get far before his hand wraps around my elbow. Spinning me to face him, Arik pinches my chin between his thumb and first finger to drag my gaze up to his face.

His voice emerges with gritty frustration, and the ferocity

of it takes me by surprise. "I missed you every goddamn day. Every fucking day, Kate. You never answered your phone once I badgered the number from Gram, and you returned every letter I painstakingly wrote to you. You sent every one of them back unopened, crushing me until I gave up and stopped trying. You fucking forgot me, forgot us, without even giving me a chance to explain. You tucked tail and ran."

Lip quivering, my eyes filling with tears I *swore* I wouldn't shed, I shake my head. Faced with his tortured expression, I'm not prepared for the guilt that surges through me.

My mouth opens to respond, but I don't get the words out before his hand leaves my face, reaching down and clasping my other arm. With my shoulder blades touching the wall, I feel his hands shake as he continues, "Do you know what it's like going from having a best friend, a friend who means more to you than anything in the world, to them being *gone*? Do you know what it's like to be cut out of someone's life with no chance? Do you know how I felt not knowing what happened, to only guess and then when I tried to explain getting shut down every single time? Do you, Kate?"

I deflate at his words, the wind sucked out of my sails until I'm adrift in defeat. There's so much pain in his eyes, and I did that to him. I was the cause of it. No matter how justified I felt in my actions, I had no right to cause him pain.

"I'm sorry. I…I never meant to hurt you. Growing up, I was so dependent on you that I knew if I opened your letters I would cave and give in. Every part of who I was then was tied up in you. I wasn't ready to face that then. I'm not sure I'm ready to face it now." In my voice, the plea is unmistakable—the appeal to not push me, to let me get there when I'm ready.

His Adam's apple bobs as he swallows. Dropping the hands that held me gently in place, he only nods.

He motions me out of the room, and I rush through the door. The messy cesspool of emotions jangling like an out of tune harmony between us, the good feelings and comfort from earlier are gone, just like before.

ARIK

Silence hangs while I pull the roast from the oven, then slice it and plate our servings. Kate is already seated at the table with her glass of wine.

I wasn't prepared for her to find out about the shop before I could tell her, not that I was in a big hurry there. Nor did I expect her to confront me about everything else before I forced her to, so her knocking on my door had me adjusting my plans fast. But I fucked that up too. Instead of having a civil conversation over dinner, I let my emotions get the best of me from the start, and I ended up verbally spewing my resentment at her.

Smooth move, asshole. Now she'll want to be your friend.

Setting her plate in front of her before sitting down across from Kate, I decide blunt honesty is probably the best way to go.

"What happened at prom? Tell me your side of it."

Visibly swallowing, she stalls her answer by taking a sip of wine.

"That night, we agreed I would drive myself, and we

would meet up there since I had to work a later shift at the bookstore. Do you remember?" Her tone is steady, almost entirely devoid of emotion like she's telling the story by rote. I don't interrupt, only nodding, encouraging her to continue. There isn't much about that night I'll ever forget.

"I walked in the gym looking for you, and imagine my surprise when Christina was wrapped around you on the dance floor while you kissed her. I was stunned, but in reality, you and I didn't have anything set in concrete, no matter that you kissed me the day before. You were free to kiss whomever you wanted. Reese, Michael, and Melody saw me watching you two and started in about how I needed to stop being pathetic, following you around, and how I wasn't worth the time or effort. You remember how they were to me."

Her voice grows desolate as she relates the details of what happened from her point of view, her mask of detachment crumbling like the hopes and dreams I had for us.

"I got out of there as fast as I could. You never even noticed I came in, so I made a plan to sneak out, but Ally found me in the hall. At that point, I was crying, making a mess of myself, and just wrecked. She ushered me into one of the classrooms, then went to get tissues so I could clean myself up. While she was gone, I heard you, Reese, and Michael come out into the hallway. I heard everything. How they thought it was funny a guy like you would ever be interested in me. About how 'it wasn't like that between us, never would be.' Those were your exact words to them." Kate's hitching breath is audible as she pauses and takes another sip of wine.

"Then they started cracking jokes about how they thought it would be so funny how humiliated I would be when I realized you were just leading me on. I've never understood why though. Why you would trick me into believing you were my friend, why you would let me think you *actually*"—her voice breaks on the word before she pulls it back, and by the clench in her jaw I see she's putting that wall back up, the one she disappears behind when she needs to disengage—"actually cared about me?" Her leaden tone confirms my suspicions. "That's on me though. I don't need the answer to that anymore. It is what it is. I didn't stick around to hear the rest. I left the next morning and started courses that summer instead of the fall."

All of this over a misunderstanding. All these years with Kate gone because she didn't confront me, call me out on my shit, something she'd never had trouble with before.

"That night—prom, do you remember exactly what Reese said?" I ask.

"Um, he mentioned something about not thinking that you'd be interested in an overweight girl like me."

"He said, 'I wouldn't have figured you as someone who wants to fuck a fat chick.' Remember?"

Her eyes bug out at the vulgarity of my statement, which I understand. Rage clouds my vision in a red haze just from thinking about it again. I have to talk myself down to continue eating. Before I move the subject forward, Kate does it for me.

"And you said, 'Because I don't. It's not like that with her.' I began climbing out the window of the chemistry lab then, so that was the last thing I heard."

"I broke Reese's jaw that night."

Her mouth parts in shock, and my eyes lock on her emerald gaze. But I plow on, beyond ready to have everything out in the open.

"What you didn't stick around for was me telling him I didn't want to fuck the fat chick because you were never that to me. You were more than what everyone else thought they knew about you. You were more than they could ever wish to be. That when they looked at you and saw an overweight, shy girl, I saw the sparkle in your eyes when you opened a new book, the curve of your lips when you smiled at me. The way you wheeze and drool when you laugh too hard and can't close your mouth all the way. The way your hair burns bright in the sunlight spread out across a blanket in a field under the summer sun. That girl wasn't the same as their petty bullshit description about your appearance, so it wasn't like that with us." I stop for a sip of wine to work past the anger the memory brings back.

"What you didn't stick around for was me and my comments about their chosen companions, which they took exception to. What you didn't stick around for was me beating down Reese and Michael until they couldn't get up. I got suspended for fighting on school property, even though it wasn't during school hours. Reese threw the first punch, so they couldn't expel me. They did suspend me and took away my walking privileges. I didn't get to walk with our graduating class. My diploma came with a postage stamp after school ended because I defended you. I don't regret it though. I'd do it again given a chance."

Breaking the stare-off, I go back to eating my dinner. Kate nibbles on the inside of her cheek, something she only does when she's thinking or nervous. I assume it's the former. I said my piece. I'll give her however much time she needs to process it. The only reason I didn't chase her down years ago to have this out was that I wanted to give her space. To trust that she would come to me and we could finally talk about it. Selfish as it is, I held on to my side of things hoping her need to know everything would bring her back to me.

Seasons turned to years before she came back, and the few times she did it was clear she had no intention of coming to me to hear my side of things. I ultimately resigned myself to avoid her when she was in town. Gram's accident changed that, and I can't be upset at maneuvering her into a position where she would have to listen to me, finally listen to what happened that night.

I focus on the food in front of me, damn good dinner that it is. Gram's roast dinners were my favorite in the Palicki house growing up. It took me about four years to beg the recipe out of Hedy, and then she had to teach me how to make it.

I'd bet that Kate isn't aware that many times when she called Gram, I was in the kitchen out of view. As soon as I learned Kate called home on Sundays, I charmed and weaseled my way into cooking lessons from Hedy, noting that Sunday was the only night I didn't have work or classes. Even though Gram never told me why Kate fled, she never kicked me out of the house on a Sunday night. She probably saw I missed Kate as much as she did.

So, I listened. I listened to Kate's excited voice tell Gram all about her life in Arizona—the mild winters, the college classes, and then later on, her work stories. I basked in her and the updates on her life in the only way I could.

Not that I'll ever tell her that.

Kate might have cut me off from her life, but I stayed very much in hers while she was gone.

I silently cheered for her when she got her undergrad and then her master's. I was a sulky broody ass for days when she disclosed to Gram that she—in her words *finally*—lost her virginity. I counted the pounds she continued to shed from her petite frame, her voice filled with so much excitement and pride that my chest hurt from the feeling of all of it.

While she ceased to acknowledge I existed, I stayed in her life the only way I could—by eavesdropping on her conversations with Gram.

Her plate is still full, and she hasn't responded to my recounting of events, so I opt for a lighter subject.

"Did I do it justice?" I nod my head toward her meal.

When she finally lifts those expressive eyes to mine, tears are swimming in them. Her shaky inhale and exhale has me on the edge of my seat.

"I don't know what to say. I didn't know. I never knew. Gram never told me."

"I told her not to. There was no reason to hurt you, and I wanted to be the one to tell you. By the time I realized you weren't going to open my letters, I told her to drop it, that you weren't interested. I didn't want to force her into the middle. I don't blame you for taking off—my words were damning enough. But I can be pissed you stayed away, that you didn't trust in me, in *us* enough to have a conversation with me."

The first tear spills over, a little stream of blackened misery trailing down the slope of her cheek. As much as the sight of that tear has me wanting to pull her into my arms, I don't. I keep my hands to myself.

"How was I supposed to know, Arik? How was I supposed to blindly trust in your feelings for me, when the only things I had to go off of was years of *friendship* and a single kiss? How was I supposed to trust when there were so many people in that damn school intent on tearing me down every single day? After hearing it for so damn long it's hard not to believe it. To believe there's some truth to what they said day in and day out."

Weariness aches like a rotten tooth, tugging at the back of my neck. The truth is, I don't have an answer for her. I can't tell her how she was supposed to trust in me, in what we were building. "I don't have the answer to that, Katie. I really don't. I'm only sorry that we lost years because of one stupid night."

Frowning, she says, "I'm sorry about it too. I'm sorry I didn't read your letters. I'm sorry I let something stupid come between us, and I'm sorry I didn't trust you or trust myself for that matter. I will say that I wouldn't mind being friends and getting to know who you are now. To catch up on all the things I missed."

I stand, moving to clear our plates, purposefully ignoring her offer of friendship.

As I stow the leftovers, Kate wordlessly starts to load the dishwasher. Once we have the counters wiped down and everything packed away, I finally speak.

"I'll take you home. I'm not letting you ride all that way at eight o'clock at night. Let me grab my keys."

Opting to use my truck since I can't fit the bike in the Jeep, I load it into the bed. The truck cab is silent the entire ride. As I pull into Gram's driveway, the sun is starting its descent across the horizon, bathing the porch in a muted pool of light.

Killing the ignition, I ignore the stagnant silence inhabiting the cab and climb out to open her door, then unload the bike. My mama raised me well, and while I'm a firm believer in equal rights and equal pay, it's ingrained in me to open a lady's door. Call it the romantic in me.

I'm sure the revelations over dinner threw Kate for a loop, and I don't discount she'll need to think through everything before we move forward. I achieved my goals this evening. I finally got Kate's side of the story, I was able to shed light on my side, and she's aware I'm part owner in the shop.

Recognizing the futility of wanting something beyond friendship with her would undoubtedly be a safer way to keep whatever relationship we have now. I shouldn't jeopardize what I've started working on getting back, but I can't deny the tug of desire for this woman.

I barely set the bike down before Kate is trying to take it from my hands.

"Here, I'll take it. Thank you."

"That's all right. I'll walk it up to the porch for you." Not giving her a choice in the matter, I head toward the steps, bike in tow.

Hands falling uselessly to her side, she follows me, and I only relinquish the bike so she can situate it where she wants it. The porch light plays over the burnished auburn of her hair, caressing her sharp cheekbones and her slightly upturned nose. She looks breathtakingly lovely with her profile a backlit silhouette.

I have no illusions when it comes to her. I've seen her covered from head to toe in mud, in sweatpants with dirty hair, and in jeans and boots on the back of a horse. I've seen it all with Kate.

Before she can turn to unlock the door, I cup her elbow and drag my hand down her arm until I tangle my fingers with hers.

The way her hand fits mine is more intimate than sex, her slender fingers locked between my thicker ones. We've held hands a lot over the years, and it always sends a jolt of awareness through me. Her hand intertwined with mine without hesitation or reluctance lights my chest on fire with feeling.

"I'm not interested in only friendship, Kate."

My demand for dinner, the business documents, all of it started as just wanting that friendship back, but it's progressed to more. I want her panting under me. I want her moans and gasps. Even if it's only one night, I'll take it.

I search her face for some sign of what she's feeling. The only insight to her thoughts is the brief flicker of her gaze dropping to my lips. That's all the encouragement I need to lean in and capture her mouth with mine.

Honeysuckle and spice. Kate's flavor hasn't changed in all this time. I pour every ounce of desire I have into the kiss, rubbing my lips across hers. I bury one hand in her hair while the other cups her face. I position her where I want her for the best taste of my new addiction with a few sharp tugs to the hair now firm in my grip. Her lips move tentatively over mine like she's unsure of what to do. As I pull back, I nibble at the fleshy middle of her lower lip, whispering, "Kiss me back, Kate," before dipping my head again and dragging her down for a deeper dive.

My control dies as our lips clash. The hand I cradle her face with falls to find her hip, squeezing her, dragging her closer while pinning her to the door. I savor every point of contact between us.

Kate emits the slightest whimpering gasp, and while I revel in the sound, I also take advantage, running my tongue over her lip before dipping inside. She's sweeter here, the wine from dinner adding to her taste, intoxicating me, until I'm lost. Lost in the kiss, lost in her.

Cock hardening painfully behind the fly of my jeans, a heavy ache settles in with a beating pulse that matches the rhythm of my heart. Shamelessly, I grind into the softness of Kate's abdomen.

Our height difference doesn't give me the angle that I need even more than I need my next breath. Frustrated, I demand more, my hands reaching around to cup her ass, lifting her to me.

Our lips never separate as she spreads her legs around my broad frame. Her legs not quite long enough to lock at the base of my spine, I use the door to hold her up, freeing my hands to dive into the glory of her hair. The heat of her core is flush with the evidence of my need for this woman.

I finally tear my mouth from hers, and with a hard tug to the silky tresses bunched in my hand, I trace a path of lips, teeth, and tongue down the slender column of her throat, devouring her.

Her soft whimpers and gasps stoke the fire in me, taking me higher and higher until we're both in flames, hands roaming, hips rocking and grinding.

I don't realize the weightless feeling that hits me isn't from the kiss until we're falling through the open door.

KATE

I BROKE MY HIP DRY HUMPING MY CHILDHOOD BEST FRIEND against the door to my grandmother's house.

It's not actually broken—that's just my pride.

But still.

Oh, how the mighty have fallen.

Quite literally.

My hip aches and screeches in protest as I try to untangle myself from Arik. The jarring pain wars with the desire still simmering low in my belly. It takes me a moment to recover from the abrupt end to all that passion.

I realized that we were going down faster than the Titanic when Arik tried to twist and take the brunt of the impact, but my flailing didn't make that an easy feat to accomplish. We both kind of timbered onto our sides, and let me tell you, two hundred plus pounds isn't comfortable to catch on the one leg still wrapped around it.

Oy, that's gonna leave a mark.

A muffled giggle has me looking up into Gram's mischievous green eyes. She's getting a kick out of our predicament.

I wait for Arik to shift enough for me to slide my leg out from under his thigh.

Clambering to my feet, I avoid eye contact, knowing my face probably looks like the polished side of a fire engine.

I peek at Arik's face, and sure enough his color is high as well. There's nothing quite like getting busted making out by your pseudo-grandmother to get you flushed.

"Uh, hey, Gram. Arik was dropping me off from dinner at his place."

Gram's cheeky grin is still in place as she clucks her tongue at us. "I gathered, and how was *dinner*?"

The emphasis she puts on "dinner" makes my face flame hotter, and God, could this be any more mortifying? Before I formulate a reply, Arik jumps in.

"Hey, Gram. Yeah, we had a good time. The roast recipe came through again, so thanks for that." Other than the slight flush, you wouldn't be able to tell he was affected at all. I sneak a peek at the fly of his pants—well, the blush and the zipper-threatening erection he's sporting.

Tearing my gaze away from that danger zone, I tune back into the conversation.

"I'm going to grab that cup of tea I came down for. Y'all have a good night now." Gram turns to head into the kitchen, and I slit my eyes at her retreating back—*the traitor.*

"Kate…"

"Arik…"

We speak at the same time. A wave of his hand has me rushing on, going with my gut instinct not to do this—not here, not now.

"Can you come by the shop in the morning to talk about the partnership agreement?"

It's a cop-out. The two seconds since I had my tongue in his mouth have started to register, and I have misgivings— lots of them.

His face gives away the second he's gonna let me off the hook and not push. I barely bite back my relieved sigh.

"Sure, Katie. I'll see you around eight."

"Thanks for dinner...and everything."

Without acknowledging my thanks, he turns, and the door shuts softly behind him.

I'm left standing in the living room alone, and it oddly feels empty now that he's gone. Turning, I climb the stairs as I pull out my phone, then fire off a text message.

Kate: Hey, you up?

The floating dots signal she's replying, and thank God for best friends.

Olivia: Yeah. What's up?

Kate: A thing happened. It was kind of a big deal thing and I don't know what to do so I need you to talk me off the ledge.

Olivia: I'm your girl.

I've never been so grateful for NAU messing up my dorm assignment. I had been standing in the hallway of what was supposed to be my new home when I discovered that NAU didn't put my registration down correctly, instead listing me as living off-campus.

If Taylor, who was the RA, hadn't let me know that Olivia had an extra room to rent in her house, I would have never met her.

Flopping down on the bed still adorned with the custom quilt Gram had made for my tenth birthday, I settle in and start writing Olivia a novel detailing the bookstore, dinner, the prom story, and everything else.

Olivia: Well shit. Here I was prepared to hate his guts. #TeamKate

Kate: Oh, it gets better. Buckle in.

Olivia: I'm ready. Hit me with it.

Kate: Apparently, he didn't get to walk with our class

because of the fight, and (shocker) he was calling me and writing me all those letters in college because he wanted to know what the fuck happened to make me run off. ALL. THOSE. LETTERS. I. SENT. BACK. He gave me a tour of his house, and while I was recovering from the spontaneous orgasm his home gym was responsible for, I come to find a rather large canvas of us made from a picture taken when we were younger...HANGING RIGHT ACROSS FROM HIS BED.

Olivia: Whoa, whoa, whoa, slow down. Let's focus on one thing at a time. To clarify, a general conversation would have saved you twelve years of misery. Do I have that right?

Kate: I wouldn't call it all misery. But yes, and there's more.

Olivia: Okay, what else?

Kate: We ate. Well, he ate. I gave an excellent imitation of it. Then he demands to drive me home after doing the dishes. I'm about to tell him goodbye at Gram's when he slides in and kisses me. It wasn't one of those innocent goodnight kisses either. It was a "hands everywhere, light me on fire and rip my panties off so he can take me in a manly fashion" kiss. Like the kiss to end all kisses.

Olivia: *O face emoji*

Olivia: Holy shit.

Kate: Yeah, I saw a kiss coming, like the "let me give you a peck on the cheek because we used to be close and I'm a gentleman" kind of kiss, not the "back against the door, legs around his waist, grinding in search of the holy-grail-of-orgasms kiss" that ended abruptly with me underneath Arik.

Olivia: Wait, back up. You had sex with Arik on Gram's porch? That's called burying the lede my friend, and friends don't bury the lede with other friends.

Kate: OH MY GOD OLIVIA. No. I didn't have sex with

him. Gram opened the door and we lost our balance and fell through it.

Olivia: Somehow this gets better and better. What happened after that nightmare?

Kate: I awkwardly asked him to come to the store under the pretense of discussing the partnership agreement. He left and I'm now texting you.

Olivia: *sigh* Kate, why aren't you with the Nordic god right now?

Kate: Nordic god? Uh, Liv, how do you know what Arik looks like?

Olivia: I may or may not have cyber-stalked him—for informational purposes—in case I needed to find and dispose of him.

Kate: Once again, OH MY GOD, Olivia, seriously?

Olivia: Hey, no one fucks with my friends and lives to tell the tale. No one.

Kate: That's good to know. So, what do I do?

Olivia: What do you mean what do you do? You see him again.

Kate: Yeah, Liv, that's all fine and dandy, but let's visit the land of logic here. I have too much shit going on to worry about my neglected vagina, thank you very much.

Olivia: AH-HA, YOU ADMIT IT'S NEGLECTED.

Kate: *facepalm emoji* Not the point here.

Olivia: Okay, real talk here. If you have a connection to this man, if there is something, ANYTHING there? Then you owe it to yourself to see where it goes. If it fizzles, then it fizzles. I would never tell you to pass up something good, not when it makes you happy. You take it and run with it.

I read her message over and over again before one last one comes in.

Olivia: Take the chance, babe. I'm rooting for you. But I also want all the dirty details. Love you, boo.

Kate: I'll think about it. Love you too. Xoxo.

While I appreciate Olivia's advice to seize life, I'm still unsure what to do with all the thoughts and feelings bouncing around my head. When Arik and I talked about what happened at prom, I didn't know how to respond. I offered to try friendship out as a peace offering, and when Arik got up to clear dinner away, I assumed he was receptive.

His declaration of not wanting only friendship was shocking, but I couldn't stop the question that flashed through my mind.

What if we were more than friends?

His mouth fastened to mine, and before I knew it, I was grinding on him like an exotic dancer trying to earn her mortgage payment.

Brushing my hands across my lips, they still tingle. I was lost the second Arik's lips touched mine.

There's a part of me that wants to explore the explosive chemistry between us, but again, that could be the neglected vagina talking.

On the other side, I'm scared. Scared that if I take this step, my heart will end up broken again by the same man.

Relationships aren't easy for me. I dated a little bit in college, but not nearly as much as some of my peers. Repeated heavy course loads didn't allow for much of a social life and then I jumped right into grad school.

Education was my focus, maintaining my GPA essential to keep my scholarships. Upon gaining my undergrad from NAU, I immediately went to work for Olivia and stayed on with her through my master's program. Olivia had eschewed additional schooling when her first book series took off. I haven't been on a date in close to two years, and I'm rusty with the flirting, the conversations, and the mating dance portion of it.

Those are just my hurdles. Taking this step would tarnish

more memories if it didn't work out. Though, I'm not convinced I can deny the pull, that deep fluttering of arousal pooling in my abdomen. It's something I haven't felt in a long time.

A knock on my bedroom door startles me out of my thoughts. A second later Gram's head pokes around the corner.

"Hey, Katie Belle, you got a minute for your old grandma?"

"Pssh, you're not old. You're still in your prime," I scoff, waving her in.

Crossing to my bed, Gram perches on the edge.

"Yeah, well, my prime takes some doing these days, but I wanted to see how you were doing. Since I pushed you into dinner and all."

Gram is the master at getting more than she gives. If she's surprised or shocked by two people crashing through the open door in an intimate embrace there is no sign of it. Her gaze rakes over me. She's always been able to sniff out weaknesses like a bloodhound and then she meddles within an inch of your life if you aren't careful.

"I don't know how I'm doing, Gram. So much happened tonight." There's a question that burns, though. "Why didn't you ever tell me Arik got suspended after prom?"

Huffing out a breath, Gram takes her time before replying, "He hurt you that night. You tried to hide it, but I know your face and there was nothing but anguish on it. The next morning you came down and announced you were heading to NAU early. I didn't even know what to think. You were packed and gone before I could ask what happened. It wasn't until after you had already left that I heard about the fight. Then Arik told me everything from his point of view, and I couldn't help but think that maybe it was for the best, and maybe you needed to spread your wings a little."

She's quiet for a minute before continuing. "You and Arik were attached at the hip, so close you couldn't think about one without thinking of the other. I felt that you needed space and time to grow, become your own person, and be *Kate*. Arizona gave you that. It gave you the freedom to find out exactly who you are. As much heartache as it caused you, I'm not sorry I didn't say anything. It also wasn't my story to tell. You needed to hear it from Arik to believe it."

I understand her reasoning. Growing up with Arik, spending every second I could with him, made it seem like I was co-dependent on our friendship. And I did blossom while away at school. I took charge of my future and my health. But the words still sting. Gram is the only family I have, and I've gotten so used to her being more of a friend that I forget she's both my mother and father and acts with my best interests in mind.

"Now tell me, did you two talk it out tonight? Did he tell you his side of the story?"

"We did. We cleared the air. I don't know what's going to happen next or where I'm going from here, but I'm glad I finally got those answers."

"Well, based on how I found you both this evening, I would guess you have an idea of where y'all are going, or at least where Arik wants to go." Her twitching lips make me smile a little.

I have missed this—the late-night chats with Gram, having her physically here to confide in, a friend as well as a parent.

Regardless of the kiss, or what I want to do about Arik, or how I feel about him and this town, I'm grateful I have Gram. Especially when feelings of this depth are confusing to begin with and come with such a complicated past.

Still, I'm not ready to commit to giving Arik and me a

chance. Part of me believes it's better to hedge my bets and protect my heart.

"I don't know, Gram. It might have been a terrible mistake. I'm not the same person I was when I lived here last. I don't know what I want. Right now, I'm trying to focus on Readers' Haven and helping you out as much as possible."

Rising from the bed, Gram kisses my forehead. "I'm sure you'll think it to death like you normally do and then you'll come to a decision that works for you. As for helping the shop and me, I can't be sorry about its current state. Not when it has you sleeping under my roof and here for me to wish you goodnight. These old bones need some rest, so I'm going to bed. Love you, darlin'. Get some sleep."

Long after she shuts the door, I'm still curled up with my pillow thinking about everything—the kiss, why I'm here in Felt, what I want to do. Sleep likely won't come easy, but I still go through my regular bedtime ritual. The usual practice of yoga, showering, and skincare routine still don't quiet the thoughts running rampant.

While I toss and turn, I decide it's best to buy Arik out of the store. Personal connection or not, buying him out of the store eliminates that tie. I shoot off a text to Rob asking him to generate the documents that we need. Less than an hour later I have them in my inbox.

Just as I finally start to drift off, I'm still thinking about Readers' Haven, Gram's hip, partnership agreements, and this small town. There are so many *things* shoving Arik and I together that avoiding him isn't going to work. While I would rather sweep everything under the rug, that isn't going so well for me either.

ARIK

I'M AT THE SHOP BRIGHT AND EARLY THE NEXT MORNING AND see Kate's bike resting against a street sign on the sidewalk. Her back is to me while she putters around the front of the store moving stuff around.

God, she's fucking gorgeous. I take the time to stare while her gaze is looking at something above one of the bookcases, and the sunlight is creating a fiery halo around her. I should be used to the sinking sensation in the pit of my stomach when I'm around Kate. It hasn't ever gone away, and I doubt it ever will.

I've been attracted to her since I started to appreciate girls from a post-puberty standpoint. I dated other girls in high school and college, but no one ever pulled me in like Kate did and still does.

Being able to wrap my arms around her, to taste her, and to catch her breathy gasps brought that attraction right back, and I'm still figuring out what to do with it. Part of me just wants one night of her under me, a night to work out the lust. Will one night be enough though?

Climbing out of my truck, juggling coffee and pastries from The Sweet Tooth, I mentally prepare myself. The brush-off she gave me last night is proof that she's backpedaling, and I'll be damned if I let her.

I shove open the door to the shop, and a bell chimes to announce my entry.

"Morning, Kate."

Turning to me, she has her hair bundled up again, and my fingers itch to tug it down so it's spread around her shoulders in all its tousled glory.

"Hey, Arik, good morning."

"I grabbed us some coffee and muffins. Ally left it black and swore that's how you take it, but I grabbed some creamer and sugar if you wanted to doctor it."

"Thanks for that, but I do drink it black. If I'm going to drink my calories, it's gonna be tequila."

"Ah, the motivations for lifting and black coffee both come back to alcohol, huh? Maybe I should stock up on tequila."

Giving a soft laugh, she says, "Well, it couldn't hurt."

There's a lull in the conversation while I sip my coffee and she fiddles around the front desk—which is still covered in paperwork—as the tension surrounding us draws her shoulders up.

"So, I have some documents here. I'll let you look over them. Let me know if you have questions." She slips from behind the desk and heads back to the storage room.

Looking at the papers on the desk, I barely scan them before I want to punch something.

"No."

Swiveling around, Kate comes back to the counter.

"No? No, what? Is something wrong with them? They're all in order."

Herculean restraint. I must have the control of a demigod when I don't rip every one of those papers to shreds right in front of her.

"No, you're not buying me out of the shop. No, I won't sell my part to you. If you want to buy in, you're gonna have to do it with Gram *and* me."

Her green eyes blaze at me, annoyed and irritated, and I don't give a fuck. If Hedy had asked me to sell my part of the store back to them, I would have, no question. I doubt Hedy even knows about this agreement. Kate likely didn't mention it. Flipping through the pages, I confirm my theory when I note that there are no signatures on any of the pages yet.

I put a leash on my anger. Only when I'm calm do I speak.

"You can't buy me out because you're scared, Kate."

"What? That's ridiculous," she scoffs.

"This is because of the kiss last night, isn't it?" I don't have to ask—I know the truth. She got in her head last night and decided to give me the shove-off, and this is her way of tying it up in a neat and tidy bow. Over my dead body.

"Of course not, but we do have to talk about that too. I appreciate you sharing everything you did, and I'm glad that we cleared the air—but I'm not in a place for anything more right now. I have too much going on."

"Bullshit." The quiet intensity in my voice has her eyes going wide.

"Arik—" I don't let her get any further than that before I interrupt.

"Bullshit, Kate. That's bullshit and you know it. You dealt with more when we were juniors in high school. You're a coward. You're scared of your feelings for me. You're scared to trust me. To take that leap with me." Giving the papers in front of me an irritated flick, I continue. "These papers give you a nifty way to cut and fucking run without actually leaving."

98

My breath is audible, and I realize I'm practically yelling at her, so maybe not so calm after all. Lowering my voice, I stay firm. "You're running away. Again. Maybe not physically this time but let's call it what it is. Emotionally you're back behind those walls, miles from here, *from me*. You don't want to take the chance on this? That's your choice. But don't fuckin' lie to yourself or me about why you don't want to."

There's a flush riding high on her cheekbones. Maybe it makes me a masochist, but my dick twitches hard. Kate in a temper always got me stirred up—no surprise that hasn't changed.

Clenching my jaw, I bite back the pleas, and the needy part of me that always selfishly demands more from her. The part of me that hid my learning challenges behind our friendship, afraid she would judge me. The side of me that was vulnerable when I finally caved and asked for her help with school. I ignore the part of me that's never been far from her—in thoughts, actions, feelings, and the ever-present consuming *want*.

That arrogant chin tips up at me, defiant, feisty, strong. There are glimmers of the girl I used to know in that determined stare.

I fist my hands at my sides to stop from grabbing her and devouring that lush mouth with mine. To remind her that last night she met me kiss for kiss. There's no wall she can hide that reaction behind.

Pushing Kate isn't the right option when I want her to do something. She won't ever admit it, but her mom leaving her with Gram caused scars, and though she came back from it stronger, it still left shadows. That doesn't mean I won't shine a light on those shadows.

"What if I am scared, Arik, so the fuck what? We don't have the best track record and, sue me, but I would rather not get tangled in something that has the potential to complicate everything—*again.* Why should I sign up for that?"

My blood roars in my ears. I have to choke back the words that want to launch themselves, words I won't be able to take back. Swallowing them down, I strive for a steady tone.

"That's for you to decide, Kate. The only thing I'm asking is that you don't disillusion yourself when you're thinking about those whys. Don't try to shove me out of the way because you're scared. You aren't buying me out of the store, so draft a new agreement. I won't be bought out. Also, I've never intentionally hurt you. I wouldn't, and you should know that after last night."

The defiant glint is gone now, replaced with a frown, a furrowed brow, and exhaustion.

"You know what they say about good intentions—it's just better if we don't go down that road, Arik."

After all the progress we made last night, she's slipping through my fingers. I try one last time.

"Go out to dinner with me tonight. Let me take you on a real date. We'll talk more, catch up, no pressure at all. Just let me spend time with you. Please."

Watching her nibble on her lower lip has fire pooling in my veins. I recall the heady taste of her, the feel of her body in my hands.

"You say no pressure, but I feel pressured. You already said you don't want just friendship. If not that, then why dinner?"

Seizing on her curiosity, I make my case.

"I want to know about what you've been up to since college. I'd bet that you have questions about me too. Let me discover who you are now. Get to know who I am. I promise, if you want it to be platonic, we'll keep it that way.

"Just dinner?" Her voice is hesitant.

"Just dinner." I pull out my most charming smile, the one that would get her in on any harebrained scheme I could come up with when we were younger.

"Platonic?" Her eyes narrow, like she doesn't quite believe me. Nodding, I don't speak because victory is on the horizon, and I can't chance her catching on to my triumph.

"Okay, Arik, just dinner and catching up."

If she wants to think that this is only dinner, that's a lie I'll let her live with for now.

For the rest of my day, time moves as if submerged in molasses. I take a call from the PTA about the town council meeting that has me seeing red. If I don't make my case to the parents, the town is prepared to use the fundraised money for new athletic gear. After getting off the call where my boss confirmed that I could be busting my ass to provide for the athletic department with those funds, dinner with Kate is the only good thing left in my day.

I understand where the parents are coming from. They have to shell out the money for the uniforms and gear if their kids want to play, but upgrading learning materials trumps football uniforms for me.

After putting together some information for the council meeting and double-checking I didn't switch any data around, I'm ready for our date a full hour in advance. Flowers I picked up from Blooming Flats sit pretty on my counter in a purple vase next to the stuffed hamper with a blanket. We used to go on picnics all the time growing up, and I'm hoping that Kate still enjoys them.

Nerves pull my shoulders tight when I think about the alternatives—that she doesn't like picnics because maybe they hold bad memories for her, or she doesn't eat fried chicken and mac and cheese now that she focuses on her health more. I second-guess myself, my choices, what to wear, what flowers to get, until I'm going insane.

No time for me to change any of it now, so I'll need to suck it up. When the clock finally says six fifty, I grab my keys and juggle the flowers and basket as I head out.

When I pull up to Gram's house, Kate's waiting on the porch for me. Not exactly how I wanted the night to start, but I'm flexible.

Casual jeans cover her short, curvy legs, and one of those skinny tank tops that make men thank God for summer drapes loosely around her torso. The shade is an almost perfect match for her eyes. Looking down at her footwear, she followed my texted instructions and wore sturdy hiking boots, which gives me an absurd amount of pleasure.

"You ready?" she asks, her tone irritated and untrusting. I don't let her lack of enthusiasm deter me. Climbing the short steps to the porch, I move in and brush a kiss across her cheek, her sweet scent going straight to my head.

"Sure am. Did you want to put these inside first?"

Taking the vase out of my hands, she buries her face in the blooms and inhales deeply, her eyes fluttering shut. The longest lashes in the world dust the tops of her cheekbones before lifting, and her gaze meets mine when she murmurs, "Calla lilies, my favorite, thank you. Don't think they'll soften me. I'm still kinda irked at you."

Chuckling, I say, "I don't doubt it."

A slight curl to her lips is all I get as she disappears through the door. Before it shuts all the way, Ben is stepping out onto the porch.

"Hey, Ben, how's it going?"

"Arik." His curtness takes me by surprise. I don't think I've ever heard him be anything less than pleasant.

"Everything okay?"

"Tell me, son, where are you planning on takin' Katie this evening?"

The unholy gleam in his eye is the only thing that stops the smile from curling my lips. Ben Dawson never married or had kids, and it seems he's taking the opportunity to play the protective Dad. Since he and I are close, I decide it's best to indulge him.

"Packsaddle Lake—I'm aiming for a picnic and a campfire."

His arms cross his chest, and he tries for a stern expression.

"And when are you planning on bringing our girl home?"

My lips twitch with the effort to hold back laughter. Clearing my throat, I respond in a saccharine-sweet tone. "When would you like me to have her home?"

Before Ben can speak, Kate's pulling open the door again. Confusion knits across her features, taking in Ben and me staring each other down. Ben breaks first and chuckles.

"Have her home whenever. I trust she'll tell you when she's had enough of you for the evening, probably sooner rather than later knowing our Katie."

"Yes, sir."

Kate rolls her eyes before saying, "Ben, you and Gram both have my cell number, but it's also on the board on the fridge. You call me if you need anything and I'll be home in no time. And no mattress acrobatics." She gives him a light kiss on the cheek and then she's at my side.

I glance over at her profile once we've gotten buckled in and are on our way. The wind streaming through the open top whips her red locks around her face. The evening air smells like the wildflowers that grow abundantly along the trail. Turning off Main Street, I head out of town toward the hills and backcountry. Kate's hands are clasped tight in her lap, and her shoulders are tense as hell.

"Lighten up, Kate. Like I said, tonight can be as platonic as you want it to be. I just want to eat dinner with you."

The path curves around the mountain and our destination becomes apparent, causing recognition to light Kate's eyes as we get farther and farther out of town.

"Packsaddle? We're going to Packsaddle?"

"I figured you hadn't had a chance to get out there yet. I thought we could have a campfire and a picnic while we catch up."

"You're right, I haven't had the time to come out here. I would have had to hike it from the ranger station since I don't have a car. I wouldn't want to bike the Jeep trail."

"It's been smoothed out some over the years, but it's still a little rough in areas. If you ever want to come out and don't feel like hiking it, you can always borrow Maude."

"I honestly can't believe you still have this thing, and you kept her name." Her laughter swirls around us as I downshift to first, and she finally relaxes into the trip. I want her at ease and comfortable with me rather than on edge.

The passenger-side tires climb an incline on the right side of the narrow road. This is one of the sections that hasn't been smoothed out and is a little tricky. Kate reaches for the top of the roll bar to steady herself as I navigate us back down to having all four tires level on the road.

"You named her." Smiling at the memory, I still remember the in-depth report she wrote for me on how it was clear the Jeep was female and therefore needed the eyelashes to feel beautiful and feminine. We almost peed our pants laughing that night.

An impish smile curls the left side of her mouth. "I helped you pick her out, Arik. Of course I got to name her. You're the one who decided to keep it."

"You can't go changing a car's name all willy-nilly. You'll give her an identity crisis."

She snorts out a chuckle and looks at me like I'm crazy. I bask in the smile on her face and the fact she's enjoying herself, and I feel ten feet tall. Packsaddle Lake outweighs distrust in her book and I'm thankful for it.

The rest of the drive passes with her giving me shit about the Jeep, my driving, about everything, and as we crest the last incline before the lake there's a lightness surrounding us I haven't felt in a long time.

The evening light shimmers softly across the lake. Dusk out here is always one of my favorite times. I park and we're both climbing out before Kate speaks again.

"I forgot how beautiful this place is. I can't believe I forgot all the green."

"Yeah, I'd imagine you don't get much foliage down in Arizona."

I'm grabbing the basket and blanket out of the back as she replies, "There's some green, especially up in Flagstaff, but it's intermixed with the reds, browns, and yellows that come with desert living. Nothing as lush as this, though Arizona is beautiful in a different way. It just gets so hot during the summer."

Shouldering the basket, I lead her toward one of the firepits that dot the lake's shoreline. There's still some light, the days stretching longer now, so I spread out the blanket next to one of the firepits closer to the water. Heading back to the Jeep, I grab a bundle of wood I brought along.

"Anything I can do to help?"

Shaking my head, I tell her, "I've got this, you sit down and get comfortable."

I join Kate on the blanket once I finish. After pulling out paper plates, I dish up the fried chicken and sides I prepared earlier in the afternoon.

"Did you make all of this?" There's a hint of disbelief, and I don't blame her for it. I've burned water trying to boil it before. Not to mention the trouble I had with reading directions.

"Gram taught me how to cook a couple of things when I was still in college. It's not every night I cook, but I've been getting better as I go along. I can't live off pizza or bar food all the time."

She searches my face for a minute as if she didn't expect me to learn how to cook or that Gram is the one who taught me.

"I guess not. This looks amazing though. Thank you."

"My pleasure," I reply, and it is. Her eyes slide shut as she takes a bite of the mac and cheese, one of her favorites if I've remembered correctly. The slight moan that slips—yep, remembered correctly—makes my jeans a little bit tighter.

Kate mumbles around a mouthful of food. "This is so good. God, I forgot how delicious cold mac and cheese is."

"Forgot? How could you forget? What? They don't have any mac and cheese down in Arizona?"

Laughing at me, she says, "No, they have mac and cheese, but I don't have it a lot. Only on special occasions, and that's usually here with Gram. Plus, I'm very picky about mac and cheese. It has to be done exactly right."

"You're telling me that nowhere in an entire state meets your lofty tastes for mac and cheese? How is that possible?"

"There is one place I love, but it's a little out of the way for pasta since I don't let myself eat a lot."

"Why don't you let yourself eat something you love so much?"

"Because my waistline doesn't love it as much as I do. I work hard to keep everything in balance."

She must be talking about her health journey. I don't want to give away that I know a lot about it already. "Makes sense. You've got some guns there, Katie Belle."

She humors me as she flexes her biceps, ripping a laugh out of me.

"Tell me about that. Why weightlifting? How was college? What's it like living in Arizona? Tell me everything."

KATE

Dinner is delicious, and the company isn't bad either. If I thought Arik would be awkward, I'm proven wrong less than ten minutes into the meal.

Conversation flows smoothly as we both talk and eat. The food is terrific and a surprise. Arik was never interested in cooking when we were growing up. But if his explanation is anything to go by, he got tired of eating like a bachelor no matter how he used to struggle with the reading, measurements, and math that come along with recipes.

We talk about everything—him going through college, changing his major to get his teaching degree, and then completing the certifications. How hard college was for him as he struggled with his dyslexia, something he doesn't talk about often. He tells me about how Ben stepped in to help him work through some of the trickier assignments.

I talk about working for Olivia while I finished up my master's degree and then decided to continue with her after her author career launched and then skyrocketed. Arik and I discuss our preferred ways of lifting weights, the routines we follow, along with plans to lift together sometime soon.

I'm thankful that whenever the conversation gets too close to the subject of me leaving or prom, Arik deftly steers it in another direction.

I assume he's trying to give me a relaxing evening, and I appreciate it. With so much turmoil in my daily life, it's nice to sit down and eat a meal with a friend—maybe more than a friend—and let everything go for the evening.

Eventually, the discussion turns to the bookstore. Arik's lighting the campfire for us as he asks, "So what are your plans there? What's the goal moving forward?"

I launch into the comprehensive plan to update the physical interior and create an online presence for the shop, linking it with the major book retailers. I tell him about the massive book signing I have planned at the summer tourist season's height.

I babble at him, my excitement for the projects evident. I talk for what feels like forever as the fire catches and bathes the darkening evening in a golden glow.

"If you need any help with it, I hope that you'll ask me. I know it doesn't seem like I'm much of a bookseller, but I did take an active interest after I bought in and learned quite a bit about the shop itself."

"I'll do that. Rob said he should have the new agreement drawn up and emailed to me tomorrow. I might have you double-check the accounting information transfer I did this week. The software Gram was using is ancient."

Arik's groan of pain catches me off guard.

"What? What is it?"

"That damn software. I've been trying to get Gram to update it for years, and she won't listen,"—using air quotes he continues in a mocking falsetto—"'*the expense isn't worth the return, and there isn't anything wrong with the current software.*' If you got her to swap to something different, I'm in your debt, especially since come tax time I handle that nightmare for her."

"Well, welcome to servitude because I switched it out this week. Transferring those files and expense reports over is why there is a shortage of wine at Sally's Saloon and Liquor store. That DOS system is gone forever, along with the antiquated cash only setup." I'm smug, and I don't even try to hide it as I break down how I have everything set up.

"We now accept all credit card types as well as cash. The new website goes live next week as soon as my designer friends finish with it. Then we'll really be cooking. Depending on the turnout for the summer signing, I have a couple of plans to get some of the more athletic authors I know for a signing and skiing event I'm playing with."

"Wow, Kate, that's a lot. Sure, I can take a look at the finances now, which should make tax time easier for us too."

I appreciate Arik trying to include me, and I can admit I was a little hurt that Gram would reach out to him first. Arik is *here*, whereas it doesn't make logical sense for Gram to bug me with the bookstore's daily needs when I am in a different state.

"Gram let you do all that?" Arik's surprise that Gram would hand over those reins ignites a little bit of pride in my efforts, no matter how I struggle with my self-worth.

"Yeah, I mean, she didn't have a choice with me investing heavily into the store. I'm now part owner. That and she saw that this was really the only way to bring the store back into relevancy once I explained everything."

"That's good of her, though she still doesn't let me file any of the taxes or paperwork. Every year I end up putting it all together for her and then she has me drop it off with her or Ben for filing."

"Really? That doesn't make sense. Wouldn't it be easier for her to file everything electronically than by long form?"

"You'd think so, but she has an aversion to filing anything by computer. It can be a damned pain in the ass."

"I hope she doesn't mind that Rob's filing the new partnership agreement that way then, because I'm not about to be mailing documents all over the state of Idaho to get the change done."

"Tell me about this Rob guy. If he's drafting business paperwork for you—for us—you must have known him a long time and trust him."

I pick up on the tension surrounding the word trust and, if I'm not mistaken, jealousy as well, though I have no idea why.

I keep my tone breezy. "Rob is Olivia's younger brother. He has his MBA but specializes in small business stuff. I've known him since I was eighteen. I met him as a freshman when I lived at Liv's place."

"Why would you live at their place? Like their parents' house?" That is definitely jealousy, and I better nip this before he makes it into something it's not, but I'm gonna needle him about it first.

"No, Olivia is three years older than I am. Rob's a year younger. Liv got custody of him when she turned eighteen and aged out of foster care. Liv, Rob, and her husband, Chase, all lived in a house there, and they had an extra room that they were renting out while we were all at NAU. When NAU lost my dorm assignment, I had to find a place to stay fast. Taylor, the RA for the dorm, let me know that Olivia had the room, and that was that. Anyway, Rob and I've been friends for years—close friends."

"What does this guy do that he handles all that?" Arik's tone is more and more belligerent, and it takes everything I have not to laugh at the sparks shooting from his eyes.

"He owns a gym, he's a personal trainer, and has a couple of black belts in different martial arts disciplines. He's the one who taught me how to grapple. He's all about proper technique, holds, submissions—you know, that kind of stuff."

I bite the inside of my cheek hard to keep from smiling. Arik's expression goes stony. He must not like the idea of me rolling around with another guy, even if it is for self-defense. I'm getting a ridiculous amount of pleasure out of making him uncomfortable. The bump to my self-confidence is nice too.

"This guy sounds fantastic," Arik bites out between clenched teeth, and I can't hold it back any longer. I start laughing so hard I get short of breath, air wheezing and whistling out of me while I try not to pee my pants.

Gasping out between chuckles, I tell him, "Rob and I were never a thing. He's like a brother to me."

Chagrin covers his expression, and that makes me explode in laughter all over again.

"Ha-ha, yuk it up."

"You walked right into that. But seriously, we're just friends. We've only ever been friends. That's all."

He shifts the subject again, seeming appeased with my explanation. "You help Olivia with the publishing side of writing? What else do you do for her?"

"A little bit of everything honestly. I maintain her records, act as her agent, run expense reports, organize her calendar, and pretty much do everything but write the actual books."

"How's the working from here going for you?"

Not quite sure how to answer his question, I choose my words carefully. On one hand, I love being closer to Gram. Working remotely from Felt has had its challenges, sure, but I'm finding my stride in the small town. On the other hand, any mention of my love of Arizona and my life away from Felt could send us straight into the conversation topics we've been avoiding.

"It's not as bad as I thought it would be. The biggest

hurdle is making sure Olivia stays on schedule since I'm not there to prod her in the ass when she needs it. She'd get a huge kick out of Readers' Haven and the changes we're making there. She's going to come for the signing in August, so you'll get to meet her then."

The conversation lulls after that as we both finish our food and lie back to relax. Crickets chirp in the distance as the first stars light up the sky and the lightning bugs flash in the distance. Arik's arm is flush with mine, his fingers playing with the tips of mine. True to his word, he kept dinner platonic. Only friendly conversation with no flirty undertones accompanied our meal. I have no idea why that disappoints me, but I don't examine the feeling too closely while we stargaze.

Something else I missed living in the city is how dark it gets out here. How visible the clusters of stars and constellations are without the pollution and the ever-present light permeating the city. Other than the small light that comes from the firepit, we inch our way into darkness.

Arik sits up and reaches into the basket, pulling out a bottle of wine and containers. With the lower lighting it's hard for me to tell what it is. I can't manage another bite after such a filling dinner.

"Here, take this," he says as he passes me a plastic cup of wine.

"What else do you have there?" I ask, sitting up as my curiosity gets the better of me.

"Some dessert, but you have to close your eyes if you want it." There is definitely a flirty cadence to his words now.

The shift throws me off for a second. Until now, dinner and hanging out has been comfortable and peaceful, like when we would camp as teenagers. Now that I'm older, I can appreciate Gram even more. Her trust in letting me run off with a boy into the wilderness for days on end goes to show how much faith she put in me to not get into trouble.

The same kind of trouble that made her a young grandmother and the guardian of a two-year-old while her daughter disappeared into the wind. Never mind that Arik and I didn't have that kind of relationship. I honestly don't think I could send my teenage daughter out camping with a boy, even if it were a trusted friend.

"Kate," he calls, and I can't see what he's doing with his back to me.

"Yes?"

"Close your eyes and open your mouth."

I narrow my eyes at his back. I've heard this tune before.

"This isn't gonna be like the time when we were fishing and you put a live worm in my mouth, is it?"

Laughter rumbles from his chest, the chuckles shaking his shoulders, his head dipping back.

"No, and I would like the record to reflect that we were seven when I did that. You were so gullible I couldn't help myself."

It's my turn to laugh now because he's not wrong.

Closing my eyes, I open my mouth and wait. He rummages around, there's a crinkle, almost like a container opening, before he cups my chin. Probably to make sure he doesn't send whatever he's holding up my nose. My skin tingles pleasantly against the steady pressure of his hand.

There's a light texture on my tongue that's sweet and tastes like vanilla air, dipped in something I can't quite put my finger on yet. I close my lips around the object, feeling the pitted skin of a strawberry.

Arik's softly spoken instruction to bite has my teeth sinking into the tart fruit as I close my lips around the stem and his fingers. The warm contrast of his skin with the fruit's juicy crispness has heat rocketing through my core and a shiver shaking down my spine.

His sharply indrawn breath confirms he feels the connection igniting between us.

"Strawberries and Gram's homemade whipped cream. Yum." My words and the mention of Gram ends the moment and I'm glad for it.

Leaning back, I open my eyes, staring directly into Arik's heavily lidded gaze, desire crackling through all that blue. I guess Gram didn't entirely break the mood for him.

I'm unsure of what to do, what to say, so I stay silent. There are a million questions in that slumberous expression, and I have no idea how to answer a single one.

An owl hoots somewhere in the distance, and some of the indecipherable emotion in his eyes clears as he leans back, grabbing another strawberry and swiping it through the cream before his lips close around the fruit.

A mixture of cream and juice sits at the corner of his mouth, just shy of his beard, ignored as he chews before swallowing the treat.

"You've...you've got some..." Motioning to my mouth I gesture, hoping he understands what I'm struggling to stammer my way through.

"Here, get it for me, will you?"

We're sitting close, close enough for me to feel his body heat. Close enough I smell the woodsy pine of whatever cologne or deodorant he uses. Close enough to watch his pupils dilate in the firelight as he leans into me, offering me his chin.

Lifting my hand, I use my thumb to wipe at the cream, but before I pull back, his fingers close around my wrist, holding my hand captive.

His tongue rasps against the pad of my finger, teeth closing on the digit in a nibble, and I go damp between my thighs, my nipples tightening and gooseflesh bumping along my skin. It's my turn to gasp now.

"Arik…" My brain is as scrambled as my hormones.

After a lingering kiss at the center of my palm, he releases my hand. Scooting the container closer to me, I'm not sure if he doesn't trust himself to feed me more or if it's a peace offering since it's clear I'm still gun-shy. Whatever *that* was, it was more than friendly.

We work our way through dessert quickly, and other than a few unintentional brushes of our hands, we don't touch again.

As the fire starts to die down, we're both lying side by side again on the blanket, staring at the expanse of sky framed by the treetops. It's quiet, neither of us speaking, as we listen to the various sounds of nature. Unbidden, a question pops from my brain into the crisp evening air.

"Why teaching? What made you decide to get into all that?"

He doesn't respond right away. He's likely trying to decide what and how much to tell me. One thing he's always struggled with is putting his thoughts into the right order before speaking, so I give him time.

"School, at least for me, wasn't easy. I mean, yeah, I had Ma and she did the best she could, but sometimes she worked multiple jobs to keep us going. So, there wasn't always time for her to help. I've never resented her for it, and I had Gram and you. We have so few programs available here that help kids with learning disabilities. I had to fumble through a lot of it myself. It's gotten better now that I understand what dyslexia is, and I navigate it easier," he trails off and I don't say anything, letting him finish his thoughts. His hand reaches for mine and he intertwines our fingers. The callus on his palm scrapes deliciously across my hand, and it distracts me in the best ways.

"If there's an opportunity to help a kid, one that feels misunderstood or confused, I want to be in the position to do so. I picked education because I've lived through what it's like to struggle to read in front of the class, because sometimes the letters and numbers don't make sense. That sometimes it all comes out backward, and it's okay. It's okay not to have the answers, to struggle with what you're reading or what the equation means. It's okay to struggle, but it's even better when they have someone there who went through the same things. Ben's the other reason. I owe a lot to him. He found a way to help me make sense of it and put everything in the right order. If I can, I want to be able to do that for someone else someday."

Once again, I'm speechless. Of course he would think to help other kids like him. Of course he would go into education with a greater goal than job stability and security. Of course his chosen profession means more to him than drawing a paycheck and a pension plan from the state.

There's so much that's different about Arik. Many things have changed about him over the years, but the core of who he is isn't one of them.

"Why Olivia's assistant?"

I sigh, taking my time to answer because my answer won't sound as altruistic or noble.

The words are there, but how he'll take them is anyone's guess since it veers toward the subjects we've worked so hard to avoid. I don't want to beat a dead horse, but part of the reason I took and kept the job with Olivia is that it let me stay away from Felt. It gave me the perfect excuse to stay away and hide.

It let me bury my past and move forward with my own story.

"It started as helping her navigate the publishing world. The marketing, the fans, the interviews. Her first book got picked up when I was a sophomore. She was struggling to juggle her coursework, her marriage, writing, and everything that came with publishing. She and Chase had gotten married quietly over the summer before her first year at NAU, and they moved into the house off-campus with Rob. Once the book got picked up, it was a whirlwind. She dropped out of college right after the first book deal came through. *Jett,"*—my voice breaks on his name but I keep going —"their son arrived not long after the second book hit bookstores and the demand for more was crazy. There were talks of movie deals and purchasing the rights to the series. By the time the third book went to editors, Liv was in burnout. She didn't want to write, and she didn't want to travel for publicity events. She started to decline book signings and didn't interact with her readers on social media as much. Her publisher wasn't happy, but she was exhausted. Jett was barely over a year old, Chase was busy with his internship, and they couldn't catch a break."

I pause, remembering the crazy schedule, the long nights, and working on the weekends while we tried to find a balance.

Taking a deep breath, I give myself a minute before continuing. "So, I stepped in. I took the heavier admin-related stuff off her shoulders. I started managing her travel calendar and being the middleman between Olivia and her publisher, her editor, and her agent. I eventually took over as her agent when they started to disagree on almost every-thing. She came out of the burnout and plowed through two more books before her world imploded and everything changed. I couldn't leave Liv then, and it made more sense for me to stay in Arizona."

Arik accepts the excuse—the reason that kept me away from Felt for years—with a placid expression. Reaching over, he grasps one of my frizzy waves, twirling the strand around his finger, and his eyes don't leave that lock of hair as he asks, "Is everything okay now with Olivia?"

"Not really. I don't want to get into it, but what she went through is not something you fully bounce back from or you get over. She's doing better now, better than before, but she still needs me."

Which reaffirms that being with Arik even temporarily isn't a good idea. Gram needs me for the shop, and Liv needs me as an employee and as a friend. I don't have much left over for anyone else at this point. Even just *considering* exploring this attraction and the thread that keeps pulling me back to Arik curdles dinner in my stomach. I can't let Liv and Gram down to chase my own pleasure.

He skates his fingers across my jaw, and we sit in silence.

ARIK

As badly as I want to ask her, I don't. Whether or not she's staying in Felt doesn't matter to me right now.

Talking to her and spending time together without it devolving into fighting and arguments has made for a pleasant evening. I should be guarding my heart against her. She's the only woman to ever really make me *want*, but I'm enjoying the night too much to let those worries and doubts hog my attention.

The light from the fire starts to die down and I let it. It's not late, but Kate gets up early every morning to get into the bookstore. With the store, Gram, and Olivia, her plate is more than full. Between that and the things I have to accomplish this week, it's about time to wrap up the evening.

Reaching over to the open food containers, I start to pack everything back into the picnic basket.

"What are you thinking?" Kate's question is soft in the evening air, a reminder of something that we both got so used to blindly asking—and answering.

Thoughts race through my head, and only by sheer will do I keep myself from throwing them out there. They're too heavy for right now. I'm not even sure that I should be thinking them. So, I hold them back.

"Nothing of consequence. Just clearing this up while we still have a little light from the fire. It's getting late though, and I figured with your early mornings at Readers' Haven, we should probably head back soon."

"Oh, here, let me help. Everything goes back into the basket, right?"

"I've got it. You sit back, relax, and I'll get it all packed up. How's Gram doing with the physical therapy?"

"She's doing good with it. She distracts herself from the work of it by talking books with her therapist. She'll have the walker for a while, but she's making good progress."

I stow everything in the Jeep and check for stray trash before heading to Kate and offering her a hand up.

Anytime I touch her soft skin, sparks fire down my arm. Her gaze flicks down, betraying her nerves. I wouldn't usually hesitate to capitalize on it, but we're in a weird place, so I step back and give her space.

My plan of being a perfect gentleman tonight won't go off the rails because I can't control myself around her when we're touching.

Linking our fingers together, we head toward the Jeep. Boosting herself into the lifted seat brings her face level with mine. I always forget how small she is. Her tongue darts out and leaves the shine of moisture on that plump lower lip.

Fuck being a gentleman. Just fuck it. I want my mouth on hers. I want to feel the silk of her hair in my hands while I taste her.

With my body in the doorframe, I tangle my hands in that mass of red hair and get a good grip. The hitch in her breath gives away her surprise.

Good. Let's go for a dive, honey.

"Remember what I said about this just being a friendly dinner?"

"Uh, yeah?" Her breath fans across my jaw, our faces inches apart.

"I lied."

Like last night, as soon as my lips touch hers, we're consumed. Kate's lips move maddeningly against mine. Slanting my mouth over hers, I nip at that damned bottom lip, a holdover fantasy from my hormone-driven teenage years. She smells like honey and tastes like home, and I can't get enough. My hands drift down her arms, rubbing lightly at the definition I find there.

Soft skin teases the pads of my fingers, and I force myself to ease up. As much as I want to claim, to devour, to conquer, I don't. She'd balk, and I have a plan. A hastily thought-out plan, but a plan nonetheless.

Letting my lips linger for one heady second, I pull back, then buckle her in and ignore the confused furrow to her brows.

By the time I settle behind the wheel, her hand is at her lips. Like she's holding on to my taste as much as I'm savoring hers. I let the silence reign in the cab, trying to put my thoughts in order.

Most people assume I'm quiet by nature, which is usually the case. On the other end of it, silence is a vital tool. It makes people uncomfortable and throws them off. I mostly use silence to order my chaotic and messy thoughts into something that makes sense, but it also gives me a solid idea of the other person because they often scramble to fill that conversation void.

"Arik, what are we doing?" Kate's never failed to fill my silences.

"What do you mean?"

Her hands spread out in front of her, and I don't stop the

slow smile on my face. Her hands fly around the cab as she uses her body to speak physically.

"I mean, what are we doing? How would you define what's going on with us? What was tonight for? What do you want from me, from this, from everything? You said friendly dinner, but that kiss wasn't friendly at all. I need rules, order, just fucking *something* to go off of."

She wants to define the undefinable. Impossible, but I give it my best shot.

"That's a lot of thinking. Does your brain ever calm down?"

Deadpan, she replies, "No. No, it does not." A put-upon sigh accompanies her statement.

"Well, okay then. I'm driving you home after an excellent picnic dinner. If I had to define what's going on with us, I would say we're feeling it out as we go. Tonight is as simple as I wanted a quiet meal with you, for you to relax, and for me to learn about the person you've become since I saw you last. I kissed you because I wanted to, and you didn't shove me off or say no, so some part of you must be curious too. You may not realize it, but I'm doing my best to give you time, to take things slow, and go at your pace. As for what's going on with us and what I want? I want to do more of this. I want to spend time with you when our schedules permit and while you're in town. I don't think I need to go into detail on what I want from this, but if you need the words—"

"No, pretty sure I got the general idea when you had me pinned against Gram's door."

The laugh barks right out of me before I stop it, and in seconds Kate's laughing with me, the tension melting.

"Good then, as long as we're on the same page. Same question back to you."

It's always been tit for tat with her. If she expects me to answer those questions, then I want her answers as well.

"Honestly, Arik, I have no idea. I know I'm here in town. I know I enjoyed the quiet meal, and I can't discount the relaxation of being out here. I know I need it, almost as much as you do. On top of Gram, Felt, you, the bookstore, and still working for Liv being her right-hand woman, it's been…" she trails off.

"It's been what?"

Another deep breath is audible through the cab before she responds. "It's been a lot. I have a lot going on. What's going on and what will happen is up in the air, but I'm trying. I'm going by the seat of my pants this time and trying not to overthink everything, but that's hard for me because planning for every eventuality is who I am. And you are right—I am scared. I'm terrified that something is going to go wrong, and it's easier if I try to avoid that, but I can't. I can't cut you out, and I want to spend time with you too, while I'm here."

"I understand being apprehensive. I am too, so we can go at whatever pace you want us to go, Kate."

"We'll both take it slow and deal with it as it comes?"

I reach over for her hand, because I need to touch her. "I'm good with that."

The rest of the drive back to town is quiet. I don't mind, not with the light breeze coming through the windows and the company.

Walking Kate to the door of Gram's house conjures the kiss we shared there, and my thoughts turn to when I'll get her alone and to myself again. Running with a half-assed idea, I blurt out, "You said you wanted to use my gym, right?"

One slender brow rises, and a beat passes before she replies, "Yeah. I mean, if that's okay. I don't mind the cardio I get from riding my bike all over town, but a solid strength workout sounds good. Why?"

"Why don't you come over Sunday morning and we'll get in a workout together? You said you take Sundays off from

Liv and the bookstore, so we could get a workout in and then get the partnership papers squared away."

"Sure, that sounds good. Six good for you?"

"That works for me."

She's standing so close. Not giving myself a chance to second-guess, I lean in and lay my lips on hers.

She meets me, and we descend into each other. With slow drags of my tongue against hers, I consume her mouth in a sumptuous kiss. I draw and draw from her lips until my head spins and arousal drowns us, until she's as wrapped up in me as I am in her. Lifting my mouth from hers, I drag in air as I watch her eyes flutter open. I reach behind her to open the door.

"Goodnight, Katie."

"Night, Arik." Once she disappears into the house, I let the grin take over my face.

The drive home doesn't take much time, and I leave the picnic basket and blanket on the kitchen island to deal with later. I'm exhausted.

Walking on eggshells to make tonight as close to perfect as I could wore me out. I pour two fingers of whiskey in a glass and head to the bathroom for a shower. Once the showerheads are set to pulse, I let the hot water pummel the tension from my shoulders and back.

I let my head drop back, my eyes falling shut as I wet my hair. I can't *not* think of Kate. The way the light plays across all those red waves of hair and the sparkle of her eyes when she's laughing. The way those same eyes shoot laser beams when she's pissed off.

The images turn until it's the feel of her under my hands, the way her legs wrapped around me, the way her hands ran over the length of my torso when I had her against the door, how they gripped my neck tonight.

My mental montage of all things Kate has my cock hardening, and as much as I want to handle my desire, I don't.

As I shower, I wonder when she will be ready to take this budding relationship to the next step. If tonight is any indication, it might be a while, and I'm not sure I'll survive it.

KATE

COLBY HUTCHINS IS A SNEAKY BUSYBODY.

One thing that's as reliable as the sun in a small town is the never-ending gossip. Everyone has been part of the rumor mill or they've added to it. The whispers and looks put an itch between my shoulder blades as I prep for the upcoming week of repairs.

Boxing up and packing away the remaining books for the remodel isn't fun or quick, so I tagged Ally for help. The original plan was to shift the store around as needed when Colby and his crew could get in and complete some of the work Gram and I decided on. A sudden cancellation in his schedule cleared out a full week for him to bump Readers' Haven to the top of the list, so I'm scrambling to get everything cleared out.

I'm quickly running out of room though, and the second floor has no space left. Only five or six boxes of books won't fit, so I plan to lug them back to Gram's house for the time being.

Measuring tape in hand as he putters around the shop

with the same leather-bound notebook he's carried everywhere for twenty years, Colby makes notes.

He's been around since I was a little girl. Being the only general contractor within about fifty miles means if something needs fixing, overhauled, or remodeled in Felt, he has a hand in it.

I don't think he'll ever retire; he's well into his eighties now. He loves the work too much. According to the one time someone asked him about scaling back before I left for college, he went on a twenty-minute lecture stating, "when someone stops doing what they love to retire, they die." We all pretty much left it alone after that.

"Okay, Kate, I'm pretty sure I've got everything I need to get started Monday. The crew will be here at six a.m. sharp."

"I'll have everything cleared out and ready for you. Is there anything else I'm forgetting? Are there any other areas that you'll need access to while y'all are in here?"

Chomping down on a piece of gum, another Colby staple after quitting dip tobacco years ago, he shakes his head.

"That should about do 'er. We aren't getting into the second floor or the storage room for the built-ins until the middle of August, so you'll have plenty of time to clear those areas beforehand. Not that those have much work slated."

I want to reopen as soon as possible, so we're doing the work on the main floor this week. After talking it out with Gram, we decided it would be best to host a Grand Reopening the third week in July, giving us just a week to get the store put back together before trying to catch the tail end of the summer tourist season.

While remodeling, rearranging, and restocking take precedence, those things also cost money, which we're not currently earning. It's a tight timeline, and I'm trying to have faith that we'll pull it off.

"Did you and Arik have a good picnic?" Colby's all innocence, but I don't believe it for a second.

I glance over at Ally, and her eyes are steady on the box she's filling up, but there's a slight smile tugging at her mouth.

I sigh, because what else is there for me to do?

"It was nice. I hadn't been up to the lake since my last visit back home, so I especially enjoyed being able to find time to get up there."

"A bunch of us were at Shorty's apartment playing poker and the like—over off Main Street—and we saw that old Jeep of his headed out of town. Couldn't help but notice you were there with him. Seeing as Martha was telling Mary Jo and everyone within hearing distance that Arik came in for the second time in a week to pick up fried chicken fixings, we all figured he took his girl out for a date."

Irked, I say, "Yeah, I'm sure you noticed with those binoculars that are never far from a poker night, huh?"

"Girls have their craft nights where they sit and spy. Us men have poker night where we keep an eye on our town. Arik's girl or not, we're looking out for you."

It's the "his girl" comment that gets my anxiety going. Aware of Colby and his sneaky ways, I don't correct him because that would add fuel to the fire. Instead, I ignore the comment and go back to taping, labeling, and hefting the boxes full of paperbacks.

In the back room, I give myself a minute. Of course, people will assume that since I'm here for a while that Arik and I would be a thing. I didn't stick around long enough to see the fallout from me leaving, or what people assumed, but no one has gotten the courage to ask or bring it up.

It's so pathetic, she follows you around like a lost puppy all the time, doesn't it get annoying having her as a constant shadow?

I shove Reese's words away, hoping that karma got him

back something fierce. I haven't had the misfortune of running into him around town, and I'm grateful for it.

Being the center of speculation with Arik shouldn't bother me, but it does. I've never been able to measure up to him and everyone's universal love for him. Why it's unilaterally assumed Kate goes right along with Arik, I'll never understand. I've been gone for years, and he's probably had his share of girlfriends, so I don't know why I'm "his girl."

The term itself isn't harmless either. It doesn't merely mean dating in our tiny corner of the world. A man calling someone "his girl" comes with the assumption that it's a serious committed relationship. Our relationship has old roots, but it's not so far progressed I'm comfortable calling myself "his girl," and this is something that could turn sticky.

As much as Gram needs me right now, I'm not staying. I can't. I have a life in another city. A life I love, one I worked hard for. I have a career, a mortgage, and all of the responsibilities that come with an independent life currently on hold hundreds of miles away.

The thought isn't a pleasant one. While I enjoy Arik's company, others assume it's something more, and that's a problem. I've never been able to shake the need to stay out of the spotlight, and being with Arik, in any way, puts me there.

I shake that off because what's going on between Arik and me is between us, not everyone in Felt. I'm borrowing trouble again, letting my fears and misgivings get in the way, and I need to stop. Squaring my shoulders, I head back out to the floor to find Colby gone.

Ally is taping up the last of the boxes on the floor. Marking the box "Paranormal Romance," she hefts it into her arms and stacks it with the other million boxes.

"So, how long did it take for that bit of news to circulate?"

Ally's reply is breezy and light. "Not long. I knew about it yesterday afternoon after Jackson texted me a string of gifs trying to pry information out of me. They went fishing together and the menfolk strategized. He thought I knew since we've been hanging out."

"Great." This is exactly what I've been trying to avoid—the gossip, the speculation.

"You remember how it is in small towns, Kate. They don't mean any harm, but you and Arik are news, and this is the juiciest bit of gossip since Tally Jessop gave birth to a baby that looked a lot more like Karl Winifred than her husband, Cody."

I do a double-take because holy freaking hell.

"Wait. Tally was having an affair with Karl?" Karl Winifred was a year behind me in school and African American. Cody Jessop, from my year, resembles a corn-fed lumberjack from the Midwest.

"She sure was, and there was a big to-do over that before she and Karl moved away once the divorce was finalized. That's neither here nor there. Give it a few weeks. Some other calamity will come along, and you and Arik will be old news. Promise."

"I hate being gossip fodder. If everyone would mind their business, we would all go on being a happier society."

"It's not malicious, Kate. Part of it comes from living in a small town, the other part of it is our community cares about each other. Usually, if there is something serious going on, the gossipers pick it up, mobilize, and help. Last year, Mark Hawkins broke his ankle after his horse threw him, and the entire town came together to help him get the rest of his spud harvest back on track and ready to sell. It's not all bad. You're just the current news that's circulating. Come on, let's head to Sweet Tooth. We'll have a Danish and I'll pry details on last night's picnic out of you."

I grab my slim wallet and phone and shove them in the

pockets of my leggings. Dwelling on something that hasn't changed in years isn't going to help me now.

"You said earlier the menfolk strategized. What does that even mean?"

Her tinkling laugh rings out. "That's something I say to get Jackson and Connor's dander up. Pretty much they go up to the lake and fish, bullshit, scratch their balls, and be men. Then there are the times they have man talk about whatever crisis they need to address. The last time they went up there for that was when Jackson caught Kathryn in bed with a tourist."

"Wait, back up. I'm gonna need you to unpack that for me."

Some of the light dims from Ally's face. "Yeah, that's the bitch Jackson was with for about two years. They were living together, and Jackson was about to propose when he came home early from a backwoods trip and found Kathryn in bed with some asshat executive on a business trip at the resort where she works."

"Oh my God. Poor Jackson."

"Yeah, it sucked at the time. He was brooding something fierce before I called in the big guns."

"The big guns?"

"Mama and Connor Murtry, though you probably haven't met him yet, hermit that he is. He and Jackson met in college, hit it off, and Connor moved here about six years back. They're bros." She say's "bros" in a pseudo deep voice—my mind reels from it all. So much has changed, but so much is still the same.

Ally pulls the door open to her shop, where deliciousness permeates the air.

Midmorning has the shop pretty near empty. Jem Woods is behind the register, switching out the morning selections with more decadent cupcakes and brownies in anticipation of the lunch crowd. A couple of employees are wiping down tables and cleaning up the morning rush mess left behind.

The two women in the corner catch my attention—Christina Hathaway and Melody Hill, twin peas in an evil pod—but I choose to ignore them.

"Hey Jem, how was the morning?" Ally leans a hip against the waist-high display case beside the register.

"Hey, it was good, brisk business. We got an order for three dozen of your Stuffed Monkey Balls. Sam is going to pick them up early tomorrow morning. The order form is on your desk."

I tune out Ally as she puts in our coffee order when I hear the distinct snorting giggle I spent years trying to ignore. I can barely make out what Christina is whispering to Melody. "It's so sad, she's so pathetic. Figures she comes back to town and latches right back on him. We all saw it coming."

"Weren't you trying to get him to partner with you for the Cowboy Courses in the fall?"

"Oh, I am. She'll be long gone by then, and he'll need consoling. He'll be easy pickin's at that point."

Turning, because God, she has some gall, I interrupt with false cheer. "Good morning, Christina, Melody. How're y'all doing this morning?"

Melody's back is to me and I must have taken her off guard because she jumps about six inches in the air before whipping around to look at me. Pasting a smile on, she says, "Oh hey, Kate. I'm doing fine, how about yourself?"

"I'm doing great, thanks for asking. I've been getting Readers' Haven back into shape. I hope y'all will come and visit us at the Grand Reopening."

Melody looks nervously back at Christina who's been sitting there with that smirk on her face. It's clear she's gonna be unpleasant before she even opens her mouth.

"Heard you and Arik had quite the picnic last night. Not

surprising that you're following him around again. You know what they say—old dogs don't learn new tricks."

Rolling my eyes, I just *can't* with her level of petty. I turn back to Ally and Jem who are taking in the show. Two disposable cardboard cups sit at Ally's elbow. Reaching to grab the one marked with a K, I take a small sip before saying, "You wanna grab a table, Ally?"

"Arik and I had a terrific laugh about it this morning." Why Christina's still talking is anyone's guess, yet old insecurities flare. The worries that I'm not enough for Arik, for Gram, for Felt rise before I beat them back. Fake it till you make it, right?

"Oh yeah? That's fascinating, Christina." Ally's sugary tone should give Christina some clue to shut up, but she's never been that bright.

"Is it?"

"What's fascinating to me is that in all these years you've never stopped being a bitter, spiteful person." Ally is spot-on about that. I was never popular in school. I chose to stay in my own world of books and Arik. Christina's bullying of me never made sense until I overheard her father berating her for coming in second to me academically. The hatred on her face the day of the recognition and awards ceremony in elementary school cemented my status as her enemy. The fact that I was overweight just threw fuel on the fire of her hatred for me, something I'll never understand.

Her being on what I assume was a never-ending pursuit to please her father, she took aim at the one place she could be better than me—being popular and getting all of the attention of our peers while knocking me down over and over again.

Outrage has Christina's cheeks bright red as she sputters out, "We did have a good laugh. He's stringing you along, and of course you're falling for it. Arik and I have gotten *friendly* recently."

Again, before I can clap back, Ally is jumping in. "Oh, really? And was that before or after he turned you down *for the fifth time?*"

I love Ally Sawyer, and I'm keeping her.

I think back to Arik's blunt honesty with me at dinner. He's never given me a reason not to trust him. Even when I thought he broke that trust, he still stood up for me—something I paid back by running away and not talking to him for twelve years. Maybe it's time for me to step out of my comfort zone and reach for something I want.

I definitely want more of those kisses.

Wicked plans to seduce Arik fill my head—our workout on Sunday would give me the best opportunity. I can take advantage of the time that we'll be alone.

Linking my arm with Ally, I tug her out of the café. While I do my own strategizing with a friend, coffee at Readers' Haven sounds much better than sticking around poisonous people.

ARIK

I'VE BEEN UP FOR OVER AN HOUR, LIKE A KID ON CHRISTMAS morning waiting for my ma to wake up. Right before six, there's a knock on the door. My desire to take it slow, to not hurry to the door, flies out the window as anticipation lights me up.

I'm unprepared for the sight on my front porch. Kate wears yoga pants painted on like a second skin and a loose lime-colored tank top that shows off her defined arms and highlights the curves I want to get my hands on. My mouth goes dry.

"Is this still a good time?" Her voice is hesitant, and it pulls my mind out of the gutter.

I'm standing in the door staring at her like a Neanderthal. Quickly stepping back, not trusting myself to speak, I nod and get out of her way. The worried expression falls off her face once she crosses the threshold. Maybe she was afraid I forgot. Stowing her bag on a hook, she pulls out a water bottle and her phone.

"Do you mind if we get started right away? I used the bike ride as a warmup."

Wrapping an arm around her waist, I pull her in, bumping my lips against hers in a friendly peck.

"Good Morning, Kate."

Color rushes into her cheeks, and a shy smile covers her face.

"Good Morning, Arik. Sleep well?"

Ushering her through the quiet house and down to the basement, I nod.

We're barely through the entryway before she's dropping her water bottle on the mat by the rack. She jumps right in to setting up the bar for squats. Lord, help me.

"You have a pretty sweet setup here. Thanks for letting me use it."

I watch her go through leg stretches while I try to reel in the lust that's tightening my shoulders—and my shorts. The way those yoga pants hug the sweet curve of her ass is a fucking crime. I'm on board for a few felonies if it means I get my hands on them and her.

As hot as the view is, a pulled muscle is a bitch, and I don't have time for that kind of recovery. Not with the *workouts* I have planned, so I start to stretch alongside her.

Ripping my brain from the gutter, I answer, "The community center is limited so you're welcome anytime."

"Hmm. I can do a lot with free weights, though I have to admit, this is nicer." Kate wraps a belt around her waist, cinching it tight before crawling under the bar and tugging her ponytail over her shoulder so it doesn't get caught under the bar.

"You need a spotter?" I note the squat bar has two hundred pounds on it, which is ludicrous when looking at her petite frame. She has soft curves, but not the musculature necessary to lift the equivalent of a grown man.

Joke's on me though when she responds, "Nah, this is my

usual. Not trying for any new PRs this morning. Thanks though."

Standing tall, hands wrapped around the bar sitting across her shoulders, she steps back from the rack. I'm in the worst fucking spot for this. With her first rep, the sage green material stretches over her ass, and my thoughts dive straight back into the gutter because she isn't wearing panties. The individual curves of her ass are prominent, her alabaster skin peeking through the thin material.

Kate pounds out fifteen reps at a smooth, steady pace. After racking the bar, she ducks under it, coming out on the other side with a smirk dancing on her lips.

"Your turn. How much do you want?"

I add additional weight to the bar while struggling to keep myself under control. She has to be fucking with me. There's no way she doesn't realize her pants are sheer. Who the fuck lifts without underwear? I certainly don't go commando when I'm lifting. I don't think Connor and Jackson do.

What the hell do I know about the underwear habits of other men though?

There's a burn in my glutes when I rack the weights, but Kate's a pro at this. Before I can get out of her way, she's already loosening the clamps and dropping the extra weights.

Back and forth, we work our way through squats, lunges, calf raises, burpees, and deadlifts. She is a beast, barely breaking a sweat as she powers through while I'm fighting to keep up.

On our next rest, I grab a bottle of water and guzzle. Not only is she intentional with her workout, but she's also quick.

"Ready for core?" Her question has my stamina crying in the corner, but damn me if I let a woman half my size knock me under the table.

Crunches, sit-ups, planks, and various what-the-fuckery I've never heard of, and thirty minutes later, I'm lying in a man-sized sweat puddle while Kate stands over me.

"You look a little peaked there, Arik. I thought you did this regularly?"

"Ha-ha, you troublemaker. What kind of sadistic trainer do you have back in Arizona?"

"Rob's not that bad. This would be a light workout for him. If you're struggling, I can go easier next time."

Easier my ass. I'm determined to keep up with her, though tomorrow I'll be paying for it.

Plopping down next to me on the mat, she sips from her water bottle. There's a subtle sheen of sweat that dances across her collar bones, and if I weren't so exhausted, I'd lean over and taste her.

"So, uh…" I'm not quite sure how to bring it up so I just blurt out, "You're not wearing underwear. I mean…your pants are see-through."

Mischief dances in her eyes as she replies, "I'm not? Well, damn, I knew I forgot something before leaving the house. That must have been it. Thanks for letting me know."

With a wink, she uncrosses her legs and starts to stand.

That wink gets my blood moving, waking me up and sealing her fate. She intentionally wore no panties, the little tease.

Reaching out, I shackle her ankle in my hand and tug her back down. She lets out a soft "oof" as her back hits the cushioned mat next to me.

I roll, holding my weight off her with one hand while the other comes to her hip before I crush my lips to hers.

Catching her gasp with my lips, I tease, entice, and cajole my way into her mouth. With long, deep strokes of my tongue against hers, we share breath, consuming each other as passion ignites between us. She surrenders to it

139

completely, her hands clawing at my hair and shoulders before coming to rest around my neck. Her breasts press against my chest, our bodies aligning now that I finally have her horizontal. Her arms come up to drape around my neck, playing with the hair at my collar while she slides her legs around my waist, bringing my center flush with hers.

The ache in my cock is unbearable as it's pressed against her body, separated from her only by thin pieces of clothing. The heat of her center against the fabric of my shorts focuses my thoughts on one thing—making Kate come for me.

Dipping my head back down, I kiss the corner of her mouth. As my lips travel the smooth column of her throat, the taste of her threatens my control and sends my senses into overload. Running my hand up her hip and under her shirt, her soft skin under my mouth and fingers is nirvana.

The scent of spicy honeysuckle surrounds her. There's a hint of musk that's addicting. Her breath catches in a throaty gasp, and her hands tug at the hair at my collar. Triumph roars through me, urging me on.

Unable to get enough, bruising our lips, I kiss her again and again until I'm lightheaded. Until my scruff turns her face and neck red, and even then, I don't stop. Branding this woman as mine is something I should have done a long time ago.

Needs swirl in a messy jumble and I'm not interested in unknotting them or picking them apart until I understand the emotions that feed those needs.

The head of my cock slides along the crotch of her yoga pants, dry fucking my way closer and closer to that delectable heat. Wrapping my arm under her hips and tugging her flush to me, center to center, I thrust.

She arches against me, hips shifting, impatient for friction.

"Arik, please."

Her plea is punctuated with a twist of her midsection, legs climbing higher along my sides, trying to get closer to me.

Trapped behind my gym shorts and boxers, my dick is begging for relief, urging me to bury myself inside of her, to rut, to fuck until I work this ache out for both of us. The fragile hold I have on myself and our earlier agreement to take it slow are the only things stopping me.

The tugs at my hair turn to pulls before her nails are digging into my shoulders. Her whimpers are fueling the fire to watch her come undone beneath me.

Neck arched and head thrown back, Kate's eyes are closed as though she's lost in sensation. I want her with me.

"Katie, open your eyes. Look at me."

Heavy lids open, and her emerald gaze is unfocused as it locks on mine.

The sounds coming from her, the whimpers and gasps, drive me nuts. Breaking my lips away from her skin, I suck air in, breathless, enchanted by her.

Her hair is spread around her in a fiery halo, her eyes reflecting the depth of her desire.

"Arik." My name on her lips is a drug I didn't know existed, and I'm already hooked.

The tremor in her legs betrays how close to the edge she is. Not faltering for a second, I piston against her, keeping the cadence steady. All my thoughts, my actions focus on shoving her over that edge. The pressure building in my core terrorizes me, but I beat it back, refusing to give in. I will not come in my shorts like a fifteen-year-old boy looking at his first skin mag—at least not until Kate does.

Upping the ante, I shove my hand under her tank top, burrowing under the sports bra. Her nipple pebbles against my palm. Scraping my thumbnail across the nub sends her hips crashing against mine, her first loss in rhythm since this started, and a strangled moan dies in her throat.

The thought of her restraining herself, holding anything back from me, is intolerable. Gripping her hips tight, I deliver a punishing thrust that almost rips my orgasm right out of me.

Just. Hold. On.

"Baby, let me hear you. *God,* you feel fucking perfect. Let go, let go for me. I've got you."

"Don't stop. So close. Don't stop, Arik."

If it's my words or something else, I don't care. When her next moan sounds, that throaty cry vibrates between us, no holds barred as her hips pump against mine, mindlessly chasing that edge.

I reach up and the flutter of her pulse under the smooth skin of her throat is a staccato beat against my thumb. Testing, I give a harder thrust, and she meets me stroke for stroke until the shaking in her thighs intensifies, and she's digging her hands into my hips, her gasps and moans coming faster and louder.

"Oh God." Bright green eyes lock on to me, and I watch the orgasm crash through her. Her eyes glaze over, going blind in pleasure while her hips are pumping against mine, dragging this on and on.

Finally letting go, my release burns up my calves and thighs, climbing higher and higher until my stomach tightens and I'm coming right along with Kate.

I don't stop, never wanting this to end.

KATE

Languid caresses from Arik stroke my thighs, my hips, and my sides. My whole body is sluggish, like I ran a marathon after the most challenging workout of my life. All thanks to the man who's dropping small kisses against my mouth, my cheeks, and neck.

Tingling in all the most amazing places, I'm so relaxed I could fall asleep right on the floor of this excellent gym. Just slide right into dreamland where it's the norm for devastating orgasms to be delivered with ease from the giant Norse god holding me.

I didn't quite plan for it to play out this way when I decided to wear my old yoga pants. I had thought there would be some flirty making out. But I'm currently unable to bring myself to care, my endorphin-riddled brain shoving the high-strung, uptight Kate to a deep, dark corner. I'm sure I'll have some misgivings later, but right now? This is just about perfect.

Prying open my heavy eyelids, the first thing I see is the arctic blue of Arik's eyes locked on me. The smug grin decorating those devilish lips takes a second to register. Honestly? He should be pleased with himself; he played my body like a maestro.

I drop my right leg around his calf and arch my hips up and hard, rolling us and reversing our positions until I'm straddling his narrow hips, hands planted on his chest. Lowering myself, I return those soft kisses. His beard tickles my lips and palms as I cradle his face in my hands.

A door closes somewhere in the house, and panic rockets through me.

"Is someone here?"

Arik's eyes are partially closed until the sound registers, and they widen comically.

"...and then they tried to tell me they weren't drinking when not even two feet from their tent was a whole fucking cooler of beer." Heavy steps are coming down the stairs from the kitchen.

"Oh shit..." Arik's words send adrenaline lighting through me. Like a runner off the mark, I roll off him and to my feet in a single motion.

Brushing my hair back, hoping it doesn't look too destroyed, I glance at Arik who's trying to arrange himself to hide the evidence of what happened. He barely manages to tug his shirt down before the interlopers cross the threshold to the basement.

Jackson pushes into the room, along with a bearded Goliath who I assume is Connor.

There's a beat of silence, their eyes scanning first us and then the room. The spread-out gym equipment litters the floor while Arik and I stand awkwardly, and I stare at my feet. My face heats, because of fucking course it does. Why not light a big fat sign saying *I just came so hard my brain leaked out of my ears*,

I can't imagine how Arik feels, since his release is much more evident than mine. Even so, I'm going to need a shower and a pair of panties, stat.

Hesitantly, Jackson breaches the silence. "We, uh...we were hoping to get a workout in before heading out and doing some kayaking on the river. Is it okay if we jump in?"

Arik looks like he's about to object.

"Absolutely. We just finished, so I'm going to get out of here."

Grabbing my water bottle and moving toward the exit, I decide the partnership agreement can fucking wait. When Arik's hand comes to rest at the small of my back, I stiffen.

"I'll walk you out." Over his shoulder, Arik says, "Be right back, guys."

The pressure of his hand ushers me out of the room, and I can feel his stare on my ass as I climb the steep steps ahead of him, emerging into his kitchen. My heartbeat thumps in my ears, blocking out the voices of the guys downstairs.

The sexy tension has evaporated. Jackson and Connor's interruption ripped through the little fantasy of a discreet affair I'd been building in my head.

Those misgivings I brushed off earlier? They rush through my head as I try to stay a step ahead of Arik. Standing there, covered in sweat, my hair is a freaking rat's nest, and I can't even imagine what they thought.

We were discovered by his two closest friends.

I'm not ready for this.

My breath is whistling through my nose as the panic and anxiety climb into my throat.

I need to run. To hide. Find somewhere private to fall apart.

I blindly turn the corner toward the front door, but a firm grip on my elbow whips me around. My body bumps into something. I slap my hands back, grounding myself against the cool, smooth wall.

"Katie, baby, stop. Do that breathing thing. The one where you count."

Count, yes. Ten, nine…

I drag air into my starving lungs while I count silently. Arik's hands play in my hair, digging in and massaging my scalp while he waits for me to calm my breathing.

Those fingers become my focus, and I use their soothing strokes along with counting to fight back the rising swell of anxiety until my heartbeat slows down.

Pulling back, I lift my head from where he gathered me against his chest.

"Better now?"

Not trusting my voice, I nod. I haven't had a panic attack in years. Structuring my life into a routine of predictability has helped me handle anything life throws at me. The upheaval in my life recently along with the strength of reemerging *feelings* pretty much guaranteed the attack, and I should have anticipated it.

"I can kick them out. Give me two seconds and they'll be gone, and we'll pick up where we left off."

The guys didn't say anything, but they didn't have to. It was pretty evident what went down, and embarrassment at almost being caught still crawls through me.

Shaking my head, I find my voice. "It's better if we don't and if I get out of here before they assume anything else. I'll leave the agreement with you to look over—you can sign it and drop it off with Gram or me anytime."

"Wait. Stop. What do you mean 'it's better if we don't'? Like don't do this today? Or don't be together at all?"

I watch as the hurt flashes on his face, unmistakable before he locks it down. Hurrying to clarify, I say, "No, I do want to try, but maybe less conspicuously."

"Conspicuous..." His lips tighten even as his eyes narrow. "Kate, are you trying to hide this, to hide us? Are you embarrassed of me?"

Open mouth, insert foot.

"No, no, not at all. If anything, it's the other way around. I would just prefer we don't broadcast our orgasms to your friends, regardless of how amazing they are. The gossip mill in the town is already going strong about us, and I would like..." I trail off because articulating the next part is going to make me sound like a self-conscious idiot, but I have to try.

"I would like it if we were discreet because you're *you* and everyone loves you, and I'm...I'm just me."

"Kate. Look at me." Again, he tilts my chin, so my eyes climb from his chest. Understanding and concern—concern for me—is evident in all of that never-ending blue.

"Baby, are you worried about what people are going to think if they know that we're together?"

"Yes. No. I don't know. I just want some time to settle into whatever this is. I want to be with you as much as possible. I'm just not ready for the whispers, the speculations, the inevitable question of what someone like you is doing with someone like me."

That insecurity is bubbling right below the surface. How can I expect to deserve someone like Arik? What makes me so impressive that I would be worth the effort? Not a damn thing from where I'm standing.

Tracing his hands up and down my arms, he says, "We'll go as slow or as fast as you need, but, Katie, people are going to know. That's unavoidable, and I don't give a flying fuck what they say, what they question or speculate. I care about you, being with you, seeing you. *That's* what I care about."

Of course he doesn't care about what others think. He's never worried about what others thought of him. Aside from his learning challenges, something he couldn't help, he's never been told he would be better *if*…he would be pretty *if*…he would make more friends *if*.

Those *if* statements shaped my life. *If* was the reason I didn't try to make friends. *If* was the reason I grew up thinking I was less-than, like I didn't belong, like I didn't matter worth a damn until I started retreating and isolating myself.

Aside from the disaster of prom, Arik never made me feel like less, never pushed me to change, to evolve into some imaginary version of Kate that would magically be worth his time and attention. His never-ending acceptance of me is what made the betrayal at prom hurt so much. And now that I know the truth, I could kick myself for ever doubting him.

That teasing glint I adore comes into his gaze before he asks, "Are you sure I can't convince you to stay? Maybe let me make you some breakfast? Then maybe we can head to town for the Fourth of July parade?"

Realizing it's the holiday throws me for a loop. With all the chaos recently, the date slipped my mind.

His friends already saw us. People are already speculating about us. We can still be discreet, but there's no reason, other than my own failings, to not spend the day with him.

Throwing caution to the wind, shoving my need to go unnoticed down, I say, "I'd love breakfast and to go to the parade with you."

I made the right decision by the grin that slides across his face.

THE SMELL OF BACON LINGERS IN THE KITCHEN. IT WAS A simple breakfast—eggs, toast, and bacon—but it was perfect. The coffee at my elbow is the only thing stopping me from slipping into a nap right here at the table.

Arik putters around the stove, sliding a new batch of bacon in the oven before he starts to clean up. It's a sight I could get used to. But I don't have long to dwell on the thought before the sound of footsteps coming up the stairs intrudes.

I have seconds to steel myself before I hear Jackson.

"Yo, Fabio, I sure hope you changed your shorts because I don't want to stare at your cum stains while I eat all that bacon I smell." Jackson walks into the kitchen and stops dead in his tracks when he sees me.

Guess they didn't realize I'm still here.

Connor's not paying attention and rams straight into Jackson. They both stumble before falling down into a heap of arms and legs.

Jackson ends up flat on his stomach, and Connor lands on top of him. Back to chest, the slight difference in their height means Jackson's butt is pressed tight to Connor's groin, and the horrified shriek Jackson yelps out says that he noticed the same thing. Laughter rips out of me before I stifle it as I whip my phone out to take multiple burst photos.

While Connor tries to disengage by pushing up to a kneeling position, it's as if there is an invisible tether attached to the two. Simultaneously, Jackson thrusts up and back with his hips, coming to his hands and knees, and they're in a disturbing parody of doggy style.

Arik's laughter roars right along with mine. He's clutching his stomach in hilarity, and I have to use the table to hold my phone steady. Together we watch the two bearded behemoths struggle to untangle without getting into an even more compromising position.

"Fucking hell, Jackson. Stop wiggling around. Let me stand up, for Chrissake."

"Dude. Get the fuck off me. Kate, stop taking pictures."

Abs cramping from my laughter, I try to draw air into my lungs, unable to see through the tears in my eyes.

When they're finally successful in climbing to their feet, Jackson advances on me as I sit wiping my eyes. I stand up, my chair clattering behind me as I bolt through the open back doors.

Suddenly, I have three giant men chasing me and my phone all over the back yard, and my laughter dies as I focus on not tripping. Graceful is something I will never be.

Their long legs catch up to me quickly. Arik aims a well-placed shove at Connor, toppling him, then tackles Jackson to the ground.

"Run, Katie, run."

My shorter legs are no match for these Sasquatches, and I'm not surprised when I peek behind me and see Connor is up and charging after me. I dip behind a huge oak tree, careful to keep the trunk between us. Giggles snicker out while I look for an exit, phone clutched tightly in my grip. Jackson and Arik are still rolling around on the ground, Arik's heft the only thing keeping Jackson from breaking away.

"It's Kate, right?"

Refocusing on the stern man in front of me, I nod. "Yep, that's me. You must be Connor."

Nodding, he says, "Well, that gets the introductions out of the way. So, how about we make this easy? You hand over the phone, and we'll all go about our day, huh?"

I grin at his cajoling tone, unexpected from someone who looks like he enjoys kicking puppies and making kids cry. I shake my head and attempt a straight face. "I'm sorry, I can't do that. These pictures need to be preserved for the good of humanity."

Eyes narrowing at me, he gives a slight nod. "Hard way it

is then." Quicker than The Flash, he darts around the tree, and in a last-ditch effort to preserve future blackmail evidence, I shove my phone down my bra.

Squaring off with me, the glare he shoots my way is formidable. "That's playing dirty, darlin'."

There are traces of a southern drawl in his words. As fascinating as that is, I need to focus on getting out of this situation.

"You're not getting this phone, Mr. Lumberjack, so you might as well give up now."

"That's where you're wrong. I'll be getting that phone. It may not be now, since I'm not keen on Arik rearranging my face, but I will get that phone."

"If I promise to only ever use the photos for good and not evil, can we agree to a truce?"

Shaking his head in rejection of my generous offer, he parries, "Your definition of good probably differs vastly from mine." And then he smiles, his face transforming like the sun shining through clouds after days of rain.

He's a handsome son of a gun, and he knows it.

It's my turn to narrow my eyes at him. "You can dim the megawatt smile there, buddy. These photos are mine."

My words wipe the smile off his face, returning his expression to the hundred-yard stare that seems much more natural for him.

Jackson and Arik make their way toward us, but I don't dare take my eyes off Connor.

"You won't win." Looking me over, Arik's puzzled when he asks, "Where's your phone, Kate?"

"She shoved it down her bra. I wisely decided I like the alignment of my nose and didn't go after it."

Glaring at his friend, Arik says, "Good choice."

A shrill beeping sings through the air, right before the

smell of burnt bacon reaches us. Arik and I look at each other wide-eyed before Jackson bolts toward the house shouting desperately, "The bacon!"

We wait until he disappears into the house before dissolving into laughter.

KATE

Bright and early Monday morning, I pull into Felt High School's parking lot. A couple of people are milling around, but otherwise the school is a ghost town. Reminding myself of the date—most of the population is likely sleeping in after the holiday yesterday—helps explain the stillness. Climbing out of my car, I head toward the camping canopies set up along the front of the building.

Being here is both nerve-wracking and weird. I haven't been back to this school since the prom disaster. Having graduated after the first semester of my senior year, the only reason that I didn't head to college early was that I wanted to walk with my class. Well, that and Arik. Even then, I didn't want to be parted from him, a feeling I'm getting used to again the more that we spend time together.

I'd been sitting between Arik's legs as fireworks lit the sky when he invited me to help out with the fundraising car wash that he's running with the help of some of the faculty. It baffles me that parents are more concerned with sports uniforms than outdated books, but I guess priorities are different here.

Wearing a bathing suit while we wash cars is not my idea of a good time, but Arik has been such a resource with the store that the least I could do is offer to help.

Hopping out of Gram's SUV, I head toward Arik, who's wearing a tank top and board shorts, and I want to climb him like a tree. After yesterday, being under him and the expert way his body worked mine right over the edge of insanity into pleasure, I'm addicted and ready for more.

"Hey, beautiful. Thanks for coming today."

Arik brushes a kiss across my lips, and the scent of him goes straight to my head. He starts to pull back, and I forget that we're in public, that people are watching us as I fist my hands in his shirt and haul him back for a deeper taste.

His hands bite into my hips, leaving behind the most delicious ache. The groan that rumbles from him is a sound I'll never get tired of causing.

Disengaging because there are impressionable minds nearby, I tease, "You're welcome. Glad I could help."

Reaching down, Arik discreetly adjusts himself in his shorts, and that's a new thrill for me—that I can affect him so easily, that the attraction between us is so strong.

"Where do you want me first?"

Muttering under his breath, I don't catch what he says at first. "Go ahead and head over to the poster table. There are a couple of kids working on them. Once we get going, we'll put them along Main Street to attract more people. I have to get the hoses set up."

"Aye aye, captain." With a saucy salute, I head over to the teenagers surrounding a camping table.

Quickly getting acquainted with the students, I jump right in. We decorate and bling out posterboard with paint markers and glitter in the school's colors of maroon and gold.

Before long, we're all standing around as the first cars

pull into the lot. Jackson and Connor are both working near Arik, all three of them looking like hunks—shirtless, wet, and their muscles bulging—as they scrub cars for donations.

I'm not the only one who notices either, as over three-quarters of the waiting cars all hold female drivers.

This car wash started innocently enough to raise money for tablets for the school but is quickly going to turn into a photo shoot for the thirsty mothers of Felt if we don't get some females out there soon.

Corralling Ally away from the donation table, I figure we can leave the school treasurer with the cash box alone.

"Come on, let's go save the men from the lusty ladies of Felt, why don't we?"

We both take off our shirts, opting for bikini tops and shorts, and we head over to the guys.

I call out, "Hey, y'all wanna swap or need help?"

Arik turns, and I relish how his mouth drops open as he stares at me in just a bikini top. My eyes lock on his until I hear Jackson shout.

"That's my fucking sister, dude. Don't look at her like that."

Connor, now drenched after Jackson turned the hose on him, sputters, "What? No. I wasn't looking at anyone like anything. She's like a sister to me."

Glancing at Ally, I watch as her small smile dies into pinched lips and an irritated eye roll. "Jesus, Jackson, stop. It's a fucking bathing suit top. Calm down, ninny." The sassy attitude that spills off her knocks her brother back a peg.

After an awkward moment or two, we all get back to work. Connor and Jackson are washing the tops of cars, while Ally and I scrub down the sides and tires as we're shorter. Arik is handling the hose now after having ripped it out of Jackson's hands. The students are in charge of drying and hopping in where they're needed.

There's a sense of community here. People get out of their cars as they wander over to the makeshift concession stand rigged up near the donation table. The friendly back and forth between students and adults isn't something I'm used to anymore. Hell, when I need my car washed, I usually just go through a prepaid one. I can't even remember the last time I saw something like what we have going on today.

A deluge of cold water swamps my back and I shriek, yanked out of my thoughts by a snickering Arik.

"What the hell was that for?"

"You were looking hot, so I wanted to cool you off."

Grumbling under my breath, I say, "Yeah, I bet." Chucking a soapy sponge at him, I put the car between us before he gets any ideas on revenge.

"God, look at the stretch marks on her side. You'd think she would have stuck to a one-piece, but no, we have to be subjected to *that*."

Standing in line waiting for the car wash are Melody and Christina. I've mostly ignored their presence, but now it's unavoidable as Christina's voice carries across the parking lot. I know they're likely here to ogle the guys, just like every other female in line, but the catcalls and comments are enough to piss me off.

Ally comes to stand next to me before saying, "Ignore them."

"No, it's okay. My shoulders were getting warm anyway. I should probably put on my shirt so I don't get burned."

Ally's eyes narrow on me, not believing my excuse for a second. She lets it go, though, and I head over to where we all stashed our stuff, shrugging back into my shirt.

Arik's eyes are on me the entire time, intense as he watches me. He says something to Connor before handing off the hose and heading my way.

"Hey, I..." That's as far as I get before his mouth is on mine. Dipping me low, his arm is a steel bar behind my back.

"I couldn't give two shits about marks on your hips. You're beautiful to me. Always have been, always will be."

As abruptly as he dipped me, he pulls me back to standing and saunters back to Connor to take the hose.

Looking over at Christina and the sour expression that now covers her face, I flash her a cheeky grin and get back to work.

Hours later, I'm showered and relaxing with a glass of wine at the dining room table in Gram's kitchen, where the Internet connection is best. My two best friends in the entire world are making friends with Ally in a video call.

Jackson had let it slip while we were saving the kitchen after the bacon fiasco that Ally was excited to have me back in town. She doesn't have many friends her age, being busy with the store and the girls.

After all her help with Readers' Haven, we've grown close. While hanging out with her today, I invited her to the video call.

Little roots are reclaiming me, tying me to the town I abandoned. People recognize me coming and going from the shop and in the grocery store. Others stop to make conversation on the sidewalk, asking about Gram and Readers' Haven. I am being refolded into the sleepy little mountain town, and it's confusing.

Being torn between my life in Arizona and settling into a routine here in Felt is throwing me for a loop and tying me in knots.

"What's going on in your head, doll?" The black-haired goddess, Taylor, has a glass of blood-red wine in her hand. She's staring directly into the camera, her gaze spurring me into spilling all my secrets.

As a virtual administrative assistant, juggling problems is

ALINA LANE

Taylor's job description, and I've always used her as a sounding board when I run into problems, both personal and professional. Compared to the things she's endured, I have no room to complain about anything in my life.

"What? Oh, nothing, just thinking."

"Whatcha thinking about?" Olivia asks. The exact opposite of Taylor's dark sultry looks, Olivia is light and airy. Her blonde hair that tends to get lighter the more she's in the sun and her dark sapphire eyes give her the appearance of a life-like Barbie doll.

"Probably Arik, based off the goofy smitten look on her face," Ally giggles into her wine, humor dancing behind her hazel eyes.

"Yes, and no. I was thinking about how weird it is for me to be back here. It's kinda throwing me off. I mean, I have a life back in Arizona, a job I love, and amazing friends. On the other hand, it's been so easy for me to jump back in here. I'm not sure what I expected when I came back, but it wasn't exactly this."

"Of course it's weird for you. Felt isn't the same place it was twelve years ago. Even though you've never shared specifics, I saw and heard enough about the terrible things Christina and Melody did to you to get why coming back here would be hard. It's also understandable you're conflicted. You adapted and built your world around another city." Ally's no-nonsense breakdown is much tidier than my verbal vomit.

"Terrible things like what?" Olivia asks. I know that tone. That's her "I'm gonna fuck some shit up" voice, and I need to head this off.

"Nothing serious," I start, but Ally cuts me off.

"I know you did not just say it was nothing serious. Christina and Melody tormented her for years, Olivia. They used to sit behind her so they could cut chunks of her hair

158

off. They printed off thousands of flyers with her yearbook picture over the body of a whale. Every day they would knock her lunch tray out of her hands or off the table. They poured paint on her. They would make farm animal noises at her when she walked by. They sliced her clothes to ribbons and then told every male in gym class that the locker room was empty. That is the definition of serious."

I'm stunned. I had no idea Ally knew about all of this. She hadn't even been a freshman when most of this happened. Christina and Melody had backed off quite a bit after they both got suspended for the locker room thing. After that they stuck to petty bullshit, like taunting me and spreading ugly rumors.

"How do you know all that? You weren't there for most of it."

"Jackson. He would tell me, and he said that if I ever saw them being mean, that I needed to step up and say something."

Jackson was there for most of it. In a school our size it's hard to miss those types of things, but I never thought that he shared that with his sister.

"Kate, why didn't you ever tell us these things?"

Olivia's eyes are brimming with tears. I know she isn't pitying me, but instead she's thinking about the shy, insecure girl who asked to rent a room from her. Now she knows why it took so long for me to come out of my shell.

"It wouldn't have made a difference, Liv. I didn't want to think about it anymore."

"That's why you latched on to weightlifting when you decided to lose weight."

It isn't a question, so I don't answer, but she's not wrong. When I gained a little bit of confidence, I signed up for a gym membership. Overwhelmed and out of my depth, Rob had found me crying in the kitchen one night and offered to show me the ropes. He taught me about nutrition—how to balance treats with healthy options. He showed me how to lift correctly and taught me self-defense.

The first time I was able to do a full unassisted pull-up, I was strong. The first time I took Rob to the mat in a grapple, I was fierce. Making the hike to the top of the San Francisco Peaks, I was fearless. I never wanted to lose those feelings. So, I kept going. I kept pushing myself, and my confidence grew, until one day I began to love myself, to love my body. I loved what it did for me, and I loved who I was. That's not a feeling easily described.

I didn't expect to come back to Felt with any good feelings. I certainly didn't have any when I left. A comet could have struck this place off the map, and aside from losing Gram, I couldn't have cared less. That's how bruised my emotions were when I left for college. I had no plans to ever return here for more than a visit, but that changed with Gram's injury.

My goal was to get in, take care of Gram, and leave again. Then the bookstore became a problem that needed solving. Arik forcing me to address the past and whatever we have now adds even more to my already burdened plate.

Those additional problems have forced me to stop and recognize that my dislike for Felt was primarily due to teenage girls' petty meanness. That and the heartbreak only a seventeen-year-old girl in the early stages of young love can experience.

"How are things going with Arik?"

Focusing on Taylor, I look at my friends and I'm thankful I have them. That they understand my need to vent or complain. Olivia and Taylor are always there for me. In the short time since I've been home, Ally's become a close friend, and I'm loving that she fits in seamlessly with us. All of them are up to date on Arik, so the question isn't a surprise.

"It's going good. I saw him yesterday, and today we helped out with a car wash for the school." My phone buzzes in my lap. Looking at the notification, I see a text from Arik.

Arik: Hey gorgeous, what're you up to?

Snapping a quick selfie of me with the computer screen in the background, I send it back without a description.

"Is that to Arik? Is he texting you right now?"

"Of course he is, Taylor, look at that smile. I haven't seen her smile like that since she hit that record with push-ups last year."

"Did you tell them about the pictures thing?" Ally asks.

Ignoring the buzz of my phone, I'm animated as I tell the girls about Jackson and Connor tripping over each other, the pictures, and the chase around the yard.

When I finish the story, Liv's looking at me with a weird expression.

"What? What'd I say?"

There's a glimpse of heartbreak in her eyes, something I recognize, but I don't understand why.

"It's nothing, babe. You're so happy and I'm happy for you. I love that this has been easier for you than you thought."

"But…"

"But nothing, it's a good look on you."

I let the subject drop and make a mental note to talk to her later. Taylor and Ally both jump in, filling the lull in conversation with commentary on the pictures of Jackson and Connor that I couldn't help but share with them. Glancing down, I read the message waiting on my phone.

Arik: Looks like y'all are having a good time. When do I get some of that?

Does he want to video chat with my friends?

Kate: I'm confused. Some of what?

Arik: Some of you. When can I have some of that?

His reply sends heat singing through me, and before I talk myself out of it, I text back.

Kate: Whenever you want.

"She's doing it again. She's making the horny face," Ally singsongs.

"No, I'm not. Stop it, guys." Denial flies out of my mouth and I realize the mistake at once.

"Ally's not wrong. You are making a funny face, and you're biting your lip awfully hard," Olivia teases.

Hanging my head, I admit, "I'm in way over my head here. We both agreed slow, but I'm sinking fast and that's a problem."

"Run it through for us." Taylor's typical response is welcome. Anytime we have an issue, Taylor tells us to run it through.

"That's the thing. I don't know what I'm doing. Am I stupid for seeing where this goes when I'm pretty sure it'll end in heartache for both of us when I go back home?"

If I weren't looking right at Olivia, I would have missed it. The slight wince is there and gone before she schools her features. Not sure what to make of it, I let it go and continue.

"Or should I take the next step and maybe it'll fade the longer that we're together? I mean, we've only recently decided to try since the floor orgasm—"

"The floor what?" all three of them exclaim simultaneously, and I want to bash my head on the table for the slip.

Resigned, I say, "On Sunday, I decided to roll the dice and I went over to Arik's place sans panties. We ended up rolling around the mats, and you get the picture."

"The neglected vagina strikes again," Olivia shouts out.

"Wait. Question. You said sans panties. Did you wear those old threadbare yoga pants that I keep trying to get you to trash?"

Olivia's yell is followed closely by Taylor's question, and

there's a second of silence before I roll my lips between my teeth and nod.

"You dirty whore, I'm so proud of you," Olivia yells, her square lighting up like a beacon. They all start talking at once, and I catch bits and pieces of their questions.

"Was it any good?" from Ally.

"Richter scale rating? Remember to be as accurate as possible. That's the best way to make informed decisions," from Olivia.

"Please describe it in a low, breathy voice. This dry spell might kill me," Taylor chimes in.

"Y'all need to stop being dirty birds."

My hope that they'll drop the subject dies when Liv continues exasperatedly, "Why? You're among friends. Ally's a wild card, but Taylor and I are in epic dry spells."

Ally snarks, "My sex life might as well be the damn Sahara."

"Okay," Olivia draws the word out, "so we're all in dry spells. There's nothing wrong with you talking to us about what's going on, and I will never understand your hang-up about it. You knew pretty much everything about Chase and me."

There's the tiniest pause before his name leaves her lips, and not wanting her to think about it too much, I sacrifice my need for privacy for my friend's mental health.

"It was amazing, like, filled me up and hollowed me right out. If I had to rate it, I would say twenty out of ten, absolutely recommend. Taylor, your dry spell is your own doing. You could date anytime you wanted." I don't say the same for Olivia, even though it's true, but I imagine the pain still lingers after four years, and I don't want to dig up ugly memories.

Taking a sip of wine, I pause then continue my thought.

"Which is why I'm out of my element here. I'm drowning fast, and it's going to end in disaster."

"What if it doesn't?" The question is a quietly spoken challenge from Taylor.

"What do you mean?"

"I mean exactly that, babe. What if it doesn't end in disaster? What if you take this step and it's amazing? What if you go to bed with Arik and it's perfect? What if it works out? What if Arik falls in love with you? What if it grows into something beautiful, something to be cherished, and something to hang on to?"

My heart thuds hard at the L-word, but I ignore it and answer from the pessimistic side of me.

"Then it hurts more when I have to leave again. He won't come with me. He can't. His whole life is here, and I can't stay." Giving voice to the fears that hold me back, that stop me from jumping without looking, has vulnerability slicing through me, a sensation I've worked hard to avoid.

"Why can't you stay? Why couldn't he go with you? Those are the decisions you need to make together. Things you can figure out later, but I see you retreating from the idea that Arik could love you, so I'll drop it *for now*. I will say if he's anything like you've told us, even a little bit, he'll handle those semantics with ease. I know you didn't ask us specifically, but I say you take the chance, Kate. Yeah, it might hurt, but the hurt would be worth it if it's true."

Raising their glasses, Olivia and Ally toast Taylor, their silent agreement uniting them.

What's some potential heartbreak in the grand scheme of things? Trying to ignore the feelings I have for Arik didn't work, and I would never hurt him to save myself. Besides, we agreed to try. We can't go backward, sideways didn't work, so forward is the only direction left to me

I can let my brain take the backseat for a while and let my

heart drive. Grabbing my phone, I shoot off a text to Arik before I talk myself out of it.

Kate: How about a sleepover at your place next weekend?

His reply is nearly instant.

Arik: Absolutely.

ARIK

Everything is turning into a fundraiser, a side job, or a way to make an extra buck.

My summer mission to raise enough money is turning into a never-ending crusade, and it's exhausting.

Thursday rolls around, and I'm a heap of shambles standing at the podium in a meeting room full of townspeople to discuss my efforts' current progress. If I didn't promise Jackson we'd grab a beer after, I would go home, soak in the tub, and pass out.

The community center is packed. Kate is sitting in the front row with Ally while they wait for things to get started. I've seen her a few times this week, but both of our schedules are insane, and we haven't spent nearly enough time together.

She's focused on getting the shop ready for reopening and I'm busy picking up odd jobs between fundraising efforts to fatten the pool of money that we've got going.

I've done car washes, bake sales, spud prep for harvest, signed on with maintenance to repaint the old gym, and even volunteered to host a raffle giveaway at the Spud Drive-in in a couple of weeks. The faculty and I are breaking our backs to get these funds together in time.

Mayor Davis is standing at the podium and announcing me before I'm ready. Public speaking isn't the puke-inspiring ordeal it used to be, but still isn't something that I look forward to.

I make my way to the front of the small stage, and Kate shoots me a wink and thumbs-up. She probably remembers all those times in school when I couldn't present a report to save my life. Thank God I'm not that bad anymore.

"Hey, y'all. Thanks for coming out tonight. I'll keep it short and sweet since it's wing night and I know you want to get back to your families." I go into detail about how close we are to the budget for replacing the schoolbooks with tablets. The needed licenses and programs that they'll need. The plans for repair and upgrading as the years go by and how the logistics of giving three hundred plus students an expensive device would go. Once I've finished my breakdown of how things stand and how far we have to go, I open the floor to questions.

Mitzy Poffenberger stands and calls out, "How are those funds going to be used if you don't raise enough to get the tablets? Will they go into the school's annual operating budget?"

Yeah, let's just jump right into me failing.

"That's a great question, Mitzy, and the short answer is no. The school's budget wouldn't absorb those funds. Instead, we would continue to fundraise through the school year. The long answer is that the funds that I've raised are under the PTA heading, so they aren't attached to the school's budget at all. The PTA graciously agreed to hold the funds until we have enough in place to replace the outdated materials and will be 'donated' to the school once we have enough money."

As expected, this starts the grumbles from the floor. I can hear a couple of outraged parents talking about the sports uniforms, and John, the school principal, is quick to step up to the podium.

"Now, y'all, everyone just calm down. These funds are still attached to the school, just with more flexibility than if the state had awarded the money directly. Nothing is changing there, so you can rest your minds on that. The funds are attached to the school but aren't under stipulation on how we use them."

"He's more than five thousand dollars away. How's he expecting to raise that much by the time school starts up in a month?"

I can't see who called out the question, and at this point, I don't care. The town meeting is dissolving before my eyes, parents shifting in their seats and some leaving. John panics, and his next words cinch the noose around my neck a little tighter.

"Mr. Beaumont here will have the funds in time, or they will be donated to the athletics department."

He just made me look like a fool in front of a hundred people, but before I can say anything, Mayor Davis steps up to the podium and shifts us aside.

"Now that we have that settled, I'm opening the floor up to Jackson and his request for volunteers for the forestry's summer programs next year."

Defeat rests heavily on me as I climb out of my truck later. I'm damned if I'm breaking my back to earn extra money for it to go to uniforms though, which just means that I have to work harder to bridge the financial gap in the next month.

O'Malley's is busy, their Wing and Karaoke night one of the week's more popular events. All the tables are occupied when I push through the door. The bar is full and the second floor that houses the band, or in tonight's case the karaoke machine, is populated with dancing people.

Half the town must be here.

Jackson's holding a seat for me at the bar and sipping from a whiskey. I lingered at the town council with Kate until she left to get some work for Liv done. Would I love for her to grab a drink with me? Absolutely, but I understand that she's got a lot to handle.

Making my way through the tables that dot the first floor, all full of people, I belly up to the bar after clapping Jackson on the shoulder.

"No Con tonight?"

"Nah, he's a dud and wanted to go home and veg in front of his TV. It's just you and me."

Cheryl, one of the owners, makes her way over to me saying, "Hey, Arik, you want your usual?" Her short bob moves with the nod she gives me when I give her a thumbs-up. Reaching under the counter, she pops the cap off a bottle and slides it across the surface to me before moving on to the next customer.

"How'd painting the gym go this week?" Jackson asks.

"If I never see another can of flat white paint, I'll die a happy man. How's it been going with the summer recreation projects?"

"It's a shit show like usual. The summer fishing camp is the only thing ready, but that's because Connor's an anal asshole. Otherwise—complete shit show."

The summer programs the state park runs usually tie in with the 4-H program, but since one of the more organized volunteers moved out of the valley two years ago, the program has declined. No one has been able to bridge the gap between funding and organizing the events, which means the programs and their offerings have decreased recently.

Making for a good reason why Jackson's drinking whiskey on a Thursday night.

"Anything I can do to help?"

"Unless you want to volunteer to get the state park service to work with the Department of Fish and Game, it's my headache to deal with. I'll figure it out, usually do. Fucking budgets."

Raising my beer in a toast, I commiserate with him.

I'll fucking buy the tablets if I have to. It might not be this year because it's going to be fucking expensive, but I'll get them one way or another.

Tuning back to my friend's problems, I dig for more information to see if there's anything I can do.

"Yeah, but it's coming up fast, isn't it? You guys usually need your budgets done soon, right?"

"Yeah, I'm pushing the wire on this, but I was thinking about asking Ally for help there. She has a good idea of what we do every year since the girls participate. Plus, she has a little more time now since she hired Jem to work full time at the bakery along with her part-time clerks."

I snort out a laugh because one thing that Ally Sawyer doesn't have is spare time.

"Good luck there."

"That was something I was going to ask you. Since Ally and Kate are tight, do you think she'd be willing to help with one of the hiking treks next weekend? One of our usual instructors can't make it, and Ally said that Kate's an avid hiker."

I hesitate before answering.

"Kate has a lot going on. She's working in the bookstore full time and the reopening is in less than two weeks. She's still working for Liv full time remotely and then trying to help Hedy get to her appointments and taking care of the house. I don't imagine she would have the time."

The selfish part of me doesn't want the few hours she's free to be eaten up with helping Jackson. I'd rather spend all the time that I can with her.

Working hard to stay in the moment and not tie Kate down until she agrees to move back home has been challenging. The more time I spend with her, the more I want to wrap her up and demand all of her, which isn't fair.

We agreed to take it slow and see where it goes. I'm doing my damnedest to stick to that.

"Just ask her for me, and let me know, will ya?"

"Yeah, I'm seeing her tomorrow, but don't be surprised if her answer is no." Even as I say the words, I know Kate will say yes. She can't say no when someone in need is asking for help. That doesn't mean I'll be in a rush to ask her to help.

Kate is going to jump at the chance to help lighten the load for Ally and Jackson. Which is just something else she'll take responsibility for. Damned if there's anything I can do about it.

"Hey, man, me and Connor still good to come over Sunday to use the gym?"

"Sure, it's open to you guys anytime. You know that." I don't understand why he's asking. They never have before.

"Well, after last Sunday, I didn't want to walk in on anything. Though now that I'm thinking about it, maybe I should try to sneak in and steal that damn phone while you have Kate distracted." Jackson's eyebrows bounce up and down lasciviously.

"You aren't getting those pictures. You might as well give it up. By now she has them saved in some dark corner of the Internet to use as leverage later."

Jackson throws his arms up. "Damnit man, you're supposed to be *my* friend. I bet if you texted her right now asking her to delete them, she'd do it for you."

Intrigued, because this is the perfect opportunity to needle him, I say, "What do you want to bet she won't?"

"If you ask her to delete the pictures, and she says no, I'll get up and sing fucking karaoke."

Grinning because this is gonna be good, I pull out my phone and open the text thread with Kate.

Arik: Hey, what are you doing?

The little dots bounce while we wait. I leave the phone unlocked on the bar next to me. When Jackson loses, he tends to cry foul, so this nips that in the bud.

Kate: Nothing much, working on some admin stuff for Liv, what about you?

Arik: At O'Malley's, listening to horrible karaoke. Normal Thursday night. But I have a favor to ask.

Kate: Sure, what's up?

Arik: Can you delete those photos? The ones you took of Jackson and Connor?

She starts to type, then stops, then starts back up. This goes on for a couple of minutes, and Jackson's leaning closer and closer to the phone the longer she takes.

When the dots stop bouncing, I chuckle. "Well, looks like we have our…" I trail off as Jackson's phone and mine chime at the same time. He wrestles it out of his pocket just as I note a new group message thread.

I open the message, and my phone shows multiple pictures of Connor and Jackson in their bromance glory. The lineup's final image is a picture of Kate flipping the camera the bird with the following message being, "I'm not deleting anything, I got these fair and square."

Jackson tosses his phone on the bar in disgust.

"Fuck. Well, fine then. At least she got my good side."

After I finish laughing at that, I say, "I told you she wouldn't. You didn't hang out with her all that often, but man, she's a redhead. She isn't doing anything she doesn't want to."

"It was worth a shot." Throwing back the rest of his whiskey, he slides off the barstool. "Let's get this fucking over with. No video."

I follow him up to the second floor, grabbing a table for us while he puts his name down for a Johnny Cash song. Christina and Melody are flirting with some tourists on the dance floor. There's a couple of local ranch hands having a beer and card game at a table, and a bunch of high school kids with nothing better to do on a Thursday night take up one corner.

I lean against the wall hidden slightly by an alcove. I'm exhausted, and every single part of me wants to go to bed. I'm also trying to hide from Christina since she has a tendency to drink too much, and I'm in no mood to deal with her tonight, especially after her stunts at the car wash last weekend. Kissing Kate in front of everyone was no hardship for me and showed the entire world that some fucking stretch marks aren't going to deter me.

When it's finally Jackson's turn to perform, I pull out my phone and get ready to record because I never agreed to his no video decree.

Not many people know that he can sing. It's not exactly a secret, but it's also not something he advertises. Regardless, it's a welcome change from the racket that usually accompanies Karaoke Night.

The smell of roses is thick and cloying as two thin arms circle my waist from behind and jar my hold on my phone.

"Hey there, handsome. Dance with me?" Christina's words slur because she's drunker than a skunk. As much as I don't want to dance with her, I also don't want a scene. I might as well get this over and done. She's drunk enough that I can handle dancing for a few seconds, and she won't notice when I bail.

I turn, keeping my hands way out of the danger zone. She's out of it, which makes it easy for me to keep her at a distance when she tries to plaster herself against me.

We shuffle side to side, Christina trying to sing under her breath, unsuccessfully. The final strains of guitar start to fade. As I step back to extricate myself from this dance, she leans forward, stumbling and about to topple over. I move to catch her so she doesn't fall and then her mouth is on mine. The stale taste of beer and cigarette smoke is heavy on her breath.

Shoving back, I wipe my mouth. "What the fuck, Christina?"

"Mmmm, you taste good, Arik. Gimme another kiss."

She is capable of being nasty, but mostly I've been able to get her to leave me alone by being polite. That's not the case any longer. As she reaches up to wrap her arms around me, I grasp her forearms and lightly push her back.

Keeping her arms locked in my hands so she can't throw herself at me again, I say, "No, Christina. I'm not interested. I will never be interested. I'm with Kate. You *know* I'm with Kate."

Her expression flips from dreamy to incensed in seconds, her anger at my rejection apparent as she tugs at her arms. I let go and cross mine against my chest, hoping that it deters her.

"Kate was a fat little nobody who finally bought a clue when she saw you dancing with me at prom. She's still a little nobody. She left town and she'll leave again, I guarantee it."

"The fact you knew she saw us and was hurt speaks more to your character than hers. I promise you I didn't enjoy a single minute of it then and I sure as shit didn't enjoy it now."

I don't let myself address her insult on Kate's weight,

otherwise I'm going to lose my shit and I don't need that kind of drama on a Thursday night in a full bar. I just need Christina to get out of here.

"You're drunk. Go home and sleep it off."

"Hey guys, everything okay here?"

Jackson's voice comes from behind me, and I turn to look at him. Then I get showered in beer.

"Oh shit, Christina, what'd you do that for?" Melody's joined our little group now too.

"It's fine, Melody." I grab a stack of napkins from the table and mop at my face and collar. "Can you get her home?"

"I'm not going anywhere. It's a free fucking country and I'll be here if I want to be." Christina's hollering now, her face red and sweaty in her anger.

"Not if I say you can't, and I say you're cut off. Pack up your shit and get out," Cheryl's voice booms from the staircase she's climbing.

Cheryl hands me a damp bar rag and I swipe at the sticky residue covering my face. The next song has already started, and I'm thankful for it, as it conceals at least part of this mess from others. Small town folk are like sharks with blood in the water—the first hint of something scandalous and they start to circle.

Pouting, Christina says, "Oh, come on, Cheryl."

But Cheryl cuts her off with a sharp swipe of her hand. "You either walk out of here on your own or I'm calling the sheriff."

Shoulders slumping, Christina says, "Fine, I'm going. But he should have to leave too."

"No. He's not doing anything wrong, but I told you if you started shit, it would be the last time you did it, employee or not. Come pick up your last check tomorrow. You're fired."

Christina's right back to rage, her head swinging up as

she yells, "You can't fucking fire me. I'm not even working right now."

Grabbing my phone off the table where I dropped it, it's past time to leave. Heading home and showering off the day is sounding better and better, especially after the clusterfuck of tonight.

As Jackson and I make our way out of the restaurant, I can only think about Kate and how she struggles with the gossip that floats around our town. She was already worried about being the center of attention, so I send up a silent prayer she doesn't get wind of what happened.

Otherwise, we're doomed.

ARIK

How does one prepare for a late dinner date and sleepover at their own house?

With nerves.

Apprehension all day Friday tightens my gut. While I'm more than happy to spend time with Kate, to have her to myself for a bit, I can only hope that she didn't hear about what happened last night.

My decision to not tell Kate is selfish, yeah, but also for her own good.

If I had told her she would have likely slammed the brakes on us. Hell, I don't even know if she would believe me if I told her that Christina kissed me out of the blue, just like she did at prom all those years ago. I don't know if she would believe that I didn't want it. Or if she would use it as a lever to shove a wedge between us.

I'll tell her when we're steadier relationship-wise.

There's chicken chili in my slow cooker, with fresh tortilla strips, guacamole, and all the fixin's set up.

Leaving my dinner prep on the counter to get ready, I shower, then have the "should I or shouldn't I" debate on trimming my beard—something I haven't had to worry about recently.

As abrasive as a beard rash is, I want to mark Kate. I want her to feel the evidence of me on her skin the next day. Thinking about the pink streaks on her neck from our foray last weekend causes my cock to twitch to attention.

It's official. I'm a fucking caveman.

Shaking my head at myself as I towel off, I'm not quite ready for the doorbell to ring when it does.

We didn't agree on a specific time, but based on when Kate gets done with the shop most days, this is earlier than expected.

Knotting the towel around my waist, I make my way through the house, and with a quick look through the peephole—no need to scare a bystander—I pull open the door.

A dark blue sundress that dips deep in the front has me praising the gods of summer. Her red curls are pulled back into some sort of complicated twist. There's makeup on Kate's face, something she usually doesn't bother with. Her eyes look bigger and more defined, and I don't mind it a bit.

Those green eyes widen as she takes in my lack of clothes, and it's no longer nerves gripping me but anticipation.

"Uh, hey, sorry. I'm kinda early, but I finished with Readers' Haven and got most of the work waiting for Liv cleared off my plate, so I thought I'd head over."

She brushes by me, and when I glance out the door, I'm happy that Gram's car is in the driveway instead of that fucking bike she rides all over town.

Grabbing her wrist, I spin her back to me. Though the temptation of her glossy lips is hard to ignore, I keep the kiss short.

"Why don't you put your stuff down, and I'll go get dressed."

Her eyes skate over my bare chest and travel south, the

subtle flaring in her eyes full of desire. The way her hands are clasped tightly has me backing off. Looks like I'm not the only one a little nervous about tonight.

In an attempt to put her at ease, I head to my room, and while I appreciate her dressing up for our low-key date, I aim for casual comfort with a pair of sweats and a T-shirt.

I find Kate in the kitchen lifting the lid off the pot of chili.

"This smells amazing. What is it?"

The sunlight is coming through the window, setting her hair ablaze, and my fingers itch to slide through those curls.

"Chicken chili, pretty simple to make. Dump it all in and then come back to shred the chicken later. Should be about done now. You want a margarita?"

Smiling, she asks, "You made margaritas?"

I grab the pitcher. "You've mentioned a fondness for them a couple of times, so I figured I'd give making them a shot. No idea on how well they came out though."

"Sure, I'd love a margarita. Is there anything I can do to help with dinner?"

"If you want to grab bowls out of the cabinet, we'll get dished up."

Kate reaches up, shifting her dress until the smooth expanse of her upper thigh is visible. The need I have to get my hands on her threatens to strangle me.

I cross to her, crowding her against the counter. Like a deer in headlights, she stills. If it's my proximity or the sudden shift in tension that has her breath whooshing out, I don't care. I can't care when I have the opportunity to touch her. Gliding my hand up her bare leg, the silky-smooth texture of her thigh is warm against my fingertips.

I nose my way in close, and her hair smells like sin and long nights. Pure craving is obvious in my tone as I ask, "You wore this damn dress to drive me insane, didn't you?"

"I plead the fifth." A soft hitching gasp accompanies her denial.

Retaliating with a light smack to her ass, I grab the abandoned bowls, reining myself in because as much as I want to get her under me—and naked this time—our first time won't be in my kitchen.

Once we're at the table, Kate's coloring is a little high, but it's always been easy to make her blush, so I move us back into safe territory.

"How're things going at Readers' Haven?"

If the sudden shift bothers her, I can't tell.

"It's going good. Colby and his crew did a great job with the remodel. I've been spending the last week getting everything put back on the floor and organized in a way I hope will help."

"On track to open on time?"

"Pretty much. I'm waiting on some of the branded stuff to be delivered, like tissue paper and gift bags. Everything else is done."

"I looked over the website," I start.

"You did?"

"Sure I did. Not having one before was a huge detriment to Gram's store, and the one you had designed is perfect. No matter how many times I offered to put feelers out, that was one part of the store she was adamant about me staying out of."

"Setting it up was the hard part. Maintenance is going to be easier."

Who's going to be doing the maintenance?

I fill my mouth with food to keep from asking. Lying to myself and not pushing Kate is working for me.

The truth of it is I don't want to know. I don't want to know if Kate is going to be around Felt after the store opens.

Knowledge may be power, but the lack of it right now suits me fine.

"This is so good. You'll have to give me the recipe. I cook —you can't grow up with Gram without learning—but I barely ever find time. Something I can just throw in a pot and then eat the leftovers for days sounds right up my alley."

"You don't cook a lot back home?"

"Nah, between work, some of the martial arts classes I take, and other stuff on my calendar, I don't have a lot of time to spend in the kitchen. I meal prep most of my lunches and dinners on the weekend, but if I'm busy, I live off cheese and crackers."

"What 'other stuff' do you do?"

Brushing her hair back from her ear, she tries to wave it off saying, "Oh, nothing really, mostly volunteer stuff."

I don't settle for the vague brush-off. "No, tell me. I want to know."

"It's just, I, um…I'm a tutor, so I help kids out with their schoolwork when I have the time."

Why is Kate beating around the bush? I keep my reply light. "Oh yeah, what kind of tutoring do you do?"

Resignation crosses her face before she says, "I'm more of an as-needed volunteer. I help out with a couple of the schools and tutor some of their struggling students and such."

There's a feeling that's settling in my gut that I don't like.

"What subject?"

She bites her lip, muffling her voice when she replies, "Reading mainly. I work with students who struggle with literacy, reading comprehension, and…" she trails off and I finish for her.

"Dyslexia."

A short nod is all she offers.

"You tutor kids with dyslexia?"

Lips rolling in, she nods again, and there's a drop in my heart.

I was never diagnosed, even years later I haven't gone through testing, but the struggles I had in school closely aligned with the disability. When Kate left, I assumed she did everything she could to forget about Felt and us. To learn she's a tutor for kids that struggle the same way I did is a kick in the chest.

"How long?" Sheer will is the only thing that keeps the words steady.

There's a beat of silence before she clears her throat, her voice coming out more assertive. "Since the summer of my freshman year in college."

Rising, I push back from the table, and I take my bowl over to the sink. I need to get up and move.

"Are you upset?"

I take a second, trying to make sense of the emotion rocking me.

"Not upset—those kids are lucky to have you. I wouldn't have made it through school without you and Gram. I'm a little surprised."

"Why surprised?"

"I would have thought you didn't want the reminder."

Dead air surrounds us. She doesn't speak for a few moments, pushing her spoon around, and I don't have the words.

Looking up from her bowl, she says, "I never forgot you. I tried. I tried so hard to forget. To forget the happy times that were stained by prom. I couldn't. After watching you struggle academically, I knew that there were kids out there that needed someone who understood that struggle."

There's a melting sensation in my chest, and I'm unsure of how to process it.

"I understand."

But I don't. I don't understand. My assumption of Kate was that she left and wrote off everything to do with me.

"Tell me about them?" It emerges as a question, but I'm hungry for more. To learn how she reaches these kids like she reached me when making sense of words was senseless.

Kate launches into a detailed description of the kids she's worked with recently and their progress, not only academically but also personally. Their ability to read and understand has a direct relation to their self-confidence. She's animated, her hands flying around while she eats and talks. There's a sparkle in her eye most would miss, but I don't. I don't miss the way she's smiling brighter than the sun, her happiness palpable.

When her spoon is scraping the bottom of the bowl, I ask, "Seconds?"

There's laughter in her tone. "I better not. It's so good I'm just eating for flavor now."

"Wanna take a walk, work some of it off?"

"I'd love to."

After clearing our dishes away and stowing the leftovers, we grab some shoes and head out the back door toward the creek that runs behind my property. The bubbling stream of water is more subdued now that the winter snowmelt has run off. Depending on the time of year, the water moves fast, but it's calm now.

The sun is still out but hidden behind the trees' tops, casting shadows and cooling the air. Neither of us speaks, but we hold hands and walk and I'm grateful for the calm.

As the light starts to die down, we turn to head back to the house. The closer we get, the more I pick up on the thread of strain tightening Kate's shoulders.

Giving our arms a little swing, I ask, "What's wrong, Katie?"

The defeated sigh that accompanies her words has my

stomach clenching. "We should probably talk. Let's grab our drinks. Can we sit on the porch swing?"

I pull her hand to my mouth and kiss the back of her knuckles. Reassuringly, I say, "I'll get them. You get comfortable."

After grabbing our drinks, I settle in on the swing and stay quiet. I'm sure whatever she has going on in her head isn't good, and I don't want to rush her, but apprehension makes me impatient.

"We should probably talk about last Sunday."

I try a joke to take some heaviness out of the conversation. "The pictures or the way you're torturing Connor and Jackson with their existence?"

My attempt succeeds, and the loosening in her frame is visible.

"No, not the pictures. What happened before."

"Okay." I don't get further than that before she's rushing on.

"I haven't dated seriously in years, and even then, it was sporadic, so I don't have a lot of experience of this kind of thing, and I'm probably rusty. The only reason I'm bringing it up—and *God*, could this be more embarrassing—is because I don't want you to be disappointed."

"Kate."

My tone has her eyes rising to meet mine, and I continue, "You could never disappoint me. I won't lie and say I haven't thought about getting you in my bed because I have, but I will say that nothing you do there could disappoint me. Experienced or not, I just want you."

A look of relief edged with anxiety crosses her features. "I want you too. I just wanted to let you know what to expect before this leads somewhere and when it's horrible and you don't want to do this anymore—"

Halting her tirade midword, I lean over and brush my lips

against hers. Not the demanding way I usually take her mouth, but softer, my lips lightly tracing hers. As I skim my nose over the tip of hers, I admonish, "Stop. You're freaking out about something that hasn't happened yet. Stop borrowing trouble."

"That's easy for you to say."

"No, it's not. I'm nervous too, but I want to be with you. That want eclipses everything else for me. So, stop and *be*." Rising, I offer her my hand and say, "Be with me. That's all I want."

KATE

Arik's request rings quietly between us. Looking from his hand to the acceptance on his face has my eyes prickling. Determined not to cry, I push the tears back and away.

I'm nervous. I'd been psyching myself up leading to our date, which was part of why I was able to plow through the setup at the store. All that nervous energy bouncing around in me like crazed pinballs has had me on pins and needles for days. At the car wash, I was ready to climb him like a tree. Even during my video call with the girls, I plotted and planned to get him in bed. What's changed between then and now?

Looking at the rough palm in front of me, some of those nerves die down. Am I rusty? Hell yes, I haven't had a proper date in years. Can I do this? Also, hell yes.

Impulsively, I place my hand in Arik's, and the way his callus scrapes against my palm has sparks arcing between us. Focusing on that, I stand and let him lead me through the house to his bedroom.

He closes the door behind us, the room dim and quiet, the

only light coming from the dying rays of the sun through the curtains as it slips below the horizon.

Wrapping his arms around my waist, he draws me into him, swaying side to side as if to a silent beat, his relaxation bleeding into me until the tailspinning thoughts die entirely.

With his hand cradling my face, his thumb brushes back and forth along my jaw before he bends to press tiny kisses along the edges of my lips, and then he kisses me thoroughly. The masculine taste of him pulls me further and further out of my head until it's just the two of us, together at the end of a day.

Feeling bold, I tug at the hidden zipper on the side of my dress before his hands brush mine aside.

"Let me," he murmurs.

The soft request gives me permission to touch him back, to undress him and run my hands under his shirt and along the muscled perfection of his abdomen and chest.

A slight dusting of hair teases my palms, tingling against the tips of my fingers as our kiss turns heated. Lips and tongues tangle, desire building between us as my dress falls to pool around my feet.

I reach for the hem of his shirt and he bends slightly, letting me tug the garment off. I kick my sandals off in the pile of my dress and take a small step back, breaking the kiss. His eyes immediately devour me as he focuses on my body in just a bra and panties.

"Fuck, Katie, you're so goddamn beautiful."

I feel beautiful as those blue eyes take in every part of my bared skin. Arik's fingers dance along my sides before coming up to brush the underside of my bra. I want us to undress each other, to remove all of the layers between us until we're skin to skin.

Sliding my hands along the waistline of his sweats, these

indecent fucking sweats, I run my fingers just under the elastic band. Impatience overwhelms me, and I push them down only to be suddenly lifted in his arms, locked against him as he kicks the sweats off and carries me to the bed.

There's a measure of decadence that comes with a man carrying you to his bed. Arik's strong arms are wrapped tightly around me, one arm under my ass to keep me close, causing more heat to build to a delicious ache, the other hand exploring, teasing, touching along my spine.

My heated center is pressed against his torso's defined muscles, amplifying the ache in my core, urging me to lock my legs at the base of his spine. He drops me down to the mattress below, following me as he kneels between my legs.

"I've dreamt of you here, fantasized, obsessed, thought endlessly of you right where I have you. If I couldn't feel you, I'd think this was another one of those dreams."

The cool bedding against the heat of my back is a compelling contrast, and his words only add to it.

My voice whispers between us as I say, "No, not a dream. I'm here." I ache to say I'm not going anywhere. I barely hold the words back, but it's not fair to give him the false hope I'll stay in Felt.

"Kate," he begins, but I sit up and take his mouth with mine. His beard is coarse against my chin and cheeks. I can't bring myself to care about the beard rash I'll have tomorrow or the looks it'll inspire. I'm too focused on the sensation of his mouth on mine, his hands on me.

The straps of my bra come loose at a flick of his wrist before he tugs the material away. Dropping his head, he presses hot open-mouth kisses across my chest, then draws my nipple into his mouth. Ecstasy swamps me, and I dig my nails into his shoulders. He takes his time sucking and nibbling across the peaks while his hands roam my exposed skin. When he isn't treating one nipple to the fucking wondrous thing that is his mouth, his fingers are pinching its tip, and it's driving me out of my mind.

I thrust against him, desperate for friction, but he drops his hand to my hip, stilling the movement. Lifting his head, desire flashes across his face. Arik's eyes are heavy, his bottom lip sucked between his teeth like he's savoring the flavor of my flesh.

"You keep that up and this will be over sooner than planned."

"Arik." His name comes out as a gasping sob. I've never been frantic for sex. Usually, it's something I can take or leave, but I'm on fire. I need more than the slow passion he is doling out with precision.

"Shhh, I've been dreaming of this for years. Let me have you."

His calm tone helps to quell some of the need raging through me. I can only nod once before he dips his head back down.

Running my hands over his back and shoulders, I reach up and thread my fingers through his hair. It's the only thing that keeps me from levitating when his hands dip under my panties, tugging them down my legs and off.

The cold air of his room brushes along my pussy and it feels positively decadent in the most indecent way.

His mouth maps down my torso, teasing nibbles and nips that give a tiny pinch before his tongue peeks out to swirl across my skin, soothing each spot before moving on.

His hands run up and down my thighs before sliding between them, pushing my legs apart to accommodate his broad shoulders. Hooking my right leg over his shoulder, he urges me farther open, and there's a moment of vulnerable uncertainty before his hands cup my ass and he's drawing my center to his mouth.

Pleasure saturates me, stealing my breath, and has me

fisting my hands in the sheets as he draws the sensitive folds into his mouth. More wet kisses press against my tingling skin, and his tongue runs from my center up and around my clit, drawing it into his mouth and softly sucking the bundle of nerves.

"Holy fucking shit, Arik, don't stop. Please don't stop."

Gasps and moans spill from my mouth as I reach down and thread my fingers through all that blond hair. He takes his time tasting me, no hurry in the meandering way he sucks at me.

My legs fall wide, the one sliding off his shoulder, as he works his hand between us to dip a finger into me. The pressure and friction are delectable, causing my hips to pump against his mouth as I hurtle closer and closer to the edge. He drags me up that cliff and back down over and over again until I'm going crazy with lust. I'm reduced to begging, pleading with him to just let me come.

I cry out, needy and desperate. "Please…"

He lets out a pained groan before his lips leave me to say, "Fuck, Katie, you're so goddamn wet, I could do this for hours."

I have no words. I would never have assumed Arik was a dirty talker. His head moves down again, lips focused on sucking my clit into his mouth as he adds a second finger.

The little bit extra is all that's needed to have fire flashing through me. I'm hurtling over the edge, just that easy, swamped in the staggering waves of pleasure washing over me. He stays with me, fingers thrusting, tongue and lips working to draw out my climax until I'm a hypersensitive puddle of goo.

His face is etched with craving, his eyes a brilliant blue. Reaching into his bedside drawer, he withdraws a condom before shoving his boxer briefs off. He rolls the latex down the thick length of his cock, his eyes never leaving mine. I'm dying to peek, but I can't tear my gaze away.

Arik arranges himself above me before dropping and fastening his mouth to mine. I taste myself on his lips, taboo and so fucking hot it reignites my desire. His hand buries itself in my tangled hair while the other grasps my thigh, hitching my leg around his waist.

The weight of his cock presses against my still throbbing center, its heat a brand.

"Eyes, Katie, I need your eyes. Open for me, beautiful."

I pry my heavy lids up as he slips along my center. He teases me, giving me the barest hint of pressure before backing off. I squirm against him, more than ready for him to fill me. A high-pitched keen is ripped out of my throat when his cock slides against my clit.

"Arik, please."

Begging isn't beneath me, not when I'm on a razor wire of thrill and anticipation.

Notching his head at my opening, his forward progress is slightly halted at the resistance of my body. Pressure invades as he delves deeper into my center, stretching me.

Reaching under me, he wraps his arms around my lower back, lifting me, altering the angle to take more of him. I'm panting against the onslaught, my chest rising and falling rapidly.

Lips brushing mine, he says, "Relax for me, baby. Relax."

Easy for him to say. God, he's so fucking thick. I concentrate on relaxing, unwinding the muscles in my core in a bid to take him deeper. He must feel it, because he presses farther and farther into me until where I end and he starts blurs.

There's an intense pressure as he bottoms out inside of me. He stills, brushing kisses across my lips to give me time to accommodate to his size, and I'm grateful for it. I'm not a virgin, but he is *substantial,* and I need a minute.

Time passes, the occasional slight shift from his hips and sucking kisses my only way to mark the time. He shallowly thrusts again and the pressure turns to exhilaration, suffusing me in rapture. I work my hips against him, silently telling him I'm ready for more.

Drawing fully back, that arm wrapped around my hips provides him all the leverage needed to pull me against him as he pushes forward, our bodies coming together in a heavy thrust, and my eyes roll back.

With a steady rhythm, he plunges in and out of my core. His lips and hands run across my body, cupping my breasts before tugging at my nipples. The maddening rhythm never falters as tension builds at my core again. His hand dips down between my legs to tease at the top of my sex in luscious torment.

I'm lost to pleasure. It's not until he's drawing soft circles around my clit that I start to get close to that edge again. Throaty groans rumble from his chest as my back arches against the bed trying to both escape and immerse myself in the sensations, the sheer feelings overwhelming me.

"Baby, I'm so fucking close. I need you with me."

The exquisite agony in his tone sends me flying over the edge. My internal muscles clenching tightly against him, my hips pumping against his, my release crashes over me, and my mouth opens in a soundless scream.

The rolling cadence of his hips increases as he chases his orgasm, skin slapping against mine, face twisting into the picture of anguish before I feel his cock kick hard inside me as his climax washes over him, leaving behind visible euphoria.

A satisfied sigh sounds before he's collapsing over me,

still inside me. Our hands run over each other, neither of us wanting to release the other as we come down from the high. His hands cradle my face, kissing me softly, in direct opposition to the fierce way his body worked mine.

"Give me one second. I'll be right back." Pressing a kiss to my shoulder, he slips off the bed before heading to the bathroom.

Replete, I focus on catching my breath, my slightly damp skin cooling in the evening air.

That was fucking intense but so amazing. I close my eyes, drifting into the light and floating between sleep and wakefulness when the bed dips.

Arik reaches between my legs with a warm washcloth and gently cleans me. Tossing the rag into the hamper, he pulls the blankets up and covers me.

"Why there?" I nod to the picture of us on his wall, impossible to miss at the size he had it blown up to.

He searches my face. I don't know what he's looking for, and I keep my expression calm.

"I wanted to remember every morning when I woke up and every night before I slept."

"Remember what?"

"A time when we were only each other's. When you were mine and I was yours without the complications life brings."

His words hit a chord in me, beautiful and straightforward, but there's a weight there. A weight that I won't live up to the imagined ideal he has for me, or that I'll let him down. A weight that we'll both end up hurt. The right words elude me, so I let the silence linger.

Settling himself next to me, he draws me into his arms, tucking me against him.

No matter how hard I try to keep my emotional distance, Arik pulls me in. Being around him has me questioning feelings I thought I got over years ago, feelings I thought were dead. I'm starting to think they were only buried, and every day in Felt is unearthing them one by one.

KATE

Arik is a cuddler. Somehow, I'm not surprised as I try to pry my way out of his bed early Saturday morning.

He has one arm wrapped around my shoulders, the other around my middle, clutching me to his chest. One of his heavily muscled thighs rests on mine, and his face is buried in my hair. I have no idea how he isn't suffocating under the abundant curling mass.

The pressing need to pee is prompting this escape attempt. Slipping my leg out from under his is easier said than done. By the time my leg is free, he's shifting and readjusting, which means his arms are dragging me back against his chest.

Rolling my eyes at the absurdity of being locked against the giant Viking warlord, I resume my gentle extraction.

I don't want him to wake up.

Don't get me wrong, last night was terrific and wonderful and so fucking *hot*. But I need a few minutes this morning away from him to process everything.

After grabbing my overnight bag from the car last night, we curled up in bed before a toe-curling round two, where I lazily rode Arik to the brink of insanity. I fell asleep to him kissing my forehead and whispering, "Goodnight, Katie Belle."

My heart lurches at the memory of it. Things between us went from "try" to heavy in the span of an evening, and I'm trying to process it all without panicking.

My bladder is about to panic all over his bedding when I finally manage to extricate myself from his death grip. He rolls onto his back, one arm thrown over his head, the other reaching to where I was as if sensing I'm gone. Soft snores and closed eyes signify he's still sleeping deeply.

I ignore the pang of emotion as I grab his shirt off the floor and slip into it. After relieving myself and washing my hands as quietly as possible, I tiptoe into the kitchen, intent on hunting up some coffee.

Muted sunlight filters into the room through the vast windows and back doors as the sun starts to climb. The mountains paint the most beautiful colors of slate and blue against the early morning light.

Managing to locate the coffee, I prep a pot, waiting impatiently for it to brew before rummaging through the fridge for some form of breakfast.

One blessed cup of caffeine in my system, I have bacon frying on the stove with eggs ready to be scrambled when arms reach around my middle.

I yelp and jump hard enough to ram the back of my head against Arik's chin.

"Oh my God, Arik, are you okay? You scared the shit out of me."

Laughing now, he asks, "Who did you think it would be? We're the only ones here."

"Yeah, well, we thought that last time too, now didn't we?"

A wince flashes across his face and he replies, "Yeah, I guess so."

Reaching out, he loops his hands around my waist and hauls me into his chest. A light kiss that tastes like reverence makes me second-guess that processing I did.

"Good morning, Kate."

"Good morning, Arik. I made coffee; do you want some?"

With a nod, he goes to the cabinet to grab a mug, pouring himself a cup. After a few sips, he pulls down plates and sets the table.

My hands are shaking so badly I manage to mangle an egg that I'm trying to crack into the pan.

"Uh, Kate, do you want some help?" His question is tentative, the words coming out stilted. Giving a testy little shove at the fridge door where I'm pulling out more eggs, it closes harder than I expect it to.

Wincing, I look down, not wanting to see his expression at me battering first his eggs and then his appliances.

What is wrong with me?

"No, I've got it. I just couldn't get all the shell out. How do you want your eggs?" A nervous laugh bubbles before I can swallow it down.

"However is fine. I'm not picky." Well, look at that. Maybe I'm just the uncomfortable one. I try to covertly peek at Arik over my shoulder, but I only see him fidgeting in his seat, alternately fisting and unraveling his hands against the surface where his eyes are locked.

There's a level of awkward between us, and I don't know how it got there.

That's a lie.

It's my fault.

I'm the reason we're awkward. I don't know what to say or how to act. My experience with the morning after is minimal, as in, I have none. I've never done the sleepover thing with boyfriends in the past. It was always my choice to go home after sex, which just goes to show how much those relationships meant to me.

Turning back to the stove, I focus on not burning breakfast. Once I have everything done, I plate and carry it over to the table. It takes me a second, but when I don't hear the noises that usually accompany a fork scraping a plate, I glance up. My eyes meet Arik's before his slide away, neither of us saying anything.

There are so many thoughts, sentences, and words screaming to come rushing out of my mouth that I need to keep it occupied. Food and coffee are my safest bet. My appetite has disappeared, so I fiddle with the handle of my coffee cup and sip the hot liquid. My fingers are wrapped around the mug so tightly that my knuckles go white.

"Kate, what's wrong?"

Unable to explain what's going through my head, I shake my head as I try to shrug my shoulders at the same time. The panic is climbing, and I'm trying not to lose my shit completely. The little processing time this morning did nothing to help.

I can't get used to cozy mornings with coffee and a view of the mountains out the window. I can't get accustomed to waking up wrapped in warmth and affection, to cuddling against his chest. I can't let myself get used to any of this because it's temporary.

I shouldn't want to get used to this.

I should want to go back to my life, the neat and ordered existence I have created for myself. A life with few variables, where no feelings threaten to consume me when this all breaks down and dies.

Because it will break down.

How can we even try to find happiness together when we live and thrive hundreds of miles away from each other?

I should want to get back to normal, but I don't.

I don't want my old normal, and that's terrifying to me.

My hand jolts at the realization, hot coffee splashing over the rim of the mug, and I nearly drop it. It clatters to the table, sloshing liquid everywhere. Hissing, I push my chair back, but Arik's hand clamps on my wrist.

"Kate, stop. Are you okay? Did you get burned?"

I swallow a sob but can't fight back the tears. I tug on my hand, needing to escape, to get out, to run.

"Kate, *stop*," Arik barks.

His grip on me is firm, steady. Strong.

I still and take a slow, intentional breath.

"Breathe, baby. Sit down and just breathe while I clean this up."

Air flows to and from my lungs a little easier by the time he sits down, though I'm still shaky. That's two panic attacks that started out of nowhere since I've been back here. Repressed feelings are probably the culprit, but I'm too exhausted to examine my mind again.

Arik doesn't let me off the hook that easily though.

"Why don't you explain to me what happened here because I'm a little confused."

Unwilling to lie, I stutter out the first thing that comes to mind.

"I'm scared."

Running his hand through the rumpled mess of his hair, he blows out a breath. "Yeah, I figured. Why?"

"Last night was amazing and perfect and I just need some time to process."

My mind is stuck on that word. Process. What does that even mean?

Eyes flashing azure fire he says, "Bullshit, Kate. You wouldn't be sitting at my table trembling if you only needed to process. Give me more credit than that. Be honest with me. Why are you scared?"

Shoulders slumping in defeat, I say, "I'm scared that we're both going to end up hurt, that we jumped into this too fast, that there are so many feelings, so much history between us and I'm scared of hurting you, but I'm terrified I'm going to get hurt again too. I can't do that again, I can't."

My explanation rushes out in a long string of insecurity and fear, but just like the panic attack itself, I can't help this either.

Warm hands slide against my palms until our fingers are intertwined. It amazes me that our hands fit so well together, his rough and large, mine slender and tiny in comparison, but they fit, they always have.

"Katie, I can't tell you what's going to happen. I can't tell the future, and neither can you. I will tell you that when I woke up and you were gone, I thought last night was a dream. I will tell you I'm not worrying about the what-ifs. I'm focused on you. On enjoying you—however long that may be, I'm *with you.* I'll also tell you that you're tying yourself up in knots over stuff that hasn't happened yet."

The patience in his tone calms my raging anxiety until it's something more manageable.

His thumb strokes along my hand as he continues, "I'm going to tell you something you used to tell me when I struggled. Have faith. Have faith that everything will work out how it should and how it's supposed to. It may be overwhelming now, but it won't always be."

Arik used to have a horrible temper, something he worked hard to control. He was angry at himself for his inability to comprehend as quickly as other kids.

He would get so frustrated when he was called on in school to read aloud, his timid voice stuttering over the words until the teacher took pity on him or he garbled his way through it

That barely contained rage often followed him to my

house after school. We would walk along the creek, and it would all come spewing out, how he hated that he struggled with the words, both reading them and mixing up their sounds.

How numbers made little sense to him and he would flip them around without realizing it. I remember telling him to have faith, to be patient while he worked his way around learning and understanding everything. It might take him longer to make sense of it all, but he would eventually understand it.

It's a good reminder that I don't have all the answers. I'm not supposed to. The reminder to live in the moment may not make sense to me right now, but it will.

"Okay, I'll have faith."

Squeezing my hands gently, he smiles at me.

"Now, with that settled, how do you feel about a day at the lake?"

I return his smile and say, "I feel pretty good about a day at the lake."

And just like that we're back on even ground.

We finish breakfast and clean up before dressing and loading the canoe onto the Jeep. We swing by Gram's for me to change into my bathing suit before driving out of town and up the rolling hills along the well-worn path to the lake.

The drive is quiet, neither of us anxious to fill the air. I'm still settling into the idea of taking things as they come, but in the back of my mind there's a giant clock ticking down to the end of this. The end of my time in Felt, the end of my time with Arik.

As we pull up to the shore, I'm surprised by how many other vehicles are around, more than there ever used to be when we were growing up coming to this lake. It isn't until a bubbly blonde waves over at me that I recognize Ally,

Connor, and Jackson setting up a camp of sorts around one of the established firepits.

I barely have time to climb out of the Jeep before I'm enveloped in her arms, the scent of vanilla wafting gently from her hair. Wrapping my arms around her, I hug her back.

"Thank God. Another vagina to balance out some of this testosterone. I have a kid-free day, and I can't handle spending the whole thing with the sausage fest."

Sputtering a laugh, I shake my head and wave at the guys.

They're fiddling with a wooden platform and attaching a trolling motor to it. I have no idea what I'm looking at as we make our way over to them.

"Didn't know you guys were bringing the dock, or I would have left the canoe at home." Arik motions to the platform with a wave of his hand.

"What is that?" I haven't ever seen anything like it. It's like a wide deck, lined with railings and only open where the motor attaches.

Jackson explains, "It's a floating dock. A couple of years ago we got the idea to build one that we can bring to and from the lake. I made this one in sections, so it's easier to put together. It's a way we could sit out on the lake but still be able to move around without having to buy a boat. Houses that have lakefront access have something similar, but those attach and detach to their docks as needed."

I've spent plenty of time on lakes growing up here and living in Arizona. Sometimes the only thing that makes the triple-digit summers bearable is the ability to drive a couple of hours to cooler temperatures and lakes outside of the city. But I've never seen a floating dock.

Ally speaks up. "It's kind of fun to jump off the side, but if you don't want to go, we'll hang at the shore while the guys go dick around."

"Yeah, Connor and I have done backflips off of it, so it's sturdy." Jackson's words give me some reassurance because I don't come close to their size, so I should be fine if it can handle their weight.

"Uh, I don't know."

"Well, you can think about it while we get set up. Did Arik ask you about the hiking course?"

Looking at Arik, I barely catch his wince before he locks it away.

Confused, I ask, "What hiking course?"

Jackson shoots him an irritated glance. "Dude, I thought you were going to bring it up to her." When Arik doesn't say anything, Jackson just shakes his head and turns to me. "One of my instructors for our hiking course can't make a class next weekend. Ally was going to take it, but it's always best to have two instructors. She knows the ropes, so you would just be support. I was going to see if you had time for it. It runs both Saturday and Sunday, a couple of hours each day."

Looking from Jackson's hopeful face to Arik's guilty one, I start to feel the stirring of my temper. Again, he's not telling me stuff. First it was owning part of Gram's bookstore and now it's this. I thought that after the mess of prom and keeping things to ourselves we would be past this, but it appears not.

"Can I talk to you? Privately?"

We walk a short distance away, putting the Jeep between us and our friends.

I get right to the point. "Why didn't you tell me Jackson needed help?"

"I was going to. But then we were talking about the bookstore, and I figured with you being so close to done you'd earned a little downtime. It's not like Jackson can't go with Ally. All he needs to do is rearrange the schedule at the station. You, however, have been working the equivalent of two full-time jobs in addition to taking care of Gram and spending what little time you have with me. I was trying to help."

"That's not the point, Arik. I could have decided for myself. Yes, I work hard, and yes, I'm exhausted and would love a weekend off, but that wasn't your decision to make. You can't keep things from me in some misguided desire to protect me. I can and have been taking care of myself for a long time now."

"Kate, you think I don't see how tired you are? The dark circles under your eyes or the way that you've lost weight since you've been home? Me not telling you about a hiking course that's going to eat up a huge portion of your weekend wasn't about protecting you—"

"Don't lie to me, Arik. That's exactly what it was about."

His jaw clenches as he bites down on his molars. Glancing at the group behind us, I confirm they're all busy setting up camp, and I'm grateful they're giving us privacy.

"Fine. Part of it was protecting you. But you have to admit that your plate is more than full. Can you blame me for not wanting to add to it?"

Sighing, I say, "No, I won't fault you for wanting to give me a break. I will blame you for keeping things from me and trying to make decisions for me. If this is going to work between us, we can't keep secrets from each other. That's not how I work. You need to talk to me and tell me things even if you disagree with how I'll respond to them."

A flicker of something crosses his face. It's gone before I'm sure I catch it, but my stomach clenches at the thought of him hiding more from me.

"Is there something else you aren't telling me?"

There's a beat of silence where a million scenarios run through my head, but I hold the worry back.

"No. There's nothing else." Leaning down, he brushes a light kiss across my lips.

"Okay. Now, did you have something planned for us next weekend that would be hindered by me helping Ally out?"

The tendon in his jaw stands out, and it's fascinating to watch him rein in his need to take charge and handle everything.

Finally, he says, "No. I didn't have anything planned."

"Okay then, let's go back to our friends."

Skirting around the car, we approach the group. They have the dock in the water, tethered by a line Jackson is holding.

"I'd be happy to help Ally with the hikers next weekend. I'll get with her on the details."

I never took part in the summer programs as a kid, and I'm curious to learn about them. After over a decade in Arizona, I'm an experienced hiker, so I know the basics and beyond. Hopefully, I'll be more help than hindrance since the terrain is different here.

"Awesome, thank you. Now we'll have you partying on floating docks and doing backflips in no time."

Arik comes to my side, his hand sliding along my lower back, and I just barely fight off the shiver from his touch.

Gathering my courage, I say, "I'm game to give it a try, but the first one to shove me over is going to pay."

Both Connor and Jackson grin, as if to say *challenge accepted.*

ARIK

I'S NOT UNTIL LATE AFTERNOON THAT JACKSON AND CONNOR make their move. They've been silently communicating, plotting against Ally and Kate when the ladies aren't paying attention.

Sitting back to watch how this will play out, I don't say anything. The guys both get out of their deck chairs as if going to the cooler to grab a beer. Kate and Ally are oblivious, standing at the railing talking about something to do with the bookstore. I should probably be listening better to the conversation, but I'm more focused on Kate in a bathing suit.

The green two-piece hugs her curves like a Formula 1 race car on the track. After swimming for a bit earlier, she pulled her shorts over the bottoms, leaving them unbuttoned. Her fair skin is turning the slightest shade of pink even though I've been applying sunscreen to her all afternoon. My diligence with the SPF is dual intentioned—to avoid a sunburn and to get my hands on her.

Even after making love to her twice last night, I'm insatiable. Thinking I was a caveman before has nothing on my thoughts now. If I had it my way, I'd drag her back to my bedroom and chain her to my bed for longer than a night. It took every ounce of my willpower to not bend her over the kitchen counter when I found her cooking breakfast.

My shirt looked fucking good engulfing her petite frame, and as I stood at the entryway to the kitchen, one thought rang clear as a bell through my mind. *I want this every single day.*

It took me a few minutes, especially after scaring the ever-living crap out of her, but I picked up on her nerves. Hard to miss that vibrating tension in the air no matter how much I'm lying to myself.

Last night was it for me. I'm aiming to keep Kate Belle Palicki, and I ain't above playing dirty to accomplish it.

Connor sidles behind Ally with a murmured "excuse me," as Jackson comes up behind Kate. Quickly, both men pounce on the women, wrapping Kate and Ally in bear hugs, keeping their arms pinned to their sides.

Ally immediately thrashes against Connor like a hellcat in a burlap sack. He lifts her clear off her feet before shuffling over to the edge and dumping her off the side of the dock.

Kate's different though. She holds herself still, feet firmly planted, and she's calculating.

"Ready for a dip, sugar?" Jackson never misses a chance to gloat.

"You think you'll get me in that water?" Kate's tone is arrogant, and Jackson misses it completely.

"I'd say so, seeing as I got more than a foot and about eighty pounds on you. It's a pretty sure bet."

"Whatcha willing to bet you go in the lake before I do?" The glee on her face is unmistakable. I'd like to think that Jackson learned his lesson with bets when it comes to Kate, but he sure hasn't.

All swaggering confidence, he says, "If you get me in that

water before you go in, I'll wear a dress to the book signing party you got planned. If I get you in, then you delete those pictures."

The grin that stretches across Kate's lips is a little scary.

"Now that's a deal."

Jackson must finally hear the excitement in her tone, because he rushes trying to lift her off her feet, presumably to toss her over the railing. As Ally pulls herself back on the raft, cursing Connor with creative venom, Kate picks up her feet, dropping into deadweight. Jackson tries to compensate, but she grabs his wrist and digs her thumb into the pressure point there, breaking his grip.

Planting her feet, Jackson's forearm still firmly in her grip, Kate hitches forward slightly and with an undulating roll, tosses all six and a half feet of Jackson Sawyer clear over the rail, his hoarse shout swallowed by the water.

He comes up sputtering lake water, catching his breath before shouting, "What the fuck, Kate Belle? Where the hell did you learn how to do that?"

"And can you teach me?" Ally chimes in while shooting Connor a glare.

Leaning against the railing, a smug-as-shit grin on her face, Kate goads, "Be sure to pick something pretty, Jackson James. I think hot pink would complement your coloring nicely. We'll have a lot of successful ladies in the house, and we wouldn't want to disappoint them."

Jackson's cursing a blue streak when he hauls himself back on the deck, and we're all laughing.

The commotion mostly dies down after that aside from some friendly ribbing. We make our way back to the shore to eat an early dinner. Burgers are firing on a propane grill, manned by the three of us, while Kate and Ally are both curled up in chairs with books.

Jackson sees me watching Kate, not for the first time I imagine, as he quietly says, "You're a fucking goner, man."

I take a drink, the frosty beer sliding down easily. "Yep, not much to do about it. I've been a goner for her for a long time."

His expression is troubled as he asks, "How's that gonna work?"

"I haven't thought that far ahead yet."

"Fuck, man. She lives in another state. Not to mention the shit that went down at O'Malley's the other night. That's a lengthy gap to bridge."

I look over at Kate. She's focused on her book with her hair bundled up and damp, tiny beads of water trailing down her neck, and all of her is beautiful to me.

I lied when I told her there wasn't anything else, that I wasn't keeping anything more from her. The lake isn't the place to get into the details of everything that went down Thursday night, and I'm sorry I lied, but I'd do it again to avoid the hurt that it's going to cause her.

I also need time to figure out how to tell her. I'm terrified that I'll tell her, and she'll see the parallels between prom and now and pull the plug on us.

"She's it for me. However it works out, I don't care. As long as I'm with her we'll figure it out together."

"Whoa, wait a minute, are you talking about moving? Like leaving the valley?"

"If that's what it takes, then yeah."

Jackson's breath whistles out before he says, "Well shit, man. I mean if that's what you want, then I'm good with it. Just think before making any serious decisions."

I nod, because his advice makes sense. Kate's been home less than a month, and we just started our relationship. As much as I would love to have her resettle in Felt, that might not be an option for her, whereas teachers are needed everywhere.

I've never thought about moving out of Idaho. It's always been home for me. Now that Kate's here, and we're together, I'd give it up in a minute if it meant I got to keep her. If it means I get to wake up to her every morning and wrap her in my arms every night, I'd follow her anywhere. Home isn't Felt anymore, it's Kate.

Connor looks at me, his face showing he gets it. He understands you have to hold on to happiness as long as you have it.

A lot of whiskey and poker at Jackson's house a couple of years back had Connor's tongue loosening enough for him to share his life before college with us. Heartbreak is a common tale. It hardened him, molding him into the surly bastard he is now.

The burgers finish up on the grill, and Ally and Kate pull the sides out of the cooler. We all eat off our laps as the sun sets, the conversation lively and fun. Even Connor jumps in a couple of times when that's not normal for him.

As we're heading home after a long day at the lake, I reach over and take Kate's hand in mine. "Stay the night with me?"

Smiling softly, she says, "I'd love to."

We take a few minutes to put the food away, then she's in my arms, lips on mine, and I'm walking us toward the bathroom. I leave her only long enough to turn on the tap and let the shower warm up. We undress each other with wandering hands and climbing desire before moving under the rainfall of water.

Warm mist envelops us. I tug her head back by the roots of her hair, wetting the strands in the shower spray. Her hands graze along my ribs, my chest, and abs setting me on fire while I pour shampoo and work it into the knotted mess of her hair, cleaning the day from her curls. As I dig my fingers into her scalp, she lets out the female equivalent of a purr, her head falling back until it's cradled in my palms.

Eyes closed, she murmurs, "That feels amazing."

Leaning down, I kiss her, the flavor of sunshine and happiness dancing along my tastebuds. I rinse the strands until the water runs clear, then reach for the body wash, lathering my hands up and running them across her shoulders, applying firm pressure to the tense muscles. She lets out a snorting grunt that makes me smile as the tension gives under my thumbs. I quickly wash the rest of her before shifting her out of the way.

Running through washing myself and my hair, I'm wiping the water out of my eyes when I find Kate watching me quietly.

"What?"

"You're so much, Arik. So many good things, so amazing that sometimes it's overwhelming. I don't know how I got here, but I'm glad I am."

Her words hit me square in the gut, serious, almost somber sounding. Looking her over, I don't see sadness. Instead, quiet happiness shines.

Unable to go one more second without her in my arms, I reach for her.

But she scoots away with a tiny step and a shake of her head. I'm confused.

"Not tonight. Tonight, I want to touch you. When you put your hands on me, I can't breathe, can't think, I get so caught up in you. Tonight, let me show you, let me care for you."

She gracefully drops to her knees in front of me. My brain catches up, and blood rushes to my dick so fast I go lightheaded. Slender hands encase my hardening length, and I have to bite back the groan at how amazing it feels as she caresses, strokes, and teases. She's driving me out of my damn mind.

Her head dips, her nose tracing along the crease where my thigh meets my groin, and having her mouth this close to my cock stills the air in my lungs until I'm hoping, waiting, wishing, and praying.

She doesn't hold me in suspense for long before her mouth finds my tip, and like a fantasy, her bright green eyes lock on mine before her silky heat envelops my cock, stealing the air from my lungs.

As her tongue teases along the underside, I'm wracked by sensation. Heaviness pools in my groin while her mouth torments me, first drawing me deep and then lips teasing as she pulls back. The water thunders around us, raining over my shoulders and down my abdomen, but she doesn't stop. Her eyes are heavy as she drags her teeth softly against the sensitive ridge along the underside of me. I'm fighting back against the urge to thrust, to bury my hands in that mass of hair and fuck her mouth until I come.

Again and again, she takes me to the back of her throat, the slender column closing around my cock, massaging me. She's not quite able to take my whole length, but her fist grips the base of me, pumping in tandem with her mouth to make up the difference until I'm on the verge of becoming a puddle at her feet.

One of her hands slips between her legs, and the fact this woman is touching herself while worshiping my dick has my orgasm firing off violently and suddenly. I'm barely able to choke out a warning.

Pumping her hand, Kate's rhythm never falters as she forces the orgasm out of me, her mouth greedy and demanding. My climax continues on and on until I can't breathe, can't think, can only feel.

She slows before she pulls back, and I slip out of the heaven of her mouth. I'm spent, my legs barely holding me up. She rests her head against my thigh as she catches her breath, one hand still between her legs.

Finding a tiny bit of strength, I bend down and hook my arms under hers to pull her to her feet, brushing my lips across hers while I hold her.

I grab towels for both of us, and we hastily dry off, our day in the sun and Kate's oral ministrations sapping my energy.

Tugging her after me, I tumble us both into bed where I find just enough motivation to love her with every part of me before drawing her into my arms and listening to her even breaths as she sleeps.

Like Kate, I'm scared, but not for the same reasons. I'm scared she's going to decide that what we have, what we're building, isn't worth the work. I'm scared that when I talk to her about Christina, she's going to run again, and this time I won't be able to bring her back to me.

I draw her tighter into my embrace while reminding myself to have patience before closing my eyes and drifting off to sleep with the smell of her shampoo tickling my nose.

KATE

THE WEEK STARTS AS INSANITY. MY DAYS ARE FILLED WITH Readers' Haven, putting the finishing touches on the store, and rushing around for the last-minute things I still need to get done.

I have books on the shelves. I have books scattered in what I hope will be appealing places around the shop. I even have a back room bursting at the seams with more books after hours of scanning catalogs, each new treasure I bought for store stock added to my already brimming to-be-read list. Book descriptions haunt my dreams, and it's safe to say that I'm getting caught up in the store, the fun of it.

Between taking care of Gram, prepping the opening, late nights at Arik's, Liv's upcoming book launch, and the plans for the signing, I'd be surprised if I have managed more than four hours of sleep each night, but I'm not complaining.

Something shifted between Arik and me that Saturday night after the lake. Sunday morning came early, and after he dropped me off at Gram's we both went about our regular days. Sunday evening, though, he asked me to stay with him again, and I did.

Every night since then, I've found myself at his house, both of us subconsciously gravitating toward one another at the end of our workdays. We both shift plans and schedules to end the day at his house, in his bed together.

The shift happened naturally as if it was the easiest thing in the world, and I've almost stopped waiting for the other shoe to drop. But there's still part of me that's holding back. A little niggling suspicion that Arik wasn't entirely truthful when I asked him if there was anything more he needed to tell me.

Since that first weekend together, our evenings have developed a pattern—we eat dinner, and then I work on things for Liv or Readers' Haven while Arik goes over lesson plans or his fundraising events. He's coming up on the deadline and still has quite a bit of money to raise. The stress he's under gave me the idea to step in and maybe save his day for a change.

After talking it over with Ally during the hiking class, I reached out to the authors attending the signing. Once I explained the situation and what I was trying to do, they couldn't throw money at me fast enough. Their donations will go a long way toward updating the learning materials at Felt High School.

Now I'm waiting at the bookstore for Gram to come in and give the all-clear to open tomorrow morning. I hope she doesn't find anything wrong because I've advertised the reopening everywhere. From the Felt Gazette to the bigger city of Jackson Hole over an hour away, everyone knows the bookstore will be open for business tomorrow morning at eight a.m. sharp.

Through the shop's front window, I watch Ben pull into a parking spot with Gram in the passenger seat, and I pass one last critical eye over the store.

Gleaming oak floors have been sanded and stained, and

threads of auburn run through each plank, tying in with the burnished cherry bookcases. The old checkout area is wholly revamped. The payment tablet is situated right next to the store's vintage cash register on an antique desk, adding a quaint touch to the digital convenience.

The furniture in the back room is new. The Storytime area is open and inviting with bright primary colors, bean bag chairs, and a reading corner with donated books shelved in old copper rain gutters along the wall.

Large plush chairs circle coffee tables, inviting people to sit for a spell and enjoy their new imaginary escape.

Capping off the full effect, soft overhead light plays across a back counter housing handcrafted jewelry and merchandise from the local gift shop and artists in the valley.

The bell over the door chimes, and Gram's eyes sweep along the changes I've made in the space she built from the ground up with my grandfather.

I planned with Ben ahead of time to let Gram do the walkthrough on her own. Mostly so that if she hated it, he wouldn't be there to see my humiliation, but also to give us time to go over everything.

Coming out from behind the counter, I ask, "What do you think?"

Gram turns to me, her eyes swimming with unspent tears, and my heart plummets. She hates it. She wouldn't be crying otherwise.

"What's wrong? Whatever it is, I can fix it. Please don't cry, Gram."

An unsteady breath whistles out, leaving me on pins and needles. Gram reaches over and hooks her arm around my waist, tugging me until we're standing hip to hip.

"Katie Bug, how did you manage this? It's wonderful."

Relief instantly uncoils the stress, and my shoulders

unknot. A giddy laugh bubbles out as I lean my head against hers.

"You scared me. I thought you hated it. I thought I messed it all up and you hated every single bit of it."

Hugging me closer, she says, "How could I? It looks so fabulous in here. I don't know how you managed to pull this off in such a short time, but goodness, Katie, you worked wonders here. I barely recognize it."

Pride sings out of every syllable, and I bask in it. It was nerve-wracking every time Gram waved me off with a "whatever you think is best." Knowing that she approves of my choices and decisions makes all the hard work, the stress, and the time crunch worth it. They make my efforts worthy.

"The changes are good, right? Is there anything you don't like?"

Gram steps away as she moves around, getting a feel for how it all works together.

"I figured with the extra room in the back," I continue, still a little nervous and wanting to fill the silence, "you'd be able to host Storytime more than once a week without it bleeding out to the main floor. Ally and I are hammering out an agreement to give customers the ability to order from the bakery to be delivered here."

When she doesn't immediately reply, I draw in a breath, unable to stem the babble. "If you're still doing them, there's room back there for the after-school tutoring sessions. After moving stuff around, there's also more than enough seating for the book club to be held out here."

"Hmmm." The sound doesn't give me anything more, so I keep talking.

"I'm not sure if you know, but the Felt Fabrics and Craft club is looking for a place to meet weekly, and you could always offer the space to them on the evenings they need it. I've been talking to Arik's ma about that a little bit. She said that they currently have it at the community center, but with the limited hours there, it's harder for them to get one of the conference rooms."

Gram turns back to me, eyebrow raised, and asks, "You've been talking to Meg and Ally?"

Her face is unreadable. There's nothing in her tone that gives away what she's thinking, so I only nod, not wanting my overactive mouth to get me into more trouble if she hates the ideas.

"That's some smart business thinking, Kate." Her shrewd gaze rakes over me, and I snuff the urge to fidget.

Turning to the back of the store, she eyes the goods offered by the gift shop. The tasteful cardstock placards note where each item came from and the local artists' contact information for further details.

"What's all this?"

"I reached out to The Galloping Gift Shop, and when I proposed they send over some of their stock for display, they offered to add a book featured here into the monthly subscription box they run. Those boxes sell like hot cakes for the gift shop, and there's already interest from subscribers in offering a book-related option. All we have to do is provide the books, which will be covered by the cost of the subscription itself. If we put the bookmarks I ordered in there along with some sort of designed postcard detailing our website and contact information, there's potential for digital sales and exposure from that avenue."

She holds her hand up, and I stop talking, not wanting to overwhelm her. Readers' Haven is a hole-in-the-wall bookstore, but unlike other independent bookstores, it didn't change with the market as it should have. The alterations I've made to the store probably look drastic and the information is staggering, but each additional source of income leads to increased name recognition and higher sales.

"Come sit with me, Bug."

We move over and I settle on the large leather couch. Gram takes the chair across from me.

"We can be honest with each other, I hope?"

The earlier triumph I found in her happy tears disappears. I knew it was going to be too many changes at once. I should have designed it better, planned only to do a little bit at a time, until she's more comfortable. Sure, that would make it a more challenging climb to relevancy or financial stability, but it's her store.

"Absolutely, Gram."

Not one to beat around the bush, Gram is blunt. "Why would you do all this? Why go through all the trouble of fixin' up the shop, reaching out to business owners around town, and set up arrangements with the clubs and programs?"

I'm confused she isn't telling me to back up, that she's not shutting my ideas and changes down. Looking her over, I note the added lines around her lips and the signs of aging and laughter that frame her eyes, and my love for her nearly swallows me.

"I couldn't let it die, not when I have the aptitude and money to help bring it back. You and Gramps built this place from the ground up. I couldn't let it go; it's home to me. The money? The work? Those are nothing compared to the certainty the store will stay open, hopefully in a successful way with the changes."

That's what I was trying to preserve. I didn't want her to lose the place that holds those memories for her, and selfishly I didn't want to lose the place with strong memories for me.

"These are smart business decisions. I should have done all this years ago. Would have saved us both from this mess."

"Wait, so you like my ideas?"

"You just said it yourself. You have the aptitude to bring this place back. I'd be stupid not to listen. Now, I want you to tell me about *your* plans."

"What do you mean?"

Gram nails me with a stare that tells me to stop bullshitting her and spit it out.

"I don't know, Gram. My whole life is back in Arizona, a life I worked damn hard to build. The longer I'm here, the more it pulls at me. The longer I'm here, the more I want to stay."

"You had a rough go of it growing up…"

I cut off that nonsense. "Gram, yeah, it was rough, but I had *you*. Every day, you were there when I woke up, every day after school, every night before bed. You were there when I needed you and when I didn't. Don't ever think you didn't do enough for me. You did more than enough."

"And Arik?"

"Arik's been there for me too."

"How are things going with him?"

Blowing out a breath, I go with total honesty.

"We're taking it a day at a time right now. It's nice to think about him without the pain from the past, though there is still a distant pang when I think about prom. I'm starting to settle in with him, but there's still that small part of me that's scared. How can I be enough for him?"

"I'm so proud of you every day, Katie. Not for this either," —she waves a hand to encompass the shop—"but for having the courage to go away for college, to stand on your own two feet, to build a career doing something you love, even in a different place. Every day I'm proud of you. I don't know where you get the idea that you're not enough, but I can promise you, you're more than enough. It's okay to be scared too, just as long as you face that fear and work through it."

"I'm worried Arik feels like he has to hide stuff from me,

that he is hiding something from me. I'm probably crazy, but we were talking about him keeping things from me and there was a look…"

"What kind of look?"

"I'm not sure, almost like guilty resignation if I had to guess. I asked him if there was anything he needed to tell me, but he said no."

"Well, I'm sure if it's important, he'll find the time and the way to bring it up. Men always think they know what's best for us, and sometimes it's easier for us if we just let them go on thinkin' that."

"Thanks, Gram, I'll try. I love you."

"I love you right back, baby. Now, let's get up. I need you to show me how all this works and where everything is for tomorrow. Then we'll go home and eat the stew I tossed in the slow cooker."

ON THE DAY OF THE OPENING, PEOPLE PACK INTO THE bookstore, milling about the shelves, lounging on sofas and chairs. I had to take the bell off the door after the first hour, its chime nearly constant. I spend the day running back and forth, trying to help everyone, while Gram is camped out at the cash register doing all the checkouts.

There's a solid mix of locals among the tourists in the never-ending droves. We ran out of all of the sideline goods I set up with other Felt business owners, and our register sang with sales. I imagine that we broke all sorts of records today. Not that the previous numbers were very high to begin with.

I'm getting ready to close, the excitement of the day winding down, when the door creaks open. Though I'm exhausted and dreaming of putting my feet up with an icy margarita, I drum up a bright smile, calling out, "Hi there, welcome to…" The words die off as Arik steps fully into the store, his eyes scanning the new design and layout, and I'm a little surprised he's here.

Yeah, he's part-owner, but like Gram, he seemed to have little interest in what I've been doing, going so far as to ask about the store but not dig into the details or show up to observe the progress or results.

Crossing to me with his space-eating strides, he wraps me in his arms, lifting me enough to twirl around while he beams at me. "It looks amazing in here."

His lips brush against mine in a slow hello kiss that has the butterflies in my stomach taking flight.

While I'm not ashamed of being with him, I still glance around the store. Gladys Merriweather and Agnes Marshall are standing by the fiction section, their eyes wide as they take in the public display of affection.

Not comfortable under their scrutiny, my cheeks heat and I drop my gaze. Arik would have to kiss me with the two biggest gossips standing not fifteen feet away from us.

There's a twinkle of humor in his eyes as if he's amused at my shyness.

Oh hell, if I'm going to be the source of speculation and gossip, I'm going to make sure it's damn good gossip.

Reaching up, I wrap my hand around his neck and draw him down to me, taking his mouth with mine in a plundering kiss.

I lose myself in the taste and texture of his lips against mine. The way his almost-too-long hair feels in my hands, the way his hands dig into my hips, and the way mine are locked around him.

"A-hem." The throat-clearing at my back breaks the moment. Pulling back, I turn to Gladys, who looks thoroughly scandalized. Bumping up the twang in my tone, I ask, "Ready to check out, ladies?"

I try not to think about the kiss that's likely going to be *the gossip* around town. I'm basking in the glow of a very successful day, choosing to focus on Arik's attention and the happiness soaring through me as Readers' Haven victoriously reemerges among the businesses lining Main Street.

The ladies gather their bags and leave the store. Flipping the sign behind them, I start the process to close up. Gram left early to rest her hip, so it's just Arik and me.

Once I have everything tucked away and the cash in the safe, Arik hugs my exhausted body to his chest, brushing his lips over my hair before asking the same question he asks me every night.

"Come home with me?"

Relaxing in his arms, I give him the same answer that I have every time he has asked.

"Absolutely."

ARIK

Summer in Felt is bittersweet. The days are long and hot, the nights short and warm.

The closer we get to August, the less I want to get back to work. Usually, the end of July is a mad scramble of last-minute plans for the school year, but this year I want the summer to stretch endlessly.

Early Saturday morning, the last weekend in July, Kate and I are in the gym, pushing through a quick workout. I'm on bench presses when she says, "So, uh, Gram and I thought of a way to help out the school and get Readers' Haven a tax write-off." Her statement snaps me out of my mental planning for the upcoming week.

Kate's swamped at the store. With the last-minute tourists of the summer wiping out most of her display and stock, she's been working harder than ever to keep things moving smoothly and prep for the signing she's got planned for this coming weekend. I haven't had time to talk to her about Christina or what the end of the summer might mean for us. Her bringing up the school, especially when I'm a day late and a dollar short on the funds raised, isn't a topic I particularly want to discuss.

The deadline for the tablets is tomorrow. I'm still almost three thousand dollars shy of the funds needed to meet the goal to secure them for the school.

"It's okay, Kate. I didn't get the money in time. I'll keep pushing for them, but for now, it's over."

I set out to do one thing this summer, and I failed. The defeat of it stings. I hate that I couldn't get the money together no matter how much backbreaking work I put into extra jobs. Between my additional work, lesson planning for the upcoming year, and stealing every moment I can with Kate, there isn't a spare minute in the day.

Watching her fidget at the dumbbells, I rack the bar and lever myself up, unsure of why she's acting so nervous. Wrapping my hands around her thighs, I tug her between my spread legs.

"But what if it wasn't over? What if I found a way to get you the money for the tablets?"

"How?"

Chewing on her lower lip and backing out of my hold, she says, "Gram and I are donating it. As long as the funds go toward the tablets, we're donating the rest of the money."

She's lying.

Being part owner, I'd have to agree to any charitable donations, and I haven't.

She has also known that I've been short for a while now—since the council meeting, to be exact. This is the first I've heard of them considering a donation. It doesn't add up.

I climb to my feet. Kate's at the far side of the rack, adjusting the weights as I slip around the bench.

She looks over at me and starts scooting away.

Where are you going, honey?

"Uh, Arik, what are you doing?"

I match her step for step, her backing up and me following. Just when I think she's about to bolt and run, her shoulders hit the wall and I've got her cornered.

I'm so close, her breasts brush against my chest. She cranes her neck to look up at me. There's anxiousness in her eyes, but there's also anticipation and desire.

Leaning down to her neck, I let my breath trail across the sensitive skin, the tip of my nose brushing along her ear.

Her inhale is shaky, catching in a soft hiccup that's both adorable and sexy as sin.

Tugging the lobe of her ear into my mouth, I swirl my tongue around the shell before pulling back to whisper, "What aren't you telling me? Are you keeping secrets?"

"Wh…No, of course not," her denial stutters out.

Skimming my mouth back down her neck, I lock my teeth around the tendon that runs the length of her shoulder and place a sucking bite. The low moan she lets out has my cock twitching behind my gym shorts.

I swirl my tongue along the bite. It's going to be red and leave a mark on her fair skin, making the primal part of me hungry for more.

I want her covered in marks from me. I want the evidence of her arousal on my fingers, my lips, my tongue, and my cock. I want to splash my release across her thighs, her breasts, her mouth. I want her saturated in me. Claimed until she accepts it, until she loves it and me.

I work my mouth toward her lips, and there's the faintest trace of salt on her skin. I nibble at the corner of her mouth before fusing our lips together. Dipping my tongue along hers, I tease before breaking the kiss and taking her lower lip between my teeth. Biting down gently, I draw a keening mewl from Kate.

Her jade eyes are hazy, full of lust and heavy.

"What aren't you telling me about the money, Katie?" I keep my voice soft, quietly murmuring against her mouth.

She stiffens, coming back to awareness, and her hands come up to my chest, pushing slightly.

"Nuh-uh, you're not going anywhere, baby." I reach down and capture her hands with one of mine, drawing them up and over her head.

"Arik, let me go." Her voice trembles, and I almost let go before remembering she's capable of breaking my grip at any time. Is she shaking from arousal?

I run my fingers along her lower abdomen, brushing at the skin above the waistband of her pants. The muscles flex and shiver against my fingers as her chest rises and falls faster, her breath panting out. Oh yeah, definitely arousal.

"Are you wet, Katie? If I slip my fingers down these pants, am I going to find you drenched for me?"

"Ungh." Her hips arch forward in a tempting offer.

Upping the ante, I dance my fingers under her belly button, growling, "If I find you wet—if you're hot for me—I'm going to play with you, tease you, until you tell me whatever you're hiding."

"Arik, please, I'm not hiding—"

Dropping a quick open kiss against her mouth, I cut off her plea. I'm willing to bet the contents of this gym she's not only wet but soaked.

Sliding my hand under the waistband, I find once again she's sans panties. Fuck, could this woman be any more perfect?

The tips of my fingers pass her mound before moving down, and I cup her pussy in my palm. Slick folds greet my hand, and as I suspected she's dripping honey all over my fingers. I add the slightest bit of pressure with the heel of my hand, and Kate lets out a wheezing gasp.

"Mmmm." Satisfaction obvious in my voice, I taunt,

"Would you look at that? So fucking slick. You know what that means, right?"

Kate starts to tug at her hands, so I tighten my grip, keeping her locked in place, and as retaliation I sink a finger into her, careful to avoid her clit.

Her internal muscles lock down on my digit, her pussy an inferno. There's nothing I want more than to throw her down and sink deep inside, so all of that plush heat is wrapped around my cock.

But first, I have other plans.

Crooking my finger, I search for her G-spot. A change in texture tells me I'm in the right spot. I barely graze it before her cry echoes in the empty room.

"Yell all you want, honey. No one's going to hear."

Her head thumps against the wall, exposing that slender throat, and I don't pass up the opportunity to send my lips cruising along the smooth skin. I bite down while rubbing at the spot inside her, pressing firmly against it. She clenches around my fingers, and she bathes my hand in even more liquid desire.

"Ready to tell me what you're hiding yet, baby?"

There's a fire in her eyes now, her breathing rapid, hips moving against my hand, desperate for relief. I feel the fluttering against my fingers, and she's so close. I haven't even touched her clit yet, and she's ready to go off like a rocket. When I remove my fingers, a hoarse cry of frustration leaves her.

"Arik, please. I can't—"

"No? Okay, we'll see what we can do to loosen those pretty lips of yours."

Pulling my hand out enough to get my fingers around her clit, I ignore the hood and focus on the sides around it, never making direct contact as I trace circles, dipping down to rim her opening before coming up and starting all over.

This goes on forever. There's not an ounce of blood in my body that isn't centered in my cock, and I'm afraid I'm going to break before she does. I'm afraid I'm going to pin her to this mat and fuck her, hard and brutal. I won't abide by secrets. I want her to tell me everything and anything, even if I haven't done the same yet.

I refocus on the tremors in her thighs, the way she twitches in need.

"Still so quiet? How about I talk for a bit, hmmm? How about I describe what your pussy feels like in my hands? How I want you in my mouth. How I want you wrapped around my dick, surrounding me, engulfing me. Should I describe what it's like when you come undone while I'm inside you?"

Punctuating my next words, I roughly thrust two fingers into her.

"It's. Perfection."

Kate yells out gutturally, and her eyes start to roll back as the muscles deep inside her shiver and clench hard before I pull back, denying her release again.

"Fuck, Arik, please. I'll tell you, just let me come."

Begging never sounded so sweet, but I don't relent.

"You tell me first, then I'll let you come for me."

The hands that are still locked in mine pull, Kate twisting her wrists and breaking my hold. She's shoving at my arms and pushing at my clothes, stripping each garment off until I'm naked. Together we work to rid her of her clothes until they're in a messy heap at our feet. Not ready to give up control yet, I pin her back against the wall, lifting her until her legs wrap around me. The blunt head of my dick is kissing the swollen heat of her core before reality intrudes.

"Fuck, Kate. Fuck, stop for a second."

Her hips stop working, stop rubbing along my cock

which is a real fucking tragedy. Stilling totally, she asks, "What? What is it?"

"I don't have a condom down here, babe."

Her gaze searches my face, and I calculate how long it would take me to run upstairs. Thirty seconds tops, fifteen if I sprint.

"I'm on birth control and I'm clean. You?"

Oh, fuck me, does this mean what I think it does?

"All clear as of my last checkup and I haven't been with anyone since then." My chest gets tight as I hold my breath.

"Then we're okay. I'm protected, and I trust you."

I trust you.

Those words ring in my ears, and exhilaration rushes through me.

"Are you sure? You have to be sure." I can barely wait for her answer, my control deteriorating by the second.

"I'm sure."

Slamming my lips on hers, I lower her down my length as I thrust up, burying myself in a single sharp thrust.

The way she clenches around me, the difference of being skin to skin is staggering. Knowing I'm as close as I can be to her without the cautionary protection between us is addicting. Everything is better, from the sensations racing through every nerve ending to the increased heat and pressure of her clutching at me. Everything is sharper, more defined.

Kate trusting me enough for this adds purity to our intimacy. Forgoing the physical barrier is akin to us dropping our emotional barriers with each other. The act of making love takes on a whole new meaning until I'm drowning in her.

Using my grip on her waist, I control the tempo with short, shallow thrusts meant to tease before plunging deep and grinding against her clit. Her arms are locked around me, her nails leaving crescent-shaped divots in the skin of my shoulders and neck. Her hips pump against mine, meeting me thrust for thrust.

Those violent ripples overtake the length of my dick, and not forgetting the original mission, I pull back before she's about to go off the cliff, keeping her poised at the head of my cock, unwilling to entirely separate.

"Why?" Her question echoes in the room.

"Tell me honey. I'll end this, right here, right now, but first I need to know."

Wiggling, she bucks against me until I tighten my grip on her hips, stilling her movement.

Eyes clenched tight, head thrown back, she's the picture of sexual frustration.

"*Fuck*. Fine, okay. I talked to Gram about donating the extra money, and she agreed."

"How? She doesn't have that kind of money, and it's not coming from Readers' Haven."

Chest heaving, her eyes are wild, desperate, and hungry as she hurries through an explanation. "The authors for the signing agreed to donate the missing proceeds but only if they were anonymously donated from Readers' Haven."

I have no words for her generosity. That she'd think of me, of the school, and the students is too much right now. Slowly, I lower her over my aching length until she's taken all of me. I rest my forehead against hers as pure emotion overwhelms me.

Kate brings her mouth to mine, the kiss both comforting and stirring. Leaning back, she opens her mouth to say something else, but I stop her with a fierce thrust. With one arm holding her, I reach around with my free hand and dip my fingers along her clit, never varying my rhythm as I circle the sensitive nub.

She's right there, the tension in her legs snapping tight right before she implodes, her legs constricting around me and her hips pumping hard as her pussy contracts with the waves of her climax, dragging me along with her. Abandoning her clit, I grasp her hips tight and shove into her with savage thrusts, prolonging her release and bringing mine to a head.

The orgasm rushes over me, heat stealing into my face, every part of my body tensing until I'm coming with a grunt, waves of pleasure so strong I get lost in them as I empty myself into her.

We collapse onto the floor, curled around each other. Breathless, replete, and sleepy.

I'm in love with Kate Palicki. The no-holds-barred, hang on for dear life kind of love.

It feels infinitely deeper than when we were kids, as if that love was younger and rooted in friendship but yanked before it had time to grow into more.

Kate's quieter than usual, but I assume it's because she's tired. We're both running ourselves ragged. After catching our breath and cleaning up in a shower, she heads in to open up the bookstore. I settle into my office, trying to focus on my work, but I'm distracted by the obstacles still ahead of us.

Namely, me explaining why I didn't tell her about the kiss. Explaining that it was less about hiding it from her and more about me trying to keep her here with me.

My motivations were selfish, but I believe that my love outweighs the selfish choice I made. I can only hope she won't fault me for it. Then there are the other hurdles we have to jump if we are going to make this work.

While my first choice would be for Kate to move back here, we need to discuss it and make that decision together. It's not just me in this. Her wants and needs come into play as well.

She and Olivia have been working through email and phone primarily, and while that's working for them so far, it may not be feasible for the long term. If I have to relocate, then that's what I have to do, no matter how much it would pain me.

Noting down to research the state licensing requirements between Idaho and Arizona, I think about moving out of Felt.

It fits like a lousy shoe pinching my toes, giving me blisters, and comes with a hefty list of things I would need to do.

I hear footsteps coming down the hall, and before I can toggle to my screensaver, Ma is shoving into my office like a whirlwind.

"Whoo-whee, Kate did amazing things with Readers' Haven. I haven't had the chance…" Her words die off as she looks to the job listing website showcased on my computer. I quickly minimize the screen, but the damage is done.

Climbing to my feet, I stammer with all the grace of a teenager caught rounding bases in the backseat of Mom's borrowed car, "You want some tea? I made it this morning, came out good." Scooting past her, I aim to make a beeline out of there.

"Arik Beaumont, you stop right there." Tone firm, she pulls out *the voice*. It's the voice all mothers reserve to stop their children in their tracks and whip any thought of rebellion from them.

Fighting the need to hunch my shoulders, to run and hide, I turn, facing her.

"Now, you tell me what I was looking at right there."

It's not a question, but she wants me to confirm it.

Stalling for time, I say, "Come on, if we're going to have this conversation, let's grab a drink while we do."

Ma follows me into the kitchen, sitting at the island while I pull out the pitcher of tea and pour a glass for each of us.

When I stay silent, Ma says, "You've always been able to talk to me about anything. This shouldn't be any different."

The almost wounded sound in her voice has my shoulders hunching further. While I've been toying with the idea of following Kate, I haven't thought through all the ramifications of that decision, specifically leaving my ma.

The same Ma who raised me alone, working multiple jobs to keep us secure and fed. Guilt drips oily and unpleasant down my spine.

"I know, Ma, but I'm not even sure if there's a reason to be talking to you about this yet."

"You're planning to follow Kate back to Arizona."

Again, it's not a question, more a statement of fact brought on by motherly intuition. Still I nod in the affirmative.

"What does she think about that?"

"She doesn't know."

Huffing out an impatient breath, she asks, "And why the hell not, Arik? You're not one to be vague. Plain-speak has always been your primary language."

"I'm trying not to rush her, to not push her into making a decision she isn't ready for. We agreed to try, to take time with each other and see what happens. I won't ask her to choose before she's ready just because I want to lock her to me."

"Oh, and you'll know when she's ready?" Her scoff has me leveling her with a stare that stops her fast.

Kate is second nature to me. How she thinks, acts, and feels are as ingrained as my own breathing.

The panic after our first night together has disappeared entirely. She doesn't struggle with the idea of people knowing we're together, as evidenced by the number of times we've been out to dinner, gone around town, and the kiss in the store the day they reopened. She's gotten comfortable with public affection, and her words earlier—her trusting me—mean we're going in the right direction.

Gaining her trust back has been hard-earned. Every time we take two steps forward, there's one back, but I can't blame her. I don't want my heart broken any more than she does. I can't discount the fact that I might lose a measure of that success when I work up the courage to be upfront with her.

Understanding on her face, Ma says, "Okay, I'll say you do know that girl, probably better than anyone else. You always have. However, I would like to note you're not giving her enough credit. To you, she's someone who needed taking care of, but something you should remember is that not only did Kate leave for and manage college, but she also built her career and life in a large city hundreds of miles away. She single-handedly planned out and implemented a renovation for a floundering business all while caring for her injured grandmother and getting involved with you. She's stronger than you give her credit for."

Ma has a point, one I haven't fully considered yet. I've also watched Kate gain more confidence each time she puts herself out there. Each time she moves out of her comfort zone, she shines. The question is, do I broach the subject of what comes next for us when we've both settled into this new normal, or do I hold off and wait for her to bring it up?

"I'm aware I need to talk to her, but part of me doesn't want to rock the boat. We have a good thing going on, and I want to enjoy it."

"There's nothing wrong with that, but you, my baby boy, are impatient to claim that woman. You have been since you were eighteen years old. But there's no sense in making plans until you talk with her, and it might be once you talk to Kate y'all end up staying here."

"I know." Even I can hear the doubt in my response. Kate did build a life in another state. She cultivated new relationships, ones that mean something to her. I don't want to move, but how could I possibly convince her to stay, to ask her to give that life up?

"Now, you don't need it, but you have my blessing. I hope...I can hope she'll choose to stay, but that's just the mother in me wanting her chicks close. You talk to her, and then you'll both make the best decision for you. Don't worry about anyone else." Her voice breaks, and I glance over and see the tears. Wisely, I don't say anything, but I wrap my arm around her, and she rests her head on my shoulder.

Ma leaves soon after that, promising to stop by for dinner and cards soon, and even that leaves a bad taste in my mouth. We usually get together at least once a month to have dinner, catch up, and hang out. That'll change too if I move.

Wandering through my house, I remember each step of building it. I had initially planned to get married and raise a family here. It never occurred to me that those plans might change. That part of my chance with Kate might mean leaving this all behind.

In my bedroom closet, I pull out my Kate box, where I confined everything related to her over the years. Popping the folded flaps up, I glance inside. Dust shifts around since it's been a couple of years since I looked at this stuff.

Right on top are the letters. Bound together with rubber bands, the paper starting to dim, no longer blindingly white. There are seventy-two of them in that bundle. I know because I used to count them when I couldn't sleep. Next to those are packet after packet of pictures taken from diaper age up through our senior year in high school. I even managed to snag the single picture Gram took of Kate in her prom dress to make a copy of it.

Years of history live in this box. Years of happiness, heartache, laughter, and love.

Kate's sad attempt at a crocheted beanie is tucked into one corner, cushioning a Christmas tree ornament that we made together one year, the first and last time we tried to whittle wood. Each item in here ties to a specific memory of our childhood together.

I pull the velvet jewelers box out. Flipping the top open, I look at the modest band crusted in tiny diamonds. I worked various jobs and saved for the whole summer to buy this for Kate. One fingertip traces over the engraving. My original plan had been to propose before she left for college and promise to be here waiting to marry her when she came back home.

How hard can it be for two adults to have a conversation about what happens next? Surely we should talk about these kinds of things, especially with the end of summer nearing. She has to be wondering too.

What if she did stay? What if she took over Readers' Haven? Gram is almost at the age where she should be retiring, and Kate has a way with the shop. She's found her rhythm and worked out the kinks over the last week, even going so far as to hire a part-time clerk. Handling her work for Olivia and the store is easier for her now.

The fantasy builds in my head, the one where Kate runs the bookstore and I teach, and we make a life here in Felt.

I get caught up until the *what if*s intrude.

What if I follow her to Arizona? I think I could be happy anywhere as long as Kate is there, but what if I can't? What if I try, I uproot my life, and it doesn't work out? What if she doesn't want me to follow her? What if this summer is only a pleasurable diversion for her? What if she doesn't want me the way I've always wanted her? What if, like me, she's holding back from telling me her feelings because she doesn't want to hurt me?

She's gotten comfortable with the idea of us, but what if that's only because she planned for it to be temporary anyway?

Plain-speak is your primary language. Kate's stronger than you give her credit for.

Grabbing my keys off the counter, impulse is pushing me out the door. I can't get caught up in my head until I hear from her about what she wants. I can build thousands of fantasies, but none of them will replace the truth. We should talk about this, the sooner, the better. If I can get her alone, I also want to tell her about Christina, and I hope for the best there.

Springing this on Kate could have disastrous results, but I have to try at least, try talking to her about the possibility of there being an us once the summer is over.

I offer a silent prayer as I drive into town.

Please, Kate, keep an open mind and we'll make this work. Be brave enough to keep trying for us.

ARIK

I'M GETTING OUT OF MY JEEP WHEN I HEAR A HIGH-PITCHED squeal. Scanning the street, I watch as Kate flies out of the store, running straight for a tall blonde and a stocky guy.

The blonde squeals and starts running to Kate. They meet in the middle of the sidewalk, jumping and shouting all over the place. My feet lock in place next to the Jeep while I watch the scene unfold. I don't recognize them, but Kate sure does.

The blonde releases Kate and then the fucking ape with her is wrapping my woman in his arms and twirling her in fucking circles, their faces close and both brimming with smiles.

Jealously flashes bright and hot, that smile on Kate's face compounding the burning in my gut.

Don't just stand here, stupid.

My legs eat up the pavement between us. Kate's laughter and giddiness is spilling out of her.

I'm nearly on them when she finally notices me. Pinning the ape with a hard stare until he drops his hand from around her shoulders, I ignore the blonde's arm linked with Kate's. I don't go to her, as much as I want to wrap her in *my*

ALINA LANE

arms—to kiss the hell out of her, to mark her as mine. I won't embarrass her like that, so I lock the caveman side of me down.

Eyes bright, she says, "Arik. Oh, this is perfect timing, you have to meet my friends. This is Olivia and Rob. Liv, Rob, this is Arik."

Stunning me, she comes over to me and reaches up, wrapping her arms around my neck, and brushes her lips across mine. While she's settled into the idea of us, I'm usually the one to instigate public displays of affection, so this is surprising. The suddenness of it has me pulling back, and the flash of hurt across her face rips at me. I never meant for her to think me pulling back was a rejection of her affection for me.

I drum up some manners. "Nice to meet you, ma'am," I say with a slight smile at the woman, taking her hand and giving it a light shake. To Rob I offer a head nod in greeting, and other than a hitch in his black eyebrow, he doesn't react to the snub. If Kate kissing me right in front of him bothered him, I can't tell.

I have a couple of inches in height on him, but he outweighs me in muscle. Kate's told me about his martial arts training, so it's unlikely I could take him in a fight. Still doesn't stop me from smirking at him. The guy has a fucking man bun, for Chrissake.

Dark sleeves of tattoos climb up thick arms still too fucking close to Kate for my liking. The only thing that saves him is the look of brotherly exasperation while Kate talks a million miles an hour about how they're a whole week early, and how she had no idea they were coming up early—that there's so much for them to do, to see.

Olivia's a smart cookie. She notices how I'm eyeing her brother and measuring him for a coffin.

"Kate, why don't you show me the bookstore? You sent

240

pictures, but I want to see it in person. Rob, would you mind grabbing my purse and the books from the car? I'm sure Arik will give you a hand with them."

She maneuvered Rob and me right into that, and before I so much as blink, she's tugging Kate into the store.

Rob walks back to their car, his steps unhurried, and I follow until I'm staring into the back of an SUV brimming with boxes.

"I've got these if you wanted to head in." Tone flat, he doesn't give anything away as he speaks.

"Nah, I'll help. What'd she do? Bring a bookstore with her? We got plenty of books about fifty feet away."

Rolling his eyes as if I'm stupid for asking, he replies, "These are the signed copies pre-ordered by her fans, who will be traveling to meet her. She signs and personalizes them ahead of time, so she isn't so busy at the actual event. Liv likes to talk with readers for a bit before moving to the next guest."

"Hmm." It's a good idea for an author, especially a wildly popular one. I can't imagine having so many people want to meet me.

Rob shuffles some of the boxes around as he says, "I don't make a habit of explaining myself, but since I would like to live till retirement, I figure I should tell you there isn't anything between Kate and me. Never has been."

"Kate told me the same, but *you* sure looked friendly to me." I'm goading him, a test, and I can't help myself.

"For one, fuck you. If you think Kate would ever have something going on with me and then take up with you, you don't know her very well. Secondly, she's like a sister to me, one I inherited through Liv. She's family."

"I trust Kate. It's you I'm not so sure about."

"I could say the same. I will say I'm aware of the truth of what happened. Still, I'm compelled to warn you, you hurt her, and you'll hurt." A sinister grin accompanies his words.

Damn me, but I'm starting to like this guy. I respect him trying to protect Kate even as it chaps my ass that he thinks I'm the one she needs protecting from.

"If you heard about me, then you know I would never intentionally hurt her."

With a slight nod, he shrugs, saying, "Still needed to be said. Here, you grab this one. It's got paperbacks so it's lighter."

Ignoring the insult, I let the subject drop. We aren't friends, but I don't want to punch him either. That's progress, I guess.

It ends up taking multiple trips and most of the stock room to get Olivia's books stored. By the time we have them all stacked and labeled among the other authors' books, Kate and Olivia are sitting on the couches. The place is empty, Kate having flipped the closed sign and locked the door behind Rob and me.

"I can't believe you guys drove up here, especially motion sick Molly over here." Kate waves to indicate Rob, and his cheeks pink slightly.

"I got motion sick one fucking time, and I'll remind you, you were the one that was driving."

Shooting him a cheeky grin, she looks over at me and after a slight hesitation gestures for me to take the seat next to her on the couch.

Unsure, I sit stiffly beside her. While I'm dying to pull her into my side, indecision stops me. Is Olivia aware of our relationship? I assume so, since Rob said something about the truth of what happened, but has Kate told them any more than that? Has she told them that aside from the store, she and I have been practically inseparable? That she sleeps in my arms and wakes up in my bed more than she doesn't?

Olivia's watching me while Kate and Rob bicker. Her eyes are a swirling mixture of colors, but they look old as fuck. I'm being weighed and measured, and I bet I'm part of the reason they decided to head up here early.

Testing, I reach over, still looking at Olivia, and pick up Kate's hand. Linking my fingers with hers, I rest our hands on my thigh. A small smile and nod are all I get, but I feel like I passed a test of my own.

We both tune back into the constant back and forth between Rob and Kate, and I have to admit it's amusing, both of them not willing to give ground, but there is zero animosity to the argument.

"You want to talk about driving records, pal, let's talk about that time I had to pick you and Sally McFearson up and then when you were in the back of…"

Rob is up and shoving his hand against Kate's mouth to silence her. "We don't talk about that, just like I don't talk about the time I found you—" Kate rips her mouth away and yells, "Concede!"

I can't say I like his hands on her mouth, but after listening to the squabble session between the two, I'm more comfortable with it. I'm also curious about how he "found" her and why her face is a bright shade of red.

"Arik, you'll have to forgive these two. When they get within five feet of each other, they either start to argue or spar."

"Yeah, munchkin, be careful or I'll take you to the mat."

"Always have to get the last word in, don't you? Well, for your information there isn't a gym in town. The closest one is Rexburg, which is about an hour away."

"Well shit, I mean—what have you been doing?"

Kate shoots me a look both pleading and a question all at once. Knowing what I should do doesn't make it any easier, still I put the offer out there.

"Uh, yeah. Kate's been using my place. You guys are more than welcome to use my basement gym. Otherwise, you have the community center. They're open till two every day of the week, and that has a couple of treadmills and a rack of free weights."

Kate jumps in, "You have got to see his setup. He has a Rogue and a whirlpool."

A look of astonishment covers Rob's face briefly before he schools his expression. "No shit? That's a pricy setup for a home gym." The unspoken question is clear—*how could you possibly afford nice things on a teacher's salary.* I didn't always have a head for finances either, but once I learned to get the numbers to cooperate in my brain, it came naturally to me.

"Yeah, well, I like being able to work out whenever, and we roll up the sidewalks pretty early here. You're welcome to it anytime. If you time it right I'll either be in there or my friends Jackson and Connor will be."

Liv says, "Ah yes, the famous Jackson and Connor."

Gaping at Kate, I say, "You showed them the pictures?"

Shrugging, she's impish as she replies, "I don't know what you're talking about."

I'm glad to see some of the sass back in her. Obviously I'll have to explain my reluctance for PDA around her friends, but that's just one more thing to talk about when I get her alone.

"A Rogue setup is nice, Kate. If you tell me they have a decent Thai food place nearby, I might just stay here, nightlife be damned. The temperature alone definitely beats the heat we left behind in Phoenix."

Olivia reaches over and smacks Rob's leg, the look she shoots him telling him to shut up.

Groaning, Kate replies, "I wish. It's pretty limited here restaurant-wise. God, what I'd give for some decent Thai food right now."

The comment stings and takes some of the wind out of my maybe-she'll-stay idea.

She probably got used to living in the city, having places stay open later, being more diverse and having so many options. What if she doesn't want to trade all that in for some better summer weather?

I won't have answers until we talk, so I push those thoughts aside. I've already started looking into moving, and if that's what it takes to keep her happy, I'll do it.

Olivia mentions something about her work, and Kate's in her element, discussing release schedules, the signing, and how it's a great place and time to announce to the fans she has a new series in the works. The conversation moves too fast for me to follow, some strange language about cover designs, marketing, and drafting advertisements for social media. I'm not surprised that Kate is in charge of most of these details, especially with the way Readers' Haven changed in such a short amount of time.

"I'm hoping to get a jump on filing the third quarter taxes when you get back, since the deadline to send those in is right in the middle of release week. You said early September is when Gram should be back up on her feet, right? Do you think you'll be back in time to help with those, or should I start the slog now?" Olivia's tone is almost tentative, as if she doesn't want to ask but has to.

Kate seems to miss it completely as she replies, "Yeah, the doctors are pleased with her progress so far. She just got the okay to start driving again, and aside from finishing out this round of therapy and the maintenance therapy she'll keep up for the next bit, she's getting around really well. So, I should be done here by then and back home in time to help with all that."

I should be done here.

Kate may not realize what she said, but I do. Five simple

words bring a crushing reality check. This is all temporary for her. I'm temporary. There was no "we" in that statement —zero consideration for me and what we have.

An ache takes up residence in my chest, one I'm all too familiar with, and I'm heartsick. Those five words confirm one of the biggest fears I have about our future, or the one I conjured up in my fool head.

She's quick to say she'd be back home, and that means she didn't consider staying here or having me go with her, so it's safe to assume she didn't consider letting whatever we have going on continue.

Once again, I'll be left behind. Maybe not forgotten, but not important enough to rate in her consideration, her plans. Again, my feelings for Kate Palicki are deeper than hers are for me. I'll just have to deal with the fallout from that by myself.

There will never be a right time to bring up the incident at O'Malley's, because just like my initial knee-jerk reaction to hide it from her, my instinct that she would use it to end things is spot on. I mean, if she's not even considering me in her decision to leave our sleepy little town behind, why would I think she'd stop long enough to hear out my reasons for keeping that night from her.

So much for talking, for figuring things out. It's clear where I stand. I guess I was only a pleasurable summer diversion. Standing by what I told Ma, I won't demand anything from her she isn't willing to give.

It's gonna hurt like a motherfucker, but I have to let her go. I was stupid for thinking even for a second that we could make this work. She's never talked about anything beyond the fall. Both of us have avoided any mention of the future. I've urged her to focus on now and have faith it'll work out, that we'll figure it out. Guess I put too much emphasis on the *now* part and not enough on the *us*.

Pulling my hand from hers, I physically retreat, ignoring the look she sends my way.

Not for the first time since she came home, there's this vast canyon of space between us. She's sitting next to me on this couch, and we couldn't be farther apart.

As they make plans to grab an early dinner after Rob and Olivia check into their Airbnb, I run through plans in my head. What I'm not ready for is the resentment and bitterness I feel over the whole situation. It's time to protect myself against further heartache. Agreeing to meet them for dinner, knowing that I'll make up some excuse to cancel, I rush to get out of there.

Once again, my dreams surrounding Kate get shot out of the sky like a duck during hunting season.

KATE

PUSHING OPEN GRAM'S DOOR, I LET OUT AN INELEGANT SHRIEK at the sight that greets me and stumble back, my shoulder jarring painfully against the doorjamb. Slamming my eyes shut, I turn around for good measure.

Not that it erases the images now imprinted in my brain until the end of time.

Thanks, Gram.

"Kate. I thought you'd be going to Arik's this evening."

Yeah, I wish I had now too.

There's shuffling around behind me as clothes are being refastened and righted. I don't look until Gram calls out to me with suppressed laughter in her tone.

"You can turn around now—we're decent. Well, mostly decent."

"Ha-ha. Are all the bits and pieces covered on *both* of you?"

"They are, you big ole ninny." There's a giggle and a chuckle.

Peeking back, I barely open my eyes, confirming that Gram and Ben are dressed before opening them fully.

Ben's hair is a disaster, standing up in spikes, a flush covering his cheeks. He's likely as mortified as I am.

There's nothing like your thirty-year-old almost step-granddaughter catching you necking on the couch.

I slam the door on those thoughts while working to shove the image of Gram straddling Ben's lap deep down until it dies a horrible death.

Kill. It. Dead.

"What are you doing home? You usually head to Arik's after closing up the store."

I do not detect a husky tone to my grandmother's voice. Nope. Not at all. It's just time to get my ears checked.

"Olivia and Rob showed up early, and we decided to grab dinner, so I needed a change of clothes."

"Oh wow. Olivia and Rob are here? How are they? Did they drive or fly? Why didn't they call ahead of time? Do they have a place to stay? They can stay here with us."

No, I'm not subjecting them to the mental torture I walked in on.

"They drove. They didn't want to ship the personalized books, and they have somewhere to stay. They're in an Airbnb for a couple of weeks."

I'm being short with Gram, but there's a very prudish part of me that never wants to address what I walked in on, so I'm not allowing her to bring it up.

Scarred for life.

Olivia and Rob have both met Gram several times when she would visit for the holidays. Accepting the two orphans in stride, she folded them into our family, winning them over.

Gram turns to Ben saying, "I'm so glad you finally get to meet them."

"I look forward to it, Hedy." Ben's still red, and I'd bet my last dollar he wants the floor to open up and swallow him whole.

I feel you there, buddy.

"Did you want to come to dinner with us? We're heading to O'Malley's. Nothing fancy."

Elation covers Gram's expression before she says, "Oh yes, please, if we wouldn't be intruding."

"Not at all. I'm sure they want to see you too. Rob and Liv are getting settled, so it probably slipped their mind to swing by to say hi."

"Perfect. I'll go get changed. Ben, you'll come too, right?"

If it's possible, his shoulders hunch even farther, until he's all but disappeared into them before he replies, "I'd be delighted."

I shoot him a commiserating smile as I skirt around them, heading up the stairs to change.

Grabbing some clothes, I make sure to look for a high-collared shirt since some of the beard rash from my time with Arik in the gym this morning is still visible across my collar bones. As much as I enjoyed it at the time, I don't want to broadcast it to everyone at dinner.

Warm heat suffuses me the more I think about it. Sex with Arik is incredible. Being less interested in that aspect in past relationships was normal for me, but with him, I feel like I never want to get out of bed.

He's a demanding lover as well, routinely waking me up in the middle of the night with his mouth or hands between my legs.

I wonder if my sudden interest in sex is more about the *who* instead of the *what*.

Somewhere along the line I gave up caring what other people thought. Instead, I've been focused on my growing affection, respect, and love for Arik.

Holy fucking shit, I'm in love with Arik Beaumont.

I wait for the panic to surge, because that's second nature with me, but it doesn't. The realization leaves behind a tingling glow, one that I'm starting to recognize is true happiness.

Arik's place in my heart crept up on me. The stolen touches, quiet evenings, early mornings in the gym, and his strong arms wrapping around me at night cemented my feelings for him. I've loved him all my life, and only I would assume that love faded away with time and distance. It's never gone anywhere. Instead it's lain dormant until the man it's tethered to reignited it.

I love Arik and I want to tell him. I want to watch his face as I tell him.

What if I stay in Felt? I can admit that leaving before was a mistake. Yeah, I would have left to go to college, but staying away for years falls on me. I let some misheard words and four immature bullies rule my decisions when it came to Felt, which isn't fair to all the other people here.

Since I've been home—interactions with Christina removed—everyone has been more than friendly, asking after me, after Gram, Ben, Arik, and Readers' Haven. People wave to me along the street, and the week after Gram came home, we had so many casseroles dropped off that we had to give some to the local churches.

Felt isn't the horrible place that I remembered it as, and the longer I'm here, the more it's starting to feel like home again.

Not wanting to be late, I rush through the rest of getting ready and ponder how to bring up the subject of staying to Arik. I'd have to figure out working arrangements with Liv, but we've gotten working from different states locked down over the past couple of months. If something comes up, we can ask Taylor how to deal with it.

It'll suck moving away from the life I made in Arizona, but nothing would stop me from visiting when I need to.

Arik Beaumont is it for me, and I don't care how it works out, as long as we do it together.

When I arrive at the restaurant with Gram and Ben, I shoot Olivia and Rob a group message asking if they've arrived yet. When I toggle back to the message menu, I notice an unread one from Arik.

Arik: Hey, I've got some work to catch up on, I'm gonna skip dinner. You have fun with your friends.

There's a flash of hurt, but I remind myself he's been patient with the amount of work that's occupied my attention lately, so it's only fair that I give him the same courtesy.

Kate: Did you want me to bring you anything? I'll have Gram and Ben drop me off at your place on their way home.

Arik: Nah, I'm gonna finish this up and head to bed early. I'll catch up with you tomorrow.

A distant alarm bell in the back of my mind goes off. I've spent the night at Arik's almost every single night since our first weekend together. The only times I've opted to return to Gram's after work is when she has an early therapy appointment and Ben isn't able to take her. Even when Arik had things to do, we'd curl up on the couch and I'd read while he worked, so this doesn't make sense. His response coupled with his behavior this morning sends a wave of "oh shit" through me.

I send one last message, hoping the response will give me some idea of what's going on.

Kate: Would you like me to make you breakfast? We could get a workout in before I have to head to the shop.

Arik: I have an errand to run early tomorrow, but you and your friends are welcome to use the gym.

On the verge of full-blown panic, I barely notice the server asking for our drink order.

My phone vibrates on the table and I snatch it up hoping that I was wrong, that Arik changed his mind, that he does want me to come over.

Arik: Goodnight Katie.

He's using my nickname, which should reassure me, but dread curdles in my gut, and I can't shake the suspicion that we just took a wrong turn.

I respond on autopilot throughout dinner when the conversation circles around to me. Struggling to focus, I tune in enough to note key details, like how Rob made a spectacle of himself by dipping Gram before giving her a smacking kiss, applause ringing out as he righted her. Ben and Rob's hearty handshake and shoulder slap. Gram resting her forehead against Liv's while wrapping her in a hug, tears making their eyes shiny before they pull it together. Ally coming over from eating dinner with Jackson and the girls to say hi and introduce herself to Olivia. The three of us making plans to get together this week and hang out.

There's nothing to do about Arik right now. Nothing to change, nothing I can alter while I'm here with everyone important to me.

Almost everyone.

We stick around after dinner, enjoying each other's company before heading out. I hug Olivia close before she and Rob take off.

Gram, Ben, and I get into the car, and Gram asks, "Do you want us to drop you at Arik's? Or would you rather take my car? I don't need it tomorrow."

"Arik's catching up on work. He said he'd see me tomorrow, so I'm gonna crash at home."

Gram's eyebrows wing up. She's as aware as I am of how many nights I haven't "crashed at home," but she doesn't say anything further. She and Ben share a loaded look before he pulls out of the lot.

As I climb into bed, I think over the day, about how thrilled I was when Liv and Rob showed up, about how I thought the moment would be perfect if Arik was there too, and then he was. Shutting off the light, I decide I'll track him down tomorrow afternoon and we can have a rational discussion of where things stand and start making plans. Arik hasn't given up on me once, and he could have thrown in the towel a hundred times, so I won't either.

I don't see him the next day though. In fact I don't lay eyes on Arik all week. Every text message replied to is succinct with some excuse as to how he's not at home, he's busy, or it's not a good time. Those are the replies I actually get—the rest of my messages are ignored completely.

I abandon my plans to track him down, pride being the only thing keeping me from driving over to his house. I refuse to shove myself where I'm not welcome, and I have an idea where everything went wrong. That damn conversation on the couch, agreeing to be there to help Liv with the tax filing. If I hadn't been so gobsmacked at having my friends show up out of the blue, maybe I would have said it differently—to include Arik in the decision—but I messed that all up.

So I wait and have faith. Faith that he'll come around. But the longer I go without seeing him, the more that faith starts to turn to trepidation.

It's not until Friday before the Romance at Readers' Haven signing that everything implodes.

After directing Rob to set up some tables for the signing, I'm heading down the stairs when I hear the tail end of a conversation that stops me dead.

"No one's seen them together all week. They have to be done with each other," Christina says.

"Maybe they're both just busy," Melody says.

"I doubt it, and honestly, after what happened in O'Malley's, I think they're done. I knew it was only a matter of time before he ditched her. He's probably waiting until she leaves again before coming around. I mean—it has to be annoying having a stage five clinger suctioning herself to you."

I listen shamelessly while they talk shit about me. Before long, my pride gets the better of me and I round the bookshelf to where they're standing, with a deceptively sweet smile cemented on my face.

"Christina, Melody,"—nodding to them both I continue—"anything I can help you ladies find?"

Melody has the grace to blush, sensing I overheard them, but Christina whips her hair over her shoulder and sneers at me though neither respond.

"Well, okay then, I'll leave you both to it. Y'all call out if you need anything."

I don't get a step away before Christina asks, "Why are you even still here?"

Taking a level of glee from her tone, I counter with, "I'm not sure what you mean?"

Rolling her eyes in exasperation, she says, "Of course you don't know what I mean." And then as if I'm stupid, she says slowly, enunciating each word, "I mean, what are you even doing here in Felt still? No one wants you here aside from your old biddy of a grandmother. No one in town gives two shits about you. Why don't you just go back to Arizona with those lame friends of yours?"

I have an iron hold on my temper, refusing to let her bitchiness get to me.

Striving for the calmest tone I can manage, I say, "I have every right to be in Felt, just as much as you. The difference between us is I'm not immature enough to play the 'this town isn't big enough for both of us' card. Grow up, Christina."

Done with her drama for the day, done with just about

everything in this town, I turn to leave. If she wants to be nasty, I'll just ignore her.

"Even Arik doesn't want you here. Did he tell you he kissed me? Weeks ago, at O'Malley's. Bet he didn't, because you are just that insignificant."

"Bullshit, I don't believe you." The words are out before I stop them, and it's clear I've played into her hand by the smirk she shoots at me.

"Here, I'll show you." Pulling her phone out of her pocket, she unlocks her screen. I want to walk away—I need to walk away—but I can't move.

There in all its glory is a picture of Arik with Christina wrapped around him, a visual flashback to prom. His hands are on her waist, eyes closed, their mouths pressed together.

I'm going to throw up.

The daily specials board that the owner insists on filling out with the date shows the kiss happening the night before we slept together the first time.

He kissed her a single day before I let him inside me, and not only did he kiss her, but he also hid it from me, emphasizing how little he cares about me.

I asked him. I asked him if there was anything that he needed to tell me, and he just stood there and lied straight to my face.

Hot bile coats the back of my throat, and tears sting at my eyes. I fight them back, unwilling to show weakness to this fucking viper.

I'm so fucking thankful when Rob's deep voice barks, "Get out."

Jumping at the interruption, a change comes over Christina in a millisecond, and she bumps up her smile, going from mean to sweet and flirty.

"What was that, honey?"

Oh, barf.

Eyeing him appreciatively, her gaze runs over his face, then down his chest before tracing lower and coming back up. Rob doesn't fall for it for a second.

"You heard me, but in case you're deaf as well as stupid, I'll repeat myself. Get the fuck out." Cold steel surrounds his statement.

All interest bleeds from her face, eyes narrowing as she scoffs, "And just who do you think you are?"

"One of the lame friends. Now get."

Tossing her hair, she's all poisonous confidence.

"You can't tell me to leave. You don't even work here."

Another voice calls from behind him, "Well, he might not be able to, but I sure as hell will. Christina, you take your mean spiteful self out of my store, and don't you bother coming back till you turn into a human and apologize to Kate."

Gram is standing behind Rob, her purse still hanging on her arm. She must have walked in during the middle of this shit show.

Melody and Christina practically run out of the shop when faced with Gram. The bell slaps against the wood before the sound dies down and I drag air in, trying to calm down.

"What was that all about?" Gram's tone is matter-of-fact.

"Christina being as mean as ever. Nothing to worry about."

The narrow-eyed stare Rob levels at me calls me on my bullshit, and Gram sees it.

"Arik, I presume?"

I nod because I can't talk. There are so many emotions clogging my throat that I won't be able to speak around them without crying. Luckily, Rob does it for me.

"Apparently, he kissed that thing a couple of weeks ago.

She was showing Kate a picture of it. I didn't get a good look at it though."

"What? No, I don't believe that. Arik wouldn't kiss her if she were the last working vagina in all the land." Disbelief is evident in both her tone and expression. Gram's gaze locks on me, and I can't hide from her. I can't hide the trembling lower lip, the clench in my jaw, all of the hurt visible.

Just like last time.

Sternly, she says, "Kate Belle Palicki. What color is your hair?"

I snort out a laugh. How is it possible to even laugh right now?

When I was younger and getting a hard time from the kids in school, Gram would remind me I'm a redhead and I didn't take shit from anyone. Even if the lesson never stuck, she'd periodically ask me what color my hair was to remind me.

I clear my throat and croak out, "Red."

Sagely nodding, she says, "Then don't you take shit from anyone. Time to pull up your big girl panties and go talk to Arik. Figure out what happened and get to the bottom of this. I'll handle stuff here for a bit."

Rob adds darkly, "And if it's true, you tell me and I'll fucking murder the bastard. No one will find the body."

On the drive over, I get pissed. Like shake the core of the planet pissed. How could Arik not tell me, not explain. Hasn't he learned anything? Keeping things from me does nothing for us.

Do I mean so little to him? Was all his talk about having faith—of trying—a joke? A way to get back at me for leaving, for never responding to his letters?

Arik's never been that kind of person, but now I'm not so sure.

ARIK

Tossing the last of my camping gear into the back of the Jeep, I slam it shut. It's my turn to tuck tail and run.

Having my feelings not be returned I could handle, but having them wholly ignored and stomped on, I can't. I've been dropping hints for the last few weeks that I don't want this to end, the subject now something that I'm tired of tiptoeing around.

What do I have to do? Spell it out for her?

The finality in her voice when she talked about going back to Arizona told me that it was a lost cause and time to end things.

It's the only way to protect myself from further heartbreak.

The only point Kate and I ever agreed on is we would both try, but I'm all tried out at this point. I can't avoid the subject of her leaving anymore. I'm done waiting for her to be ready to talk about it, and sitting next to her on that damned couch, the reality of the situation slapped me in the face.

The only difference between the past and now?

Now I read the signs better.

Better for me to get my head on straight before I talk to Kate.

I'm locking the front door when I hear a car pull down the drive. Anxiety floods me when I see Hedy's SUV pull in, blocking my Jeep.

Hardening my heart, I finish locking up the house and pocket my keys. I shove my fists into my pockets, hoping the physical barrier will stop me from grabbing her and begging her to love me back.

Kate shoves out of the car and we both speak at the same time.

"We need to fucking talk."

"Hey, I'm about to take off, what's up?"

Dark sunglasses obscure her face, and for a second I wish I could see her eyes but then dismiss the thought. I don't want to witness what she's feeling, especially with what I'm about to do. Right about now I wish she had never come back to Felt.

Her statement registers, and of course she wants to talk. Well I don't. I won't keep playing this game of merry-go-round with her. I'm done with all of it.

I don't get the chance to speak again before she does.

"What's up? You're asking me what's up after blowing me off for a week?"

Guess that whiskey in my bag is going to be more for erasing memories than helping me get my head straightened out.

This is gonna fucking hurt.

Brick by brick I build my argument, defense, and façade before I speak.

"I wasn't blowing you off, I've been busy. I go back to work on Monday and have a lot on my plate." I brace myself. "Which is why it's probably better if we end things now."

Face unreadable, she stares at me, the angry flush across her cheeks the only giveaway to her mood. Years seem to pass before she speaks.

"You want to end things?"

"Yeah, with you going back to Arizona soon and the school year starting, it's probably a good idea to call it now. It's been fun and all, but I've got a lot to get done before classes resume. Though you're welcome at the End of Summer Pep Rally. Principal Phillips still wants to thank Readers' Haven for the donation, but you could probably get Hedy to handle that."

"So that's it, then. It's been fun and what's done is done."

Hating the flatness in her tone, I steel myself against it.

Just get through this and then whiskey. So much whiskey.

Bumping up the warmth in my tone, this is my last-ditch effort to get her out of here. "Yep, sounds about right. It was a great summer, and I hope we can still be friends, maybe hang out when you come visit Hedy."

Being one of the few people that has witnessed Kate's temper go thermonuclear, I can see we're moving into the danger zone by the subtle thinning of her lips and the way her jaw tightens down.

The flatness from earlier? That's gone now, as her voice cracks like a fiery whip when she bites out, "Friends? You want to be friends when you can't even be honest with me?"

There's a roaring in my ears. Kate's voice is barely audible over it. My focus, my mission is to get her out of here. If I'm making myself the bad guy, so be it. It'll keep her from knowing what I'm thinking, what I'm feeling. All of it for her own good.

I flash her a smile and hate myself a little more for the fakeness of it all.

"I am being honest. I'm busy, you're leaving. There ain't anything more to it than that, sugar."

Ignoring the nickname, her tone is quiet as she replies almost cordially, "No, Arik? There's no other possible reason you could be calling it off?"

Unable to do *this* a second longer, I say, "None that come to mind, now if you—"

I don't get to finish my sentence before Kate is yelling, "How about the fact you kissed Christina, you jackass. How about that for one of your reasons?"

Oh shit.

I don't wipe the guilt from my face fast enough before a startled gasp comes from her as she takes two steps back, her arms coming up to wrap around her middle as if physically wounded.

"Oh my God, it's true. You kissed Christina."

Immediate denial springs out of my mouth. "Of course I didn't, Kate." I've never been able to see her hurt without trying to fix it, and no matter how hard I'm fighting to get through this, to get it done, old habits die hard.

Shaking her head at me, she doesn't believe me, not that I blame her. I watch as she backs up farther and farther, both physically and emotionally.

"I asked you. I asked you that day at the lake if there was anything else you were keeping from me. You lied. You lied straight to my face." Quieter, she continues, "I should have known. I should have trusted my instincts."

"What should you have known?"

"I should have known this was too good to be true. That you were keeping secrets. I should have protected myself, because even now, just like in high school, it was all Christina."

Two tracks of tears fall below the darkened lenses of her glasses, and the roaring gets louder. "I didn't kiss her, Kate, she kissed me." As soon as the words are out of my mouth, I wish I could swallow them back down.

Kate finds her anger again, and I try to drown out the words, words I don't want to cut me deep, all of these stupid words. Her fisted hands drop down to her sides.

"She kissed you? That's all you have to say to me? How about, 'She kissed me, and *I didn't bother telling you about it*'? How about that, Arik? How about 'she kissed me, and I talked you into my bed the next night with bullshit words of being together'? How about how I should have faith everything would work out? How about that?"

Each question is a sharp slice to my vital organs, but I force myself to continue, to play the angle I have, to finish this before I disappear into the woods and drink myself blind, deaf, and dumb.

"Why would I tell you? You were never planning on staying. You never once thought about us past you leaving for your beloved Arizona."

"Oh no, you don't get to put this back on me, Arik. You deliberately withheld this from me before weaseling your way into my pants. To charm the pants off me quite literally and get the notch on your bedpost you missed all those years ago. Well I sure hope you fucking enjoyed yourself. I would never have expected this from you, so bravo, Arik. You have the whole world fooled into thinking you're this amazing guy. Too bad for me I fell for it, huh?"

As she rails at me, my heart rate beats furiously, the roaring louder and louder until her voice becomes muffled as if coming through a tunnel. Each breath is like a sharp staccato of glass shards against my ribcage. My head is spinning, and I can't keep up.

How did we get here?

How could it be so promising and then end like this?

She turns to leave, but twists around before reaching the vehicle, firing a parting shot I'm barely cognizant of.

"Who's to say I wouldn't have stayed? Did you think

ALINA LANE

about that before you gave up on the *faith* you preached? Before you decided to use me and play with me and my emotions. Did you think of that before you chose to keep your secrets? For what it's worth, I hope you and Christina are"—her voice breaks before she slips the final nail in the coffin—"very happy together."

I don't try to stop her as she climbs into the car, my head foggy as I try to piece together everything that's happened since June into some sort of sense. Of how we got here. I stare forever at the retreating vehicle until both it and the dust plume following it disappear like the hope I held on to for so long.

Something wet hits my arm, and I look up at the sky. I wouldn't be surprised to find black clouds and rolling thunder with pestilence and frogs raining down from above. I'm confused when all I see are white fluffy clouds scattered around blue skies. It's only then I realize it's not rain hitting my arm. No, not rain at all. Just my tears.

Not long after, I head out. Not to the lake—there are too many Kate memories there—but to a small spot I found a year or so after she left the first time. Situated right at the base of a jagged rocky incline, the area is naturally devoid of trees for about twenty feet across on all sides. It's far enough back off the ranger trail that I could camp out here for weeks with no one the wiser.

Setting up my camp takes me no time at all, and as the sun starts to fade across the sky, I'm almost through my first bottle of whiskey.

Kate leaving is for the best. She wouldn't have been happy here, and I'm not sure I could have been happy anywhere other than Felt. The hurt at having her even for a short season will eventually fade, and luckily, other than teaching I don't have anything else going on in my life. As long as I do right by my students, who cares if I get skunk drunk every night.

There are so many new memories of Kate, so many fresh and inviting, it wouldn't have mattered if I had gone to the lake or not, because even now, she's everywhere.

My mind decides right now would be a great time to play through the greatest hits of Kate memories. The gasping laugh she can't contain when I tickle that spot on her ribs. The way her hair spread across my pillow and got every-fucking-where. Tucking her in my arms at night, burying my face against her neck, and breathing in her honeyed scent as we drift off together. Waking up next to her to watch the sunlight dance across her freckles. The fire in her eyes when she's challenged, her temper when riled. There are so many things I love about Kate. Things I'll always treasure. Things I don't get to have.

It's useless to think about this shit that twists me into knots, mostly when I did everything I could to kill *us*.

Hell, I'd be surprised if Kate's still in Felt by the time I head back. She's never had a problem with leaving before, and if her sporadic visits over the years are anything to go from, I doubt I'll see her around town.

Probably time to start distancing myself from Hedy and Readers' Haven too. If I have to, I'll let Hedy buy me out so it doesn't get sticky between us. She's good friends with my ma, so I need to keep the break there as clean as possible. Distancing myself from Hedy means distance from Ben, and that's another cut into the sucking wound.

Ben, who's more like a father to me than the pissant who bailed on Ma. He tutored me all through college, taking up the torch Kate left behind so I didn't fail. From walking me through the process to get my teaching certifications to me taking over his position at the school after he retired, Ben's been a large part of my life for a long time.

The more I think about what I'm losing, the more I drink. The more I drink the more I rationalize that breaking things off before they went too far was the best possible outcome. I did it for Kate's well-being. My decisions weren't selfish and self-serving—I was just protecting myself from inevitable heartbreak. Pouring whiskey down my throat makes it easy to vow off love entirely. Sticking to one-night stands with tourists—it works for Jackson—seems like a fine idea to protect my heart, because feeling like this fucking sucks.

The whiskey trying to leave my body has me lumbering my way out of my chair. Stability proves to be troublesome, especially since the fire died down and I can't see two feet in front of me. Shuffling around the camp, I knock shit over left and right. The first bottle of whiskey made me unsteady, the second is insurance I'll wake up hating myself tomorrow.

If there were a way to obliterate my memory from June forward, I would without hesitation.

Unbuttoning my pants takes a couple of tries, my fingers clumsy and thick as I lean against a tree. I manage to get the job done, and as I'm emptying my bladder, which is probably ninety percent alcohol at this point, I think about Kate's parting shot. The last twist to the knife I stabbed into my soul.

"Who's to say I wouldn't have stayed? Did you think about that before you gave up on the faith you preached? Before you decided to use me and play with me and my emotions. Did you think of that before you chose to keep your secrets?"

There's something about what she said that has goose-bumps prickling on my arms, but I'm too drunk to possibly interpret it now.

Before I can dig deeper at her words, the ground rushes up and everything goes black.

KATE

Those times you get undeniable proof that you've been an idiot? Those times suck.

Crying into your best friend's shoulder the night before an important event you planned, implemented, and are in the middle of orchestrating is even worse.

Still, I take comfort I have Liv here. This would be so much worse if she were back in Arizona. No stranger to heartache—though hers was vastly worse than mine—she sits with me quietly. Probably to make up for Rob pacing the floor with promises of various methods of torture and pain against Arik as soon as he finds him.

Rob took one look at my face when I walked through the door of Readers' Haven and called Liv while Gram flipped the closed sign and sent Kelly home for the day.

Somehow, I found myself shuffled into a car, Gram thrusting a bottle of emergency wine at Rob, and driven to their Airbnb.

Leaning my head back against the couch, the throb that comes from nonstop tears bangs like a drum against my skull.

Wiping my eyes again, I take a sip of wine. I would give my left ovary for a carton of ice cream right now. Emotional eating and I go together like heartbreak and misery.

"Ready to tell me what happened? I got the backstory of the nasty bitch from Rob, but what happened after that?"

Reliving it is something I'm not interested in, but Liv's a big fan of talking shit through, so I humor her.

"Christina showed me the picture, and sure, it was pretty clear, but I built it up in my head that it was a misunderstanding. When I got to his house, Arik was locking up and leaving. I'm not sure if she warned him to give him a head start, but anyway, he was on his way out of town."

Blowing out a breath, I gulp at my wine. Yeah, alcohol isn't the answer, but it's giving me the courage to get through this.

"Anyway, as soon as I get out of the car, he's trying to give me the brush-off."

Tears continue to drip down my face, so I grab another tissue before continuing. "I give him the 'what for,' and he says how it's been fun, but we might as well call it. That with me going back to Arizona and him going back to work, it's *easier* if we end it now."

Liv's arm runs up and down my back, soothing and calm, while I'm hiccup-sobbing everywhere, and Rob is about to run a hole through the carpet. "What did he say about the kiss?"

I don't want to tell her, because it still fucking hurts.

I suck in a shuddering breath before launching into the explanation of what he said, how he looked, and how his reaction was different than the Arik I've come to know and love again. I tell her about him trying to turn it around on me and me not staying.

Gently, she asks the question I assumed I would have

gotten from Arik before things went sideways and upside down.

"Were you thinking about staying?"

If someone had asked me six weeks ago if I was planning on moving back to Felt, I would have responded with a "hell no." I like my life in Arizona. I like my job, my hobbies, and my friends. Coming back to Felt was supposed to be a temporary inconvenience, but it turned into so much more. What doesn't make sense to me is that Arik tried so hard for me to see the potential between us, to see that we could be something. He convinced me it was okay to take the plunge, to try with no pressure, no strings. Then out of nowhere, it's all, "thanks for the hot fuck, have a nice life." None of it makes sense.

Realizing I haven't replied to Liv, I say, "I guess it goes back to not having your cake and eating it too, because if I could have found a way to make it all work, I would have *tried*."

Oh, how I hate that fucking word now.

"I would never want you to stay in Arizona if you're happy here, and we could figure out the working remotely more efficiently. I want you to be happy, and while I would miss you, I wouldn't stop you from moving where you'd be happiest."

"Guess it's a good thing we don't have to figure it out then, huh?" Self-deprecation is one of my many and varied talents, included amongst my inability to trust, lack of self-confidence, and absolute shit taste in men.

Those are all fixable. No dating, no relationships, and never falling in love again pretty much takes care of the last three.

It hurts so fucking bad, and if swearing off relationships avoids this kind of pain in the future, I'm a fucking fan of it.

Guzzling the remainder of the wine in my glass, I reach

for the bottle to refill when there's a knock at the door. Liv looks at Rob and me quizzically before Rob heads to open it.

I'm not expecting to see Ben on the other side, but then it clicks that Gram must have told him what happened.

Ben and Arik are close, they have a history, and I love him for how he is with Gram, but if he's here to defend that bastard I'll slam the door in his face.

Rob backs up and Ben comes in, sitting next to me on the couch. Taking my hand, he just holds it, in his silent comforting way.

Not ready for more ugly crying, I lean my head against his shoulder and focus on breathing, on getting through tonight and tomorrow. After that I'll take it a day at a time until I no longer feel like a part of me is splintered and broken.

"Katie,"—even the normal nickname friends and family use hurts because I hear Arik's voice every time someone uses it—"there's something you need to see, sweet pea. Will you let me show you?"

"What is it?" I don't want to get up. I don't want to move. I want to drink more wine and wallow in the puddle of my tears and self-pity.

"It's something you've likely needed to see for a long time. Come on now, up ya get."

Ben stands and with his hand still holding mine hoists me off the couch. Still unsure if I should follow him, I look over at Liv and Rob who both give me encouraging nods.

Liv says, "Could it get any worse?"

She has a point.

The car ride isn't as silent as I thought it would be.

Clearing his throat, Ben asks, "Did you know I tutored Arik through college?"

Is it rude to tell your grandmother's first boyfriend and

first relationship in nearly three decades to fuck off? Asking for a friend.

Ben continues, not caring if I want to hear this, and I turn to the window, unable to tune him out.

"It was his first summer back from Boise State, and Meg was worried about him. He wouldn't talk to her about anything—coursework, classes, grades—he clammed up tight. She assumed it was because he was still sore over you, and part of it likely was. Meg asked me to step in and I did. He and I spent a lot of time talking while fishing one day. I came to find out he was struggling hard but trying. He barely made it through that first year by the skin of his teeth. I offered to help him, and through tutoring him on video calls, over email, and long weekends where I drove up there before exams, I came to love him. He's a son to me. I never had kids, so saying that means something to me. Been stuck on Hedy most of my life, so I can understand how Arik feels."

Ben stuck on Gram is something I want to hear about, but when I'm sober. I shrug my shoulder instead of responding.

He continues his story, telling me about how Arik got his teaching certifications, how he took over Ben's position at the school, how he set up a tutoring program. How everything Arik touches turns to fucking gold until I want out of this car.

"Ben, why are you telling me this? I didn't break it off. Arik did."

"Hmm."

Recognizing the road we turn down, I almost jump out of a moving car.

"He's not there, so you can turn this car right back around."

"I'm aware he's not here, Kate. He'd skin me if he knew what I was about to do."

I'm so confused. If Ben's like his dad, why are we even here? Shouldn't he be consoling Arik or some such bullshit?

There's a green SUV sitting in the driveway, and all I can do is groan.

Standing on the porch, still in his uniform, Jackson is waiting for us. Ben pulls up and parks. I don't want to get out of this car. I'm going to sit right here and out-stubborn two men until we turn around and Ben returns me to Olivia's. Or Gram's. I don't care where the bed is, I only want sleep.

"I know how you feel right now."

Rolling my eyes, I don't quite bite back the scoff.

"Huff and puff all you want, missy, but I do know how you feel. I'm going to tell you a story. It's not pretty, but it has a mostly happy ending. You hear me out and after I'm done, you still want to go home? I'll turn around and we won't ever talk about this again."

I perk up a bit at that. "One story, then you'll take me home?"

"If that's what you want."

"Okay."

"Once upon a time, there was a strapping young man that worked at the lumber yard outside of Jackson Hole. He was best friends with a scrawny nerdy kid, who was more interested in books than anything else. One day, the two best friends decided to go for a drive and found themselves in Felt, Idaho. Now a lot of this wasn't around back then, but the Buffalo Diner was. At the time it was called The Teton. Stopping for a drink before we gassed up and headed out, who should we find except the most beautiful redhead working behind the counter."

I'm familiar with the start of this story. Gram worked at the diner for the summers to earn money through high school before her daddy died and she took over the farm. I didn't know that's where she met Ben though.

"Naturally, we were friendly enough and she pointed out some of the local attractions for us to go see, but I was a goner from the first second. We didn't stick around too long after that, having to get on our way and all. But I made it a point to stop in Felt every Friday afternoon during the summer. Greg…"

I gasp, some of the dots starting to click, but Ben stops me with a pat on my leg.

"Yup, that strapping young man was my best friend and your grandaddy. Now, where was I? Oh yeah, so Greg would sometimes accompany me, and other times he would have to work. I liked the visits he had to work the best, though I'll lie if you ever tell anyone.

"Hedy and I became friends, though I hoped, wished, and prayed for more. What was a stunning woman like that going to ever see in the shy, geeky, nerd like me? That label wasn't as cool back then as it is now, I'll have you know.

"You look so much like her, sometimes I look at you and I see her, standing behind that counter pouring pops. Does my heart good.

"Hedy and I got close. Her daddy died right around the time she was running The Teton, trying to work the farm and help her mama. God, but her mama was plain helpless. Hedy ended up quitting her job to take care of her mama and the farm, though her mama passed away shortly after that. So, one fine September day I drove into town, making my usual stop only to find out Hedy no longer worked there, and after I drove to Hedy's place, I was surprised to find Greg, working the land with Hedy. I remember that day like it was yesterday. Her head was tipped back as she was laughing at something Greg was saying before he kissed her.

"Broke my damn heart to pieces. Later it'd come out that Greg had the same thoughts I did. He had been visiting her without me around. Not because they wanted to go behind my back, but because they fell in love with each other."

"What'd you do?"

A mirthless chuckle leaves his mouth. "I got pissed. I was so mad at the both of them thinking that they'd kept this from me, that they kept it a secret to make me look like a fool. I had it out right there with Greg, punched him square in the jaw." Ben chuckles lightly before continuing. "Though I imagine I did more damage to my hand than his face. Once I calmed down enough to look past the assumed betrayal, I saw Hedy crying. She was worried she and Greg would lose their best friend over something neither of them could help. I was sore for a while, but the longer I stayed away the more I missed them both.

"Eventually, I got over the hurt and started coming around again. The thing is Hedy hadn't promised me anything. We didn't have that kind of relationship, not like she and Greg did. They both bounced happiness and love off each other anytime you were within two feet of them. Greg proposed and I stood up for both of them at the wedding. I'm godfather to your mama in fact, something I don't think your Gram ever told you.

"Even though my love for Hedy never went away, I focused on her happiness, having love and being secure. When Greg died, after most of the grief passed, I thought that it was my time, that she would see me. But she didn't. She was focused on you, on making Readers' Haven work, and juggling other responsibilities. So again, I waited. I waited another twenty years for her to be ready, to recognize that we could have something, and I don't regret it."

The tears that track down my cheeks aren't from my heartbreak anymore. I had no idea Gram and Ben had such a complicated lovely story. I remember Ben being around a little bit when I was younger, but not very often.

"Why are you telling me this?"

"Two reasons—the first being I know how you feel, being the one picked on, the one no one liked. I know what it's like to have a best friend and then something happens to shatter that bond and the pain is so bright you have to get away from it. I understand thinking it'll never be your turn. But secondly, I also understand what it's like to put my wants and needs aside for someone I love. I think if we really, truly love someone, there isn't much we wouldn't do to preserve their happiness."

"What does that have to do with us being here though? Arik never thought of me like you do Gram. No one's ever thought about me like that."

"Hmmm. I imagine if you think about it for a bit, it'll come to you. Now Kate, I'm a man of my word. I'll take you home if you want, but I believe there's something in that house you need to see." Holding his hand out to me, he asks, "Trust me?"

I do want answers, but going into that house has the potential to break me completely. It feels so much like home. I saw myself fitting into that house, tucking myself in with the man who built it before that short-lived dream got yanked out from under me.

As if summoned from the recesses of my memory, Arik's voice rings through my head, and though it hurts, I listen.

Be brave, Katie. Take a chance.

I slip my hand into Ben's, he squeezes mine before letting go, and we climb out of the car.

KATE

As we climb up the steps to the porch, Jackson opens his mouth to say something, but Ben shakes his head, and the words die.

Apparently Jackson rates a key to the place because he unlocks the door, and we shove into the dark foyer. Flipping on a couple of lights, he leads the way back to Arik's room. We all pause at the closed door.

I don't want to go in there.

"I don't think we should do this. If he wanted her aware of them, he would have shown them to her himself," Jackson whispers to Ben.

"This here is one of the cases where we're acting in his best interest even if it goes against what he wants. Let's just get it done."

That doesn't sound ominous or anything.

Exhaling in a huff, Jackson shoves the door open and pushes inside. Ben follows, and after mentally pulling my big girl boots on, I inch in.

It looks the same as the first day I was in here—bed made,

the door to the bathroom slightly open, loose change on the dresser.

Then I notice it. The wall across from Arik's bed is empty. Unimaginable pain rips through me.

Gram gave it to me right after you left. I had it made into a canvas.

Then the next time I looked at it, lying in Arik's bed after the first time we made love.

"Remember what?"

"A time when we were only each other's. When you were mine and I was yours without the complications life brings."

I'm so confused. How could Arik say something like that to me when the night before he was kissing Christina in a bar? How could he say wonderful heartfelt things when he didn't mean any of them? Why would he take down the portrait of us? Was it all a lie?

Jackson sees where my gaze is locked, though there isn't much light in the room.

"It's not what you think. First, you're going to look at something, and then we'll talk, but you'll want to brace yourself."

Having someone who faces down wildlife more terrifying than heartbreak every day telling me to brace myself isn't a good sign. It's not until I see Ben shoving an old box back to the top of the closet and what's in his hand that I start to freak out.

"No."

"Kate, if I told you that these letters are important to your happiness, that you should read these, not for Arik but for yourself, would you believe me?" Ben's question takes me off guard.

"I'm feeling like I can't believe a whole lot going on right now."

The small smile that tugs his lips is both commiserating and humored. "I can imagine how that feels, so I won't tell you that you need to read them, but I will say you could save yourself some trouble guessing at the whys if you just look at them."

Damn him, but I do want answers. None of it adds up, not a single second from the bookstore to me confronting Arik earlier. If my so-called answers are in letters written twelve years ago, then I'm a monkey's uncle, but I'll still give it a shot.

My hand trembles as I reach out to take the letters from Ben.

"I'd appreciate some privacy."

Leaving quietly, they're both somber. I plop down on the bed and flick on the bedside table lamp.

These letters feel like a bomb I defused by returning them all those years ago.

Pulling the top one open, I unfold the paper. Arik's shaky handwriting stares up at me from the page.

"Kate,

I hope you're well. You should be headed into your end of year exams and I hope you do well. I don't know a lot about what major you decided on, but I hope it makes you happy. This is going to be the last letter I write to you, unless I hear from you. I'm still not clear on exactly what happened the night of prom, but I have a pretty good guess.

I never meant to hurt you. Nothing you saw was accurate that night. For that I'm sorry.

This letter is really to tell you all the things I was afraid of telling you then. All the things I held back because I didn't want to pressure you or hurt you in any way.

You're the best person I know. I'll cherish my memories of us always. You are and will always be the most beautiful woman to me, both inside and out.

Kate, most of all, I want to tell you I love you. That's always been something we say to each other in the spirit of loving each other as friends, but it turned on me. Where? I have no idea. But it did. Somewhere along the line my feelings shifted from friendly affection to something so much deeper, more abiding. You likely don't or won't ever return those feelings and I..."

Choking on a sob, I have to stop. My breathing is fast—way too fast. I'm seconds away from hyperventilating my way into a panic attack. Slow steady breaths help to rein it in as I count backward from ten. When I get back under control I read some more.

"I'm sorry about it because you'll likely never read this letter. But I needed you to know I love you, am in love with you, probably have always loved you. If there's one thing I could wish for, it would be a chance to say those words to your face.

I had so many promises I wanted to make to you, so many plans for us, but those shifted to where we are now. The love I have for you? That love doesn't die. It waits quietly and patiently to be reclaimed. The hope that I'll have another chance has slowly died over the last several months, but I'm holding on to it.

I wish the best things for you. If you ever need me, I'll be there. If you decide to come home for summer break and want to talk, I'll be here.

Loving you always,

Your Arik

I don't try to hold in my ragged weeping. There's no use.

Like prom, I assumed Arik purposefully hurt me, that he was using me for amusement or some other sick reason, and like prom I jumped to conclusions and believed the worst about him. I ranted and yelled at him, ignoring the despair that peeked through at moments when he wasn't wearing that charming sleazy disinterest.

Like prom, I refused to hear his whole side of the story and I hate myself for it. All of this, every single minute of misery over the last twelve years between us is my fault. All the hoops I made him jump through, the moments of suspicion and doubt, he painstakingly took those walls down brick by brick for me to only throw them up again at the first hint of potential trouble. I pushed him away until he broke things off in the worst way to protect me from the brunt of heartbreak. He's playing the bad guy and letting me go.

I don't deserve him. I haven't earned him. But damned if I'll let him go.

I set the bundle on the nightstand. I want to read more, but I need details first.

Pushing the bedroom door open and heading out to the living room, I find Ben and Jackson watching ESPN.

Men.

They both stand up as soon as I come in. The first thing I do is walk up to Ben and wrap my arms around him, because I don't deserve him either.

Not only did he see what was going on, he's going against what Arik would want to make it right. I'll never forget that, and I vow to do everything possible for him and Gram.

"Tell me about Christina at O'Malley's."

Blowing out a breath, Jackson runs his hands through his hair. "Well shit, okay, sit down. You look really pale, Kate. Do you want some water?"

"I'll get it." Ben's hands brush along my shoulders as he heads for the kitchen.

"Thanks, Ben." Jackson focuses back on me and slumps onto the couch. I curl up in the opposite corner. "Arik and I met up for a beer at O'Malley's on karaoke night after the council meeting. We made a stupid bet which I lost because you're stubborn. Anyway, I had to sing a song. I didn't see all of it, but Christina was there. She was drunk and hanging around a bunch of tourists. Then she roped Arik into a dance."

Ben walks back into the room, uncapping a bottle of

water for me and urging me to drink, so it takes a second for me to get what he said.

"Son of a—" My temper flares, but Jackson cuts it off.

"A dance he wasn't interested in. He wanted none of it, okay? He was trying to avoid a scene. So then after the song, Christina stumbled and Arik tried to catch her, and she got the perfect angle to plant one on him."

"I'll plant one on the…Wait a second. How the hell did she get a picture if she was wrapped around him?"

I didn't notice it right off the bat, but the more I remember the picture, her arms *were* wrapped around his neck, *both* of her arms.

"Melody probably took it. Cheryl came up and she and Christina got into it and she got fired. We left pretty quick after that. He wasn't trying to hide it from you, Kate. Your relationship was still new, and Arik was aware of how you feel about being the center of gossip or attention. Considering what prompted you bailing before, he wanted to let it die down before telling you, I'm sure of it. Should he have told you? Yeah, probably, but I understand his reasons for not telling you."

"Typical guy response there, Jackson."

"It's what I am, and the only point of view I got. I'm only saying there's more to this than meets the eye."

Christ on a cracker, this got messed up so fast.

I don't know how to fix this, only that I will, but first I need some sleep. Wine, multiple crying jags, and very little food have me exhausted and rundown.

Ben helps me off the couch. "Let's get you home and tucked in. You have the signing tomorrow. We'll figure out what to do after that."

He's right, but that doesn't make it easier to swallow. I have a commitment to Readers' Haven and all those authors.

Before we leave, I run back to grab the letters. Technically they're not mine, but I'm taking them anyway.

The drive home is silent. I clutch the letters to my chest while climbing the stairs and falling into bed. I don't have the chance to read any of them before I tumble into an exhausted sleep.

The signing is madness. There are bodies everywhere, with a line that wraps clear down Main Street. I have to run for more pens, more water, more snacks, lunch for the writers, more everything.

The day flies by in a blur, but I focus in long enough to catch the highlights. There's the couple who flew in to meet Breanna and Claire after devouring their collab from last year. A group of television executives interested in buying the rights to Stella's dragons for a BBC series. The local teenagers who lost their minds over Fancy's announcement of a new romantic series surrounding a ballet company's drama. Olivia almost beaning Jackson with a hardback when he strode in, royal-blue mini dress riding indecently up his hairy thighs. Her catching him naked in the stock room. Him staring at her like a starving man looking at a steak for ninety percent of the evening.

When I tried to pump Liv for details, anything to distract me from the misery that is my life, I got a blush in response. When I asked him? I got a cocky smirk.

Definitely something there, but I can't pry it out of either of them right now.

That's okay, I'll bide my time and catch them when they least expect it later.

By six, my feet feel like boiled sausages in my shoes. I've walked, jogged, shuffled, stomped, and paced over ten miles today easily. As I flip the closed sign, there is a collective sigh of relief behind me from my exhausted authors. Not only has it been a fabulously busy day with a turnout beyond our wildest dreams, but peopling for hours on end has drained all of us.

At least Norma Marie didn't joke about stabbing someone.

She has a weird sense of humor like that.

Staying busy kept my mind off Arik, but now that I'm sitting and don't have anything left to do, he creeps back in.

Robyn Elyse, affectionately nicknamed Pinup for her love of all things vintage, plops down next to me on the couch saying, "Perk up buttercup or your face'll stick like that. What's eatin' you? We just had a hell of a day."

That immediately gets the attention of all the other authors, and they zero in on me. Rehashing this again doesn't sound like fun, but I trust these ladies and we've grown close over the years of working together, so I summarize what's happened and end with, "Now I don't know what to do."

Tara Carr is the first to speak after I finish.

"That Christina is a flaming piece of shit."

"*Right?*" Robyn treats us all to a southern twang version of the word.

"I'm gonna shank that bitch in my next book," Norma chimes in, and I knew we would hear something stabby from her eventually, but it still makes me laugh.

Soon enough everyone is talking. Tamara is creating alibis for each of us and announces she needs a shot of Jack to deal with this. Iannah provides critical information on how to hide a body and submits that the ocean is the best dumping ground. Stella offers to hex Christina to a decaf existence.

I barely catch it, but Iannah is murmuring, "Fuckity fuck fuck. I just can't."

Hattie, one of the quieter ones of the bunch but willing to crack up and let loose with the rest of us, asks, "What do you want, Kate?"

I say the first thing that comes to mind. "I want Arik. I

want him to stop hiding things from me, to stop trying to protect me—I just want him."

"Are we talking HFN or HEA here, hun?" Fancy's question comes ringing from the back of the room.

"Ever. I want the Ever After."

Claire's voice rings loud and clear over everyone else. "Fuck me running, ladies. We got a woman in love, mid black moment. Let's get to work."

Breanna cries, "What trope?"

"Second chance." That comes from Olivia.

"Who's the asshole?" Norma calls out.

The shop door jingles open.

I answer that one. "Both of us. Me first, then him."

Stella has to stand on a chair to be heard over the cacophony. "Black moment?"

Gram has returned after her midday break to rest her hip a bit. Ben follows her closely, holding her elbow as she takes in the chaos. There are various best-selling authors standing on chairs, rumpled and tired from a full day of mingling with fans. Women who are gearing up for war in the name of love. Gram cocks an eyebrow at me before saying, "Ended it *for her own good* mixed with a little *she's too blind to see what's in front of her.*"

The authors chatter behind me as I stare at her. I'm not surprised she knows, but I am shocked she isn't more upset with me, especially given her past with love.

Calling out loud enough to be heard over the din, Gram says, "I was hoping the burst pipe would have settled everything, but it looks like I'm getting involved again."

Ben's face splits in a sly grin as he helps her to a chair.

"What do you mean the burst pipe...get involved with what? What are you talking about?"

Gram's smirk says it all. Realization dawns, and I can't help but yell at her.

"You *planned* this whole thing?"

"I wouldn't say planned, but I did help the pipe along in the back. I tried to do something years ago, but Arik—that kindhearted fool—didn't want to worry you."

"How? Why? What even…" I can't form words.

Gram tugs at my hand until I sit on the arm of her chair. Ben's busy opening wine and pouring it into plastic cups as she starts to tell the story.

"I knew you and Arik were right for each other. I also knew you needed to grow a little, to come into your own. Taking a page from Ben, I waited. A couple of years back, I thought you might finally be ready. I let Arik find me upset over the store. I fibbed about it being in trouble, but instead of calling you like I wanted him to, the blasted man invested"—she puts the word invested in air quotes—"into the store. Messed my plans up good. I was about to take additional measures, but…" she trails off, her unspoken thoughts clear.

But Liv needed you.

"So again, I waited. A couple of months back, I started thinking it was time, so I started planning. I had my…accident, and I decided to capitalize on the timing. Ben called Arik when it happened, and Arik did what we assumed he would by calling you and voilà. You were home."

"But the tax accounting, the records, the filing. You can't fake those things."

"I didn't have to. Yes, Arik did all the accounting. He generated statements and forms for the store, but who taught him to do that?"

Ben.

"I never let him file anything on behalf of the bookstore. Fed him a bunch of bullhonkey about sticking to paper filing. When he dropped them off, I would shred them and then file the correct documents electronically with Ben's help."

Glancing at Ben, I see the sheepish smile he's sporting isn't guilt. It's pride. He's proud of their scheming.

Gram keeps talking about how she recruited Rob and Liv to drive up here early when Arik and I were taking our sweet time of things. Rob for the jealousy factor, Liv because she could nudge me along. How she reached out to Taylor, Liv, and then Ally when we rekindled our friendship to talk some sense into me over our girls' night chat. Showing me the letters, her idea. She tells me how she purposefully turned off the main water line over the winter, then back on causing the pipe to burst since it had frozen over. Gram had a hand in all of it.

"That's why I couldn't find an insurance statement or claim. You never filed one."

"They would have found I did the damage and that would have gotten sticky. So no, I did the bare-bones repairs and shut down the shop."

"And the website? The one with the store name that you knew nothing about that's 'down for maintenance'?"

"Guilty as charged. I had that website for years, damn near gave me a heart attack to unpublish it."

We're all silent, marveling at her genius. The juggling, maneuvering, and finessing she would have needed to do to get this off the ground is astonishing, but I still have questions.

"What would you have done if I didn't want to stay?"

"Honey,"—she takes my hands in hers and looks at me— "this was never about you staying. This was about you being *happy.* Would I love it if you moved home? Absolutely. But would I be okay if happiness meant you and Arik moved to Arizona? Of course."

"Did you know about the kiss?"

"I did. But I also knew that there was more to the story.

I've been silently willing him to talk to you about it, but the boneheaded man didn't."

"Why didn't you tell me?"

"As much as I would have loved you coming home and fixing things for yourself, you're just like me. Something has to smack you in the face before you realize it's there. Especially something as subtle as love." Ben comes up next to Gram and she takes his hands, looking at him.

The love on her face is so evident, so plain. I don't know how I missed it during all those video chats, all our talks of plans and of how my life was going. I've been so blind.

Tears burn my eyes. They're so frequent lately I barely notice them until Gram wipes a fallen one away. "You ready to get your man back?"

The authors cheer behind me, their catcalls and whoops deafening.

One small problem remains though.

"Uh, Gram, how exactly am I gonna do that?"

The mischievous glint in her eye has us all waiting, then to no one's surprise she says, "I have a plan."

ARIK

Waking up Sunday is about as much fun as Saturday. My head throbs horribly, my stomach pitches, and once again there's piss on me. I didn't learn my lesson, though, because I immediately reach for the open bottle of whiskey. Damn my metabolism, I'm no longer drunk. Just fuckin' hungover.

When I can't find the bottle, I'm more irritated than anything. The ache I've been working hard to drown is still there, still pounding away at the empty shell where my heart used to be.

Saturday morning, when I realized I wasn't going to be at the signing, to participate in it, I reached for the bottle. I kept reaching for the bottle until I vomited, then I reached for it some more. Today's my last chance to get a handle on the hollow feeling before I head back to school tomorrow.

Luckily, the End of Summer Pep Rally is handled by the athletic department because I am less than useless. I just have to show up.

Easy enough.

Sunlight beats through the top of the tent, mocking me in my pain and brooding, shining bright above the canopy of trees, and for a second I hate that too. I hate that the sun is shining when my whole life is likely going to be dark.

That last thought is a little more tortured than expected. I force myself to roll over, stomach sloshing and rolling. Breathing through clenched teeth, I wait for my stomach to calm. I really don't want to throw up again.

Making it to my hands and knees, I hunt for a bottle of water and some of the aspirin I packed.

When I can't find the water, I dry swallow four of the pills at once and wait impatiently for them to kick in.

Shoving out of the tent, I'm met with a face full of ice-cold water. Stunned, I tumble backward, my foot hooking on the lip of my tent, and I crash down.

Squinting against the sunlight, I see Jackson lowering the bucket, flanked by Connor, Ben, and Rob, all wearing severe frowns.

Jackson's the first to break the silence.

"Hey there, Arik, fancy finding you here. You fucking stink, man. Come on, get up now."

Connor comes over to help Jackson as they hook their arms under my pits. I'm dusting the seat of my pants off when a bare-knuckled punch slams into my face, sending me reeling again.

Cartoon birds are circling my head, and I lie back and pray I don't have a concussion. Once I'm convinced I don't, I prop myself up on my elbow.

"Anyone else gonna take a shot?" I don't blame Rob. I had it coming. If I had a sister and a douche did to her what I did to Kate, I'd punch him too.

Rob is shaking out his fist as he advances on me. Connor, who almost matches him for size, bumps him back. "Yeah, he's an idiot, but it's not his fault he was dropped on his head as a baby."

"I fucking warned him. He didn't have to deal with the

fallout of his little altruistic breakup. I did." Rob turns my way. "You hear that, dickfucker? You broke her fuckin' heart to pieces. Is that what you wanted?"

Being the bad guy and hearing about it are two completely different things. Still, the thought of Kate hurting, even by my actions and decision, stings like a motherfucker.

"No. I didn't want to hurt her. I didn't want her to have to make a decision she wasn't ready for, so I made it for both of us."

Rob sneers, "Yeah, and how's that going for you? You smell like piss and vomit. Your eyes are bloodshot to hell and back. If the empty whiskey bottles are anything to go off, you're hurting as much as her."

Connor chimes in, "I'm getting eau de depression. Anyone else smelling that?"

Jackson picks up the ball, saying, "Eh, for me it's more cologne de ass fungus."

Ben's been quiet through the whole tirade, the antics, and the punch. When I look at him, another arrow of hurt pierces my chest.

Fuck it, what's one more person I've disappointed?

And because I can't help myself, I ask, "How did the signing go?"

Ironically, it's Ben who replies, "Without a hitch. Katie did right by Readers' Haven."

"Is she still here?"

"Flew out before we woke up this morning. Left Hedy a note saying goodbye."

A fissure runs through my chest, cracking the cavity open and spewing poison through the rest of me while I bleed out.

Left behind again, forgotten again. It must be my lot in life. Yeah, I broke it off because I thought it would be best. I thought

Kate being back in Arizona was best for her—living her life, having her career and her friends. Tutoring dyslexic kids because she fucking gets them, she connects with them, and can draw them out of the invisible shell the disability puts them in.

What I didn't count on was how much being right would hurt. I don't feel vindicated. I ran her off, proving my theory that she wasn't in as deep as me. I'm not happy she's hundreds of miles away. More than anything I'm sad, lost, and confused.

There isn't enough alcohol in the world to erase this.

Once again, Jackson and Connor drag me to my feet. I watch Rob warily, but he doesn't move. He just stands there staring me down.

"How'd you guys find me?"

"The permit you grabbed out of my Jeep has a GPS tag on it. I'm always misplacing that damn thing."

Of course, it would be my luck. I run away only to be thwarted by Jackson's failsafe.

"It's getting late, boys. Let's pack this shit up and get home. Hedy wants you three over for dinner." Pointing to me, Ben says, "She's still sore with you, so I'd keep my distance for a bit."

I have no plans of going anywhere near Hedy. While Kate's tizzy is a flash burn thermonuclear blast, Hedy's is the atomic bomb mixed with a nuclear reactor explosion. Steering clear of her is the best solution for all parties.

It doesn't take us long to clear the campsite and clean up the mess two days of heartache caused. Ben takes my keys because I'm in no shape to drive. Connor, Jackson, and Rob trail us to drop me off, and then they'll take off.

The ride home is quiet. Ben lets me brood silently from the passenger seat until we pull onto the road leading to my house.

"Why, Arik? Why would you sabotage it and throw it all away?"

I'm ashamed of it but I tell him the truth anyway. "I was hurt. She was making plans *right in front of me* to leave. She didn't even look at me, Ben. I'm sitting there, planning on telling her I love her. Telling her I want to make a life with her. And she's making plans to leave—*again.* I twisted it around in my head to where I was doing what was best for her, what would make her happy. I hurt her for her own good. Those are lies though. I did it because I couldn't stand the thought of her breaking my heart, or her staying to make me happy and being miserable."

"You know the story between Hedy and me. You've seen first-hand that love requires patience. You let a single state-ment—heard with a hurt heart, insecurities, and doubt—rule your actions. Completely selfish actions. What about what Kate wants and needs? What about talking to her like an adult? Facing your fears together and coming out stronger—again together—for it. I'm not mad, Arik, but I sure am disappointed. Disappointed that two people who are more suited for each other than anyone else in a hundred-mile radius can't get out of their own way long enough to talk about the hard stuff, make compromises, and safeguard their love. I can be disappointed at that."

"I'd do it over if I could, but I can't. Kate's gone and I'm not likely to get a third chance from a Palicki woman."

We're pulling into my driveway when Ben offers one last parting piece of advice.

"You're right about that. But I will say if you're ever given a chance at love again, that you'll remember this feeling right here, right now, and do things differently."

I don't bother to respond. He of all people should know my love is tied up in a feisty redhead living in another state.

Once I'm in the house, other than showering off the hell

trip in the woods, I don't do shit except fall into bed and hide from the misery in sleep.

Monday morning comes bright and early. With my stomach still touchy from the vast amounts of alcohol I ingested over the weekend, I limit breakfast to coffee before I grab my files and head into the school. Both the campus and hallways are brimming with parents here for the open house and kids excited for the pep rally. Kids mill about thinking this year will be different. This year they're going to change, suddenly become more mature, more sophisticated.

I want to tell them to stay young and carefree as long as possible, because with age comes wisdom but also complications, loneliness, and regret.

I take myself and my rain cloud of pessimism into my classroom where there are tablets everywhere. A sticky note on my desk only says, "Setup instructions are in your email."

I didn't think Kate and Hedy were going to follow through with the donation. I prepared myself to come into school this morning to have my fundraising defeat thrown in my face.

I've just gotten them organized when I realize the rally is about to start. Principal Phillips disapproves of stragglers from the staff, so I double-time it down to the gymnasium.

The marching band is finishing up, and our single PE teacher and coach for about every sport we have is riling the students up, getting them pumped. The town residents are cheering right along with him, since ninety percent of Felt is here in the stands. I smell the popcorn and other goodies offered to students and parents.

We go through the normal announcements—tryouts for this and signups for that—then Principal Phillips comes out to take the microphone. The earsplitting screech has everyone wincing and groaning. I don't think there has ever been a successful microphone pass off in the history of academia.

"Sorry about that, y'all, one of these days we'll figure this out. I wanted to welcome everyone back to Open House and to the start of another successful year here at Felt High School. I have a couple of things to go over before I release you to meet your teachers this year."

John drones on and on about upcoming committee meetings and the various school extracurriculars students can engage in.

"Earlier this summer, we got the unexpected treat of one of your alumni coming back to Felt to help the family business get back up and running. During her time here, she found it in her heart to make a much-needed donation to our school. Kate Palicki, whom some of you know..." I tune him out as he runs through Katie's accomplishments and scan the crowd. Smiles are everywhere, aside from the sour look on Christina's face, but I ignore that.

"She couldn't be here today to accept our thanks, but her grandmother, Hedy, is. Let's give Hedy a Timberwolves welcome."

The crowd goes nuts. Gram is an institution in this town, and almost everyone knows her. Deciding to cut out early, I'm almost through the doors when the voice that haunts me rings out. I whip around so fast I tweak my neck. Unable to see through the crowd, I climb the side of the bleachers and hang off the rail to get a glimpse.

Kate's hair is a crazy mess tumbled around her shoulders, kinky curls flying in every direction. She has a bright smile in place, and her eyes are clear and mostly calm, though there's a slight tremble as she starts talking.

"Hey, everyone. Wow. Thank you so much. Now, I know what you're thinking. You're thinking she doesn't look like anyone's grandma. And I really hope I won't be one for a long time,"—the crowd chuckles at her joke—"but that's getting off-topic. Principal Phillips is right. We did donate the rest of the money for your new tablets, but we didn't do it for the recognition. We did it because every one of you deserves the best education possible."

She clears her throat before continuing. "I had a little bit of a hard time in school. I wasn't the bravest, the prettiest, or the most accomplished or popular. None of those things bothered me much, though. The only thing I regret was that I didn't dream more; I didn't wish for more."

I couldn't be prouder of her than I am now. Love floods out of me toward her, this woman I need.

"My best friend went to school here as well—kinda hard not to with a town this small—but not only did he go here, he came back to teach you all. He's also responsible for most of the funds being raised for those new tablets that we hope you'll use to learn, dream, and hope. Arik came back to help you with your education while living the example that things get hard, they get tough. But if you're patient enough, if you have enough faith, it'll all eventually make sense."

Her voice wavers, but she swallows hard and keeps going.

"Arik, you wrote me letters every day for months after I left as a result of what I mistakenly believed happened in this very gym. I didn't read them. I didn't want to remember you or the hurt. I didn't want to dream or reach for more, not when the fall crushed me. I recently got the chance to rectify that situation. In response I decided to write you a letter telling you all the things I couldn't say then."

A hush of anticipation hangs in the air. People who were hanging back by the sides of the bleachers push closer, eager to catch every word.

"Dear Arik, I hope this letter finds you well, though I doubt that to be the case with how we left things. I have so many things to say to you, but words aren't my strength, so I'll likely fumble my way through this."

I jump off the side of the bleachers and shove people out of my way, but for every person I move two more get in my path. Kate's voice rings out as I'm working through the crowd.

"First and foremost, I'm in awe of you. You're so inspiring to others. People that are like you and those that are different. Like you, I hold close all of the memories we share, good and bad, because they're the reason we are who we are today."

People clog the aisle, and I lose all my manners, skirting around them and bumping them out of the way as she continues.

"There are so many things I want to apologize for—being scared, doubting you, not trusting you, not talking to you. The list is endless. What I regret the most is not having faith in you, in us. But there is one thing I'm not sorry for. The one thing I won't apologize for and refuse to regret is loving you. You've had my love through all stages of my life. Like our connection, it changed and evolved. You've had my love through the happiness and heartache, through the sunshine and the rain."

The need to get to her, to put my hands on her, to tell her I love her, that I'll always love her, overwhelms my ability to breathe. I clear the heaviest part of the crowd as she starts to read the next part.

"You had my love yesterday, you have my love today, and you'll have my love tomorrow and every tomorrow after that. To steal your words, the love we have doesn't die, it waits patiently to be reclaimed. I'll wait—it might not be patiently because I'm only capable of so much—but it'll be here waiting for you. All of my love and loyal devotion for you. Yours, Kate."

I'm running as she finishes the letter, tucking the folded paper in her pocket and wiping at her eyes. When she looks up from her shoes, our eyes meet and then I'm wrapping her in my arms, sweeping her up while I kiss her.

I pour all my reverence, love, and desire for her into the kiss. Her arms are locked on my forearms, holding tight like she never wants to let go. The feeling is mutual.

The crowd cheers enthusiastically around us until the subtle clearing of a throat at my back intrudes, forcing me to break the kiss.

Staring into Kate's clear green eyes, I've never been happier in my life. I have so many questions, but Principal Phillips breaks the silence.

"Arik, why don't you skip today's open house. You and Ms. Palicki can find a quiet place *off campus* to talk."

Ignoring the screaming people behind us, I grip her hand and start to push through the crowd. Once we're outside, I whip her around and kiss her again. I'll never get enough of kissing this woman.

"I have so many questions I want to ask," I tell her, "but first I need to apologize. I'm sorry I let you think you weren't everything, that I let you think you don't mean everything to me."

Kate's shaking her head before I get through the first apology. "No, you don't have anything to be sorry for, other than lying to me. You were just trying to protect yourself, and so was I. I'm so sorry I didn't see through it; I didn't give you the benefit of the doubt. That I didn't talk to you about my feelings, about what I wanted. That any time you tried to bring up what would happen with us next, we avoided the subject. I almost let my blindness and anger ruin this—again. Just don't lie to me again. You can't protect me from all the hurts in life. You have to trust that I can handle it."

"I promise. I'll promise every day if I need to. I thought

you left. I'm so fucking sorry. Ben told me you left after the signing." I'm confused, and my mind is racing a mile a minute as we make our way to the Jeep. "What is this, Katie? I need you to spell it out for me. I need us to be on the same page."

Her laughter spills out, throaty and carefree. "Boy, do I have a story for you. But first, take me home, Arik. We have a picture to hang up."

"About that. I'm sorry I took it down. It just hurt to look…wait, what do you mean home? Does that mean…" I'm too terrified with hope to finish the sentence.

"That I'm moving back to Felt? Yeah, you see there's this giant Viking I'm pretty fucking crazy about, and luckily I have the most amazing boss—"

I cut her off, fastening my mouth to hers again, elation wiping out days of suffering.

Lips brushing hers, I murmur, "I love you, Katie Belle."

Her reply is instant. "I'll always love you, Arik."

We may not have all the answers yet. It may take some time for us to find them, but I have faith that we'll walk through life together and handle all those questions together.

With reclaimed love holding us strong, there isn't any storm we can't weather.

EPILOGUE - ARIK

Early October at Packsaddle is peaceful. There are no other cars on the shore as I park the Jeep. The air is cold and dry; we'll likely get our first snowfall in a couple of weeks. Living in Arizona thinned out Kate's blood, and she's bundled like we're in the Arctic.

"If you think I'm getting in that water, you're out of your mind." A shiver accompanies her words, and I can't help but chuckle at her sitting in the passenger seat of the Jeep. The heat is cranked as high as it'll go, but she's still cold.

"Nope, just a lunchtime picnic." The finer details have already been taken care of, so Kate thinks today is just an impromptu date.

"Okay, but don't think I'm not above throwing you into the water if you try any funny business."

Laughing at the way her teeth are chattering as she threatens me, I climb out and head to the back to get the basket.

Kate lays out the blanket, then I hand her a thermos of hot chocolate, some cold fried chicken, and the sides. I keep waiting for her to catch the menu's significance, but she doesn't put it together.

While we eat, we talk about my students and the changes and events she has planned for Readers' Haven.

Gram has scaled back over the last month, leaving Kate to run the store and work for Olivia. When Kate told me how Gram manipulated and schemed to get us together, part of me wanted to wring her neck. The bigger part of me is so damn grateful I could have kissed her. Plus, I have to admire that streak of genius and how easily she played us.

Kate still works for Olivia. They've found their stride in the long-distance working arrangement. Olivia and Taylor miss having Kate close, but it's something we've been working through together.

After we finish the meal and pack up, I link my fingers with Kate's, and we walk down the shore, then turn into the tree line. I'm leading her to a specific location, but there's still no recognition the farther we get from the water.

This area is mostly overgrown. Pine trees are so thick that we change directions multiple times to skirt around them. A couple of years ago, there was a destructive fire up here and most of the trees burned down, but the one I want made it through unscathed.

As the trunk comes into view, Kate's still chattering about the things she wants to get done when we get home.

"Olivia said the moving company should be here by Wednesday with my stuff, so I'm hoping to get ahead now to have time to sort through some of that. I'll be happy to have a car again."

It's not only your 'stuff' showing up.

It probably isn't the best idea to keep a secret from Kate, but I don't think she'll hold this secret against me. Today is for other plans though.

I pull us to a stop and wrap my arms around her, brushing my lips across hers.

"Do you remember this place?"

She looks around us and confusion covers her face.

"Um, no. Should I?"

It has been over a decade, so I don't hold it against her for not remembering. I'll tease her though.

Theatrically I clutch my chest while arranging my face into the picture of anguish. "As a sensitive teenage soul, I asked you a crucial question under that tree right there." There's a towering pine directly behind her. Reaching over her shoulder, I point it out. Her gaze follows my hand, and understanding lights her face. She whips around the trunk, circling the base of it until she finds the old carving from that spring day.

"Oh my God, I can't believe it's still here." Her back is turned to me, fingers tracing the outline of our initials across the rough surface. I drop down to my knee and pull out the ring box.

When I told Gram and Ben I had planned to propose to Kate, they were enthusiastic but worried I was moving too fast. Kate had uprooted her life to move back to Felt, while taking over the store and continuing with Liv.

I've waited over twelve years to ask Kate this question, and I won't wait a minute more. If she says no, then I'll have to convince her to say yes or keep asking until she does.

Ma was thrilled, recognizing it was a foregone conclusion. Jackson wished me luck, and Connor...well, Connor's reaction is another story.

Before Rob and Olivia left, I made sure to get their blessing. That was a fun conversation to say the least.

Our closest family and friends rallied behind me, helping me with the details, because our love story is as much theirs as it is ours.

"Katie."

She turns, and finding me on bended knee, she gasps, her hands flying to her mouth.

Some say it's an antiquated tradition to get down on one knee, but I'd get on both knees for this woman.

"Years ago, I asked you a question under this tree, my heart full of hope, happiness, and plans for our future. Those plans didn't work out so well for us, but I don't regret the years apart because they brought you back to me and helped shape you into the woman I love. I'm going to ask you another question under this tree with the same heart full of hope, happiness, and plans. Kate Belle Palicki, will you marry me, be my wife, my partner, my lover and most importantly, my friend"—my voice cracks on the last word and I have to clear my throat to continue—"for every day we're given?"

What I'm hoping are happy tears trail down her cheeks, and her breath catches on a sob. I'm holding mine because this is fucking nerve-wracking, but I wait. I'll wait as long as she needs because love like ours doesn't die.

Those bright green eyes lock on mine and she starts nodding.

"Yes, I'll marry you."

I'm off the ground sweeping her into my arms, laughing as we spin in circles. I can't kiss her, touch her, or hold her enough as elation and joy flood me.

Sliding the ring out of the box, I slip it on her finger. It's a perfect fit.

"Arik, it's so beautiful. How long have you been planning this?"

"The proposal itself? Since the first day of school. The ring's waited a little bit longer for it though."

She searches my face, catching my meaning. "You've had this ring all this time?"

"I was going to ask before you left for NAU, but I didn't

get the chance. It's not much, but we can get you something better."

"Touch this ring and you'll lose a hand. It's perfect. I love it and you."

"Here, let me show you something."

I slip the ring back off her finger, and Kate lets out an irritated grumble.

Laughing at her attachment, I angle the band so the engraving is visible.

"'My undying love,' but I don't understand, what's the date?"

"That was the day we got Maude stuck in the mud. You were helping me push her out when you slipped and fell. Covered head to toe in muck and instead of getting upset, you laughed. That was the moment I realized I was in love with you."

"Oh God, Arik." More of her tears fall as I continue.

"That was when my feelings shifted, when I realized I didn't only love you like a friend. I lied in that last letter I sent you. I knew the whole time exactly when I fell for you. Since that day, you were it for me."

I cup her face in my hands and capture her lips with mine. The taste of her is something I'll never get tired of.

On our way back to town, Kate keeps admiring her ring, rubbing her fingers over it and staring at it in the sunlight. Her left hand holds every ounce of her attention until I pull into the driveway.

I open Kate's door for her, and linking our fingers, we make our way up the porch. I'm shoving the door open as several voices shout out at us.

"SURPRISE!"

Balloons are everywhere, there's a *Congratulations* banner across the entryway to the kitchen, and streamers hang from the ceiling. All of our friends, coworkers, and family are crowded together holding noisemakers.

"Did you plan this?" Kate's bewildered gaze meets mine.

I'm as stunned as she is, and I can only shake my head as I look at Ben and Gram who are both wearing small smiles.

"We figured we would throw y'all an impromptu engagement party. We got champagne chilling, and we put some food and treats together. We're gonna have a party."

"What would y'all have done if she'd said no?"

Jackson calls out, "Drink all the champagne without you," and everyone laughs with him.

I tuck Kate under my arm before announcing, "Well, that won't be necessary. She said yes."

She holds her hand up, showing off the ring on her finger, and the group cheers loudly.

Surrounded by the people who love us and to the sound of their applause, I dramatically dip Kate and kiss her.

Food and drink circulate, people mingle in the house or on the back patio, making small talk. Kate and I haven't separated since coming home, and we're making our way back through the house when a giant moving truck pulls up, closely followed by an SUV.

That secret I didn't tell her about has officially arrived.

Peering through the front window, she shoots me a confused glance. I shrug and play dumb.

"Movers? They weren't supposed to be here for two more days."

"Well, come on, let's go see what's what."

We barely make it to the deck before Kate screeches, running across the lawn. Olivia throws up her arms, yelling, "Hey there, neighbor!"

Kate stops so fast, she almost face plants.

"Neighbor? What are you doing here? What's going on?"

"You didn't tell her?" Olivia questions me.

I shake my head. The original plan was to tell Kate once the sale on Olivia's house went through, but Olivia wanted to surprise her and swore me to secrecy, though she didn't think I could pull the surprise off.

"Tell me what? What's going on? We agreed no more secrets, Arik!"

At this point people are spilling out to the porch around us to see what's happening.

Kate's gaze is still pinging between Olivia and me.

"Liv asked me to find her a house here in Felt," I say. "The purchase went through two weeks ago."

"Liv?" she asks.

"I'm moving to Felt." Olivia starts singing loudly and off-key, "Reunited and it feels so good."

As Kate laughs, hugging Olivia, I hear Jackson's harsh whisper from behind me. "Fuck."

THANK YOU SO MUCH FOR READING! I HOPE YOU LOVED KATE and Arik!. If you'd like a bonus peek at their happily ever after sign up here!

KEEP IN TOUCH WITH ALINA LANE
Facebook: AlinaLaneAuthor
Instagram: AlinaLaneAuthor
Readers Group: Happily Ever After Addicts
Amazon: Alina Lane
BookBub: Alina Lane Author
Goodreads: Alina Lane

INTRODUCTION

Reclaimed Love Bonus Epilogue

Here's more of Kate and Arik that I hope you enjoy!

Happy hugs and positive vibes to you all!
Love,
Alina

ARIK

"WHAT THE HELL ARE YOU DOING?"

Kate's struggling to get the clamp secured on the squat rack bar and I know she isn't about to do what I think she's doing.

Twang!

The clamp springs shut, securing the weight to the bar, and I look my wife over in disbelief.

Spandex sports bra, skintight yoga pants, all that curly red hair bundled up into a tail.

Oh yeah, and the eight-and-a-half-month pregnant belly poking out from the waistband of her bottoms.

Pregnancy hasn't slowed Kate down at all, if anything she's got more frantic energy than ever, and I've lost sleep trying to catch up with her.

I figure I'd better get used to it now, especially with a baby on the way.

"Working out, what does it look like I'm doing?"

Green eyes that I have the pleasure of waking up to each morning spark irritable fire at me and I stifle the chuckle that wants to erupt.

Kate's hormones are all over the place. One minute she's so happy she's pinwheeling through the house, and the next she's crying over a diaper commercial. If I didn't grow up around women, it would be alarming to say the least.

"Katie, baby, you're not squatting anything at eight and a half months pregnant. That's not happening here."

That defiant chin tilts back and I'm preparing to be roasted, when her lower lip trembles and a tear tracks down her face.

See what I'm talking about with hormones here?

"Baby, what's wrong?"

I have no idea what's going on, for all I know her toast could have been buttered wrong this morning, pregnancy is strange and foreign land for the both of us.

We talked about starting a family, somewhere down the line. We never anticipated Kate throwing up for a week straight at the start of winter following our wedding. We assumed it was a bad stomach flu and I nearly broke the chair at the doctor's office with how my knees went weak and I crashed into the damn thing when the doctor delivered the news.

The plan was to wait, to time it when the bookstore was further along and easier to run, to time the birth to happen at the start of summer, so I didn't have to work while Kate was at home alone with our newborn.

Just like Kate and I though, we went about it in our own way, but I have faith that it'll work out for the best.

Kate sniffles back her tears and I can't take it when she cries. Gathering her up in my arms, I ask, "Talk to me, baby. What's going on?"

"I'm fat, Arik! That's what going on. I'm fat, I'm hot and sweaty even though it's like twenty degrees below zero outside, I can't fit into any of my old clothes, I haven't seen my feet in weeks, but they feel like over-cooked sausages.

The stretch marks are ugly as hell, I'm itchy and my vagina is becoming the world's most dense pube forest! I'm starving all the time and no matter how much I pay attention to my diet, I'm gaining weight like a hog and I feel ugly and horrible and horny all the damn time."

Holy shit.

"Baby—" I don't get farther than that before she's plowing ahead.

"No, don't tell me I'm beautiful, I don't want to hear it. Hearing it and feeling it are two very different things and I feel a million times less than beautiful right now."

"Come with me." I pull her from the basement, making sure to follow her up the stairs, in case she slips. We make our way through the kitchen and into my office where I sit her down in my chair.

Leaning over her, I pull up my email and tell her, "Close your eyes."

I find the file that I'm looking for and pull up what I want, expanding the image to fit the screen.

I bulldozed her into getting maternity shots done in the middle of her second trimester, even though she was less than thrilled about it. Winter in Felt can be hard, there isn't much to do or many places to get out to, so going stir-crazy is a definite possibility. Kate was halfway to bat-shit when I came up with the idea.

I didn't know that, when I finally got the files this morning, I would fall even more in love with her, but I did.

"Okay, when you open your eyes, I want you to remember that no matter how shitty you feel now, that you're always the most beautiful person in the world to me, swollen feet, sweat, hormones, and pubes aside. Nothing is gonna change that, Katie. Go ahead and look."

I can't see her open her eyes, but I do hear the slight hitch in her breath, I see her hand come up to cover her mouth and, shifting, I look down at the woman I love.

Stunned shock is the only way that I can describe the look of wonder on her face as her eyes eat up the picture on the computer monitor. I capitalize on her silence, saying, "You are actively growing our child, Katie Belle Beaumont. You have the best pieces of us safe inside your body right now. There is no amount of weight you could gain that would take away from the beauty of that. Your body is responsible for protecting and nourishing the most important piece of our lives and there's so much beauty and strength in that. I don't know how you don't see it, but let me show you how I see you."

On the screen is a picture of Kate, surrounded by the sky, painted in dying sunlight, and snow-packed forest. At her back is the same lake where I fell in love with her. The red glory of her hair spills fiery curls down her back and sets her apart from her surroundings like the goddess she is.

One hand is on her belly, on our baby, her head tilted down while her eyes are on the camera, and the touch of witchy with the beauty of our *place* was enough to make this my favorite picture.

Kate put a spell on me years ago and I've been willingly ensnared since.

I click through the genius of our photographer and with each image more of Kate's strength, determination, beauty, and love pour onto the screen.

Kate will always be her harshest critic and I will always be her biggest supporter, urging her to see herself like I do.

I should have seen it sooner, the requests for salads and healthy food to replace the junk that we kept around the house. The ever increasing walks that she was taking, and when the weather was bad, the workouts on the treadmill.

The first thing Kate asked her doctor about what being

able to stay active during her pregnancy and I could kick myself for missing the signs.

She was ridiculed, teased, and bullied for years over her weight. Of course that would be a concern for her now, but it shouldn't be.

Pointing to the screen, I say, "This right here? This is magic in its purest form. This is how I see you every single day. I hear you and your concerns for the weight gain, baby, but we've talked to Dr. Allen about it. You're in the normal range, you're not gaining too much weight too fast, your health isn't at risk. That's what's important. That's what we should focus on. We can walk more, we can find low-impact stuff to do, but you can't be squatting heavy weight this far into your pregnancy."

Kate swivels around and there are still tears in her eyes, but the small smile on her lips says they're happy tears, instead of the angry, frustrated ones from earlier.

I dip my head and lay my lips on hers.

There isn't ever a day that I don't want to kiss this woman, she feels like forever and tastes like eternity and I'll never give that up.

KATE

Pregnancy is a fucking war on the body and a battle on the heart.

Years ago, I fell in love with my body and what it did for me. I fell in love with the strength of it, the capabilities of it, and the beauty in it.

Somewhere between September and now, I lost that love with my body. With every appointment, I've been increasingly aware of my weight, the number on the scale steadily creeping up at every single doctor's appointment, and I've come to dread my checkups.

Instead of being focused on the unbelievable amazingness of the baby we were bringing into this world, I was stuck on the number on the scale—again.

I thought I hid it well enough from Arik. Keeping my requests to clean out the pantry bland enough that he would think I was trying to eat better because of the baby and our health, not my recent obsession with a stupid number that in no way should ever define me, but he saw right through that.

Not like my rant downstairs didn't clue him in or anything.

Being pregnant is hard. The bladder kicks and rib

punches are enough to wake me up in the dead of night and the sheer exhaustion that suffocates me daily is more than I can handle on a good day. I don't even wanna talk about the bad ones.

I'm horny all the damn time, but far along enough in my pregnancy that any kind of intimacy takes planning and a flexibility I lost along with the ability to tie my shoes.

The nausea, Charlie horses, and hot flashes are enough to drive me to drink—if I was actually allowed to do that.

Pregnancy is also breathtaking though—sometimes in a very literal sense. What started out as flutters and rolling somersaults turned into violent gymnastics and bulging skin.

Arik likes to video the movement of my tummy and I know that he wants to capture every second of my pregnancy, which is what prompted the maternity shoot.

At first, I wasn't on board—at all. Take my picture while I look like a bloated heifer? No thank you. But he wheedled enough to get his way and looking at the images painted on the screen he was *right*.

I look like magnificent glory and that warm spark of pride I used to have in my body flickers back to life.

I shouldn't be focused on a number, I should enjoy and embrace the awe-inspiring beauty of my body.

Arik's lips move against mine and, like always, I get lost in him. Heat pools damn near everywhere and I'm a panting hot mess of twitching need by the time he pulls back.

Desk and office sex has been off the table—literally—for a while now, so no matter how badly I want to get my husband naked, I need to move us to a more comfortable location.

See what I'm saying about logistics?

Arik must see the calculation on my face, because he hooks his arms under me and sweeps me into his arms.

His tendency to lift me made me really uncomfortable when I started to show my pregnancy, and, terrified that he would throw out his back, I made him put me down more often than not.

Now? Knowing how he sees me, I let him have his way. Trusting that if the weight of me is too much, he'll put me down.

My feet gently lower to the floor and I waste no time in shedding my sports bra and leggings, though those take some effort to get off—damned spandex.

As soon as we're naked—hello brawny husband body— we both climb into bed and arrange the pillows how I need them to be comfortable. Just the proximity of him is enough to send shivers racing through me and anticipation of his touch curls through my limbs until I can't wait to get my hands on him any longer.

Arik lifts my leg and draws it back over his thigh, the drag of his fingers along my skin maddening enough to send me squirming against his touch. Sliding his hand down to find me drenched, his fingers swirl around the center of me causing the breath to stutter in my chest and the ache between my thighs to a flashpoint of need.

"Fuck, Katie. You're so damned wet."

Two fingers thrust into me and, as much as I love him for trying to prepare my body, they're not enough. I need more.

I reach down and circle the heavy length of him in my fist. There's moisture beaded at the tip of his cock and knowing that I excite him that much, even looking like I do, is enough to turn what started out slow and easy into something much more frantic.

I line him up with my entrance. He pulls his fingers out of me just as I'm wiggling my hips back. The head of his cock stretches me, and I hear him suck my arousal from his fingers. It's added fuel to the fire.

Shoving my hips back, I give in to him. We both touch,

thrust, and move with each other until we're lost. Lost to the pleasure, lost to our senses, and lost to one another.

Like always with him, I get swept away.

Sometime later, snow falls quietly outside and Arik's tracing light circles on my stomach. Opting to stay in bed for the remainder of the day we just cuddle. Thinking back to his words about my body and what we should focus on, I know I can do better. I know I'll struggle occasionally, but I can trust Arik to pick me up and point me in the right direction.

The baby is kicking against his hands and doing jujitsu on my bladder and I'm a good two seconds away from needing the bathroom again, when something inside of me pings and then there's a flood of liquid suddenly covering the bed.

Arik jumps up to get a towel, because sadly this isn't the first time there's been an abundance of liquids in bed with us —damned tricky pregnancy bladder—but the sheer volume of it stops me dead in my tracks.

My face must be shocked, because Arik says, "I'll get the sheets changed and the cover cleaned up while you shower. It's okay, baby."

Clueless lovable man that he is, he doesn't know what to make of me when I start to laugh hysterically.

"What? What's so funny?"

"Arik, that's definitely not pee. I'm pretty sure my water just broke."

His hand trembles against the towel that he's using to try to wipe up some of the fluid still leaking from my body.

If I thought he would panic, I was wrong. Kissing my belly gently, he murmurs to the baby, "Happy birthday, bug."

Elation, excitement and love – so much love – shine in those blue eyes as he says, "Looks like it's time for our next adventure, Katie Belle."

ALSO BY ALINA LANE

Love Reimagined

Turn the page to read the first chapter of Reclaimed Love.

LOVE REIMAGINED

JACKSON - AUGUST

"SUCK IT IN, JACKSON."

My sister, Ally, is fighting the dress zipper at my back, and with every inch gained, I lose more blood flow to my torso.

I have got to stop making bets.

"Bro, I think you got the wrong size."

Connor's not wrong. Not only did I have to *search* for the damn thing, I had to guess what my size would be.

And based on the compression to my guts, I guessed wrong.

Earlier in the summer, I had Kate locked in a bear hold on the floating deck we use during days at the lake. I was threatening to throw her in when she bet me that I'd be the first to go into the water. Stupidly, I let my ego get the better of me and took that bet.

Who'd have thought a tiny thing like Kate could actually toss me into the lake? I sure as hell didn't, hence the current loss of my ability to breathe freely.

Ally's snorting giggle has an edge of hysteria to it, and I've either traumatized her or she's laughing at me. Likely the latter.

"Good call on the girdle. You look like a busted can of biscuits with it, so I can't imagine if you didn't have it."

Whipping her phone out, she takes a couple of pictures, and I don't even try to stop her. Not like it's the first time I've been photographed in embarrassing situations.

I turn back to the mirror to take in the final touches on my humiliation. My shoulders bulge against the dainty strap circling my neck, and my thighs are going to hulk out of this thing any second. I look like an overgrown ape in this dress, but anything for friends, right?

Knowing I wouldn't get my arms into anything with sleeves, I had decided to go with what Ally called a "halter," and I'm glad I did. At least it's on.

The black stilettos on my feet pinch my toes and I have a new appreciation for women everywhere.

God, please let me get through this without breaking anything, and I swear I'll never complain about how long women take to get ready again.

"Ha ha, you two," I say. "Let's get this over with." Grabbing my keys and a duffle that contains a change of clothes, I head out, wobbling and tilting as I try to walk.

"Oh my God. I'm going to pee my pants," Ally wheezes through a laugh. "Jackson, loosen your hips, you look like a clown on stilts trying to walk like that."

I fucking feel like I'm on stilts. Did I have to get such a high fucking heel?

I cross my eyes and mimic her in a high-pitched voice. "Suck it in, loosen your hips." With a sad shake of my head, I tell her, "There are times I wish I had a brother instead of you."

She ushers Connor and me out the door of Ma's house

with a queenly wave, and I realize my next problem about two seconds later. I can't drive in heels—at least, not without driving us into a ditch. Kicking the things off, I'll leave them on the truck's floorboard until I get us to the bookstore alive and well.

As I slow to turn onto Felt, Idaho's Main Street, I press the clutch and another seam pops somewhere on the dress. At the rate I'm going, I'll be walking into the shop with my ass hanging out.

Not the first time that's happened.

Readers' Haven comes into view, and I have to admit, Kate knew what she was doing when she decided to remodel the store. Warm light glows from the storefront, and there are people all over. I planned this trip toward the latter part of the evening, hoping that the crowd would have died down, but I'm not that lucky.

After parking on Main, I ease out of the driver's seat, careful not to flash an innocent bystander. I'm glad that I brought a change of clothes. I don't want to be in this get-up —or these fucking shoes that double as torture devices—a minute longer than I have to.

The spandex girdle I ordered—and no, I don't want to talk about how I know what a girdle is—is about the only thing stopping Jackson Jr. from making his presence known. The damned thing is squishing my internal organs until I'm sure there's going to be permanent damage.

There are both familiar and strange faces in the crowd around me. The townsfolk are giving me some looks, but I couldn't back out of this bet.

"Hurry it up, would you?" Ally calls as she hustles past us. "If I don't get my books signed because you can't find your damned courage, I'll never forgive you."

Connor and I share a look of exasperation before working our way to the front of the store.

The crowd that still stretches around the front of the building means I'm going to be standing longer than I care to.

I wave Ally and Connor to the line, saying, "I'm gonna go around the back and be seen so I can change."

A short trek around the store later and I check the back door to the shop. When the knob turns, I count my lucky stars and push into the back room. Hopefully I can grab Kate, show her I fulfilled my end of the bargain and then use the upstairs to change, my duty done.

As I'm stepping into the store, the heel of my shoe catches on the threshold and I nearly go ass over elbow trying to steady myself in these skyscrapers. There's a brief moment when I think Ally's right, that I'm going to break my ankle.

I have eight different trails to hike this week. I am not about to be chained to a damn desk because of footwear.

With a shuffling stumble, I avoid disaster and get my feet back under me, just in time to see a book flying at my head.

It makes a tumbling arc through the air straight for my face. I have a split second to appreciate the aim and the force behind the throw before I snag the book. Once I have it firmly in my grasp, I take in the pitcher with impeccable aim.

Fuck me.

A gorgeous blonde, one with about a mile of hair waving softly from a face that models wish for, stands in front of me. She's dressed in a black tank that skates over subtle curves. I note the nipped-in waist and mile-long legs encased in form-fitting jeans as I trail my eyes lower.

The flash of lust that shoots through me has me thanking God for this girdle and that it hides the way my dick twitches in appreciation.

One hand full of book, the other empty, I raise both in the universal gesture for "it wasn't me."

"Sorry," I tell her. "I'm sorry. I didn't mean to startle you. Is Kate around?"

Suspicious sapphire eyes narrow on me, and I don't blame her. A six-foot-three guy in a too-small dress and heels comes stumbling in the back door, I'm gonna assume he's drunk, high, or both.

"Who's asking?"

Swallowing hard, I say, "Jackson Sawyer. She knows me, I swear."

My voice didn't shake, your voice shook. Shut up.

Like my name holds all the answers to the universe, she immediately relaxes, shoulders falling, legs straightening from the ass-kicking stance I missed at first because I was focused on the flying book.

She cocks an eyebrow, cool as a cucumber. I, on the other hand, can still feel my heart rocketing in my chest from the one-two punch of nearly falling off these heels and her stunning beauty.

She turns to leave, saying, "Follow me," as she heads to the door.

"And you are?" I assume she's a visiting author since I know everyone in town.

"Olivia Carter."

Ah, the best friend. Kate hasn't said much about her, but I know that she and Ally have gotten friendly recently.

"Uh, if it's all the same, could you just send her back here?"

She looks back over her shoulder with a smirk painted on a mouth that makes men beg. "No can do, cowboy. She's running her ass off and busy. You want Kate, you come out here."

Well shit fire, yes, ma'am.

I got my orders so I march behind her, reveling in the way her biteable ass moves in those jeans.

What used to be a quaint, cluttered bookstore now looks fresh and clean, like a boutique in a bigger city. Gleaming wood floors are highlighted under the low lights of the store. The big bookcases we moved around at the beginning of summer are polished to a shine. The furniture's been moved to accommodate a long table, and it's *busy*.

Fuck my life.

Kate's standing at the checkout counter with her part-timer, Kelly, showing her something on the tablet they have situated there.

"Hey, Kate, your mascot is here," Olivia calls.

Mascot is right. I inherited my joking nature from my dad. There wasn't a dare he wouldn't take, and he never missed the opportunity to make a corny joke. He'd have loved this—the way Kate brought back the store, the way she conned me into a bet so I'm stuck in a dress for the night. He'd be here snapping pictures, probably dressed up right beside me, if a heart attack hadn't taken him from us my sophomore year in college.

Kate looks up from the tablet and smiles, but it doesn't reach her eyes. Even with whatever makeup magic she worked on her face, the dark circles, exhaustion, and heartbreak are all there.

The memory of listening to her weeping a few days ago over the letters Arik wrote her after high school has my temper at him surfacing.

Neither of them would be hurting if they would have just talked to each other without the shadows of their pasts looming over them.

But what do I know about successful relationships?

You can't trust that organ pumping away in your chest to make the right decisions in the long run.

The heartbreak written all over Kate is another reminder of that.

She drums up some enthusiasm, and there's a tiny spark in her eye as she comes around the counter to wrap me in a hug.

Squeezing her tight, I rub my hand down her back. Kate and I weren't really friends growing up—that honor belonged to Arik, the douche—but she and I have gotten closer since she's been back this summer, and I hate seeing her like this.

There's a muffled laugh and snort, and if she's able to find some humor in the situation, then I'll roll with it and accept my ribbing.

Teasing, I say, "What do you think? I make this dress ten times sexier, don't I?"

She takes a step back, and her green eyes dance a little more as she views the whole ensemble. "Your legs"—a giggle pops out—"look amazing. I wasn't expecting the shoes either. Those are a nice touch."

Cocking a hip and praying I don't break the damn thing, I strike a pose and demand, "Show me off, woman. A dress like this needs to be admired by the masses. What are you waiting for?"

With an exaggerated huff, Kate rolls her eyes before leading me to the table of authors. Faces and names whizz by me, and I do my best to catch a couple, but it's not long before they're all a blur. I recognize some of them because Kate promoted the event all over the town paper, something that I still read daily.

"This is Olivia Carter. She writes paranormal romance," Kate says.

Olivia extends her fingers toward me, and when we touch, electricity zips up my arm to nail me in the spine. I drop her hand after giving it the perfunctory shake.

Olivia Carter —she's Kate's best friend and also her

employer. She and her brother came in from Phoenix for the signing and are hanging out for the next few weeks, if the news around town is accurate. The grapevine in Felt is strong enough that I'm inclined to trust it.

Maybe blondie is looking for a good time while she's here for her friend? The better question is can I get her alone long enough to charm her into my bed? Only one way to find out.

Those thoughts get pushed back for later exploration, and I aim my most alluring grin at Olivia while saying to Kate, "We've met."

"You have?"

"Yep." Olivia shoots me a look meant to shut me up.

So naturally I say, "It was brief though. Kinda hard for a proper introduction when a book is flying at your head."

She turns to Kate. "It was nothing. He just caught me off guard."

Kate's snickering as she asks, "And you threw a book at him?"

The dimple in Olivia's cheek pops as she nibbles on the corner of a lip that begs for lush kisses. "Yep. Sure did."

Kate dissolves into more giggles, her smile going from wooden to more natural, and even though it's at my expense, I'll take it.

Neither Kate nor Arik deserve what's going on, but my hands are tied, and I can only try to be a good friend to them both.

We continue our two-person parade around the store. People have their phones out now and are snapping pictures of me with the authors, some with their fans. I get into character, sitting on laps and draping myself over the table with books around me for an impromptu photo shoot. Everyone is laughing, and someone convinces me to catwalk my way through the store for videos.

I only eat shit once, crashing against a couch, and after that everyone unanimously agrees that I should ditch the heels.

About done with the whole thing—I don't know how women breathe or walk in these get-ups—I track down Kate.

"Hey, you got somewhere I can change?"

Glancing around the shop, she takes in the dwindling crowd before answering, "Sure, either use the back room or the second floor. The powder room is tiny, and you won't have as much room."

"I'll use the storeroom—that's where I left my change of clothes."

"Okay, go ahead and head back. I'll keep a lookout."

I'm shutting the door to the storage room when I realize my first problem. I didn't bring underwear, and I couldn't fit briefs under the girdle, so I'm commando.

The second problem becomes apparent when I reach back for the zipper.

You know that one place between your shoulder blades that you can't reach no matter how bad it itches? That's right about where the zipper to this damn straitjacket is sitting. No matter how I contort myself, I can't grab the damn thing.

Reaching under the hem of the dress, I drag the girdle off. Maybe removing twelve layers of plastic wrap from my ribs will give me more flexibility.

The small metal tab is between my fingers and my shoulder is about to pop out of its socket, but the zipper is stuck. Either I stretched this dress enough that it's not coming down, or this is the universe's way of getting back at me for something.

Dress rucked up around my waist, ass out in all its splendor, I'm cursing a blue streak, about to rip my way out of this eyesore, when the door behind me opens.

Thanks for the lookout, Kate.

READY FOR MORE? ORDER YOUR COPY OF LOVE REIMAGINED here.

ACKNOWLEDGMENTS

Woofty… Where to start?

First of all, thank you! Thank you for reading and I sincerely hope you enjoyed your trip to Felt.

Nick – thank you for being my biggest supporter. I wouldn't be here today without you and I count my lucky stars that you embrace my brand of chaos.

Sax, Jennipoo, Mellie Mel, and Kan – thank you for always having my back, for always being there. I don't know what I did to deserve you, but I am so grateful for your friendship. I couldn't imagine better ride or die ladies.

Claire and Bre – you two are the missing pieces of my puzzle and I would be lost without you. To all the wrong answers, eye candy, alpha reading and cheerleading I am so grateful for the friendship that we've developed and cultivated. Y'all are stuck with me forever.

Maria Luis, Lucy Score, Claire Kingsley & Addison Cain – I don't have words to express how much your support, words of encouragement and willingness to assist a newbie like myself mean. Thank you for everything you do in our community and everything you've done for me to get me here.

Jessica Snyder – Kate and Arik wouldn't be what they are without you. I couldn't have told their story without you pushing me to be a better writer, always being available to answer the questions I send you at all hours, day and night and offering invaluable insights.

The Happily Editing Anns – Thank you for your eagle eyes and the amazing edits you provided me to work with. Your advice and experience are something I appreciate immensely and adore.

Kate Farlow – You didn't miss a beat when I came to you with the littlest cover concerns. Thank you for answering every question I threw your way and giving my book baby the beautiful cover Kate and Arik deserve.

Members of RWR – Thank you for being the best place on the internet. The positivity, encouragement and motivation to write brought me to this point and I am so thankful for you all.

Thank you to everyone who helped me create, craft and hone Reclaimed Love into what it is. Y'all are the real MVP's here.

ABOUT THE AUTHOR

A pocket-sized powerhouse, Alina lives with her personal Hunky Hero and two children in Arizona. Slathering on sunscreen and living life to its fullest she enjoys hiking, camping, fishing and rock climbing in her desert backyard.

When not hard at work on your next literary escape, you can find Alina embracing her bad-assery on Call of Duty, binge reading or shopping for nail dip sets to compliment her book covers.

Sign up for her newsletter to stay up to date on the latest Alina news.

You can follow Alina on:

Website: AlinaLane.com

Facebook: AlinaLaneAuthor

Instagram: AlinaLaneAuthor

Readers Group: Happily Ever After Addicts

Made in the USA
Columbia, SC
17 April 2022

59099833R00202